COPYRIGHT 2018

Elias was sweating now.

The sun was higher, and he'd developed a raging headache. He wiped his forehead with his sleeve. At the wellhead, he came across a valve with a loose bolt where it connected to the pipe. As he crouched to tighten it, he discovered the thread on the screw was worn, and the bolt wouldn't tighten. Then he heard a distinct hissing coming from the pipe. It grew louder and louder.

His adrenaline spiked.

He turned to his co-workers and yelled, "The bolt's not tightening. It's going to blow. Run! Now!"

M000191571

Praise for A.M. Halvorssen

"The book is great! Full of action, and highly relevant in today's environment. Even though it is fiction, the climate science is accurate. I will definitely buy this book when it is out."

~Trude Eidhammer, climate scientist,
National Center for Atmospheric Research
~*~

"A. M. Halvorssen exposes the greedy practices that cause climate change, and the people who will kill to cover it up and destroy the world in the process. This suspenseful tale carries more truth than fiction."

~Karen C. Whalen, author of the
Dinner Club Murder Mystery series
~*~

"...a gripping international cli-fi thriller for our challenging times."

~Dan Bloom
The Cli-Fi Report

Dedication

To my children

Acknowledgments

I want to thank the following people who have helped me during the process of writing this book:
Anne Abrahamsen, Tom Blomquist, Wencke Braathen, Betty Castillo, Marit Christie, Christine Cohen, Lori DeBoer, Karen Douglass, Hege Gudrun Eliassen, Colleen Ostlund, Brith Walstad Pulido, Mandy Setliff, Rachel Weaver and Karen Whalen.

~

I especially appreciate the help of Trude Eidhammer, a climate scientist at National Center for Atmospheric Research, who read the manuscript and confirmed the accuracy of the climate science.

~

I'm very grateful to my editor, Ally Robertson, at the Wild Rose Press, who believed in this project.

~

Most of all, I want to thank my better half, Rafael Castillo, for reading the manuscript, critiquing it, and providing moral support throughout the process.

Prologue

Elias knew he was being watched. He rubbed his eyes against the dry Moroccan desert heat.

It was midmorning and already stifling. He scouted the perimeter from the gas field to the distant Atlas Mountains, taking in the rocky, sandy wasteland with pockets of shrub before entering the maze of pipes, machinery, tanks, and trucks. A member of a nomadic Berber tribe, Elias was accustomed to the heat, but the stress and fatigue of the past few weeks were taking their toll. Massaging the back of his neck, he felt the sun bearing down on him, warning him.

Shaking his head, Elias stopped to check his phone again and frowned. He was hoping to hear from Zakia; she was one of two people he could trust with the information he was carrying.

When he'd stumbled upon the transfer of a deed for a large tract of state-owned land traditionally used by nomadic Berbers into his company's name, Oddleifur Oil & Gas, he decided to tell the media. That's where Zakia came in. Elias wasn't comfortable releasing the information. Yet, why was the company insistent on doing hydraulic fracturing—extremely water intensive as it was—in the desert? He'd considered quitting earlier, but he needed access to the company files to prove the wrongdoing. He couldn't turn back now, even if he was putting himself in danger.

Elias reached the wellhead where he met three workers who'd been assigned to help with the malfunctioning equipment he'd been ordered to fix. Reluctantly he took the lead, closely followed by the young men, scrambling around the pipes and pumps, checking the fittings. He attached a manual pressure monitor, a high-tech version of a manometer, to the valves to test the pressure in the pipes. The whole time he worked, he sensed the smell of the rotten eggs, which was common, though this seemed more than the usual amount.

He was sweating now. The sun was higher, and he'd developed a raging headache. He wiped his forehead with his sleeve. He came across a valve with a loose bolt where it connected to the pipe. As he crouched to tighten it, he discovered the thread on the screw was worn and the bolt wouldn't tighten. Then he heard a distinct hissing coming from the pipe. It grew louder and louder.

His adrenaline spiked.

He turned to his co-workers and yelled, "The bolt's not tightening. It's going to blow. Run! Now!"

Elias heard the ear-splitting explosion and his own scream.

Chapter One

The day's deadlines were looming. Zakia Karim walked quickly to her favorite French sidewalk café, five blocks away from her newspaper's office. She wound her way on the crowded sidewalk between tourists taking photos of the elaborate mosque next door with its turquoise blue dome, and locals going about their business. The torrential rains of the past few days had stopped and Rabat was lush and green. Zakia smiled; she appreciated the early spring rains.

Crossing the noisy street, she paused to avoid a fast-moving moped which had squeezed between the cars and trucks, carrying a family of four sandwiched on a single seat. Reaching the curb, she just missed stepping on a stray cat soaking up the sun. She rushed into the popular Joyeux Café, her green eyes adjusting to the darkness, and saw an empty table back in the corner, near the hookah smokers. Being a lone woman in a café could bring unwanted attention, especially since Zakia had short-cropped hair not covered by a hijab. In Morocco, mostly men frequented the sidewalk cafés. All Zakia wanted to do was eat a quick lunch, not be harassed by a bunch of gawking men in robes with nothing better to do.

She slid into a wooden chair and sighed. These days she hated to spare even a moment for lunch. She was eager to land a career-changing story, one that would propel her to a senior reporter status. Lately, her spouse, Benjamin Atkins, who worked at the World Bank in Washington, D.C., had been hinting that he wanted to make a permanent move to the United States. She feared her career would stall there; she felt pressured to prove herself in Morocco in order to move to a senior positon in the United States.

When it was her turn to order, she smiled at the proprietor and said "Bonjour," hoping that her good nature would hurry the process. It worked and she had just started to eat her habitual *croque monsieur*, prepared here with mutton instead of ham, when her phone rang. The proprietor frowned, but she shook her head apologetically and answered it anyway. It could be a source.

Instead it was Mohammad Yasin, one of her colleagues in Marrakesh. Mohammad worked as a reporter on the news desk at a sister newspaper that covered the Al Tarife region in the south and surrounding areas. She remembered vividly that when they'd last spoken, he'd said, "Zakia, your passion is going to kill you one day." They had both laughed.

Mohammad sounded tense. "Zakia, I have an interesting story for you."

She perked up. He had dispensed with the usual Arab tradition of catching up on family matters before getting to the point.

"What's going on?"

"Something big." His sharp tone made her uneasy.

He didn't speak for a moment, and then cleared his throat. "Several people died in a blowout at a gas well near Al Tarife. The story's just breaking now."

Zakia's stomach churned. She had an uneasy

feeling she knew where this was going. "Isn't that where Oddleifur Oil is located?"

"Yes," he said. "Weird thing is the well is still on fire, but the authorities are chasing reporters away. I know the fire chief, but he wouldn't let me through and, instead, threatened to confiscate my camera."

"How can I help?" she said. Her adrenaline surged with the thought of a potential new assignment.

"Well," he paused. "I thought you mentioned once that you had a friend working there."

"Elias Mansur," she said. "You have a good memory."

He sounded sarcastic. "That's how I get so many press awards," he said. "I remember things. Make connections."

Zakia didn't answer. In fact, her old boyfriend, Elias, did work for Oddleifur Oil. Zakia had been in love with Elias in a way that could not happen in Morocco until you were actually married. But his ongoing friendship after she'd married Benjamin was awkward for her. He had kept in touch over the years— just casual contact, yet disconcerting. After they had a chance encounter at the tenth reunion of their classes at their Alma Mater, Columbia University in New York, three years ago, he had begun sending her holiday cards. Even though Benjamin was an even-keeled American, she could tell by his forced smile when the cards appeared in the mail that he was not thrilled about it. Holiday cards seemed innocent enough, but married women just didn't write to old flames in Moroccan culture.

Especially not if your firstborn was Elias's boy and you weren't married to Elias.

Fighting against temptation, she'd never told Elias or Benjamin. She hadn't found out she was pregnant until after she'd broken up with Elias and was involved with Benjamin. Elias was too controlling. Not daring to take the test, she had been unsure who the father was for several months. After talking to her sister, Tahra, Zakia had done a lot of soul searching and decided it would be best if she went ahead and married her latest lover, Benjamin. Tahra was her only living family member and they were close, even if she lived in Chicago. She had said that her chance of a journalism career if she married a nomadic Berber was highly unlikely. Zakia had not told Benjamin there was a possibility that she might be pregnant by another man.

Then four days ago, Elias had sent Zakia an e-mail, asking to meet with her. He mentioned something about nomadic Berbers, water rights, and hydraulic fracturing. She hadn't told Benjamin. And she hadn't responded because part of her wondered if somehow he had figured out that Dani was his son.

Zakia cupped her chin with her right hand and leaned her elbow on the small table. *Something isn't right.*

"Well," said Mohammad. "Can I have Elias's phone number?"

"I'd have to dig to find it." Zakia slumped as she remembered the e-mail with guilt. "Can I get back to you?"

"Sure." "But make it quick. I want to find out what's going on from an insider. There's an absolute information blackout."

Zakia felt a twinge of anxiety in the pit of her stomach. "All I know is that Elias is one of the

6

engineers working in operations in the data center trailer."

"Good, then he'll know exactly what happened. This whole operation has a secretive feel to it lately. I used to cover it routinely as part of my beat, but information has been drying up ever since they started moving into fracking in a big way."

They agreed that Zakia would call him as soon she found Elias's phone number and hung up. By then, her food was lukewarm and Zakia had no appetite. She pulled up her e-mails on her phone and thought about writing Elias back, then thought better of it. Against her instinct, Zakia would stick to her plan. She had decided she wasn't going to tell him about Dani before her son turned eighteen. She'd let Mohammad talk with Elias.

****

Zakia's shoulders tensed up as she hurried into the small, noisy newsroom at *Le Journal du Maroc*. She wondered how she could wangle her way into covering the explosion herself. Plus, she needed to reread the e-mail from Elias to see if she had somehow missed something about his tone that may have been conveyed in the short message.

But what?

She loved her job at *Le Journal* because the paper was one of the few in Morocco, let alone the Arab world, that had not been shut down for being outspoken about issues the government believed were too sensitive. It had grown in popularity during the Arab Spring because the publishers had played an effective balancing game, choosing their battles carefully. That was another reason she didn't want to move to the States. Landing a job there was very difficult, as newspapers were slashing the newsroom staff or even closing down in many places.

The moment she sat down, her long legs butting up against the desk, her colleague, Fatima Darzi, a petite powerhouse, came over to her little cubicle. "Zakia, I've been looking for you."

"Why? I just returned from a quick lunch."

Fatima smiled. "Good, you need to eat. You've been working too hard. You look tired."

"The story of my life." Zakia smiled. She'd worked with Fatima at the paper for what seemed like forever. Fatima was content to write social stories. The two were miles apart in their career aspirations, but still good friends.

While Fatima told her about her morning tribulations, Zakia began zipping through her e-mails, looking for the one from Elias and wondering if she had accidentally deleted it. Fatima, who lingered, looking at her own phone, gasped. "Wow, look what came across the wires just now. A terrible flood in the area around the Serbian town of Obrenovac, over ten people dead so far."

Zakia's heart raced. "Obrenovac? Are you sure?"

"Yes," said Fatima, her eyebrows drawing together. "What's wrong?"

"That's near where Benjamin is on a job this week," Zakia bit her lip and pulled her phone out of her bag.

"Have you spoken with him recently?"

"I called him earlier today and got no response. The cellphone system must be overloaded. I'll try again now." Zakia fingered her thin gold necklace as she tried calling him.

"Thank the stars. There you are. I was beginning to stress out about you."

"I'm fine. I've tried calling you all morning," said Benjamin. "Record-breaking rainfall in the region caused huge flooding last night."

"Just hold the line Benjamin," Zakia turned to Fatima, "Let's try getting it live."

She straightened up in her chair, searched and found a livestream of the report on her computer and turned up the volume. They watched soberly as helicopters flew low over the town where flood waters had swept through. Soldiers rescued people off rooftops.

Zakia spoke into her cell, "This looks awful; where are you now, Benjamin?"

"On the outskirts of Belgrade east of Obrenovac. What a disaster. I'm stunned. There were scores of people hauling suitcases along the road heading this way, looking like refugees—they're the lucky ones. The authorities are urging everyone to get out of the area. I'm not sure when we'll be getting to the airport, but I'll call you later if the phones work. Or I'll use Skype. Love you!"

"Be safe," said Zakia, finally breathing easy again. "I love you too."

The news reporter on the screen said, "Cyclone Tamara has brought record rainfall to the region and caused the Sava River and its tributaries to overflow their banks. It's the heaviest rainfall in 120 years." In the scenes from the center of Obrenovac, people were wading through nearly waist-high water, carrying their most treasured possessions. Some rescuers were in rowboats with elderly people and families with small children. Debris was floating everywhere and some cars were bobbing around.

A couple of reporters in nearby cubicles had gathered behind Zakia and Fatima to see what the commotion was all about. "That doesn't look good," muttered one of the reporters.

"Be quiet," said Zakia. "I want to hear this."

They all watched in silence while the reporter wrapped up his coverage. "This flood fits the pattern of climate change. The heat is creating more moisture in the atmosphere, causing heavier rainfall, hence more floods."

Fatima turned to Zakia. "There always seems to be flooding somewhere on the planet."

"But they seem to be getting worse." I have a friend, Fiona McPherson, who's a climatologist. She's often called on to advise policy-makers and corporate executives. She's told me that extreme weather events are going to happen more and more often."

Fatima shook her head. "Thank goodness Benjamin's okay."

Zakia breathed out a sigh of relief. "Yes, my stomach was starting to act up." With Benjamin gone so often, she was used to his being away for weeks at a time, but then something like this reminded her how important her marriage was to her and how much she loved Benjamin. She hoped Elias wasn't intending to upset things.

When the coverage switched to the inauguration of a new university research center in Casablanca, the other reporters wandered back to their cubicles, talking amongst themselves. Fatima lingered. "Do you want to take a break? Let's go get some coffee."

"Just a minute." Zakia peered at the screen. Now that she knew Benjamin was safe, she was ready to dive back into her story lead. "I want to see if they are covering the gas blowout near Al Tarife."

They watched for a few moments longer, but nothing was mentioned, and Fatima playfully pulled Zakia out of her chair. "We'll just make Jasem work on editing our stories even later tonight. Aren't bosses meant to be working twenty-four-seven?"

"Indeed. Yet, I don't understand what's going on with the media," Zakia pondered as they walked to the breakroom. "Why wasn't a blowout at a gas well in the Sahara, where several workers were killed a few hours ago, mentioned on the local news?"

Fatima shrugged. "That is peculiar."

As they poured coffee and prepared tea, Zakia considered telling Fatima about Elias, that he worked at Oddleifur Oil and had tried to contact her recently. Instead, she and Fatima compared notes on stories they were working on and then finished up after their editor, Jasem Essa, poked his head in the breakroom and gave them a dirty look.

****

Zakia went back to her desk, intending to find out what was going on at the gas well, though it was anyone's guess as to whether or not Jasem would approve of her picking up the story. At the outset, he had seemed to have mixed feelings about her career aspirations, even though he had given Zakia her first job after university. Then, four years later, he was very supportive when she decided to pursue her master's degree in the U.S., and hired her back again after she graduated. She'd had a chance to stay in the U.S. after her studies, but decided to return home to Morocco.

Having grown up in Casablanca with a multi-cultural background—her father an English businessman of Syrian origin and her mother a French-Moroccan singer—Zakia had wanted to be a part of Morocco as it changed with increasing globalization. Yet, being a woman in a male-dominated profession, she had to fight more to get the most sought after stories.

Zakia scrolled online to see if any mention of the blowout had made it into any other newspapers or into the blogosphere. She found nothing, not even video coverage on YouTube, Twitter, or Facebook. Zakia suspected that the story was being suppressed. Otherwise some footage would have appeared on the domestic news by this time. She'd written some pretty good stories, such as the expanded series on the Arab Spring, but this one, somehow, seemed different.

The well blowout, coming so closely on the heels of Elias's trying to contact her, made her uneasy. She broadened her search to encompass all news within the last two years, and the only stories she could find on the oil and gas well in that area was that the company was expanding its hydraulic fracturing operations.

Zakia contacted a friend from high school, Rafid Bera, now a geology professor at the University of Rabat, to ask what exactly hydraulic fracturing was.

"Hydraulic fracturing and horizontal drilling, often referred to as fracking, is a method used to recover oil and gas from shale rock," said Rafid. "Drilling is done vertically, thousands of feet below the surface, then horizontally, before directing a high-pressure water, sand, and chemicals mixture at the rock to release the oil and gas inside. The method uses millions of gallons of water per gas well."

"That sounds like an awful lot of water."

"Not an ideal energy source for places with an arid climate and water scarcity. Fracking also has negative environmental impacts, especially the wastewater."

"Thanks for all the info. I'll be in touch."

She turned to research fracking accidents by poring through the internet, including research papers, scientific papers, and accident reports. There had been several explosions on fracking sites in the U.S., for the most part due to sloppy operators. Could that have been the cause of this explosion? And what did that have to do with the story not being covered?

****

The afternoon passed quickly and it was nearly five when Zakia finally looked up Elias's phone number on the list provided by the alumni association of Columbia University and called Mohammad. She realized that she'd been putting it off. Guilt was getting the better of her.

"*Salam*, Mohammad. Have you learned anything new?"

"*Salam*, Zakia. The person in charge at the gas well is being very tight with information," he said. "I probably need to go back down there myself, but they still aren't letting any reporters in."

"Well, what can you tell me?" Zakia was pleased that her suspicions were well founded. "Anyway, I have Elias's number for you."

Zakia heard no response.

"How bad was it?" she asked.

Mohammad hesitated.

Zakia held her breath while she pulled her hand through her hair.

"All right," said Mohammad, sighing. "I didn't want to be the one to break the news, but since he's already come up in conversation, I need to tell you. The company released Elias's name as one of the victims."

"Oh my God," Zakia dragged in a deep breath, the room started spinning. "No, no. It can't have been Elias."

"I'm afraid so. Oh Zakia, I might as well just tell you. He was burned so severely, he was pretty much incinerated. They identified him by his ring, a black sapphire stone. One of his co-workers recognized it as being Elias's ring from Columbia University. They still have to check the dental records, of course."

"Oh, no. Please, no," she moaned. *What a horrific way to die.* She leaned back abruptly in her seat, the tears rolling down her face. Dani would never get to meet his real father and Elias would never know he had a son all because she had kept the secret and now it was too late. "No, it's not possible," she wailed.

"I'm so sorry," said Mohammad. "You and Elias were close, I take it?"

Zakia swallowed hard. "Yes, Elias was a good friend of mine, a long time ago." Zakia, struggling to regain her composure, added, "Mohammad, thank you very much, but I will have to get back to you."

She hung up and wept quietly at her desk. *This can't be true.* How could she possibly explain it all to their son Dani? Nauseated with guilt, she sat there for a long time.

Fatima was suddenly at her side. "You look awful. What is going on?"

"You remember I told you about the friend I met at Columbia University, Elias Mansur?"

"Yes.,"

"Elias was incinerated in the fracking blowout."

"No!" said Fatima, wide-eyed. She bent down and hugged Zakia.

"Here is this nomadic Berber boy who was chosen by the tribe to get an education, excelled in his studies and became an engineer, and now he is gone. I just can't believe it. I'm so angry, what a waste of a life with so much potential!" Zakia's eyes welled up again.

"May God have mercy on him. That's tragic," said Fatima with a sad smile. She squeezed Zakia's shoulder.

"It's worse than that," Zakia hesitated. She'd never confided this to her friend; what would have been the point? But now she wished she'd been more open. "He was actually more than just a friend. I dated Elias in New York when he was studying engineering and I was getting my master's. Then I met him again three years ago at the tenth reunion for both of our classes at Columbia."

"Honest?" asked Fatima with an incredulous stare. "You never told me that."

"It never seemed to be the right time to tell you. We were actually an item before Benjamin came along."

"That makes it even worse. Did Benjamin know about him?"

"Benjamin never met him, but he knew we had been good friends." Zakia hesitated again. She wanted to tell Fatima everything, but she felt uncomfortable admitting to her friend who was more traditional, that she'd had sex before marriage. For a long time, she'd even managed to convince herself that Benjamin was Dani's biological father. But, as Dani had gotten older, it was clear he took after Elias in so many ways. Dani had his mother's olive-colored complexion and the dark hair and Elias's brown eyes, whereas Benjamin had light brown hair. Benjamin had never suspected anything, not having met Elias, but he wouldn't have missed the striking resemblance if he'd met him now.

Her plan of waiting to tell Dani who his biological father was until he turned eighteen had just disintegrated. She would have to rethink the whole universe. One thing that would never change, she surmised, was her guilt.

Zakia wiped her eyes and sniffed. "Oh, my God, he sent me an e-mail four days ago and wanted to meet me, but I did not respond. You know how it is. You can't just meet a man alone in a café, what with the conservative factions these days, and I definitely couldn't bring Benjamin along. I feel awful that I didn't contact him."

"Was he involved in something sensitive?"

"I don't know, maybe." Perhaps Elias had wanted to meet with her for another reason. "I aim to find out."

After Fatima left, Zakia, blew her nose, took a deep breath and decided she would get to the bottom of Elias's death, *whatever it takes*. She would do it for his son. Elias would never willingly have been involved in something that was unsafe. There had to be more to the story.

Chapter Two

A few hours later, she was still doing research. The day staffers had left and the night reporters and editors were just getting started. Zakia finally got up from her computer. The light in her boss's office was on. His office resembled an aquarium, with glass walls on three sides. It was big and airy, fitting for a senior editor, who happened to be portly. She knocked and walked in. He looked up at her, surprised, and she got straight to the point. "I want to cover the accident at Oddleifur Oil."

"Oh, you've talked to Mohammad." He leaned back from his desk with a sigh. "The answer is no. You're not driving off into the desert on your own. You know that is not going to fly under any circumstances."

Zakia narrowed her eyes. "I am as able to cover this piece as well as the next person."

"Not alone you can't," he retorted.

Zakia had no answer to that, but she intended to go, no matter what.

"I would not be able to face Benjamin if something bad were to happen to you because I'd sent you out to cover a story in a place that can be dangerous even for a man to travel to."

Zakia paced. She didn't see any reason to bring Benjamin into it. After all, he was stuck in Belgrade. "This story could be really important, especially since the authorities are trying to suppress it."

"I have my doubts about that," said Jasem. "Don't let your passion get in the way of common sense."

Zakia smiled grimly. "Don't you always preach that the media's purpose is to gather information, present the news accurately and honestly to the public, and serve as a check on power?" She crossed her arms and gave him the raised eyebrow.

Jasem took off his glasses and rubbed his eyes. "Yes," he said, wearily. "Censoring media coverage is not acceptable, even if we see it happening far too often. Freedom of the press is a battle worth fighting."

Zakia sensed she was making progress. "Furthermore, fracking on the outskirts of Al Tarife, is, as you well know, not far from Western Sahara," she said, pressing her advantage. "That's always going to be controversial."

"Yet, you as well as anyone knows that, after the Arab Spring, even if the crackdown on opposition groups has been loosened somewhat, questioning or standing up to the government on any issue even remotely related to Western Sahara could land you in jail, or worse." He gave her a meaningful look.

She knew what he meant. There were other risks involved too. Several political dissidents and environmental activists had landed in jail on dubious charges or joined the ranks of the disappeared.

"I'll invent a cover story. Infant mortality among nomadic Berbers might sound convincing," she said.

Jasem frowned at her. "Maybe. But it's always personal with you, Zakia, isn't it? Your stories are all driven by passion. What's the connection for you now?"

Zakia began sweating. Journalists were supposed to

be unbiased, and for him to point out her weakness didn't sit well with her. But she couldn't leave her conscience at the door.

"Well, I found out that Elias, my friend from Columbia, was one of the victims," she admitted.

Jasem nodded. "I am very sorry to hear that. That's heartbreaking." Jasem turned abruptly to the window, as if he had spotted something outside, and didn't move for a moment.

"I guess that brings it all back—your parents' accident." Fifteen years ago Zakia's parents had died in a car crash in the morning fog outside of London after having visited her grandfather in Oxford.

"Yes, it does," Zakia said. Her eyes squeezed shut.

"Okay. I give up. You can go, but only if you are accompanied by one of the male interns here."

Zakia stiffened with anger. She didn't need a chaperone. "That won't be necessary. I can take care of myself."

"Please Zakia; stop pretending you're living in New York. Remember, journalists have been arrested in rural areas and assaulted in jail. The intern can pose as your driver."

"But…"

He turned. "This is nonnegotiable. You should leave for Al Tarife first thing in the morning. Nassar, the intern I have in mind, will be back from Casablanca then. It's about a six-hour drive to Al Tarife. Mohammad said the gas well is still burning."

Zakia didn't like his terms, but there were no other options. "Good. We'll leave as soon as possible in the morning. Only one more thing: I need a car with air conditioning."

"You drive a hard bargain." Jasem smiled. "You can borrow my car, but I want it back in one piece."

"Thanks." She grabbed the door knob to leave.

"Oh, Zakia. You might consider wearing a hijab."

"That's not how I was raised."

She walked out without a backward glance. She had some preparation to do. It was getting dark and Zakia could hear the call to prayers from the nearest minaret.

****

When Zakia let herself into their small apartment that evening, she felt a pang that Benjamin was not there to greet her. He commuted across the Atlantic every two weeks for his job. They'd had this arrangement for quite some time so his absence wasn't normally an issue, but the death of Elias had shaken her. She longed to hug Benjamin, welcome him home, and then—at the opportune moment—share the news about Elias with him.

He'd surely understand her need to investigate Elias's death, once she explained what had happened.

She could tell by the lovely aroma of saffron, lemon, and chicken in the apartment that Nura, their cook, had made dinner.

"Dani, Harris," she called. "I need to talk to you."

She put down her computer bag in the hallway and went into the kitchen to make tea, putting a heaping spoonful of mint leaves into her grandmother's elegant glass teapot. Her sons came into the kitchen, their eyes lighting up. Harris, her eleven-year-old, gave her a hug, while Dani, her ever-hungry thirteen-year-old, lifted the lid off the pot on the stove and took a whiff.

"Smells good," he said. "Can we eat?"

"Give me a moment. Why don't you set the table while we talk?"

"What's up, Maman?" asked Harris.

"First, I wanted to tell you about your Dad. He is fine and at a hotel in Belgrade now, but he was working in Serbia, not far from Obrenovac, where a huge flood swept through. Ten people have died so far. We need to count our blessings." The emotions of the day, especially about Elias, hit her again, but she held back tears. She gave Harris another hug, then Dani, holding onto him for a moment longer.

"How bad was the flood?" asked Dani pulling away.

"Obrenovac has had torrential rains for the past few days, unlike the regular rain in the spring. There hasn't been so much rainfall in 120 years."

"That sounds really bad," said Harris. "But Dad is fine?"

"Yes, thank goodness. He called me when he got to Belgrade."

"A 120-year flood; that's a lot of years," said Harris. "Is that also connected to the climate change that you've been talking about?"

"It follows the pattern of climate change for sure."

"When do we see Dad again?" asked Dani.

Zakia looked at him for a long moment—he looked so much like Elias—then caught herself. "He needs to go to Washington first, and then he'll be back here in about a week." She thought again about Elias's death and was tempted, in her guilt and grief, to tell Dani everything.

He gave her a puzzled look. "What's up?"

She hesitated. *No,* she told herself. She couldn't tell

21

Dani about his biological father now. This was neither the time nor the place. She'd wait for the right moment.

"Nothing. Just thinking about what a handsome young man you've become," she said.

Dani flushed. "Maman!"

"Can we call him on Skype now?" asked Harris with a smile.

"In a little while. The other thing I need to tell you is that I am covering a story outside Al Tarife tomorrow."

"Is that going to be safe? It's out in the desert, isn't it?" asked Harris, his eyebrows drawing together over his green eyes.

"Yes, no problem, it will just be an overnight trip. I've spoken to Nura. She'll spend the night here," said Zakia. She looked at Dani, but didn't say anything. Dani didn't notice; he was busy setting plates on the table. "You will be fine, Nura always prepares delicious food, right? Maybe she'll make your favorite lamb tagine with prunes and almonds tomorrow."

"Yes, you're right about that. She's nearly better than you are at cooking," said Dani.

"That's good," said Zakia, arching her eyebrows. "As long as it's only *nearly*."

Zakia often came home late, and Nura would prepare dinner for her boys. Being a family split on two different continents was temporary. Zakia was not happy with the arrangement, but after arguing about it, she and Benjamin had agreed they would live with it for two more years until Harris finished middle school. Dani had already been accepted to a prestigious high school in Chicago, and was looking forward to living with his aunt Tahra and his cousins. Zakia often found herself drained, operating in practice, as a single mom. Tahra had happily made the move to Chicago some years ago after she had gotten a bachelor's degree at Northwestern University, so she wasn't around to help.

****

After Dani and Harris had spoken to their Dad and had retired to their room, Zakia got on Skype with Benjamin. "I'm so glad you are safe," said Zakia. Dani and Harris were so relieved when I told them you were okay. I figured I had to tell them about the flood."

"Yes, that just makes good sense. They are old enough to hear about such things now."

"I hope you found a room for the night."

"No problem. Belgrade has no flooding issues. I'm staying at my usual comfortable little hotel."

"That's good. Oh, I've also got some other news." Zakia decided she didn't want to worry Benjamin, so she would play it cool. "There was a blowout at a gas well in the desert. It's southeast of Agadir, not far from Al Tarife. I need to go cover the story. I just thought I'd let you know."

Benjamin remained quiet for a moment before taking his time answering her. "Why do *you* need to go? I'm sure you have lots of other stories you can cover. And someone else can go to the desert. Besides, is it wise that you take off when I am out of the country? Normally we alternate, remember?"

"This has to be dealt with now. The boys will be fine. Nura is staying the night. And, I'll stay safe. I'll have a driver along, a male intern," said Zakia, lightly.

"I'm not happy about you going to the desert even with an intern in tow. I wish you could focus on issues that don't take you into dangerous areas. Just running out of gas can be a problem in the desert country, for heaven's sake."

"Not to worry, we're bringing a jerry can with extra gasoline. You need to remember that this is my job. Reporters have to follow wherever the story takes them."

"Still," insisted Benjamin. "You seem adamant about covering the story. Why?"

Zakia added, as if in passing, "Elias Mansur was killed in the accident."

Benjamin was quiet for a moment, rubbing his chin as he always did when he was starting to get upset. "Wasn't that your good friend at Columbia before we met?"

"Yes," said Zakia. She tried unsuccessfully to sound unaffected, but started crying softly.

"Oh, jeez." Benjamin ran his fingers through his hair. "I'm sorry about you losing your friend. But that explains a whole lot."

Zakia sniffed. "I guess so." She held her tongue about the truth.

Benjamin peered at her. "Are you distraught because he was killed or because you had a more serious relationship, even after we met at Columbia?"

Zakia felt herself flush. "Well, we did date before I met you. But that was a long time ago. Then I saw him again at the reunion three years ago, but nothing happened."

"How come I didn't hear about that?"

"It was just a dinner, remember? No big deal, I met up with you at the hotel that very same night. Let's just drop it shall we, *please*." Pulling herself together, she said, "I'll stay safe on my trip; don't worry."

Benjamin gave her a dubious look.

"And, you needn't be so protective, you're practically stifling me."

"Well, you know perfectly well what I mean." Benjamin's downturned mouth said it all. She hoped it wasn't about Elias.

Zakia figured she would tell him at some point, but it wasn't going to be now.

"Not to worry. I'll be extra careful."

Chapter Three

Zakia and Nassar arrived at the gas well at around five in the afternoon. Nassar was able to drive close enough, so they could see the drill site. It looked like a war zone, smoke everywhere. He stopped the car next to a large sand dune that was trying to drift across the road.

Zakia and Nassar got out of the car. From where they stood they could see the fire was extinguished, but oil and gas still spewed from the well, creating a roaring noise. The smell of rotten eggs was everywhere. The site was in an uproar, with people running around, moving equipment from trucks, while one man stood in the middle of the activity, shouting orders. A handful of men worked fiendishly at plugging the well.

The drill was still standing tall, but below it, half-burned pipes, hoses, and other damaged equipment were covered in soot and scattered everywhere. A couple of makeshift fire engines were parked nearby, seeming useless. Three large, water trucks had broken windows and blackened exteriors. One had been totally burned out and was tipped on its side.

"*Ya Allah*," said Nassar.

Zakia took a deep breath, trying to put Elias's last moments out of her mind. This looked like a scene from hell. Had he suffered any? What was she going to tell Dani?

She pushed it all out of her mind as the stocky, middle-aged man who had been shouting orders spotted them and picked his way across the rubble-strewn ground toward her and Nassar. He looked tired and gave them a dirty look.

"Let me handle this," Zakia muttered to Nassar.

"Good afternoon," she said before the man could say anything. "Zakia Karim with *Le Journal du Maroc.*"

He scowled at her and opened his mouth, but Zakia continued: "What happened? What caused the blowout? When will it be plugged?"

The man folded his arms, his eyes protruding. "I am the production supervisor and you have no right to be here. No interviews and no pictures, please." He directed this last bit to Nassar, who was aiming his camera at the destruction.

"But," said Nassar, looking at Zakia.

The supervisor took a threatening step toward him. "This is private property," he said. He waved Zakia away. "You need to call the central office in Rabat if you want information on the accident."

Zakia pursed her lips. "Could I speak to one of the employees?"

He put his hands on his hips and glared at her. "Absolutely not. We have our communications manager in Rabat."

"Fine!" said Zakia in a curt tone. "Here's my card if you change your mind."

She shoved it in his hand and said, "Come on, Nassar."

"Are we really leaving? You're not letting him push you around, are you?" he asked, trailing her as they walked quickly toward their car.

"Just follow my lead," she said quietly.

She could feel the man's gaze drilling into her back as she walked away. At the car, she turned to see him walking back to the gas well, confident that he'd run her off. She lifted her smartphone to steal a picture of the drill site just as a large plume of black smoke belched out of the well. Zakia got into the car and Nassar drove off in silence.

Once they got onto the main road, Nassar asked, "Why'd we give in like that? What about freedom of the press?"

Zakia gave him a smile. "There's more than one way to report a story. We're going to find someone on the inside."

He grinned. "I like your style."

"Don't," she said. "It'll get you in trouble."

****

The small town of Al Tarife was close to the fracking operation. Nassar drove slowly through its narrow streets. The brick and mortar houses, huddled together, gave way to a beautiful mosque, facing the traditional central plaza with a colorful, open-stall marketplace, selling food, clothing, and Islamic artifacts. Nassar parked near the plaza and they walked to the food stalls. It was a noisy place, with throngs of people chatting and milling about and music playing on boom boxes at several of the stalls. The smell of spices was intoxicating.

A nomadic Berber family, with their flowing, colorful clothing and weathered faces, stood near a booth brimming with olives of different varieties. Zakia was reminded of Elias and how proud he was of being part of a nomadic Berber tribe. She had often thought how Dani's life would have been so different if she had married Elias, although it would have been a nightmare for her. Yet, as he got older she had noticed how Dani had the seeds of some of Elias's unique but wonderful qualities. He had been a proud man with integrity.

"This looks good." Nassar stopped in front of a stall with mounds of *briouat* pastry stuffed with chicken, and lamb stew bubbling in a copper cauldron. "Want some? It smells like home-made cooking."

"Help yourself," said Zakia. "I have something I want to check out. We'll meet up by the car in about a half an hour. Try not to get into trouble." She smiled.

"I'll do my best," he said with a wide grin.

Zakia followed the nomad family through the marketplace as they inspected the wares at various booths. She wondered if they might have traveled near the fracking operation and if so, whether they knew anything. She was also curious about them, about Dani's heritage.

Finally, she sidled up to a stall selling dates where the older nomad woman, her face rugged and wind-chapped, was standing and tried to strike up a conversation.

"These dates are beautiful," she said. "We do not get such fine dates in Rabat. My sons would love these."

The woman looked at her, but kept silent, then walked off.

Zakia, undeterred, followed the family along the rows of food, and decided to approach the younger woman in the group, the one wearing a wine-colored robe. She had wandered a short distance away and was admiring a headscarf in all the rainbow colors at a stall on the edge of the marketplace. Zakia walked up to her. "What a pretty headscarf," she said, softly. "That would look very nice on you."

The young woman, sucking in a quick breath, said, "Really, do you think so?"

"Yes. It complements the color of your robe."

The young woman nodded. "Thank you."

She wondered if this young woman might have known Elias, but didn't want to name him just yet. "I'm a journalist and I've come to investigate the blowout at the gas well, where there were several deaths involved. I've not had much luck at the fracking operation, the supervisor sent me away. I was wondering if you'd heard about it."

The woman's eyes widened. She looked around her, then lowered her eyes and said in a quiet voice, "I can't talk about it."

"Please," said Zakia. "I had a friend die in the accident."

The woman put down the scarf, clutched her hands together and looked up at the sky. "Yes, we passed by the wellsite early yesterday, and heard what sounded like a bomb detonating in the direction of the site." Her voice grew loud for a moment, catching the attention of several other marketgoers, before she caught herself and reverted to a whisper. "We saw fire in the distance and heard screams."

Zakia shivered, but forced herself to focus on the woman, giving her an encouraging nod.

The woman leaned into Zakia. "When we doubled back to see if anyone needed help, we were met by an angry man who seemed to be in charge. Before we could get close, he told us to leave at once or he would call the police, you know, the *gendarmerie*." The young woman shook her head.

"Yes, that was probably the supervisor we met. Not a pleasant fellow." Zakia hesitated a moment and then asked if they knew Elias Mansur's family.

"Yes," she said, looking surprised. "You knew him? Elias was my distant cousin. There aren't that many Berbers living the nomadic lifestyle anymore, so we keep in touch."

Zakia nodded. "I met him at university. It's so sad."

"Yes. What a horrible death. His parents are devastated. He was their oldest son. They are trying to claim his remains. They are in mourning now and would like to retreat into the desert to bury him, as is our custom." Zakia thought she should know where Elias's remains would be buried for the sake of Dani, but asking might give too much away at this point.

She took a deep breath. Somehow, talking to one of his tribespeople made Zakia feel Elias was in their midst. "It's tragic," said Zakia. "He had such great plans to help his tribe."

They stood in silence for a moment and then Zakia asked, "Did you know anything about his job or the company he worked for?"

The woman nodded. "I can't say much about it. There are lots of rumors swirling around Oddleifur Oil. But I can tell you that the fracking operation has polluted one of our water holes on our traditional lands." She wrung her hands. "It's less than a quarter mile away from the gas well. Thousands of gallons of toxic wastewater have spilled from a leaking pipe and into the ground water."

"Did Elias know about this?"

"I think he had talked to his father once or twice about our water. He said he would get in touch with a human rights organization that could help us. We are at our wits' end. The little rainfall we used to have is practically gone now with the drought, so the water holes are our only source of water." She rubbed her eyes. "Now we barely have that."

Zakia wondered if Elias had gone out on a limb. Oddleifur Oil couldn't have been happy with him had they found out that he was working against them. "Has there been any progress?" she asked. Some men standing nearby looked at them curiously, so Zakia pretended to admire the scarves, picking one up and wrapping it around her neck. The stall owner came over and she quickly took it off.

"Let's keep moving," she said. "I appreciate the information you are giving me." Zakia and the woman moved to another stall displaying purses with ornate embroidery.

The woman looked around cautiously before leaning in, to speak to Zakia. "We have spoken several times to the local authorities, but they have pretty much ignored us. Elias said to give them some time, that they could help," she said. "Now I don't know what's going to happen."

"Maybe the human rights organization will be able to help," said Zakia. "If we can prove that Oddleifur Oil is poisoning your water, it would make a compelling human rights story."

"Would that help us?" asked the woman, swallowing rapidly.

"It would call attention to your plight. Not many people know what's going on with your tribe," she said. "Awareness-building is the first step. I hope to write a piece on this." It was the least she could do for Elias…and Dani, she thought. She took a deep breath.

"Thank you, that's very kind of you," said the woman.

Zakia asked how she could get in touch with her and was somewhat surprised when the woman dug a cellphone out of her bag with a smile." Let's exchange numbers. By the way, my name is Lina Nawabi."

"My name is Zakia Karim," Zakia grinned. She couldn't help but marvel how the nomads had never had telephones in the desert, but they had leap-frogged right into the era of cellphones. Exchanging phone numbers was a good idea. It would offer Dani a connection to his father's family, when he was finally told about his biological father.

They said goodbye and Zakia started walking out of the market to find Nassar. On the way, a memory of Elias kissing her passionately at Columbia on the steps by the statue of the Alma Mater all those years ago, flashed into her mind. She stopped for a second, feeling both angry and sorrowful. She had to write the story about his accident, now more than ever.

She caught up with Nassar, who was leaning against the car with his hands in his pockets, and they agreed to drive out to the fracking operation again early the next morning.

****

That night in her room at *Pension Rashid*, Zakia propped her computer open on her bed so she could use Skype. She was surprised when the internet connection worked instantly—great Wi-Fi for a boarding house. She Skyped first with Dani and Harris and made sure they were okay, then with Benjamin.

"I really miss you," said Benjamin. "How could you go on vacation without me?"

Zakia smiled. "Oh, yes, a lovely vacation spot—here with the cockroaches. We'll have to come back on our second honeymoon."

"Is it that bad?"

"At least the toilet works. How was your trip back to Washington?"

"I got one of the last seats on the morning flight. And your visit to the gas well?"

"It looked like a war zone."

"That sounds terrible, but newsworthy."

"Clearly something suspicious was going on. The supervisor practically pushed us out of there and refused to let us talk to any of the employees."

Benjamin frowned. "Meaning there's more to the story than meets the eye as you usually say, right?"

"Yes, indeed. The intern and I will find out more tomorrow. We're going to hit the sack now."

"I hope it's not the same sack," he said drily.

"I don't know about that," she teased.

"Remember, make sure you stay safe," he said. "Seriously!"

"Don't worry about me," she said.

****

The next morning, when Zakia hurried to the car with her overnight bag, Nassar who was already there offered her a coiled snake pastry bursting with almond paste and flavored with cinnamon and orange flower water. Then he showed her a thermos. "I brought tea and an extra cup," he said. "I thought we should get an early start."

Zakia took a bite of the pastry, "Warm and delicious. Thank you. Wonderful of you to think ahead," she said. "You're a good teammate."

They got in the car and Nassar turned the key. Nothing happened.

"What?" He tried again.

Silence.

"Oh no," said Zakia, She bit back a curse.

They got out of the car.

"Wait up. Lucky for you, I know the mechanic in town. Neighbors from when I grew up in Marrakesh have a repair shop a ten-minute walk from here. I was hoping to connect while we were here, so I have his number." He pulled out his phone, stepped away and called.

Zakia, unable to stand still caught the tail end of the conversation. "If you can come right away." Nassar clicked off the phone.

"Now what?" Zakia held her breath.

"They're coming,"

"When?"

"They're on their way."

"Thank you Nassar. I don't know what I would have done without you."

Zakia and Nassar spent the rest of the morning, updating colleagues and working on other stories, waiting for the car to be repaired. When he got the call saying it was ready, Nassar walked to the shop and drove the car back to the boarding house. Nassar explained that one of the spark plug caps had been missing. Not having the part at hand, the mechanic had to order it from the neighboring town an hour away. That's why it took so long.

"What does it mean that the cap was 'missing'?" Zakia frowned. "Jasem is not going to be happy."

"The mechanic said the car may have been tampered with, but they couldn't say for sure."

Zakia sucked in her breath, and then shook her head. "That's not a good sign."

But I owe it to Elias. I can't back off now.

****

Before noon they headed back to the gas well. This time they chose a back road, which was shielded from view by the large sand dune. They parked at the other end of the operation. When Zakia stepped out of the car and around the dune, she saw a worker walking out of one of the trailers.

Zakia called out to him, and then muttered to Nassar behind her, "Go, and stay in the car and be ready to take off."

"You're the boss."

The worker looked around, squinting, and then walked across the expanse of ground toward her.

"What are you doing out here?" said the young man. "You'll get in trouble for trespassing."

"I just want to find out what happened with the blowout. Not much to ask."

He scowled. "I'm not supposed to talk. You should go." He turned and started to walk away.

Zakia ran after him. "If people don't know what happened, there might be more accidents."

"Don't bother me," he said, without stopping.

"Was this even an accident?" shouted Zakia.

The man stopped and looked at her with a startled

expression. "Do you really think it could have been on purpose?"

"I am just speculating, but we won't know without transparency."

He folded his arms across his chest and regarded her for a moment. "I shouldn't tell you this, because they haven't told us much, but some of us workers have started piecing things together."

Zakia's heart pounded. She was pretty sure Elias's death was suspicious. "Why don't we meet somewhere, where we can talk?"

She could see his jaw muscles working. Then he fixed her with a sharp look. "I'll meet you at the marketplace in Al Tarife at four this afternoon. Call this number if we miss each other. The marketplace can be crowded." He scribbled his number on a small scrap of paper and thrust it in her hand, looking around nervously the whole time. "Don't tell anybody about this."

He took her business card without comment, stuffed it into his pocket and jogged back to the trailer, quickly opened the door, and then let it bang shut behind him.

Zakia wondered if he would show up for their meeting. She looked at the scrap of paper and saw that he had also written his name on it—Tariq. She realized that if something was sketchy about the accident, he was risking his life. Zakia stuck the phone number in her bra. *Just in case.*

Turning to go back to the car, she saw the supervisor step out from another trailer. He was carrying a rifle and, judging from his flaring nostrils, he was ready to use it. Zakia began running toward the car and Nassar drove toward her in a hurry. The supervisor hollered something she couldn't make out. She saw him bring the rifle to his shoulder as she grabbed the door handle of the car, tore it open, and dove in.

Zakia heard a shot. The bullet had cut through the air inches above the open door.

Nassar, panicked, hit the gas and the door swung shut.

Zakia could see the supervisor in the rearview mirror, aiming the gun at them again.

"Look out, Nassar," she yelled.

Two more shots missed as Nassar swerved and raced out of range.

They sped along the dirt road and soon turned onto the pavement, the car fishtailing. "That was close," said Nassar, grinning. "The first shot was just inches from your door. Jasem would not have been pleased if the bullet had hit his car."

"What do you mean?" shouted Zakia. "It was just inches short of my head, for heaven's sake. I heard the bullet whiz by just above my right ear."

"That was awesome. Do you get shot at a lot in our line of business?"

Zakia gave him a sour look. "Just drive."

"Shouldn't we go to the police?"

Zakia thought about it for a moment. "We were trespassing. I think the only people who would get in trouble would be us."

****

When they got back to Al Tarife, it was three in the afternoon. Zakia was starving—she'd forgotten to eat yesterday evening, as she often did when she was working in the field, and the morning pastries weren't enough to sustain her through gunfire. She figured Nassar was hungry, too. "I'm famished. Let's head for the food stalls and find some lunch."

Nassar agreed. They parked close to a kebab stall, bought assorted kebabs and tea before settling down to eat on a small bench overlooking a little park under the shade of an acacia tree. Kids were running around, kicking a soccer ball, and Zakia, for a moment, missed her sons, remembering how they played soccer when they were little, before shifting their interests to Jiu Jitsu.

"Mmm, it smells so good," said Nassar as he helped himself to grilled chicken on a skewer and Zakia followed suit.

Her cellphone rang and, to her surprise, it was Dani calling.

"Hi Maman," Dani said, a slight quiver in his voice.

"What's up?" said Zakia. "You sound out of sorts."

"Well, I've been trying to convince Harris that everything is okay, but I'm worried."

"What is it?"

"We just got home from school and a big, angry man came to the door asking for you."

"Did he say what he wanted or where he worked?"

"No, I asked for his name. He said you'd know. Maman, what is going on? Who was this guy?" Dani said, his voice still trembling.

"Where's Nura?" Zakia asked, trying to keep her voice level.

"She left a note saying she went to the pharmacy. Said she'd be back in twenty minutes, that's about fifteen minutes ago."

"Just text me when she arrives," said Zakia sounding even-keeled despite an urge to panic. "No need to be afraid. I'm sure this person was just someone from work having a bad day. But please don't answer the door from now on, unless the person actually gives their name first, and you recognize them through the peephole."

"Okay, Maman, I'll do that." said Dani. "You'll be home tonight, right?"

"Don't wait up, my dear. It will probably be late. Ask Nura to stay the night again. I love you so much."

"Okay, I love you too," said Dani and Zakia hung up.

Zakia's hand was sweaty as she put her phone away.

Nassar gave her a quizzical look. "Problem at home?"

"Yes, strange," Zakia said. "Someone showed up at our apartment and wouldn't give his name." Dani sounded worried. I hope I convinced him that everything's okay. But, seriously, I have no idea who it might have been."

"That is odd," said Nassar. "Is your address listed in the phonebook?"

"No, it's unlisted, but I'll have to focus on that when we get back to Rabat. The cook is going to stay with them overnight again. Hopefully, they'll be fine," she said unconvinced.

Nassar stood up and took his paper plate to the trash bin.

"I guess it makes sense to visit my old neighbor, the mechanic, to thank him for fixing the car on such short notice."

40

"Good idea," said Zakia.

Nassar looked surprised. "But now that I think about it, shouldn't I be there when you interview the Oddleifur Oil employee?"

She could manage an interview on her own. Plus, her contact—Tariq—might feel threatened. "No, you go see your friends and thank them so much from both of us. The marketplace is right here, I'll be fine. I will call you when I am done."

****

It was time to meet Tariq. Zakia strolled around the marketplace, waiting for him. She got Dani's text. Nura had returned right after Dani called and was happy to stay another night. *Great! Love you,* texted Zakia. She sighed, very much relieved.

There were mostly men milling about on the plaza, a few couples, but no single women. A group of men looked in her direction and snickered. She turned her eyes to the ground and hurried past them, conscious of her slacks and uncovered head.

Where's Tariq? Maybe he'd been frightened by the shooting incident.

She regretted that she'd told Nassar to take the afternoon off. The rural custom, especially for religious conservative families, normally required that a woman be accompanied by her husband or a male family member when going out.

Zakia stopped in front of the scarf stall again, pretending to admire the merchandise, thought about buying a scarf, but was annoyed with the idea. After a few moments, she saw Tariq walking towards her. He looked around nervously.

He walked up to her. "Salam," he said.

41

"Salam. Thanks for coming." She introduced herself without shaking hands.

"Tariq Nagi," the man said in a tense voice, "Shall we walk along here and talk? It will look more natural."

Zakia rubbed the back of her neck. If someone were to catch on that they weren't related, she could be in serious trouble. She pushed that thought aside. She needed to concentrate on her work. "I think that's a good idea, Cousin," she said deliberately, emphasizing the word "cousin."

"Okay…Cousin," said Tariq, smiling for the first time.

Tariq had deep worry lines on his forehead. He constantly looked over his shoulder as he and Zakia walked along the food stalls.

"Stop looking around," whispered Zakia. "You look suspicious."

"Sorry. Let's get this done quickly, shall we."

"Agreed," she said. "What happened when the gas well blew?"

Tariq grimaced. "I had the day off but was reading in my trailer when it happened. I was one of the first ones on the scene. I found Elias's body." Tariq's voice went husky and he wiped his eyes. "It was gruesome."

Footsteps approached behind her, and she turned her head. Three *gendarmerie* stood not even a foot away from them. She froze, her heart pounding.

The oldest of the three officers, a grey-haired man, addressed her. "I'm Captain Awad. Are you Zakia Karim?"

Zakia, made her voice sound stronger than she felt and answered, "Yes." She straightened her shoulders. "And I am a journalist. How did you know my name?"

"You need to come with me to the police station. We have reason to believe you are involved in terrorist activities."

"There must be some mistake," said Zakia, her eyes widening. "I'm here covering a story. Nothing more. We still have freedom of the press in this country, don't we?"

The officers ignored her and put cuffs on her wrists. Her insides twisted.

"I don't know who this woman is," said Tariq, as the officers put cuffs on him too. "What grounds do you have to suspect me?"

Zakia followed the officer out of the marketplace, feeling the stares of the bystanders upon her. Her lips and chin were trembling.

Chapter Four

Zakia was taken to a building that looked more like a shack than a police station, made of cinder blocks and a tin roof. Inside it was extremely hot, even with a couple of ceiling fans running. Captain Awad disappeared as soon as they got to the station. One of the officers led her into a room and ordered her to stand while another policeman ransacked her handbag, dumping its contents, including her laptop, onto the table. "Be careful with that," she said. "That's my livelihood you're tossing about."

"You've got more serious problems to tend to," one of them said.

Zakia kept silent. She needed to figure out what was going on before she decided how to handle this.

An officer stood in front of her and did a thorough frisking. It was quick, but Zakia cringed as he ran his hands over her breasts. He leered at her.

Finally, she was left to sit at a table in the small, oven-hot room, wondering how she was going to get a phone, since they'd taken hers. A few minutes later, Captain Awad showed up. He sat down across the table from her, stared at her and said, without preamble: "What were you doing in the desert, outside of Al Tarife yesterday and earlier today?"

If she were in the U.S., she could have called a lawyer. Here, she wasn't sure if she'd be able to get in touch with anyone. She had to sound confident. "I was interviewing nomadic Berber women about infant mortality for a special interest article I am writing for my newspaper."

"But you were seen on private property at Oddleifur Oil's operations."

"Well, as a reporter, I thought it my duty to check on that incident, since it had just happened and we could see the smoke."

"So you admit you were at the gas well?"

"It's the nomadic women I am writing about," Zakia answered calmly.

"Then why did you meet with one of the company's employees at the marketplace? Upon further questioning, Tariq told me that you asked to meet him."

"Oh, that was just a chance encounter. I felt unsafe at the marketplace. You know, a woman alone in rural areas, and Tariq seemed sympathetic. I was going to ask him to escort me to my colleague who is visiting a friend at the local car repair shop."

Awad frowned, but didn't argue with her. She couldn't tell if he was buying her story or not. "Do you really care about the nomadic Berbers?"

"Yes, I do." She looked him straight in the eye.

"Then you know that they have been having some trouble with their water holes," he said quietly. "My brother-in-law, a farmer, said that the crops are drying up in these parts."

Zakia was silent. She didn't know what to say. Was he trying to trap her into revealing the real focus of her investigation?

Finally, she decided to go out on a limb. "I don't know how it all ties together, but I am getting interested in that side of their story."

Awad smiled slightly, seeming satisfied with her answer. She didn't know what he was up to, but he changed the subject. "How many nomadic women have you managed to interview? They are usually a little skittish about talking to outsiders."

"A handful. There are advantages to being a woman reporter, you know." Zakia realized that either she was becoming a good liar or Awad was sympathetic to the plight of the nomads and wasn't a friend of Oddleifur Oil. Whatever his reason, she hoped his sudden shift in questioning meant she could walk out of here rather than languish for months, even years, awaiting trial.

Three hours of questioning went by before Awad left her alone in the room. She was thirsty and worried. Zakia had a brief thought about Nassar, but promptly dismissed it. He could drive back to Rabat on his own. All she could do was sit and wait. She thought about Tariq and what might have happened to him. She wondered if he would still be willing to carry on with the interview they had begun at the marketplace.

After another half hour, the captain returned, carrying a glass of water, which he offered her as though it were the finest tea. She thanked him and drank it in one go.

"Your boss has corroborated your story," he said as he sat down. "You are free to go."

She was thankful that she had communicated her cover story to Jasem. She wanted to bristle at Awad, but instead she simply nodded.

"I am sorry to have detained you," he said, and then paused. He seemed to be searching for the words.

"But the company has been most insistent that we find and arrest you for trespassing and harassment." He tilted his head and looked at her, curiously. "In fact, someone from the government was said to have specifically named you as a terrorist." He drummed his fingers on the table for a moment. "It might be better if you left immediately and kept a low profile if you plan to continue this investigation."

Zakia shivered in the heat. Someone in the government knew she was investigating this story and, moreover, wanted to stop her? Would her newspaper and reporter status protect her from a smear campaign? "Obviously they are mistaken," she said. "Sometimes women in this field become an easy target for traditional thinkers."

"That may be the case. But I think you should tread carefully with your story on the nomadic Berbers...however it plays out."

"Thank you," she said. "I'll be more discreet."

He nodded, wished her luck, and left the room. Shortly, another officer, the one who groped her, returned with her bag and flung it on the table. Zakia's shoulders tightened. Yet, this time the officer avoided making eye contact with her. Forcing her trembling hands to cooperate, she picked up her bag and walked out of the room, through the small lobby, and out into the evening. She took a deep breath of cool air, and caught the sweet scent of cabbage rose. The square was nearly empty.

She walked quickly away from the station, texting Nassar as she went, asking him to meet her by the marketplace. Walking around alone this late at night would only invite more trouble.

****

After a few minutes, Nassar pulled up in the car and she climbed in.

"What happened to you?" he said. "I was about ready to call the police and report you missing."

"I was arrested."

Nassar whistled: "I missed all the fun."

She looked at him with narrowed eyes. "It's not funny. I need to get home."

They drove in silence.

Halfway home, Nassar said, "Have you noticed that the same car has been following us since we left the marketplace?"

Almost asleep, Zakia rubbed her eyes. "Can you lose him?"

"I'll try." Nassar concentrated on ducking through alleys and side streets on a back road, trying to shake off the car that was following them.

"Just keep driving," said Zakia.

As they pulled out of a side street near a mosque, a pair of headlights came up in the rearview mirror. Nassar swore under his breath. "Now what do we do?"

Zakia looked up and scratched her chin. Who might be after them now? "Speed up, turn the corner and quickly park in the street, by some houses with your lights and motor turned off."

After nearly driving over a lone pedestrian, Nassar pulled up in front of a house, turned off the lights and the motor. He and Zakia ducked down on their seats and held their breath. A few moments later, they saw the headlights flash across the windshield as the car sped by, then disappeared. Nassar grinned. "All gone."

"Well done," Zakia responded with a sigh of relief

as she straightened up in her seat.

They waited a few minutes, to make sure the car was really gone. Then Nassar drove back to Rabat, all the while keeping an eye on the rearview mirror.

****

Nassar dropped Zakia off in front of her apartment building at nearly three in the morning. The street in front was peaceful, but Zakia peered out of the car window for a moment, waiting to see if someone would pop out of the shadows. She thanked Nassar and told him to get some sleep.

"You, too," he said. "Thanks for the adventure."

She turned and walked up to her door, shaking as she stood on the front stoop. The terror—being shot at, arrested, groped, accused of terrorism, and followed—had begun to sink in.

She unlocked the heavy wooden door, feeling an odd sense of relief that it had been locked. She put down her purse in the hall. Dani came out of his room, his hair standing on end. He was always a light sleeper.

"Hi Dani," she said. "What a relief to see you!"

He wandered sleepily over to her and hugged her. Then he pulled back and looked her over carefully.

"Maman what happened to you? You look awful. Are you okay?"

The events of the day piled up and Zakia's voice choked with tears. "I was taken in for questioning at the police station in Al Tarife, just as I began to interview a man for a story I'm working on." Dani flinched when she started sobbing. "They held me for more than three hours. It was horrible."

"Oh, Maman," he said biting his lip. "Why didn't you call me?"

"I was helpless; they had my phone," she said, wiping her eyes.

Zakia and Dani hugged again, this time, for a long time. Thinking of Elias's untimely death and her own arrest, made her think, once again, about the secret she was keeping from her oldest son.

By this time, they'd awakened Harris, who was a heavy sleeper. He came stumbling out of the boys' room. "What's going on? There are still four hours left before we need to get up for school."

"Maman got arrested," said Dani.

Zakia didn't deny it, but she felt a headache coming on.

"Wow," said Harris. "Let's call Dad."

"No, you two go back to bed," said Zakia.

Nura had also woken up and walked into the hallway. "Welcome home, Madame Zakia," she said. Then she frowned at Dani and Harris. "You two should be in bed. You have school in the morning."

"We just wanted to make sure Maman was okay," said Dani.

"We'll talk more in the morning," Zakia said to her boys, and then turned to Nura. "Thanks for taking care of them for an extra night."

"No problem," said Nura. "Would you like some tea?"

"Yes, please. I'm famished. I need to eat something right now or I will pass out."

"There's lamb tagine left from dinner if you like."

"That would be wonderful. Thank you. I'll wash up and change into my nightgown."

"Go on then," said Nura, disappearing into the kitchen.

Exhausted, Zakia undressed and then noticed a scrap piece of paper fall on the floor. Ah, yes, Tariq's cellphone number. She put it on the nightstand, and decided to take a shower. Having been pawed by the policeman had made her feel dirty.

****

The next morning, after they finished breakfast, Zakia asked Dani and Harris to get ready for school while she tried to Skype their father. "He's most likely asleep already," she warned. "It's past midnight there."

He answered immediately.

"I hope we didn't wake you," she said.

"No, I was working late, trying to finish a report. We're looking to fund a large solar panel project in Morocco actually. I'm excited that there are moves being made towards renewables."

"Sounds good," said Zakia. She called the boys to join her.

Dani and Harris crowded around behind her to see the screen. "Maman got arrested," said Dani.

Benjamin looked shocked. "Is this true?"

"It isn't the whole story. I did in fact get arrested and taken in for questioning in Al Tarife yesterday, just as I was interviewing an employee of Oddleifur Oil. They didn't press any charges though, thank goodness."

Benjamin said, "I'm so sorry Zakia. That's terrible. I wish I were there to put my arms around you." He gave Dani and Harris a grim look. "Boys, you will have to do a better job of taking care of your Maman."

Zakia laughed. "Don't be ridiculous, Benjamin."

"I'm just kidding," he said. I will wrap up here, but unfortunately, with my work load I won't be able to get away for another few days."

"We'll be fine. All good journalists are expected to be arrested at least once in their career," said Zakia.

"Oh, Maman, don't talk like that," said Harris, shaking his head.

"She's pulling your leg," said Dani, bumping purposely into him with his shoulder.

"Stop that. I know she is."

"Okay, Benjamin; Dani and Harris need to get to school and I have to call my boss. Talk to you soon."

****

After the boys left, Zakia stayed in the kitchen, poured herself another cup of tea and sat back down. She stared out the kitchen window at the big tamarisk tree and sighed. She had skirted telling the details about the arrest to Benjamin, especially in front of the boys, but now she worried that she was on some sort of international terrorist list.

Zakia called her boss.

Jasem answered the phone after a few rings. "Jasem," said Zakia, "I'm back home and safe. Thanks for corroborating my story with the Al Tarife police."

"You're welcome," he said. "Nassar filled me in. I'm glad my car made it back in one piece. What was it like being arrested?"

"It was terrifying. All the time, I expected something awful to happen to me—a woman—with all those men standing around."

"You just got rattled," said Jasem, trying to make light of the incident. "But you do need to be more careful. Always have someone with you. I thought that was why I sent Nassar out there with you."

"That was my fault."

"So tell me, did you get to talk to anyone at the gas

well?"

"I did meet with one of the workers, a man named Tariq. He's the one I started interviewing at the marketplace when I got arrested, but at least I got his phone number. I'll give him a call, that is, if he'll still talk to me. I never saw him again after the arrest."

Jasem sighed, "He could be long gone by now."

Chapter Five

On Friday morning, Zakia arrived at her office an hour early hoping she'd have a better chance at connecting with Tariq before he started his shift at the gas well.

He answered the phone after Zakia's third attempt with a curt "Salam." She wondered if he was dodging her. Zakia reminded him they had met at the marketplace.

He sighed. "I can't really talk right now, Cousin."

Cousin? Zakia thought of the possibility of his phone being tapped, so she carried on with their little game. "Auntie sent me to her kitchen to show her how to make the family recipe."

"I get it," said Tariq. "Yes, I was also asked a few questions about the recipe."

"Auntie said you insisted on meeting me at the marketplace first, to buy some fish. I said you had misunderstood."

"I guess I did." Tariq sounded tired.

"I got stuck in the kitchen for three hours. The food smelled awful," said Zakia.

"I'm sorry to hear that," Tariq's voice was sympathetic. "I was sent out of the kitchen as soon as the white beans were cooked."

"Look, we really need to work on this recipe together. Why don't you come eat with the family this weekend? It will make Maman happy."

"If we must," responded Tariq. "Okay then, your uncle can wait by the entrance to Café de Paris outside the Old Medina and drive us to the house from there. Does tomorrow at three o'clock work for you?"

"Yes," said Zakia. "See you then, Cousin."

Right after Tariq hung up, Zakia heard a second click on the phone. She stared at her cellphone. *Right, I get it. Tariq figured it out; someone is probably listening. I better buy a disposable phone for these calls.*

Zakia spent the rest of the morning researching Oddleifur Oil. On the company's website she found that Oddleifur Oil & Gas Morocco had its parent company in Iceland, although it was now majority-owned by a Chinese company. Typical, thought Zakia. The Chinese invested in energy worldwide, even in Morocco. But she didn't find much more than the standard PR fluff. She did, however, come across an announcement that the company was one of the sponsors for an upcoming energy conference to be held in China. That looked interesting and she made a mental note to check on it further; maybe she could talk to Jasem about it.

Reflecting on her research, she wondered what angle was going to be the most effective. She thought about what Awad, the arresting officer, had said about water holes drying up. On impulse, she typed in "theft nomadic Berbers' water rights" into the search engine.

Two websites in Tunisia came up. She tried again, this time targeting chat rooms. She found an internet forum run by one of the Moroccan opposition groups, and scrolled through the threads. The nomads and their allies weren't as low tech as the government figured because here was loads of information.

It became evident to Zakia that her government wanted to use the nomads' tribal water rights and the lands they traditionally used for pasture to enable Oddleifur Oil to expand the fracking operations, drilling thousands of feet below the desert sands. She read further, getting more excited, when a name jumped off the page.

Elias M.

He had told his people, "We need to organize or we are going to lose out to the oil and gas company. I have proof, but can't share it yet."

"Oh, Elias," moaned Zakia. "What did you get yourself into?" She tried to think like Elias. Had he stumbled across some proof of illegal doings or had he just been contacting her with a hunch? Was the blowout staged as an "accident" to get rid of Elias? The trail was all over the place.

****

Later that morning, Jasem called her into his office. "Sit down." He pinched his lips. "I have some news."

Zakia sat opposite his desk. "What's up?"

He rubbed his temples. "I've been reprimanded by Hakim. Our esteemed publisher is not happy. This is very serious. I'm sure you'll understand."

"Why on earth would he do that?" Zakia asked.

Jasem frowned. "He was not at all pleased with your investigation of the blowout at Oddleifur Oil. Even Sigurd Agnarsson, the CEO, called to inform him of your encounter at the gas well and the arrest. Hakim has ordered me to pull you off the story. It's way too sensitive and not worth jeopardizing…"

She cut him off. "What do you mean?"

"Zakia, you need to lay low. The government considers this a sensitive area because it's so close to Western Sahara. Maybe you should take off on a foreign assignment. Essentially, get out of the limelight."

Zakia narrowed her eyes and wrinkled her nose. After studying in the U.S., she longed for Morocco to embrace the freedom of the press much more seriously. In the U.S. at least, they had the basic ideals of how media should operate in a democratic society, trying to reveal the facts, even if the practice was not always exemplary.

"For heaven's sake, why are you caving to the higher-ups?"

Jasem waved his hand at her. "Not much good we can do if we're unemployed. You remember the journalist who was jailed on extortion charges when he published an article exposing the Cedar Mafia?"

Zakia nodded.

"Just pipe it down a notch. I'm officially pulling you off the story." Jasem lowered his voice. "So just do it under the radar."

Zakia knew he was right, even though she didn't like it. She thought for a moment, and remembered the upcoming energy conference she'd read about. "There's an energy conference coming up in China. The oil and energy minister is speaking in Chongqing. Perhaps I can get some more information by asking the minister in person. I bet I'd have a better chance of doing that on a trip abroad."

Jasem nodded thoughtfully. "As it happens, the Chinese have invited the oil and energy minister *and* his entourage, including reporters. I have the invitation right here somewhere." He rifled through the piles of papers and files on the table next to his desk, finally fishing out a fat envelope. "Here it is. I got this invitation several weeks ago, inviting us to send someone, but I didn't give it much thought. Then I forgot all about it."

"That's unlike you, to forget an invitation," said Zakia.

Jasem smiled. "Do you want it or not?"

He told her it was a five-day trip, all expenses paid. Spouses and family would need to pay their own way, of course. It included a three-day mini cruise on the Yangtze River, starting in Wuhan. That sounded perfect, thought Zakia. She could take the boys, get out of the country, and keep investigating.

"As I understand it, the Chinese are planning on large investments in the Moroccan energy sector. That could be a safe angle," said Jasem.

Zakia took a deep breath. "Yes, I've also read about that. However, I'll still be sticking to my story."

He frowned. "Did you not listen to what I just said? Actually, I wonder if Abdullah wouldn't be a better candidate, especially since you are already in trouble," he said, waving the envelope around.

"Wait a minute," said Zakia, starting to sweat. "This is my story. I've already been arrested once. I'll be careful not to upset the publisher again."

Jasem laughed. Then he looked serious. "I am worried about your safety, Zakia. You know I consider you one of my best reporters—diligent, persistent, and always acting with integrity—but your stubbornness is driving me crazy. Furthermore, your risk-taking seems to surpass what even I consider safe."

"I'll be fine. The official story is that I'll be covering the Chinese investments in the Moroccan energy sector. And I'll bring my sons along as my escorts."

"Aren't they a bit young for that? Do you think that is wise? There's a lot of pollution and you can't drink the tap water there. Besides, most people don't speak English, let alone French."

She thought about what he said, but wasn't worried. It was a regular tour group, for heaven's sake.

"Dani and Harris are about to have their midterm break with no plans and Benjamin isn't arriving for another week. I prefer them being with me rather than staying with friends. Even though it is a spur-of-the-moment trip, it would be good for them to visit China. They could learn plenty. Besides, the ship is run by some European outfit. It should be safe. We'll learn some basic phrases in Mandarin on the plane."

"Sounds like you've already got it all planned. Guess I won't stand in your way."

"I appreciate your support," she said.

Jasem shook his head. "We should review what questions to ask. The delegation to China leaves early next week so we don't have much time."

"Thanks." Zakia rolled her eyes, thinking of all that needed to be done in such a short amount of time.

"What about visas? Doesn't that take months?" asked Jasem.

"I've look into it." she said. "I happened to notice this conference as I was checking Oddleifur Oils' website earlier. It's one of the conference's sponsors. I've got contacts. It can take as little as two days to get a visa."

"Good, then get on it." He handed her the envelope. "You have to give me two other stories while you are there, one being a travel story."

"Agreed." When Zakia walked out of Jasem's office, she was already making plans in her head for intercepting the oil and energy minister. Jasem may be willing to cave into their publisher's politically motivated requests, but she wasn't about to let the story go. And she'd keep her appointment with Tariq.

Chapter Six

On Saturday, after delivering their passports to the Chinese Embassy, she dropped Dani and Harris off for their Jiu Jitsu lesson and hurried to meet with Tariq. He was visiting his parents who lived in Rabat. Zakia had called him with the disposable phone and they had agreed to meet at a newspaper stand around the corner from Café de Paris just opposite the Old Medina. That way, they would arrive at the café together.

Zakia walked across the Old Medina, the large, colorful, covered market, teeming with locals and tourists and caught a whiff of some exquisite spices. She found Tariq leafing through a glossy magazine by a news stand. "There you are, Cousin," he said a little too loudly. "I was worried you would be late." As a precaution, they walked into the café arm in arm, pretending to be related. The traditional café, one not mobbed with tourists, was located in the Old Town, a picturesque neighborhood with several colonial-style hotels, surrounded by narrow, arched alley ways.

Zakia grinned at him. "Not to worry. I said I would be here. Let's keep our voices down. Why don't I find us a quiet table in the back and you can get us some tea?"

Tariq ordered two teas at the counter, waited a few minutes, and then brought their drinks to her table and sat down.

She took a sip of her tea. "What exactly are your duties at the gas well, Tariq?"

Tariq combed his hand through his hair. "Oh, I connect the water hoses to the drills."

"And what did Elias do?"

"He checked the water pressure and made sure the machines were working properly." Tariq fidgeted with his spoon and his left knee kept bouncing. He spoke in subdued tones, constantly looking around "I'm really not comfortable here. Let's make this a quick meeting, shall we?"

"We'll make it short," said Zakia. Tariq's nervousness was contagious. Perhaps this meeting was a mistake.

"Elias was a team player and everybody liked him. I did want to mention that Elias spoke fondly of you," said Tariq, out of the blue. "We were roommates, you see."

His comment took her by surprise and she felt guilty about her own behavior; she hadn't been nice to Elias. He'd gotten in touch when they were done with their studies and back in Morocco, but Zakia had ignored his overtures. Yet, she had felt her hands were tied. If she had met with Elias she would have felt compelled to tell him about Dani and if he had seen Dani, he would have known the boy was his.

Zakia had to press on. "Tariq, what went wrong that day?"

"At first I thought it was caused by the usual short cuts. The company has been using a new method of oil and gas production in Morocco—fracking. I'm sure you've heard of it."

Zakia nodded. She noticed a man standing in the

front of the café eyeing them. A shiver went down her spine. Then he disappeared.

"We were always under pressure to get things done faster. We barely had any time to think. And the hours were long. We were tired most of the time, too little sleep."

"Clearly, lack of proper labor standards." Zakia made some notes.

Tariq sighed. "Yes, you got that right. The day of the accident Elias was called in to fix something. I thought it was strange. He was usually in the control center, maintaining the systems, working at a higher level. At the time, I assumed we were short staffed. But I've been thinking about it and there had been a bunch of odd incidents surrounding Elias these last few weeks."

Zakia straightened up, her eyes wide. "What do you mean?"

"Well, I began to realize that Elias was unhappy with Oddleifur Oil. He didn't say much to me, but he was out of the trailer at all hours, working late or visiting his tribal community. He was under a lot of pressure at work. It seemed like he might be in some sort of trouble with upper management." Tariq rubbed his forehead.

"And what were the odd incidents you're referring to?" prompted Zakia.

"Slashed tires on his car. His computer was stolen and somebody had broken into his files at work—but now when you add them up, well, you know…"

Zakia's stomach was in an uproar.

"I volunteered to go down that fatal morning, to work on the equipment, but my boss told me specifically that it had to be Elias." His voice rose and he kept fidgeting with his paper napkin. "The really weird part was when—not an hour after the accident—our boss came to our trailer, seized all of Elias's personal belongings, and asked me a lot of questions about whether or not I knew what Elias was doing in his spare time. I told him I wasn't Elias's babysitter, pretended I knew nothing and wasn't interested, but the whole incident made me uneasy."

"Why don't you just quit?" asked Zakia, "Are you sure you're safe?"

"I've put in too much time with this company to start all over somewhere else, especially since I don't have a university degree."

"Why are you talking to me then?"

"Because it seems like the right thing to do. And the whole thing doesn't sit right with me," he said and pushed his tea away. "I want to find out what really happened to my friend."

"So do I." Zakia didn't know what to say after that, but Tariq filled her silence.

"The blowout was horrific. Elias died instantly and we couldn't do anything. The other victims might have survived, had they been treated more quickly. I was part of the crew ordered to contain the fire. None of us was trained or equipped for such an accident, even though we all knew it could happen—the worst case scenario. It was as if the owners wanted to make money as fast as possible, but they weren't prepared to take responsibility for the risks involved. It's criminal."

Zakia nodded. She worried that meeting with her might get Tariq in the same sort of trouble as Elias had landed in. "That's the sort of information I want to investigate," she said. "But we probably shouldn't be seen together for too long. Someone might notice us."

"I agree. I was thinking, if the accident was actually that—an accident, then the main cause of the explosion should come out," he said, lowering his voice.

Zakia shivered at the implication. She barely dared to make the accusation—so much was at stake—she too brought her voice down to a whisper. "Is it possible for someone to sabotage the operation intentionally, yet make it look like an accident?"

Tariq's jaw dropped. "You mean murder!" he said rather loudly.

Zakia looked around to see if he had caught anybody's attention. "Keep it down, someone might hear you."

He nodded. "Right."

"Tariq, do you know if Elias was planning to release information about the company and if so, what kind of material it might have been?"

"He did say he had gotten in touch with friends from Columbia University, but he didn't elaborate. Did he contact you?"

"Yes." Zakia shifted in her chair. For all of his postings on the internet forums, it seemed like Elias had deliberately kept his roommate in the dark. He must have known he was in danger.

Tariq rubbed his eyes. "After the accident, of course, there has been talk of changes in procedures— more checks on safety issues, and so forth. A similar accident—assuming it was one—will not likely happen at this fracking site any time soon. There are discussions about a pay raise. I think they are desperate not to have us all quit and they want to avoid suspicion."

Through her research at the land office, Zakia had found a connection between the nomads' traditional lands and the lands owned by Oddleifur Oil. She didn't think that Tariq knew about it, but asked him anyway. "What do you know about Oddleifur Oil buying up the nomads' traditional lands and polluting their water holes?"

He shook his head. "Very little. But I did overhear our supervisor, Rahim, talking to someone on the phone about compensation, but I'm not sure if it was related to the nomads or not."

"What did you hear?"

"Just that 'if they know what's good for them, they'll take the money and run.' He may not have been referring to the nomads, but I'm beginning to see a connection."

"They shouldn't have their traditional lands jerked out from under them," Zakia shook her head.

Tariq leaned in and murmured, "I've also heard a rumor, and it's just a rumor, that some of the tribes are being moved further east, far beyond Al Tarife. It's outrageous. I suspect someone is preparing the ground for the oil company to move in."

"The government must be involved in these maneuverings. But we better get going. I'll go first. Thanks for meeting with me. Let's stay in touch."

Tariq smiled grimly. "Yes. Just call me if you have any more questions." He sat back and looked around the café. "You best be careful...Cousin."

****

After the boys went to the movies that night, Zakia

riffled through the day's mail. At the bottom of the pile she found a letter from Elias.

She gasped and then froze. Holding the letter close for a moment, Zakia sat down. It was postmarked over a week earlier. *Typical, the mail is so unreliable in Morocco.* She tore open the envelope with trembling hands. It was the standard Easter card with a note enclosed. She struggled to read through watering eyes.

Dear Zakia,

I am writing to you as you are a journalist with international connections and I only have a couple of people I trust, who I believe can help me. I sent you an e-mail asking to see you, but wanted to explain more in a letter because I feel like my e-mail account might have been compromised.

Zakia took a deep breath and continued reading.

I have discovered some inconsistencies at my company that have me worried about the operation's safety and ethics. I've also found proof that Sigurd Agnarsson, the CEO at Oddleifur Oil Morocco, is trying to seize my people's traditional lands to expand its fracking operations. It appears someone in the government is colluding with the company. Don't try to contact me directly; it's too dangerous. Can we meet at Hotel Villa Andalusia next Saturday at 2 p.m.? This is urgent. Use discretion and tell no one where you are going, not even Benjamin.

Zakia dropped the note as if it had caught fire. *Oh, my God, we were to meet today. Yet, Elias has been dead for five days.*

"It's not fair," she shouted as she picked up the note, and then blew out a series of short breaths. She paced around the kitchen, hugging herself. If she'd answered the e-mail, perhaps she could have convinced Elias to leave the country, or at least the company. Maybe he'd still be alive. *Poor Elias. And poor Dani.*

Then she pushed her shoulders back; she needed to do something with this information. She thought about calling Benjamin, but she didn't want to arouse his suspicions about her relationship with Elias. The only person she knew who could handle this situation, she concluded, was Jasem.

When Jasem picked up, his voice had a stern tone. "Did somebody else die? This better be good," he said. "I'm in the middle of watching a gripping movie with my wife."

The whole story came spilling out, "I met with Tariq today, here in Rabat. We discussed the circumstances surrounding Elias's death that pointed to foul play. Just now, in today's mail, I find the annual holiday card for Easter I got from Elias, sent nearly two weeks ago. Elias wanted to meet," Zakia paused. "Today!"

"Oh my," said Jasem.

Zakia continued "He writes that something suspicious was going on at work." Zakia's voice was shaky. "I might have been able to prevent my old friend's death," she blurted out.

"Calm down Zakia," Jasem interrupted, "That note is not proof of murder. And there was nothing you could have done about it. Get off of that guilt trip. You women are so good at that."

"But what do we do now?"

"You are treading on dangerous ground. We can't run the story as you well know."

"We can't just ignore this," she said. "This man

68

was killed, for heaven's sake, and we're talking about the land and water rights of the nomads. That's a human rights issue. And it looks like someone in the government and Sigurd Agnarsson are in cahoots."

Jasem grumbled, "If you make these allegations public, you will have signed your own death warrant."

"But it's wrong, and you know it," she said.

"Look, I want to support you in this, but I can't. It's too dangerous. I can't stop you from publishing this elsewhere, of course. But just don't do it now," he said.

"Okay, Jasem. Thank you," said Zakia. "At least that's something."

After she hung up the phone, she sat at the kitchen table with her head in her hands, thinking about how things had changed so quickly in her personal life, and yet, how the politics in Morocco weren't changing nearly fast enough to suit her. As the agent for Rolls Royce in Morocco since the 1950s until he died, her father had managed to work his way around corruption when selling airplane motors to the whole Arab world, but said it probably would take many generations to change the culture. She wished that she could talk with him now.

That night on the sofa with the boys, Zakia Skyped with Benjamin. He seemed more supportive of their upcoming trip to China than when they'd last spoken, though still concerned.

Zakia told Benjamin about the meeting with Tariq. "We discussed among other things, how Elias's death may not have been an accident."

Benjamin glared at her, rubbing his chin, "Zakia, is it Elias's death that is driving you?"

"No," said Zakia adamantly. "I am just trying to

get to the bottom of the story."

She looked at Dani and then Harris who were sitting on either side of her. Harris had a little frown on his face and Dani was smirking.

"The boys were wondering what to get you on the trip," she said, changing the subject. "They are all excited about going and we are almost done packing."

"Good," said Benjamin, "Just surprise me. I am really glad you boys are going along to protect your Maman."

They signed off Skype and Zakia stood up to go to the kitchen, when, Dani asked, "Why are you so focused on Elias?"

Harris tipped his head to one side, "Yes, who is this Elias?"

Dani looked at her with raised eyebrows. She thought how unfair life was. This would have been a perfect moment to tell Dani the truth, but she couldn't. Not now.

"We went to the same university together and were just good friends. That's all," she lied. Lying to your children is allowed in an emergency, thought Zakia.

In bed that night, she wondered if she was being naïve taking her boys along to China.

Chapter Seven

Zakia and her boys left their apartment just before dawn. The taxi was waiting to take them to the airport. The driver got out to open the trunk. While they were loading their cases, Zakia noticed a black car across the street. She could barely make out two men sitting in the car. One of them wore a wine-colored fez. She glimpsed a distinctive scar on the face of the other. Then they held up a map, but constantly peered over it in Zakia's direction. The car and the men in it made her uneasy. She hurried the boys along into the taxi. As their taxi drove away, she turned around to look. The black car waited a few moments, then pulled out behind them.

Her mouth went dry.

"What's wrong, Maman?" asked Harris.

"Nothing," she said. "Just trying to make sure I didn't forget anything." The car appeared to follow them for a while before it was lost in the morning traffic. *Good, it was probably just a coincidence.*

It was nearly six o'clock in the morning, when Zakia and her boys joined the group of fellow journalists headed to China. After she hustled Dani and Harris through security, Zakia glanced behind her and gasped when she recognized the two men at the other end of the terminal; they were the same men who had been casing their apartment that morning. She put her arms around Dani and Harris, steered them through the crowd and arrived at their gate without further incident. If she'd had the presence of mind to write down that license plate number, maybe she could have found out who was tracking her. Moreover, the men hadn't threatened her, so what was there to report?

Despite the joy of being with her sons, she had a nagging sensation that all was not well. Zakia kept reminding herself that things would be fine, that they were joining a guided tour and not traveling alone.

At the gate, they ran into another reporter on the trip, Omar Latif. He worked for an old newspaper in Fez, which was one of *Journal's* biggest competitors, although they didn't slip as many stories past the censors as her paper did.

"Zakia, great to see you!" Omar boomed. His wife looked at her and smiled. "Are you headed to China, too?" he said.

"Yes, last minute, I was added to the press entourage."

Omar smiled broadly. "Wonderful! We'll have to get together for drinks on the ship. These trips are marvelous."

"Well, I hope to interview the oil and energy minister about drilling activity in the desert," Zakia stopped short, catching herself from telling Omar about the blowout. They had shared information before, but she was not sharing this time.

"You mean the blowout at Oddleifur Oil."

Clearly the story had leaked. Zakia held her tongue.

Omar gave her a worried look. "I wouldn't do that if I were you. You might stir up more than a story."

Zakia crossed her arms. "I guess that's a possibility?"

Omar patted her on the back. "You were always the daredevil journalist. Remember, we're not exactly in New York now."

He must be trying to put me off the scent. "Well, what have you picked up on the blowout?" she asked.

"We were told not to cover it," Omar kept a poker face. "I'm writing on energy and trade issues. Pretty harmless. But I'm sure it will be a nice trip, regardless."

"Yes, I'm looking forward to a change of scenery." Zakia smiled.

Omar and Zakia agreed that they would try to meet on the ship. Dani and Harris were already lined up to board the plane, so she excused herself to join them.

****

Arriving at the airport outside of Wuhan, after switching flights in Paris and Beijing, they were greeted by a guide holding up a sign with the ship's company name, *Red Dragon Cruise*. He wore a green polo shirt emblazoned with the name and logo. A large group of people from the U.S. and Europe joined the Moroccan entourage and Zakia saw Omar and his wife standing on the outskirts of the crowd. The guide said his name was John. He had a heavy Chinese accent. "My Chinese name is too difficult for you to pronounce," he explained.

The Moroccan group was split into two buses. Zakia and her sons ended up on John's bus. The bus pulled out from the curb and headed to Wuhan. Winding through the center of Wuhan to the county museum, the bus passed the old and new parts of the city and Zakia was struck by the sea of building cranes;

there must have been hundreds.

John turned on the mike and, pointing out the window on the left, said, "Over there you can see the new, impressive Greenland Center, a 2,000-foot tall tower, one of the tallest skyscrapers in the world,"

"Awesome," said Dani. "I wonder if I should study engineering and build something like that."

Zakia took a deep breath to avoid looking shocked—was Dani following in his biological father's footsteps? "That would be an amazing career."

Dani smiled shyly.

****

Arriving at the Hubei Provincial Museum, John's group was greeted by a docent, who spoke no English. With John translating, Zakia and her boys stuck close to him, while the docent walked them through exhibits that portrayed Chinese history through the millennia. They all wore headphones, so John could translate simultaneously. The collection was extensive and Zakia enjoyed listening to the ancient set of bronze bells, the Bianzhong Bells.

Two hours later, while they were looking at an extraordinary horse and carriage from the Ming Dynasty, Zakia heard someone shouting down the long hall. She could have sworn it sounded like Omar.

"What's going on?" asked Dani.

"I'll check it out. Come on, follow me," she said to her boys.

Zakia and her sons pressed through the crowd and found Omar in an argument with one of the tour guides and a museum security guard. He was red-faced and waving his arms. "But you have to call the police!" he said. "I know my wife. She wouldn't take off like this."

Zakia put a hand on his arm. "Omar, what's the problem?"

The security guard glared at her. "Madame, we have this under control. Please go back to your group."

Zakia pulled herself up a little taller and held out the Moroccan Press identification badge on her neck lanyard. "I am a friend and colleague of this gentleman. I am also a reporter."

The guard rolled his eyes. "More journalists to contend with. You all think everything is such a big deal."

Omar bristled at that. "No, my friend Zakia can help. I know that something has happened to my wife and I insist that you contact the proper authorities at once." He folded his arms and glared at the guard.

"Your wife?" said Zakia. "Where is Alba?"

"She excused herself to go to the ladies' room and has been gone almost an hour."

The guard smirked. "Maybe she's still in there."

Omar turned on him gruffly. "I sent someone in to check. She is not there."

Zakia scowled at the guard. "We're here as part of the press envoy of the Moroccan government. Do you want to turn this into an international incident?"

The guard reddened, then pulled out his cellphone and started speaking in rapid Mandarin.

Omar looked at her with pursed lips and new respect. Then he said, "Thank you so much for your help. I feel desperate. This is so unlike Alba."

"Well, let's make a plan to search for her in the museum while we wait for the police," she said. "This is a big place. Maybe she got lost or has fallen asleep someplace. We're all so jetlagged."

Omar agreed. Zakia turned to Dani and Harris, who were up for a hunt for the missing Alba and wanted to go in different directions but she insisted they stick together.

They ran through a few thousand years of Chinese history. Dani seemed pleased that they were doing something adventurous. As they hustled through yet another exhibit hall, Harris—who appeared not to be dealing well with the jetlag—moaned that he was tired and he would like to sit down and wait for them. Even Zakia admitted she was drained when she got a call on her cellphone.

It was Omar. "They found Alba," he said. "Please meet me in the lobby. I could use your help again."

When they got to the lobby, they found Omar sitting beside Alba on a long bench, patting her hand and looking relieved. Alba was sobbing quietly, while she rubbed her left knee.

"Alba," cried Zakia, rushing toward her. "Oh, thank goodness they found you. Omar was beside himself." Alba looked wilted, dusty, and distraught. Two policemen had arrived and were talking to the museum employees and taking notes. Then John showed up.

Omar rubbed Alba's arm. Tears streamed down her face as she spoke, "I had gone to the bathroom, and, when I came out my tour group was gone."

"We must have just moved to the auditorium to listen to the bronze bells," said Omar.

Alba continued, her face puffy and running with make-up, "I panicked and ran outside, wondering if the group had gone off to lunch without me. Then a black car with tinted windows swerved up to the sidewalk, two men got out and dragged me to the car. I tried to fend them off, but they threw me into the backseat and drove off in a hurry. On the highway, the men began questioning me in English."

"I was so scared," said Alba, shivering. "I didn't understand what was going on."

"But now you're back, thank goodness," said Zakia smiling. "How did you get away?"

"Well, they thought I was a journalist." She held out her lanyard with the press badge. "I insisted I was not, but was married to one. That disappointed and angered them. They drove off the highway, and dumped me out of the car while it was still moving. I bumped my knee on the ground, but I'm okay." She rubbed her knee again.

Harris was taking in the story with wide eyes and Dani muttered "wow" under his breath.

"I'm so sorry this happened to you," said John, who had been watching from the sidelines. He suggested their group move to the gift shop. Zakia asked him if he could keep an eye out for her boys, while she talked to Alba. He nodded and led the group away.

"Alba, do you need to go to the hospital?" asked Zakia.

"She's fine," said Omar. "She just needs some ice on her knee."

"I'm asking Alba," she said, giving Omar a sharp look. "Alba is the one who was thrown from a car."

"My knee hit the ground, but it's not serious. I'm okay, just a little shaken."

Zakia privately thought that Alba was lucky to be alive. She thought about Elias and the men who appeared to have followed her to the airport and shuddered. Her pulse raced at the thought that the kidnappers might have been after her. There weren't too many Moroccan women with journalist's badges on this tour.

She swallowed hard. "Do you know if they were targeting journalists or female journalists in particular?"

Alba furrowed her brow. "I don't know."

Recognition dawned in Omar's eyes. "I noticed you're the only woman journalist on this trip. The rest are wives of journalists. You think they're after you?"

Zakia kept her voice steady. "Just wondering," she said. She didn't want to share all this with Omar. This was her story. "Probably just a coincidence." *What am I saying? I don't believe that for a second.*

She asked how Alba had gotten back to the museum. Apparently, she'd convinced a store owner in the neighboring town to drive her back to the museum. He had been so shocked by her appearance—a disheveled tourist—he'd taken pity on her and, after much hand gesturing, drove her back to the museum on his moped.

"Why didn't you call the police?"

"I knew Omar would take care of that." She leaned against him. He smiled and put his arm around her.

Zakia rejoined her sons, embracing them both. "Alba is going to be all right." They were heading out toward the buses. Despite the drama, it looked like the tour group was still on schedule for their lunch.

When they arrived at the restaurant, Harris followed his mom like a newly hatched chick, chasing mother hen. While they were sitting at the long tables, waiting for their food to arrive, Harris had scooted his chair close to his mom's and was looking around the room every time someone walked in the door. Finally, Dani said, "Harris, what's your problem? Are you scared?"

Harris scowled and gave Dani a sidelong glance. "Lay off, why don't you. I just want to protect Maman. You remember what Dad said, don't you?"

"I think it's nice to have two bodyguards," Zakia said evenly. "But I'm the boss and I assure you that everything will be just fine. No one is going to hurt us in China." *I can't be sure of that. Here I go again—lying to the boys, but it's also an emergency.* "We're here to have fun, so let's enjoy it."

Dani gave Harris a triumphant smile and Harris stuck his tongue out, but they kept their bickering to a minimum for the rest of the day. Which was good because Zakia was exhausted. Her head was spinning. *We've only just arrived, and someone's already been kidnapped.*

Sitting there with her sons, it occurred to Zakia that she should just cancel the trip and fly home with her boys, but she convinced herself that once they were onboard the ship they would be safe, just as if they were on an island—no one gets onboard without being noticed. Furthermore, she had a job to do. She desperately wanted to know what happened to Elias.

Chapter Eight

The afternoon had become much warmer. As the Moroccan group and the other passengers boarded the Red Dragon Cruise destined for Chongqing, they were thrilled to be handed refreshments at the elaborately decorated and brightly lit ship's lobby encased by an elegant spiral staircase with a view to the top floor. Zakia and her sons got their keys and found their cabins on the starboard side. After dropping off their bags, they decided to explore the ship. They passed a small exercise room and a tiny library with a couple of card tables and a few books. There were two large lounges, one on each of the two lower decks. Zakia thought they would be quite safe on the ship and she said as much to her sons.

The ship was not big, but luxurious, with small shops and a tailor. Harris gently poked Zakia's arm. "Where is the game room with the Nintendo and other video games, big flat screen TVs, and foosball tables? My friends who have been on cruises said they always have game rooms onboard."

Zakia laughed. "I guess they skipped that part. Maybe there are too few kids on these trips. But I'm sure we will have enough to do." She was actually pleased that Dani and Harris weren't going to be stuck in front of a computer whenever they had down time. "Did you see the daily itinerary? We're off to see a pagoda on a mountain top tomorrow morning, and then a spy museum starting with the Qing dynasty in 1636."

"That sounds pretty cool," said Dani.

"Sick!" said Harris.

They walked for what felt like a long mile exploring the ship. As they headed back in the general direction of their cabins, they came across a wing of the ship that had a guard at the end of the passageway. They stopped and peered down the carpeted hallway.

"What's with the bodyguard?" asked Dani.

"That must be where some VIP is staying," said Zakia.

They turned to leave and she recognized a well-dressed, elderly man striding toward them down the passageway like he owned the place. Two solemn-looking large men were in tow behind him. The thick carpeting made their arrival almost soundless.

"Who is that?" whispered Harris.

"That's the oil and energy minister," she muttered. "Be polite."

The man looked annoyed, just for a moment, and then smiled broadly and stopped in front of them. "Hello," he said in a gallant tone. "I am Gamal Samara."

"Nice to meet you, Minister Samara," she said. "We were just exploring the ship. It's very pleasant."

His smile was plastered on his face longer than normal. His gaze flicked from her to the boys and back again. Zakia shifted uncomfortably. He reminded her somehow of an older Al Pacino in the *Godfather* movie.

Then she remembered that she hadn't properly introduced herself. "Good afternoon, Minister, I'm Zakia Karim—part of the press pool and these are my sons."

His mouth twitched when she mentioned the word "press"—she could only guess why he did that—but he quickly recovered and grinned. "You boys should be proud that Morocco values freedom of the press," he said. "Then he leaned forward, and added nearly in a conspiratorial whisper: "Unlike some countries I can think of, such as our host on this trip."

Dani nodded politely in response. Zakia touched her boys on the shoulder and asked them to go unpack their things and start getting ready for dinner. They agreed and took off.

Samara watched them go and turned to Zakia. "I am glad you are here; I knew your father. He was a great man for assisting in the negotiations of the trade agreement between Morocco and the UK. I admired him greatly and considered him a friend."

The mention of her father came as an utter surprise and she didn't know what to say. They stood there stiffly. Zakia was bursting to ask him some pointed questions, now that she had him to herself. He was a notoriously difficult man to land an interview with. In fact, he had not given a private interview in at least two years and his office had not returned her calls for earlier articles, even if they were run of the mill.

Zakia's rational mind was telling her to wait, yet the impulsive part of her nature won; she had to take advantage. "Yes, freedom of the press indeed. I was curious, what about the blowout at the gas well near Al Tarife? Why wasn't that made public?" Zakia immediately regretted being so aggressive. *Great! Hopefully, he'll still answer my question.*

Annoyance flickered across Samara's face and he

folded his arms across his chest. "Oh, that was an unfortunate accident," he said, dismissively. "They've already changed all the safety procedures. Nothing to worry your little head about. I don't think your father would've been pleased if he knew you investigated those types of stories. I am sure he had different ambitions for you."

Zakia stood there, her mind racing. Had he just invoked her dear, dead Papa? Her father had, in fact, encouraged her to pursue her passion and had helped her land her first job. But before she could formulate a response, he continued, speaking slowly and loudly, as though she were deaf or stupid: "You should be doing some travel pieces or writing on the arts or perhaps an article on infant mortality among the nomadic Berbers."

"Is that so?" Zakia was glad that Samara couldn't see her heartbeat pounding. *The nerve. How dare he?* Blaming exhaustion, she smiled and excused herself, as she hurried off to find her boys.

****

After dinner, Zakia and her boys headed to their cabins. She hugged them goodnight and waited while they figured out who had the key and then entered their cabin.

Across the hall, as she was about to put the keycard in her own door, she noticed the door was already open. She knew that she'd checked the door, pulling the handle when she left for dinner. She was sure someone had entered her cabin.

Holding her breath, Zakia pushed open her door, peered inside, then stepped into her cabin and found the light switch. She exhaled, relieved no one else was there and found her things much as she had left them, except that her carryon, perched on the luggage rack, had clothes peeking out of one side as if it had been zipped in a hurry. *That's strange.* She thought she'd locked it. She grasped the closet door and found the mini-safe was broken into and her laptop was gone. She swore under her breath.

Zakia straightened, ran her hand through her short hair, and looked around her cabin; a chill ran down her back. She wasted no time calling the front desk and told them what had happened. In a calm voice, the clerk said someone would be right up to give her a new keycard.

"Thank you," she said. "Also, could you please change the lock on my sons' cabin? Just in case."

This was supposed to be a safe place.

"That won't be a problem," said the clerk. "I'll let my manager know about the computer. Can you file some paperwork in the morning?"

"Sure," she said in a cool tone, swallowing her anger. "Thank you."

Zakia sat on the edge of her bed, waiting for the new keycards. She was certain the theft had to be connected with her investigation. Someone was after her research. She'd had a nagging feeling about this trip all along, beginning with that strange car idling across the street from their apartment. Both of the boys had picked up on her worries. She wished Benjamin had been with them.

A little nausea roiled in her stomach. At least she had backed up all her data on the cloud.

She heard a knock on the door and opened it a crack to see a young woman wearing a purser's uniform standing there. "I have your keycards, Ms. Karim.

Zakia thanked her and took the keycards and put

them on the nightstand.

She wasn't sure she could sleep now, so she decided to Skype Benjamin on her cellphone. Zakia was determined not to tell him about the computer disappearing. She'd leave that for another day. Instead she told Benjamin what had transpired in her conversation with the oil and energy minister.

Benjamin listened to Zakia with increasing agitation. Finally he interrupted her. "I'm concerned that he knew your cover story. Obviously, everything is connected—the police, Oddleifur Oil, and now we know, also the oil and energy minister. You should have waited and not given him any clues of your interest in the blowout story."

She smiled at him, even though she didn't feel it in her heart. "I couldn't help it; he was so provocative and patronizing, typical of our male culture. Plus he mentioned his connection to my father. Remember the trade deal I told you about?"

"Yes, I remember. Be careful, Zakia," said Benjamin. "Your father had a lot of connections, but I am not sure they'll be able to protect you."

Zakia didn't want to fight with him over this. "I will, however, try to lay out the nomads' case in regards to fracking, perhaps at one of the dinners while we are still on board ship." She really wanted to ask Samara more about the blowout.

Benjamin continued to frown at her, "I still don't see why you are so keen on this story, what kind of relationship did you have with Elias that you never told me?

"I told you we dated, that's all." Her lips pressed together in a slight grimace.

"Honestly, I find that hard to believe."

"Come on Benjamin, give me a break, I'm wiped. I need to get some sleep now. Talk to you soon. I love you."

Benjamin, slowly shaking his head, reluctantly gave up. "Love you too," he said with no warmth.

Chapter Nine

At breakfast, Harris announced that while they slept, the ship had traveled southwest and then northwest on the Yangtze, arriving at Jiangling, a small town by Chinese standards, having just a half million people. Dani rolled his eyes. "Why do you make this stuff up?"

Harris looked smug. "I don't make things up; I looked it up using the ship's Wi-Fi on Maman's phone."

"Oh, you're such a showoff," said Dani.

"Yeah, well, you're just ignorant," said Harris.

Zakia reminded them not to fight. Everyone was looking forward to the hike up the mountain to see the pagoda, the famous Shibaozhai Temple. "I hear it's beautiful," she told them.

Dani and Harris continued to tease each other, but as soon as they got off the ship, they were too absorbed with the spectacular view of the mountainside covered by temperate rainforest to continue bickering. Once they reached the bottom of the trailhead, Zakia and her sons set off at the front end of their tour group, right behind John, who, she noted, seemed out of shape, his breathing labored. He struggled to keep ahead of the pack. The trail was quite steep.

The scenery was breathtaking, with lotus blossoms, bamboo plants, dove trees and more. She was glad that the day was overcast, so it wasn't too hot. Half way up the mountain to the temple, they came upon an ancient building tucked against the mountainside, surrounded by dense forest.

Zakia paused to look at it, motioning her sons to stop. "What's that?" she asked John.

"That's the monastery for the monks who belonged to the temple," he said. "It is hundreds of years old and has not been occupied since World War II. It looks somewhat preserved on the outside, but the interior is falling apart."

"I need a travel story for my newspaper. This would be ideal," she said, feeling drawn to the dark cracked windows and decorated doorways. Zakia caught a glimpse of a courtyard inside, where she saw ancient statues, stained and pitted from the weather.

John frowned. "It could be dangerous."

Zakia pulled out her camera. "I won't go into the building itself. I just want to get some photos of the courtyard."

The rest of their group paused briefly and decided it wasn't worth their time to explore the monastery. John excused himself. Dani and Harris asked him to wait. They turned to Zakia and asked if they could go with him. She said no. When they insisted, she gave in, saying they had to promise to stay close to John. She saw all three of them hurrying after their group.

After exploring the monastery, snapping photos along the way, she returned to the path and realized that the place was quiet except for some birds chirping. She couldn't see the group.

She hurried up the trail, wondering how long she'd been engrossed in the monastery. For the first time, she noticed just how wild her surroundings were. She walked faster. She was a little worried about Dani and Harris. Should they get lost, they had no way of communicating, since their cellphones were left at home and John had collected all the headsets, saying specifically that on this outing he did not want to interfere with their enjoyment of nature. "No comment can describe such a beautiful landscape," he had said.

Zakia hurried up the mountainside. Twenty minutes later, she came around the bend and saw her tour group admiring the pagoda perched on the edge of a cliff. She didn't see Dani or Harris among the group. She looked over the edge and saw a sheer drop to the rocks by the river below.

John spotted her and came up to her. He was visibly sweating.

"Where are my sons?" she asked him, panic creeping into her voice.

"They decided to race up the mountain side ahead of us about thirty minutes ago and I haven't seen them since," he said.

"How could you let them run ahead?" She looked down the steep path she had just covered.

John shifted uncomfortably. "I told them to wait for me because I have a bad knee. But they just took off."

Zakia's pulse raced. Words stuck in her mouth.

John gave her an apologetic look. "I thought they might have caught sight of a monkey troupe, but they should have been back by now."

"You should have been more forceful," she shouted, loudly enough that the other people in their group turned to look at them.

"Now just a second," said John. "You didn't ask me to bring a leash. You should have been looking after your own children."

Zakia blinked back tears. "It's not your fault. I spent altogether too much time in the monastery. I'm sorry. What do we do now?"

John pushed back his shoulders. "I will call the ship's captain, and he will alert the cruise ship's owner, and the police." He frowned at her. "I don't want to scare you, but please don't yell at me again. We'll assemble a search team from the ship's crew."

"I can't just stand here doing nothing," Zakia said, wiping her eyes. Other members of the tour group were huddled a small distance away, pretending not to hear anything. Alba's kidnapping, not twenty-four hours earlier, flashed through Zakia's mind. She shuddered. *Now what have I done?*

"We'll do something," said John. "While we wait for the crew members, we should all search here by the pagoda, and then go back to the ship. The police will have arrived by then."

It was midafternoon when the ship's crew arrived to help. By this time Zakia had looked and scrambled all around the mountainside, even climbing high on a dangerous rock outcropping, managing to trip and scrape her leg in the process, hoping she could get a glimpse of Dani and Harris. But they were nowhere to be seen.

She watched the rest of their group meandering down to the ship.

"I think we better go," said John, gently. "Your sons are clearly not in this area. I'm sure we'll hear something soon. Some of the locals are joining in the search. They know this area very well and will notify us if they find your sons or see something unusual."

"I'm going to call their father from the ship, but I'll come right back to search some more. I'm not giving up on them." Zakia was numb with fear. She allowed John to lead her back down the trail to the ship. As she passed the monastery, she felt as though a week had gone by since they'd begun the trip to China, yet it had only been a couple of days.

****

Back on board, Zakia went to her cabin and Skyped with Benjamin. She braced herself, knowing Benjamin would not be pleased.

He yelled, "Dammit, Zakia, you know how the boys are—competing all the time. For God's sake, they don't even have a cellphone or any other way of communicating. You should have stayed together." Benjamin rubbed his chin.

"They were with John, the guide. He sat at our table for dinner last night on board the ship; he's a good guy. It's not as if I abandoned them. It seemed so peaceful up there. I know they didn't follow my instructions, but it's not like them to be so careless," said Zakia in tears. "I wish you were here."

At that, she couldn't stop crying.

"I will catch the first flight out of here. We'll find them."

"Benjamin. There's more," Zakia whispered.

"What do you mean?"

"I haven't been straight with you. Someone tailed us going to the airport, and in Wuhan the wife of another reporter was kidnapped outside the museum we were visiting. Luckily, she made her way back safely.

That night on the ship, my cabin was broken into while we ate dinner and someone stole my computer."

"Great, that's just great," snapped Benjamin. "You take off with our boys and you totally lose it. Knowing what else was going on, you should never have let the boys out of your sight. I don't know what's gotten into you. He rolled up his sleeves and loosened his collar.

"Nothing has gotten into me. I'm investigating a story, but that should have nothing to do with our children." Zakia blew her nose.

"Clearly, someone is making the connection. Who knows what could have happened to the boys." Benjamin's face had turned ashen. "I'll get there as soon as I can."

"What if they didn't wander off, but something else happened to them?"

"Let's not let our imaginations take off."

"I'm really sorry, Benjamin," muttered Zakia.

They made plans for his arrival, but it didn't console her. They signed off.

Sitting on her bed, Zakia thought for a moment. Having an Anglican father and a lapsed Catholic mother, she had grown up an undetermined Christian, yet she thought, now might be the time to pray.

Instead she went down to the ship's lounge. A few other passengers had gathered there to receive updates, and though they seemed surprised to see her, tried their best to console her. Another hour had gone by with no word of Dani and Harris.

Zakia was about to head outside again when she saw two police officers walk toward her in the lounge. She stiffened, thinking the worst.

"We need to talk," said the older of the officers.

"Let's go over there, where we can be alone." They walked to the far end of the lounge and Zakia sat down on the sofa. The officers took the lounge chairs.

"Did you find my sons?"

"No, but we need to ask you some questions. Have your sons ever run off before? And how old are they?

"No, they haven't. Dani is thirteen and Harris is eleven. They are good boys, never been in any trouble."

"Have you got any pictures?"

Zakia bit her lip. She took out her cellphone and pulled up a photo of Dani and Harris standing in front of the lavishly decorated Mausoleum of Mohammad V in Rabat. "Here," she said, handing them her cellphone. Seeing the photos of the boys taken just two weeks ago made her heart ache.

The older police officer smiled at her and returned the phone. "Good-looking boys. Please send me the photo in an e-mail."

She selected the photo he wanted and he dictated his e-mail address to her.

"Thank you. We'll be in touch." The policemen got up and left. Zakia rubbed her arms and looked around. The other passengers in the lounge were staring at her, but they quickly shifted their gaze to the view of the Yangtze. The smoggy twilight was giving way to darkness. The search for the boys would be suspended when it got dark, John had said. She gave a loud sigh, her plan to go back to join the search party dashed. She trembled as she pulled out her notebook and wrote down some of her thoughts, as if reporting on her own situation. Thirty minutes later, she looked up to see John walking into the lounge. He looked pale.

"Zakia, we need to talk. Shall we go to the

library?"

"What's happened? I spoke to the police a few minutes ago. Have you had any word on Dani and Harris?" Zakia began wringing her hands.

"Let's just have some privacy, shall we?" he said.

She felt nauseated and light-headed on the short walk to the library. Never had she experienced such a sense of dread. The ship's captain was waiting for them. He greeted her and offered her a glass of water. She declined.

John closed the door. "Please, take a seat Zakia," he said. He handed her a piece of paper.

She sat at one of the two small card tables, and took the note, her hands trembling. "What is it? I can't read this."

John sat down next to her. "The crew's search team found the note tucked in the ceiling of the first level of eaves of the Pagoda. It's in Mandarin. It says your sons have been kidnapped." He shook his head.

Zakia gasped, "Kidnapped? That can't be true." She stifled a sob. Crying was not going to bring them back.

"I'm afraid it is," said the captain. "A terrible crime."

Zakia took a deep breath. *Okay, now I'm angry.* At least, she thought, they weren't lying dead in the bottom of the cliff below the Pagoda.

The captain, in a steady low-pitched voice, chimed in. "The kidnappers say you are to proceed to Sandouping, a town close to the Three Gorges Dam. There you are to hand over a million U.S. dollars."

Zakia nodded and squeezing her eyes shut. "That's an awful lot of money. But I'll do whatever it takes to get my boys back. Anything!" She would reach out to her contacts to see if they had information on who might have captured her boys. "Can't we find them?"

"There's not much you can do at this point, besides arrange for the money," said the captain. "The kidnappers added a further peculiar bit in the note," the captain continued. "Does this mean anything to you? It says: 'Let this be a warning to you: Stay away from the investigation. Or there will be more bodies to deal with.'"

The blood rushed from her head. "I am investigating a possible murder," she murmured. "I can't believe it. How can so many people be involved in my reporting business?"

Neither man said anything. The captain scratched his cheek and John had a thoughtful expression. She sat up. "Someone is trying to frighten me. Guess what? They've succeeded. It's one thing to arrest me and try to intimidate me, but to kidnap my boys—now they have crossed the line." She slammed her fist on the table and John and the captain both flinched.

"You were arrested?" said John. "What for?"

"I was researching a story about a blowout at a gas well in Morocco and somebody didn't like my line of questioning."

John looked at the captain and they both nodded, as if she didn't need to say anything more.

For a moment, Zakia thought that they could be in cahoots, but decided to stay focused and added, "And where am I going to get this money?"

John patted her awkwardly on the shoulder. "Don't worry about the money. I'm sure the ship's owners can help. They don't like bad publicity. We will inform the police, of course."

The ship's captain nodded in agreement.

"At least it sounds like your sons are still alive," said the captain.

"I pray you are right," said Zakia, shuddering.

****

When she saw Alba and Omar in the ship's lounge, waiting for her to return, the sight of familiar faces threatened her composure. She wiped her eyes, but when she slumped down on the empty sofa opposite them, the flood gates opened and she started sobbing.

Alba came over and sat next to her. "They will find them. I am sure of it."

"It may not be so easy," said Zakia. She took a deep breath and blew her nose. "They've been kidnapped. We have a ransom note."

Alba clutched her chest and Omar said, "That's dreadful."

"I will never forgive myself for letting this happen." Zakia's shoulders dropped.

"The first thing we need to do is identify possible motives for kidnapping them," said Omar. "Was this the same outfit that came after Alba earlier? Or is this a random incident?"

"Even though the kidnappers are asking for money, it seems more like a cover," Zakia suggested. "I think the real reason is to dissuade me from pursuing the blowout story."

Zakia pulled out her notepad and began, with Omar's help, to make a list of journalists and sources that might be in the know. They'd compiled a list of about twenty sources, with e-mails and phone numbers when Zakia looked up to see the oil and energy minister striding into the room. Samara was flanked by his body guards.

"Well, there's someone to ask," muttered Omar quietly, lowering his eyes. "He's living lavishly, even for someone in our government. I've heard that he's involved in some questionable dealings."

Zakia wanted to ask him what he meant, but then Samara was upon her.

"It's terrible news about your sons." His voice sounded anything but sympathetic. Then he added almost on impulse: "It's too bad your sons' training in martial arts didn't help them get away."

"I mentioned my sons are taking lessons in martial arts?"

Samara narrowed his eyes at her and stared, daring her to accuse him of any wrongdoing.

She dropped her gaze. She forced her tone to be noncommittal. "I'm afraid I don't remember it ever being mentioned in front of you. But so many things have happened I'm all mixed up now." *He didn't get that piece of information from me. He knows everything about us.*

"I hope they find your sons," Samara said with an air of practiced compassion.

His tone was so perfect that Zakia did not buy it for a moment.

Then he shook his bloated index finger at her. "But had you been a traditional Moroccan mother, you would have stayed in Rabat with your sons, and none of this would have happened."

She heard Alba give a little gasp and Omar grunted and shook his head.

Zakia's cheeks burned and she recoiled as if he'd

slapped her face. She was about to defend herself when he turned and walked away, his bodyguards trailing after him. Her intense love for her boys would never dampen her drive to get her story out, especially this one. *But are the risks too great?*

She couldn't believe what Samara had said. He seemed oddly interested in her personal life for such a high-ranking official. What did he care what she did with her life? He wasn't the morality police, like they had in Iran or Saudi Arabia. The fact that he seemed *so* offended by her working as a journalist was odd. He showed a little too much interest in what she was up to.

Alba gave her a tight hug. "Just ignore him. He's a male chauvinist. We seem to have all too many like him in Morocco, sadly."

This just confirmed her suspicion that Sigurd Agnarsson was probably bribing someone in the government to help Oddleifur Oil expand their fracking operations, as Elias had assumed. Samara might be just the one in a position to profit from such dirty deals. Her heart raced. She wondered if he was involved in the kidnapping of her sons. Did he know where her sons were? If so, she needed to tread carefully.

She was tempted to tell Alba and Omar or the ship's captain about her suspicions, but held back. She had no proof yet, and bribes and kidnapping were serious allegations.

She needed to think about these things, alone. She looked up to see Alba and Omar staring at her with wide eyes. "He's not someone I'd trust," said Omar in a whisper and looked around the room. "But whatever you do now, Zakia, be careful."

"I will." Zakia blew her nose again and stood up,

promising Alba and Omar that she would keep them updated. She excused herself and hurried to her cabin. He had kindly agreed to let her borrow his computer for the evening.

****

Zakia Skyped with Benjamin, "I don't know what to say," she sniffled. "I have horrible news. Dani and Harris have been kidnapped," she cried.

His mouth fell open. "There must be a mistake." Then he frowned and shook his head in disbelief.

"They found a note from the kidnappers. Benjamin, I don't think I can survive if they are gone," said Zakia wiping tears.

While Benjamin absorbed the news, she told him the kidnappers were asking for ransom. She skipped the part about them threatening her with killing their sons if she didn't stop her investigation. What good would it do for him to know this, so many thousands of miles away?

"How much are they asking for?"

"A million dollars."

Benjamin rubbed his temple.

"What are we going to do?" Zakia blew her nose.

"I'm at my wits' end." His brow furrowed. "But somehow, our sons will be found. We will get hold of the money. I'll make some phone calls. We should be able to get a loan somewhere. Then, after our boys are safe, we will leave Morocco and move to the U.S. Maybe live in Chicago, close to your sister."

Moving was the last thing on her mind. "The captain said we could borrow money from the ship's owners. They would like this to be resolved with the least amount of publicity. I suspect having tourists disappear on their guided tours would not be good PR."

Benjamin leaned forward, as though he were peering into her eyes through the camera of his computer. "Stay strong. I am heading to the airport in a couple of hours."

Zakia nodded. She was feeling better already for having talked to Benjamin. As soon as she got off their call, she connected with her sources to see if anybody knew anything.

Zakia was surprised to see it was only seven p.m. She wondered where the boys were, and what they were thinking. They were probably hungry by now. Were they hurt? "What have I done?" she muttered tearfully.

Chapter Ten

She didn't sleep that night. At six a.m., she heard a knock at her door. Daylight had begun to stream in through the porthole. The pollution was so strong in this region you couldn't see the sun. She opened the door to find John standing there with two cups of coffee in hand. He offered her one with a wry smile. "I figured you hadn't slept much and could use this. Please, meet me in the library as soon as possible."

She took the cup without argument although she normally didn't drink coffee. But nothing felt normal this morning. Zakia threw on some clothes and headed to the library. Her hands were sweating.

"Did anything happen overnight?" asked Zakia as she entered the library, fearing the worst. If it were good news, John would have shared it already. She took a seat across the card table from John.

He hesitated. "The captain instructed me to deliver a message." He fished a piece of paper out of his shirt pocket and showed it to Zakia. She looked at him quizzically. The note was written in Chinese characters, like the first one. He read it to her: "The kidnappers contacted the cruise ship's owner at three in the morning, instructing the ship to dock in Sandouping, where we are to deliver the money in exchange for information on where we can find your sons."

"But we haven't put together the money yet," she

said with a frown.

John nodded. "Don't worry. Your husband connected with the ship's owners and the money will be there when we dock."

"I wish I had known earlier. I haven't slept at all." Zakia wiped her tired eyes.

John flushed. "Sorry, I meant well."

"It's not your fault, and thanks again for the coffee." *It's all my fault.* She wanted to scream. What if they didn't find Dani and Harris or they were found dead? *Okay, I have to stop this line of thinking.* She bit her lip hard.

"As it happens, my wife works for the state police," said John. "She did a bit of investigating of her own and sent a message to a couple of senior officials who are willing to help."

"Please thank her for me." Zakia sat a bit straighter.

"They are sending a helicopter over to Sandouping to get an aerial view. Copters can often make a big difference in such searches. The timing is essential."

"Is that standard procedure?"

"No. But if one can impress VIP visitors from Morocco, it's worth it."

"That's wonderful. I don't know how I can repay you."

John looked down at the floor. "I am sorry I wasn't able to keep up with your sons on the trail. I had no idea something like this would happen."

Zakia shook her head. "It's nothing to do with you. Someone must have been tracking us, waiting for the right opportunity."

****

The morning dragged on. Despite no sleep, Zakia was determined to do everything in her power to rescue Dani and Harris. *If only I'd kept a closer eye on them.* At one point, she caught herself knocking on her sons' door to call them for breakfast. Working on Omar's computer she tried to find clues to the kidnappers' identities. So far, no leads.

At ten a.m., the ship docked at Sandouping. The rest of the Moroccan contingency was headed for a tour of the Three Gorges Dam. Zakia was told to wait on the ship until the deal was made with the kidnappers, but she had no intention of doing so. She watched the other guests disembark, looking for a moment when she could slip away unnoticed. Alba broke away from the group for a moment to give her a big hug. Zakia looked around, and then forced herself to walk at a slow pace following Alba off the ship.

She hadn't gone five steps along the dock when she heard one of the crew members calling to her. "Ms. Karim! Where are you going?"

She kept walking, but he grabbed her arm. "What are you doing?" she said, trying to pull away.

The crew member didn't let go. He scowled at her. "Ms. Karim, I have orders to make sure you stay on board."

Zakia wiggled out of his grasp, but managed to trip on an uneven plank and fell on her knees and grazed her elbow.

"Damn!" yelled Zakia, "That hurt." Tears sprung to her eyes.

"Oh, no, so sorry, Ms. Karim," said the crew member crouching down beside her. "Are you okay? We must get back on the ship."

"It's okay, I'll take care of her," said John as he walked straight over to Zakia and knelt beside her. He looked at the crew member with a set jaw. The man grumbled, but walked back to the ship, shaking his head.

"Are you all right?" asked John.

"Yes, thank you. I'm fine." She sat up, rubbing her elbow.

Zakia stood up abruptly and then took off, jogging along the dock toward the visitor's center. John hurried after her. "Where do you think you're going?" he called.

"To find my sons!" She picked up her pace.

She was so distracted that she almost ran over the considerably shorter man walking toward her. "Pardon me," she said without thinking, pausing for an instant.

He nodded. "Madame, are you Zakia Karim?"

"Yes, I am," Zakia said, looking at him with interest. "Who are you?"

"I'm with the police. We'd like a word with you. Please follow me," he said.

John caught up with her. "Do you have some ID?" John asked him, holding his arm in front of Zakia as if to protect her.

The man fixed John with an amused stare, then slid his hand into his jacket and pulled out a leather wallet with a badge.

John nodded at Zakia. "Given the circumstances, you can never be too sure."

"Shall we?" said the policeman, gesturing toward the hill where the visitor's center was perched. As they walked, John followed them until the officer turned to him and said: "We just need Madame Karim, if you please."

Zakia turned to John with a shrug and went with the policeman. "I'll see you later."

"I'll check in with my wife to see if she has any updates."

"Thank you!" called Zakia.

The officer led her up the hill and into the visitors' center. Zakia's attention was caught by a model of the Three Gorges Dam dominating the entrance. She stopped to examine the model to get her bearings. The police officer waited a moment.

"We need to hurry," he said.

Zakia followed him through the building to a back office, where he saluted his superior, waiting behind a desk. The policeman who had brought her there grabbed a backpack from underneath the desk and sat down in a chair, securing the backpack on the floor between his legs.

The man behind the desk stood up and introduced himself. "I am Police Chief Wue and you are Zakia Karim, I gather," he said as they shook hands. "You've already met my sergeant, doubling as a courier today. That's the ransom money he's guarding. I've been brought in with the sole mission of dealing with this case. You must have some friends in high places."

"I guess. Thank you," she said.

"This is a nasty affair, but we'll do the best we can to save your sons," Wue said.

"Do you have any idea who might be behind this?" asked Zakia. *I have my suspicions.*

He shook his head. "Not at this time. Our sources say this doesn't seem to be the work of our local criminals. There seems to be some outside influence."

"I see," said Zakia, her suspicions confirmed. "Will the kidnappers show up for the exchange?" she asked.

"I think that they'll stick to the plan. There's no reason to think they won't," he said. "Anyway, we have a Plan B."

Zakia was glad that the police were involved, but worried that if the kidnappers got wind of their involvement, the whole deal could end in disaster. She hadn't covered kidnappings before, but she knew it was easy to bungle the tradeoff.

"What's the backup plan?" she asked.

"We're not at liberty to say." He was pleasant sounding, though reserved. "Tell me about your sons. I have the photo of them you sent the police officer in Jiangling. What were they wearing on the day of the kidnapping?"

Zakia struggled to remember. "Um...., right, both wore shorts. Dani wore a sky blue t-shirt. Harris's was yellow."

"We'll just wait a few minutes while your tour group returns to the ship. This operation focuses on safety."

Twenty minutes later, Zakia heard the distant sound of a helicopter.

"Right on time," said Wue, smiling.

"Wait a minute! What's going on here? I thought the helicopter would be brought in if the kidnappers didn't show."

Wue put up his hand. "Calm down, it's going to be fine. We know what we're doing."

He turned the office lights off, stepped over to the window and opened the blinds. "Look. The drop point is over there, at the west end of the dam. We have information that the kidnappers are on the ground and their point man is in position, waiting for the money. We have the place surrounded. It's just a matter of time."

"Let's just give them the money as we agreed to do," said Zakia.

"Just wait." Wue turned to Zakia. "We can't be encouraging these kidnappers."

"Do you know where my sons are?"

Wue wore a pinched expression. "Not at this time."

Zakia wasn't about to risk the deal falling apart. "You aren't interested in rescuing my sons, are you?"

Wue didn't answer, but was focused on what he was seeing out the window.

She looked over at the sergeant guarding the backpack. He was craning his neck sideways away from her to look out the window behind him.

Without hesitating, Zakia stood up, grabbed the backpack, flung it on her back, and ran.

"Wait! You can't go outside now! You'll get shot," Wue called after her.

Zakia kept running down the hall.

She didn't have a specific plan, other than to reach the meeting point. *I have to save my boys.*

She ran through the building, past the model of the dam, and out the door. She heard the police officers yelling behind her. She headed toward the dam, feet flying, Wue pounding the pavement behind her.

She had almost reached the west end of the dam when she saw a man who looked like a tourist with a camera dangling on his chest, but his hostile demeanor gave her the notion that he must be one of the kidnappers. He wore a blue baseball cap emblazoned with the word "Tigers."

Her boys were nowhere to be seen.

The man looked at her for a second, and then fled, throwing the camera aside as he ran.

"Wait," she cried after him, in a panic. "It's me, the boys' mother. I have the money."

At that point, SWAT team members swarmed toward her like ants. They surrounded her, aiming their guns at her. She realized the chase was over. She stood still, taking deep breaths, trying to calm herself and plan her next step.

"I told you we were going to handle this," said Wue, coming up beside her, his sergeant, following close behind. The SWAT team stood at ease. Wue's nostrils were flaring. "You just interfered with a major police operation. That can have dire consequences for you." The sergeant grabbed her arm so hard it hurt. Then he tore the backpack off her back.

Up ahead, the man with the baseball cap ran ahead of another SWAT team. He had slipped through their 'net' and joined three other men.

In the distance, she saw a policeman running up the long outdoor escalator to the lookout on top of the hill above the visitor center. Other policemen were already positioned closer to the dam. It was just like in the movies, only Zakia was in the middle of it and her sons were still missing.

A moment later, a SWAT team ran across the main part of the dam in hot pursuit of the four men who were beginning to lose ground.

"What are you doing?" Zakia yelled at Wue. "Where are my sons?"

"Madame, I heard you were a crazy journalist,

but," said Wue, "you must seek cover. It's not safe here."

Zakia gave Wue an icy stare. "You double-crossed me."

"You're not running this operation," said Wue. "We'll arrest you if we have to."

"Is this about catching the kidnappers or freeing my boys?" Before he could answer, Zakia cut him off. "I'm not going anywhere until I find my sons."

Just then, she heard shots. She jerked her head around and saw one of the kidnappers, the one with the baseball cap drop to the ground. The police caught up with him and hauled him up by his arms. A dark crimson stain pooled on the back of his white t-shirt.

She watched as the police closed in on the other three. One of the kidnappers stopped, hesitated a moment, and then jumped from the dam into the roiling water. He disappeared.

"*Mon Dieu*," she said.

"Instant suicide." Wue shook his head.

"You would be safer taking refuge at the visitor's center. But in the interest of time, even though it's against protocol and my better judgment, you can help us if you cooperate."

"I'll cooperate, if you focus on finding my sons," Zakia slumped her shoulders.

"Okay," he said and then turned to his sergeant. "Let her go."

They walked toward the dam, passing the policemen who were carrying the wounded kidnapper on a stretcher. The other two kidnappers reached the end of the long dam and disappeared, with the SWAT team following far behind.

If the kidnappers were headed in the direction of the boys, they were their best ticket out of there. She turned to Wue. "Do you have another backup plan? Are your people going to search for my sons on the other side of the dam, over by the locks? They're still filling up, right?" Zakia had noticed the ships crammed into the locks on the other side of the river, nearly reaching the top one. She remembered John telling her that the whole process of moving through the five locks would take about four hours.

Wue smiled and shook his head. "Now that's better, constructive ideas are welcome." Wue radioed the helicopter pilot to fly over the locks.

"When we learned of the drop-off point, the control center for the dam called in extra security," said Wue appearing more relaxed.

The helicopter, which was nearby, moved into position above the locks.

Zakia heard yelling from the walkie-talkie. Wue stepped away, pulling the walkie-talkie free of its holster.

He talked for a moment, and then turned back to Zakia. "The helicopter pilot has spotted something in the empty lock at the top. Something colorful."

Zakia drew in her breath. Her heart raced.

A voice crackled through on the walkie-talkie again. Wue grinned. "The pilot says they've spotted two people and one of them is waving something yellow. It could be your sons down there."

"Thank God," said Zakia, looking up and lifting her arms to the sky.

Wue frowned. "We have to move fast. Two of the kidnappers are still at large and the lock is about to fill."

He got back on the walkie-talkie.

Then with a grim look, Wue began barking instructions into the receiver. Zakia couldn't understand Mandarin, but she got the gist. Something was amiss.

"What's going on?" she asked Wue's sergeant.

"There's a problem. The dam control center isn't responding to our calls. Someone is being dispatched to stop the machine that automatically fills the lock."

"Isn't there an emergency button or alarm system or something?" Zakia looked around, eyes widened. "Please..., don't you have children?"

All three of them turned toward the locks, looking helpless. From this distance, it was hard to tell what was going on. They could see the helicopter land above the lock and the SWAT team racing toward it.

Finally, Wue's walkie-talkie crackled. He looked somewhat pale as he grabbed it. Then he broke into a grin.

"They were able to stop the lock from filling. But it was a close call."

"Thank heavens," said Zakia, so lightheaded that she nearly lost her balance.

They hustled across the dam, Wue in the lead, to the top of the locks. Zakia, still dizzy, was falling behind, but she pressed on and caught up with Wue.

They stood a distance away from the top lock, but Zakia thought she could make out, in the far corner, two tiny figures. It had to be her boys. Zakia's heart raced. The lock looked like a huge, empty swimming pool, many times bigger and deeper than an Olympic-sized pool.

She watched as the SWAT team rappelled down into it, while the helicopter hovered over the lock, ready to receive the boys.

In a few moments, she saw Dani and Harris being hustled along the bottom of the lock to the ropes tossed from the hovering helicopter. The SWAT team members helped them on with their harnesses.

"Dani, Harris!" she shouted. They couldn't hear her. Zakia watched as her boys, each harnessed to a SWAT team member were lifted into the helicopter. She didn't exhale until she saw them both safely inside the helicopter and the sliding door slammed shut. Then it took off.

Zakia and the policemen ran over to a large grassy area on the other side of the lock where Wue signaled the pilot to land. As it landed, draft from the rotor flattened the grass and dust blew into her eyes.

The door slid open and Harris stepped out, bending over to avoid the rotor, followed by Dani. They both ran to Zakia.

They came with such speed that they almost knocked her over. She put her arms around both of them, feeling their warmth. "My brave boys are back." Zakia smiled.

"Hi Maman," said Harris, looking pale and dirty. "I was so scared." He started sobbing and she held him closer.

Dani was the first to pull away. "We rescued ourselves!" he said.

"What do you mean?" she asked.

"We managed to get out of some kind of machine room and make our way out to the lock."

"That was lucky. Or we wouldn't have found you so soon," said Wue.

Zakia cried and laughed simultaneously. "I won't

let you out of my sight until we get back to Morocco, young man."

Wue asked Dani and Harris if they were okay walking for a while. And after they nodded yes, all of them crossed the dam, Zakia walking arm and arm with Dani and Harris. They were hungry and tired, but otherwise seemed unscathed, at least physically.

Thirty minutes later, when they reached the dock by their cruise ship, Wue said he wanted to interview them further. Zakia asked if that could wait until the boys had eaten and rested. Wue agreed and she invited Wue to meet with her in the library in an hour. He saw them safely onto the ship and said, "I have to see about the two kidnappers that got away."

It seemed like the whole Moroccan contingent was waiting for them in the lobby of the ship. The crowd cheered and applauded when they saw Zakia and her boys. Omar shouted, "I'm so glad you two are safe."

John was also there, running interference between them and the rest of the group. "How wonderful to see you. Welcome back, young men. We missed you," he said. "Let me arrange for some food and bring it to your room, while you rest." He leaned into Zakia so the boys couldn't hear, "Just to let you know, we've given you a state room now and a police escort."

"Oh my, a suite sounds wonderful, but a police escort?"

"Yes," said John. "Wue ordered it. After the kidnapping in Wuhan and this one, it makes sense. They don't want your trip interrupted any further."

"I want to take my boys home as soon as they've rested. We're not safe here. I'll tell Wue the minute he's back. The boys are clearly shaken. I can't risk any more incidents and it's obvious we've not been protected."

"That will all change now. As I mentioned, you will have an escort at all times and the ship has additional security. We've been given our orders—if you were to leave now, it would be bad publicity for Chinese tourism."

"You can't stop me from leaving."

"If you leave, you'll be brought right back here. If you were to make it to an airport they would stop you from boarding your flight. So, you see, there's no point."

"I understand." Zakia understood only too well. The Chinese authorities were not easily dealt with. With the police escort, she thought, at least they might be safer.

"I'll show you to your state room now."

When they all arrived at the suite, a policeman was standing at attention at the door. "Thank you John," said Zakia.

"See you shortly," he said.

The boys were thrilled with their new accommodations. Once they had collapsed into bed, Zakia sat and watched them for a while. Then she closed the door to the boys' cabin, sat on the sofa in the sitting room area and Skyped Benjamin. When he picked up, he looked pale.

"I've been calling you all afternoon."

"Dani and Harris are safe now. I got caught up in the rescue effort." she said. "The boys are asleep."

"Oh, what a relief," said Benjamin, rubbing his eyes. "But what did you mean by 'caught up in the rescue effort'?" She saw his frown.

"It's too complicated to tell you just now. I'll fill you in on that bit later, when I'm not so exhausted."

"So they took the money?"

"Not exactly, the police got involved," she said. "Our guide, John, has a wife in the state police. She was able to pull some strings, so we owe them big time."

"Thank goodness for that. Well, I am in Paris now, trying to book a flight to China," he said. "But I've got a serious problem. I can't get a visa on such short notice."

Zakia sighed. "To be honest, I wanted to travel straight home after the boys had rested, but the authorities have decided otherwise. We have no choice in the matter. It seems they don't want the bad publicity for their tourism industry. I guess we could contact the embassy in Beijing and make a stink about it, but I've been told that we will have a police escort at all times. I guess you could say we're no longer in danger. Besides, it's only two days until we fly home."

"I don't like the sound of that, but a police escort should make a difference. And you're right, it's just a couple of days," said Benjamin.

"Yes. Now look, they moved us into a suite; see." Zakia, moved her phone slowly around the cabin. "They want us to be all together. The bedroom is right there—see the door? The boys are sleeping, so I won't go in there. The security guard is posted outside our cabin twenty-four-seven."

"That's good. How are the boys doing?"

"They seem okay, so far. They were a little shaken, but thought their kidnappers were just 'lame'. They don't seem to realize what danger they were in and I'm not sharing, at this point." Zakia downplayed how frightened they still seemed.

Benjamin agreed. "Good thinking. That way, they'll probably get over it sooner." He paused then added, "It may take me longer, though."

"Me too. Anyway, having no other choice, I'll attend my conference in our hotel in Chongqing and we'll see you in Rabat in two days as planned."

"I think it's better if you just stay with the boys."

"I've spoken to Alba, Omar's wife, she's volunteered to stay with them while I'm out. And with security guards all over, there should be no problem."

"Are you sure about that," Benjamin looked grim.

Zakia took a deep breath "Let's not argue about it. We've been through such an ordeal. I'm totally spent. We'll see you soon."

Benjamin said, "I'll meet you at home then. Just check in more often, will you please?" And let me talk to Dani and Harris as soon as they wake up."

"Will do."

****

While the boys were wolfing down the pizza that John had managed to wangle for them, Zakia headed for the library to meet with Wue. The chief looked tired and rumpled, but he stood up, shook her hand, and inquired after Dani and Harris.

"They seem fine. I think they will bounce back soon enough. Thank goodness," she lied. Her brain fought an impulse to scream. Since she couldn't leave, she decided to pretend all was well. *I'll reassess everything once we get back home.*

Wue smiled, "Yes, thank heavens for the resilience of youth." He gestured to a chair. "Won't you sit? I have some news."

Zakia sat down, wondering what was next. Even though she worked in the industry, being on the receiving end of bad news was something entirely different.

"The good news is that the last two kidnappers have been caught. They're from a gang in Wuhan. Clearly, two guns for hire."

"Well, at least we know that much," said Zakia.

"However, they refuse to tell us who they were working for. I'm sure we will find out eventually.

Wue looked at her as he tilted his head. "Are you going to continue with the investigation? It's obviously getting out of hand." He cleared his throat. "I suggest you look for another story. And you should contact the Moroccan authorities once you get home."

"I'm afraid the authorities may be involved."

"Not good," he said. "It will be more complicated then."

They sat in awkward silence for a moment. "Are your sons awake yet? I'd like to speak to them now." said Wue.

"Yes, they are. I'll go fetch them."

As she got up and turned to go, she said, "Thank you for all your help. I'm sorry I gave you a hard time."

Wue laughed. "I wouldn't have expected anything else from you, now that I know you better."

****

Dani talked to Wue first. He described in a calm voice how they had raced up the hill, just past the pagoda, to see the view from the top. "We were startled by a man wearing a gorilla mask and another with a skeleton mask. They said we had to come with them and grabbed us. I thought they were kidding at first."

Wue nodded. "Go on."

"Anyway, I tried to tackle the gorilla-masked guy, but then he pulled out a gun. That freaked us out. We couldn't use any Jiu Jitsu moves to get out of that situation." Dani looked at Zakia. "Even with the junior black belt we worked so hard to get."

Zakia nodded, her mouth dry.

"They forced us down the backside of the mountain, then onto a speed boat on the Yangtze," Dani continued.

"Don't forget to mention," added Harris, wringing his hands, "the boat was disguised as a fishing boat." He cleared his throat, "I asked him why he was doing this. What did he want from us?"

Dani frowned at his brother. "The gorilla-masked guy said, 'Just don't give us any problems kid and you'll be okay.' Then the other guy said, 'We deliver, the client pays, it's a win-win situation.'"

The boys said that they'd stayed the night on the boat as it traveled down the Yangtze and had eaten a plateful of noodles. Early the next morning, they were blindfolded, their hands bound, and dragged onto land.

Dani explained how they were taken from land onto another boat where they heard two new voices. Still blindfolded, they were locked in a smelly storage room, where they could barely move. The boat set off and a short time later, it stopped and they were dragged onto land again, across a grassy area, and then they were thrown into a place with loud machines.

"It sounded like turbines." Harris shook his head, "But then we heard a constant, loud thunderous rumble. We didn't know where we were."

Dani shifted in his seat. "The two newcomers tied

us to some pipes, turned off the lights, then took off our blindfolds and left. So we never saw their faces. When they left us, Harris got really scared."

"No I didn't. I just felt a little lost." Harris rubbed the back of his neck. "But then I remembered the itinerary. We were supposed to stop by the Three Gorges Dam."

"Good thinking," said Wue.

"We just wanted to get out." Harris's eyes blinked faster than usual. "After struggling for a while we were able to loosen the rope around Dani's hands, he found the light switch and untied my ropes. The door looked like one of those on a submarine, air tight with a big metal frame and a lever you had to pull down to open the door. It took both of us to work the lever but then we managed to open the heavy door and walked into what looked like a giant, empty swimming pool. We figured it had to be the locks by the dam. But we couldn't get out of the lock. We tried yelling but nobody answered." He bit his lip.

"Then, later, we heard the helicopter," Dani chimed in. "Harris took his t-shirt off and waved it around and then the helicopter hovered just over us."

"That was awesome," Harris wiped his eyes.

"That's quite a story," Wue proclaimed.

Wue asked them to confirm that there were four kidnappers. He asked if all of them seemed to be Chinese or if anybody seemed like they spoke another language. Dani and Harris answered as best as they could. The kidnappers all spoke English with Dani and Harris, when they spoke to them at all, and the boys said they couldn't make out what they said amongst themselves, but it had sounded Chinese.

"Did they hurt you?"

"Nah," said Dani. "We just got a little shook up."

"I'm glad you're okay," said Wue.

"Can we go now?" asked Harris while rubbing his hands down his pant legs.

Wue nodded and Dani and Harris stood up to leave. Zakia gave them both a hug.

Holding back tears Harris said, "Why were we kidnapped Maman?"

Zakia hesitated, and then said, "I don't know." *No need to share my suspicions at this time.*

Turning to Harris, Dani said, "Don't you remember the guys said they wanted money?"

"Yeah, that's right," said Harris seeming satisfied with the answer. Wue's eyes connected with Zakia's.

"Now please go and meet John in the lounge. He's teaching everyone how to play mahjong. Don't worry about the police escort. He's here to keep us safe."

"Do we have to play mahjong?" asked Dani.

"Yes, I want you to focus on something else just now. I'll be there shortly."

After they left, Zakia turned to Wue and said. "Can you find out who was behind this?"

Wue nodded. "I'm sure we will. I have some theories, but since this may have international connection, I will have to work with Interpol."

Zakia touched her temple and closed her eyes. "Please keep me posted."

Wue smiled. "I'll let you know the moment we get any news. Do me a favor and watch yourself and your sons. I think you may be in over your head, if you don't mind my saying so."

Zakia nodded. She took a deep breath, worried

about Harris who seemed to be reliving the terrifying experience all over again. She would need to watch him closely. *But I still need to attend the energy conference, so I can talk to Samara. I can't just give up now.*

Chapter Eleven

Arriving in Chongqing the next day, Zakia and the boys looked out the larger of the two portholes in their suite and saw the contours of a huge city, obscured by a veil of smog. They could see the strong yellow light in the direction of the sun, but no blue sky.

After they docked and went on the outing to the zoo to see the giant pandas, Zakia settled Dani and Harris into their hotel suite to do homework and watch some TV. Alba arrived soon afterwards with a box of chocolates. The boys smiled. "Thank you Alba," said Zakia, and then turned to her sons. "But first you have to get started on your homework." She gave them both a hug, and headed out the door. Giving a nod to the guard in the hallway, she hurried off to the conference. *Is this safe? Alba was already a victim of kidnapping. Yet, there's a fierce looking policeman standing outside the suite.*

Zakia attended two panels and took notes, though she wasn't focused at all. She kept thinking about her boys' kidnapping and how lucky she was that her sons were found alive. And then her thoughts turned to the threat she had received not to continue her investigation. Samara did not enter her mind until it was his turn to speak. The minister's speech had the usual elements of cooperation between countries to promote progress in the energy sector. Nothing new. Next, she found herself standing next to him at the dinner buffet.

"Good speech," she said, "Your emphasis on the growing need for energy is important."

"Oh, hello," he said, looking at her with interest. "I hope you're boys are recovering okay—what an ordeal! I think most anyone else in your situation would have flown home with her sons by now," said Samara.

She frowned. "Yes, they are fine, thank you. But I'm on an important assignment and have a conference to attend." *Would you have said that if I'd been a man?* "We didn't see you at the zoo. Have you been ill?"

He smiled warmly. "I'm fine. I had matters of state to attend to," he said. "Were the pandas cute?"

While they went through the buffet line, Zakia told him all about the pandas, wondering the whole time if he had been involved at all in the kidnapping. Finally, they were standing at the end of the line, holding their plates awkwardly, until Samara looked at her and said, "Well, here we are. Would you care to join me at my table?"

"That would be my pleasure," she said forcing a smile. They set their plates down.

Samara held out a chair for her, "Thank you," said Zakia, settling herself into the chair.

He sat down next to her, took a sip of water and then turned to her and said, politely. "This hotel is like a fortress, so we need not worry about your family's safety anymore. Soon enough we'll be back in Morocco."

Zakia pulled out her notepad. "I am happy to hear that. I am quite drained from the whole incident—a mother's worst nightmare. I still don't know who's behind it." *But I can guess!*

Samara took a bite of his chicken, chewed it, and then gave her a sidelong glance. "Indeed, it is unusual, even for China."

"I'm sure it was a local gang," she said. *Not likely.*

He looked surprised. "Are you sure? It seems like you may have angered certain quarters."

Zakia coughed. "I'm just doing my job," she said. "It's unlikely that my routine coverage would cause any concern."

Samara narrowed his eyes for a brief instant—so brief she almost missed it. Then he poured himself more water. "The Chinese have promised to keep us informed and we have already begun our own investigations in Rabat, in case there are links from the kidnappers to some elements in Morocco." He kept his eyes on her face.

Zakia said, "Oh, I can't imagine there'd be ties to Morocco," she said brushing the idea away with her hand. "Why would there be?"

Samara focused on his chicken again. "It is unfortunate. I think someone was mistaken at Al Tarife," he said. "No one should be arrested for doing one's job."

"Exactly," said Zakia. Was he threatening her? Before the conversation could take a turn for the worse, Zakia changed her angle. "I had a question for you," she said. "I've been wondering how fracking impacts the nomadic Berbers. Doesn't it force them to lose their water rights and the use of their traditional grazing lands?"

Samara paused with his fork in midair. He looked pale. Then he seemed to recover and gave her a broad smile. "My grandmother was a nomad."

"Really?" said Zakia. "Is she still alive?"

"Sadly, no." Samara put down his fork. "Her tribe was forced to settle in a town near the Atlas Mountains. She never got over that." With an empty stare he said, "Nomadic Berbers shouldn't be forced to live in squalor either, as they often do when pressured into becoming city dwellers."

"I agree. And what about their water rights?"

Samara looked somewhat embarrassed. "Those rights benefit society as a whole. A small minority can't hold back progress."

"And if that minority is going extinct as a people? If we want to preserve their culture we have to act differently, wouldn't you think?"

The minister gave her a stiff smile.

Zakia continued. "I understand our government has begun a huge project to use renewable sources of energy that are much more feasible for our climate, specifically, solar panels. I mean, they don't emit methane or carbon dioxide—that's got to be progress." She knew she had gone from asking questions to lecturing, but she wasn't going to pass up an opportunity to convince a politician.

The minister looked annoyed. "As a matter of fact, that's not something my ministry is focused on right now. Besides, I don't think the project will fly. Investments have already been made in oil and gas ventures—for the next thirty years or more." He gave her a searching look, and then said. "I trust you are done interviewing me? Have I answered all your questions?"

"I have one more question," said Zakia. "I've read that blowout accidents are rare. Do you know what caused the blowout near Al Tarife?"

"No, I don't. That is not my area of responsibility. It's usually left up to the company and the police, though I do review certain of the more complicated cases."

"Ah, I see."

Samara's eyes narrowed. "Why are you asking?"

"Just a routine question." She looked down at her lap, rearranging her napkin.

"Now are you done?" He squinted at her.

"Yes, thank you," Zakia looked up at him again. No point in asking anything else.

"Good." He turned to the Chinese Energy Commissioner seated on his left, leaving Zakia alone with her thoughts. He didn't speak to her the rest of the dinner. She made small talk with a Chinese businessman seated on her right, and another participant, a local bureaucrat, across the table, and left as soon as she was done eating.

Walking back to her room, Zakia thought about how Samara seemed like such a smooth operator. If he was involved in seizing the nomads' lands to sell to Oddleifur Oil, could he also have been embroiled in the murder of Elias?

****

Before bed, Zakia checked her e-mails. She found one from Fiona, her Scottish friend and "go-to" person on climate change. They hadn't talked for months. Dr. Fiona McPherson had been one of the best professors she'd had at Columbia. After graduation, they stayed in touch and became good friends.

She glanced at the first sentence of the email. Fiona wanted to get in touch immediately. *What could be so urgent?* The e-mail would have to wait. Zakia needed to get some sleep to get up early the next morning to catch the tail end of the conference and then get to the airport with her boys in the afternoon.

As she was falling asleep she thought about her career and how it seemed to be careening to crazy places and how this might be affecting her family. *Am I being a bad mother? Will my marriage survive?* She began to think she wouldn't be safe in Morocco either. Perhaps the only option would be to move to the U.S.

****

Zakia and the boys landed in Rabat late on Saturday, took a taxi home, and collapsed into bed. Benjamin arrived then next day, just before dinner. He hugged Dani and Harris for a long time and then turned to Zakia and gave her a long kiss. It appeared they wouldn't be fighting about anything that night.

Over dinner, Zakia was glad to see Dani and Harris laughing and joking with Benjamin. She worried Benjamin might bring up the kidnapping and she was ready to discourage him from doing that in front of their sons.

After the last bit of food was gone, Zakia started clearing the plates and Harris got up to help her. Benjamin told Harris that he'd help Zakia with the dishes, and that they could go see a movie if they wanted to. "Your mom and I need some time to talk."

Dani and Harris hesitated, looking at Zakia for permission. Her stomach clenched. She nodded at them. "Yes, go on. Just be careful and come straight home."

After Dani and Harris left the kitchen, Zakia faced Benjamin, "Can't we just enjoy each other's company tonight?" she said. "I haven't seen you for a while."

Benjamin frowned. "I think we need to talk about what happened in China."

"I'm a little worried about Harris," said Zakia. "He seemed so anxious when he was interviewed by the police chief after the ordeal."

Benjamin responded. "Oh, he'll be all right once he gets back into his normal routine. If not, we'll find a therapist."

"I don't think it's that serious. You know how it is in Morocco. Everyone doesn't have a shrink like in New York."

She handed the plates one by one to Benjamin, who dried them with great energy and put them in the cupboard.

As he finished drying an iron pot, Benjamin took a deep breath. "You want to tell me what happened? Everything was so confusing. I felt I was just getting snippets of information. Let's figure out, in retrospect, what could have been done differently and talk about what we should do now."

Zakia felt her cheeks flush with anger. "I guess next time I should bring a leash."

Benjamin slammed the pot down on the counter. "This isn't funny." He snapped at her. "This is serious."

"Without a sense of humor, we might as well pack it in and move to an island," she said. "Only very soon, some of the small islands are not going to be habitable, if not gone—overtaken by rising seas."

He paced around the kitchen. "Oh, you're always going on about climate change."

Zakia folded her arms. "I can't help it. We have two sons and maybe we'll have grandchildren one day."

He rubbed his eyes. "We can't worry about that all

the time or we'll wear ourselves out."

He looked so tired and she knew he was trying. "So, what do you want us to do?" she asked. "Clearly, there seems to be more to the story than what I've uncovered so far. And the truth needs to be made public. But I do realize that investigating my story has gotten tricky."

He took her hands in his and looked at her, his shoulders drooping.

"Tricky? It's downright dangerous. That's why I think we should move right after Dani and Harris finish their term at school. They will get used to the new place, whether we stay in Chicago or not. Your sister always said we could stay with her for a couple of weeks. Then we look for a rental. The best thing would be for you to call it quits on the story."

With a vacant stare, Zakia freed her hands from his and sat down at the kitchen table. "I'm with you on the safety issue, but I can't quit the story."

"Yes you can, but you are not *willing*. If you want to continue investigating the story, you need to take the option of moving to the U.S. more seriously," said Benjamin.

"I'm not really happy to leave Morocco, you know. This is my home, and my people. I wanted to improve things through my work. I'll be lucky if I can be someone's assistant at one of the big papers in the U.S. The small ones won't have any openings."

Sighing heavily, he said, "I realize it's not easy, but we can't stay here. You are endangering the whole family. It's time to be flexible."

"That's easy for you to say," responded Zakia. "Even if I do quit my job, I'd still have to wrap up the other stories I've been working on before I leave. And it's already the tenth and Dani's graduation is only two weeks away. That's not enough time to pack, move, and find myself another job in Chicago."

"That's a timing issue, those are minor details. My question is: Are you going to quit your job and move?" Benjamin's face was less tense.

"I'll think about it." Zakia gave him a glassy stare. *I'm not ready to make such a decision now!*

Benjamin walked to the chair opposite Zakia's and gripped the back of it. She could see his jaw muscles working. Then he said he was going out for a coffee.

He waited for a moment, time enough for her to say she would join him. But she didn't. "I'm not in the mood for a noisy café," she said.

Benjamin's expression fell. "Sleep well then." He turned and left the kitchen. She could hear the door to the apartment open and shut. He was gone.

She washed the remaining pots and went to bed, alone. She lay there feeling the emptiness of the bed without Benjamin. She was more and more convinced that Benjamin was right. By staying in Morocco, she was putting her family at risk.

Chapter Twelve

The next morning, Zakia found Benjamin drinking coffee on their balcony, while reading his e-mails. Zakia hugged him and whispered in his ear that she had thought long and hard about it and agreed to move to Chicago. "Our boys come first," she said. "I don't want to fight with you anymore."

He jumped up with a broad grin and hugged her. "I think you made the right decision."

Zakia nodded. Fate was taking over, and she didn't like that she was losing control.

He sat down. "I did mention I have to be back in Washington in two days. I'm sorry it's such a short visit, but we will all be together again in Chicago soon and it will be great."

"I guess I'm doing the packing myself?"

"Oh, no worries, I'll be back to help with that. And since you have to stay a bit longer, we'll leave first and you can join us later."

"I guess that makes sense." Zakia looked out over the lovely lush garden, with its red roses and yellow jasmine trees. She and Benjamin had found their apartment when Dani was just a year old. She would miss it. It was centrally located; she could get almost anywhere on foot.

"You're not going to get sentimental on me, are you?"

"No, but we've had a good time here. I hope we can find someplace nice in Chicago."

"We will. Let's tell Dani and Harris about the move at dinner tonight." Benjamin beamed.

"Good idea." Zakia smiled.

****

An hour later, Zakia arrived at the paper. Fatima gave her a big hug and offered her a cup of tea.

"Thank you," said Zakia.

"I'm glad you're back and everyone is safe. The boss wants to see you."

Zakia savored a sip of her tea then took it with her to Jasem's office.

He smiled at her. "Welcome back," He gestured to the chair for her to sit. "Tell me what happened in China. First, I want to hear all the details about your sons' kidnapping and rescue."

Zakia laid it all out for him.

"That must have been terrifying." Jasem pulled his hand through his hair

"In all my life, I've never been so frightened." Zakia, squeezing her eyes shut.

"Did you get a chance to talk to Samara?" asked Jasem.

"Yes, I sat with him at the conference dinner. I asked him about the effect of fracking on the nomadic Berbers. He mentioned his grandmother was a nomad.

"That *is* interesting," said Jasem.

"He seemed to agree with me when I told him one should evaluate if the nomadic Berber culture is worth preserving before we eradicate it."

"Well that was progress. Fancy you educating the oil and energy minister. However, remember you are a journalist, not an advocate of a cause."

She hesitated. "I'm producing a story, not making recommendations. Samara seemed a little too attentive, but he wasn't forthcoming about the blowout. I sense he's in it up to his eyeballs," she said. "I asked him if he knew about the cause of the blowout incident. He said no. I bet he was lying."

Jasem gave her a curious look. "Sure. But please keep all of this to yourself until you have concrete evidence."

"I will," said Zakia.

Zakia went back to her cubicle. She turned her attention to Fiona's e-mail. Fiona explained that she was in Iceland doing research. She needed a favor from Zakia. Could she go to a weather station in the desert near Al Tarife and collect some temperature readings as soon as possible?

Fiona said she'd done some breakthrough research and needed some more climate data to confirm it. *I have a deadline on the latest report and no one else to turn to. The North African countries had not been very helpful in responding to the requests for data, especially Morocco.*

Zakia grumbled to herself. She wasn't keen on going back to the desert, but Fiona couldn't have known that, so she read on. *Oh, by the way, you'll never guess who contacted me out of the blue: Your old boyfriend Elias. He said he had something really important he needed my help with, regarding the nomadic Berbers' water rights, fracking and climate change. Now I have to admit, I only just read the e-mail yesterday—I've been so busy, I think he wrote it almost three weeks ago.*

Zakia's chin dropped to her chest. Fiona obviously did not know that Elias was dead. She sat back in her chair, took a deep breath, and signed on to Skype.

She was relieved when Fiona responded right away. Fiona's sky blue eyes looked red-rimmed, as though she had not slept or had been crying, and she looked even more pale than usual. "Zakia. Oh my God. I'm just beside myself!"

Zakia didn't want to get sidetracked, so she launched right in. "Fiona, I have bad news." Zakia paused for a moment. "Elias died in a fracking incident."

"Elias? Could this day get any worse?" said Fiona, the shock clear on her face. "Like I said, he tried to get in touch with me recently, I've been crazy busy lately and hadn't gotten back to him and now all sorts of terrible things are happening..." She trailed off for a moment, then with an intent look said, "How did that happen?"

"At this point, it's not very clear," said Zakia in a subdued tone. It was odd that Elias, after all these years, would have written to Fiona. "He was killed in a blowout accident at the oil company he worked for. But I think it may not have been an accident."

Bringing her hand to her mouth, Fiona gasped. "I can't believe it. You think it was murder?"

"That's what I'm trying to figure out. He tried to get a hold of me too. And someone was determined to stop him from giving us some vital information."

Fiona stared at her, eyes widening, "I'm so sorry, Zakia. I want to help you, but someone tried to assassinate the Pope just twenty minutes ago."

Zakia shook her head, "What are you talking

about? I've heard no such thing and I'm in a newsroom for heaven's sake."

Fiona shook her head. "I just got a call from the Vatican."

Zakia gave her friend a skeptical look. "Sure you did."

"I did. I was one of the advisors for the Pope's 2015 environmental encyclical calling for action on climate change. The group continues to keep the Pope updated on such issues."

"You never mentioned that."

"It was confidential."

"Why secret?" asked Zakia.

Fiona pursed her lips and looked regretful. "For our safety. Many factions would prefer the Pope had not pushed the truth on the climate science."

"Are you saying that your work on climate change is dangerous?" asked Zakia, surprised.

"Very much so, and now we are exposed because our names have been leaked." She gestured wildly around the room. "That's why I was immediately informed about the assassination attempt. Any one of us could be next."

"Wow, that's a lot to take in. What happened?"

"The Pope gave a speech in New York this morning, at the United Nations, a special forum addressing climate change and sustainable development. While he was being driven to lunch, a sniper shot at the car and hit his good friend and advisor Federico DePietro who was sitting right next to him. The bullet hit him in the back of the head. He was pronounced dead as soon as the paramedics got to the scene. I met Federico once, but only briefly. He was a gracious man. It's so sad."

Zakia's mind whirled. It was terrible news, but Jasem was going to love getting the jump on the international media. "I'm so sorry to hear that. That's just shocking!" she said. "Do you mind if I let my editor know?"

Fiona shrugged. "Fine with me. I'm still trying to take it all in and I don't know much yet." She leaned forward, looking haggard. "To be honest, this is too close for comfort."

"Let's hope it was just a random nut case."

"I wish, but they've asked us all to take precautions and not to travel anywhere for the time being."

"I guess that makes sense then."

"Unfortunately," Fiona sighed. "That's why I need to ask you this favor."

"Wait a minute. In your e-mail, you mentioned a weather station close to Al Tarife. Last time I was in that area, I was investigating the circumstances around Elias's so-called accident at the gas well there. When I went to interview a fellow employee of his, I was arrested and accused of terrorism. Can't you find somebody else?"

"What do you mean arrested?"

"Yes. No doubt, someone wanted to send me a message about staying away from Oddleifur Oil & Gas Morocco. I was released after three long hours of questioning."

"Hold on. You said Oddleifur Oil. I'd forgotten. That's where Elias worked, right? He used his private email when he wrote me. As you probably know, Oddleifur's headquarters are here in Iceland." said Fiona.

"Yes, I picked up on that," said Zakia.

"I was approached by Halgrim Thorsson, Oddleifur Oil's CEO, here in Iceland a few days ago. He heard I was visiting and wanted to learn about climate change and the company's options to transition to renewable energy. We even talked about methane leaks and fracking. After three meetings, it was clear I would just be a pawn in his green wash PR campaign."

"That's unfortunate."

"Yes, and it's outrageous." Fiona raised her voice. "I looked him in the face and could see that he understood the consequences—that their 'business as usual' approach threatens both the stability of the global economy and the longer-term future of the human species." Fiona glared, and then took a deep breath. "I witnessed, firsthand, the intricate patterns of denial and self-deception he was adopting. It makes me so mad."

"That is extraordinary. I understand your anger."

"After the first meeting," continued Fiona, "he showed me a write-up of our collaboration published in their internal company newsletter. Elias must have seen the article and wanted to tell me something in that regard. We know that methane leaks occurring during the fracking process contribute to climate change, but I didn't understand what Elias was referring to when he wrote, 'the nomads' water rights'."

"Wait a minute. It makes sense. Elias wrote me that Oddleifur is colluding with the government trying to expand its fracking operations." Zakia gazed straight into Fiona's eyes. "It seems someone in the government has illegally seized lands traditionally used by the nomads to sell them to Oddleifur.

"Then *that's* the connection. I've done extensive

research on fracking and climate change. Fracking emits methane which is more than eighty times more potent than carbon dioxide as a greenhouse gas in the short term," said Fiona. "The leaks are much worse than previously reported."

"Elias probably figured public pressure might put a stop to the expansion, thus saving the nomads' traditional lands."

"That makes sense," said Fiona.

"I need to get back to the gas well and see if I can find proof of what happened to Elias. I must find out more about how all these things are tied together. If you had sent him proof of the methane leaks from fracking, and I had published an article on it, he would not be doing his employer any favors. Perhaps a reason to remove him *by accident.*"

"That's a serious allegation."

"Yes, it is." Zakia's pulse quickened. "Okay, collecting your climate data will be the official excuse for my trip. You see, neither Benjamin nor my boss would be keen on me going back to the gas well. So, how do I collect the data you require?"

"There are a few weather stations in Morocco, all run by the government. The closest one to the desert is near Al Tarife." She hesitated, and added: "I cannot connect directly with my climate colleagues there, because then the government would figure it out. You have to go and speak to them in confidence and collect the data in person. I would have done it if I weren't stuck here in Iceland. I'll e-mail you the specific data I need."

"Okay," Zakia said. "I should be able to do this."

"Thank you for doing me the favor," said Fiona.

"You don't need to talk me into it. But please do come visit me if I land in jail."

Fiona laughed. "Good luck." Then she looked serious for a moment. "And I'm very sorry about Elias. I know how you felt about him."

If only, thought Zakia, but she thanked her friend. Then, pushing the pain from her mind, she murmured, "I just want justice."

Zakia logged off Skype. Her instinct told her that going back to the desert was a really bad idea. But an accident report could shed light on what caused the explosion. Anything else indicating Elias was no longer in the good graces of his employer would be helpful. *But what if I'm arrested, again?* A shiver went down her spine.

Chapter Thirteen

Zakia tracked down Nassar eating kebabs on a bench in the corner of the courtyard next to the newsroom. He looked up, blushing when she approached him.

"I didn't have time for lunch today," he said with a darting gaze.

"Relax. I'm not your boss." Zakia smiled.

He laughed. "Thank goodness."

When she broached the topic of going to Al Tarife again, he looked excited, and then he slumped.

"Jasem's not going to allow it."

She grinned mischievously. "We're not telling him. We're heading out on Saturday."

"For real?"

"Yes. And you're helping me with something important, even if he finds out and gets angry later."

"As long as I don't lose my job."

"You're helping on the climate change front. It's not for the newspaper." Zakia wasn't telling anyone of her hidden agenda—visiting the gas well again. It was for her story, not the newspaper this time, since they wouldn't print it anyway.

"What are we doing?"

"We're picking up some climate data for my friend Fiona, a climatologist."

"Isn't this something scientists should be doing?"

asked Nassar.

"I wish," said Zakia. "Someone is trying to prevent the data from being reported. If we can do it, we will help the scientists confirm yet another piece of the big climate change puzzle. Which has, I'm sad to say, become a political issue."

"Okay, that makes sense. You can give me more details on the drive there." They agreed to meet at the office on Saturday morning.

Then Zakia remembered that they needed a car. "Nassar, since we can't use Jasem's car this time. Have you got access to a car with air-conditioning?"

He laughed. "I will check with my uncle. He has a beat-up old Chevy, but it's got air conditioning. I'll get in touch if that doesn't work out."

"If not, I'll rent a car."

****

Next, Zakia needed to get hold of Tariq, hoping he would join them. She went across the street to the pay phone and used her new disposable cellphone to text him the number, hoping he would be free to call her back from another payphone. She waited. Ten minutes later, the pay phone rang.

"Hello Cousin," he said. "Any news on our third cousin?"

Zakia quickly realized he was referring to Elias. "I'm calling on a different matter," she said. She told him all about needing to go to the cooking facility outside Al Tarife to get some accurate temperature readings for the meat.

After a moment, Tariq responded. He didn't sound enthusiastic. "Cousin, I don't think I should get involved with any more of the cooking."

"Dear Cousin, I need you to go with us because you know the area better than we do. I will pay you to join us." She said this, not knowing what he received in hourly wages or where she was going to get the money.

"If my aunt finds out, she will be very cross." Tariq sounded hesitant.

"We'll make sure that doesn't happen. Don't worry, we'll be careful not to take any unnecessary chances, *in sha'Allah*."

"Yes, *in sha'Allah*." said Tariq. "I'll do it because our third cousin was very kind to me. Anyway, I happen to know just the right person to help us. He works in the kitchen. But you cannot under any circumstances share these secrets outside of our family."

"Not a soul," Zakia promised. "We will go on Saturday, when most everyone has the day off. Where can we pick you up? Will you be at work?"

"No, I've been staying with my friend in Al Tarife since the accident. It doesn't feel comfortable staying at my old place—too hot. I'll text you where we can meet."

"Thank you," she said. "I don't know how much you know about the science of changing meat temperatures in the recipe, but one thing is for sure, your children and grandchildren will have to live with the mistakes we make now."

"I don't think there are any children in my future," said Tariq. "And you don't need to lecture me about changes in temperature. I'll set it up so we can meet with my friend, you'll see."

Zakia looked toward the heavens as she let out a breath. They were halfway there. Maybe they could get in and out without any problems. Benjamin might not have to know.

****

When she got to the office early Saturday morning, the sun was just starting to warm the air. Nassar was waiting for her at the entrance. He looked a little run down and was clutching a brown paper bag as though it held treasure. Friday night must have been a late one, she thought.

"What's in the bag?" she asked.

"I picked up some *bocadillos* with tuna and olives."

"Wonderful," said Zakia. "I didn't even think about lunch. Thank you. You are most resourceful."

Zakia was relieved that they were heading out, even though Nassar's uncle's car looked barely roadworthy. They made good time heading out of Rabat and the drive passed quickly. An hour away from Al Tarife, she heard a pop.

"What was that?" asked Zakia, her head jerking back. "It sounded like a shot."

Nassar shook his head. "I think it's a flat tire. Relax."

Nassar pulled over, got out of the car, and examined the tire. "It's a flat tire all right," he called to Zakia. I'll take care of it." Zakia offered to help, but he waved her off, so she passed the time trying to center herself by examining the shrubs and tiny flowers by the highway. Then she saw a car in the distance, switching lanes and bearing down on them fast.

"Hurry up, Nassar. We've got company."

The car slowed and pulled over in front of their car. A young, bearded man stepped out. He strode down the highway and right up to Zakia, close enough to touch her.

"Why haven't you got a hijab on?" he yelled.

"What do you mean?" asked Zakia, standing her ground. "What do you care what I wear on my head?"

The man gave her a scowl and she bit her tongue, regretting her words. The stranger moved close enough to Zakia that she could smell his stale breath.

"You are an abomination before Allah," he said, his nostrils flaring.

She desperately hoped he didn't have any weapons.

Nassar had been watching them, but at this he got up and squeezed between them, holding up his hands to the man. "It's okay, she's my sister and she has a fever, so I insisted she take it off to get some air. She's been begging me to put it back on." He glared at Zakia, who finally stepped back, realizing that this man might be more trouble than he was worth.

"Isn't that right, sister?" said Nassar, in an even voice.

On cue, Zakia had a coughing fit.

The stranger looked at Nassar pressing his lips together.

"Let me assist my sick sister," said Nassar, reaching into the car's backseat and passing Zakia the scarf that she had left there earlier.

She wrapped it around her head and shoulders to fashion it into a makeshift hijab. It wasn't something she enjoyed doing, but the way the man was staring at her made her quite uncomfortable.

The stranger looked pleased and nodded in approval at Nassar, who nodded his head in deference. Then he turned to Zakia. "Make sure you do not take it off. Goodbye and Allah be with you."

The stranger walked back to his car in silence, made a U-turn, and headed north.

Zakia leaned against the car, a wave of nausea coming over her.

Nassar took a deep shaky breath, rubbed his neck and walked around in a circle for several moments.

"That was close," said Zakia. "Men like that make me so angry." What made her even angrier was that she couldn't convince them that women ought to have a choice in what they wear.

"And I'm not even a Muslim." This had not been a problem on previous trips to rural areas. Again, she wondered if Benjamin wasn't right about moving to the U.S. It saddened her that her beautiful culture was being undermined by religious radicals.

"Do you think he was convinced?" Nassar peered down the road as he rubbed his hands. "At least he's not going in our direction."

"Let's get out of here," said Zakia.

Nassar finished fixing the flat tire and they drove the last hour to Al Tarife in silence.

****

When they pulled into the main square, Tariq was waiting for them on a side street. "There he is," said Zakia.

Nassar pulled over and Zakia waved to Tariq, who nodded and looked around, then ran over and hopped into the car. Zakia introduced him to Nassar.

"Nice to meet you, Nassar," said Tariq, eyeing Zakia's hijab with a curious look, but he said nothing. "Does she have something on you, too, or are you also a volunteer?"

"I'm always up for an adventure," said Nassar.

"Let's not waste any time in case someone from Oddleifur Oil catches us in the vicinity," said Zakia, adjusting her sunglasses and tugging at the hijab in irritation. She would wear hers so she wouldn't attract any more unwanted attention, but she was losing it as soon as she could.

****

Arriving at the old weather station, Tariq stood there smiling as Nassar tried to open the door to what looked like an abandoned shack. The door was unlocked, but stuck. After an impatient grunt, Nassar smashed into it with his shoulder. The door gave way and Nassar disappeared into the shadows.

"Wow," he cried.

An army of lizards came pouring out.

Tariq jumped aside.

Zakia screamed, and then smiled in embarrassment. "Wasn't expecting that."

Nassar ducked back out. "That was close," he said, shaking his legs. "I felt tiny teeth biting my ankles as they stormed by."

Tariq grinned. "Good thing these lizards are not poisonous. Yet most people think they are."

Zakia decided the weather station was as good a place as any to pull off the head scarf. She shook her head. "Overheating and fear are not a good combination."

They all three stepped inside and Tariq closed the door behind them. One small window barely gave sufficient light for them to get their bearings after the scorching desert sun.

As Zakia took in the room, she realized she had a

146

major problem. The weather station was clearly abandoned. The room was mostly empty—just a beat-up, dusty desk and chair, though she could tell, by the lines in the floor, that there had been more equipment in the station.

"Oh, no," she said. They had made all this effort, and for what?

"Appearances can be deceiving," said Tariq. He walked to the back wall and knocked.

Nassar gave Zakia a quizzical look. "What's he up to?"

"I have no idea."

After a few moments, the wall panel slid aside and out stepped a good-looking young man dressed in jeans and a button-down yellow shirt. "Hello Mon Cher," he said to Tariq, kissing him on both cheeks, French style. "Who do we have here?"

Tariq reddened a bit, but said, "These are my friends Zakia and Nassar. They need that data you said you could provide." He turned to Zakia and Nassar. "This is my friend Maati Tawfeek, one of the climate scientists here."

"It is my pleasure to help you," said Maati. "Follow me."

He led them into a well-lit, spacious room with computer monitors blinking and daylight coming through skylights. Nassar was in awe. "This looks so high tech. What's with the shambles in the front room?"

Maati looked at him with approval. "This is a serious research station. We have to throw would-be thieves off the track," he said. "We feed the lizards so they stick around. Otherwise this place would be emptied in a flash and our beautiful equipment sold on the black market."

"That makes sense," said Zakia. "Thanks for letting us come. Here's the list of data I hope to collect from you. Zakia handed him Fiona's email. This will be invaluable for my friend, Dr. Fiona McPherson."

Maati sat down at a computer and started tapping keys. "Oh, I've read some of her research papers. I too have seen alarming increases in the number of record high temperatures even in my short time out here. Our government has not wanted our climatologists to cooperate, but I guess that's not surprising with the oil interests having the upper hand."

He smiled at Tariq. "My partner works for the enemy."

Tariq frowned. "Stop it," he said, uncomfortably. "I'm just trying to make money to pay for college and this was the only job available. I'll get out as soon as I can, I promise."

Maati reached out and touched Tariq's hand for a moment. "I'm just teasing," he said. "You know how much I respect you."

Zakia smiled.

It took a few minutes to download the information onto a flash drive. Maati explained what he was giving them and what it meant. Zakia took notes. "I apologize that I can't help more, but please let your friend know that I appreciate her work."

"I'll tell her. Thank you for all your help," said Zakia.

Maati handed her the flash drive. "Guard this with your life," he said, in a serious tone. They talked for a short while longer. Tariq was antsy to get out of there, while Maati was interested in talking about his work.

Waving his arm, Tariq was able to herd them toward the door. "We need to get going."

Outside the weather station, Zakia decided it was time to spring the idea of a new visit to the gas well.

As if reading her mind, Tariq looked at her with suspicion. "You have a look on your face that suggests you are up to no good."

"No I don't," said Zakia. "I was just thinking that since we were in the neighborhood, we could drop by the gas well to see if the supervisor might have any information about what caused the blowout or who's behind it. He probably had to file some kind of accident report." Zakia prayed they wouldn't catch on that this had been her plan all along.

Nassar shook his head. "I agree with you, Tariq. This woman is going to get us in trouble. We should go home while we're ahead. We have what we came for—the climate data."

"We've already had plenty of drama working with you," said Tariq.

"But this is important, our friend Elias died. We need to find proof that it was murder and who's behind it."

Tariq was silent and Nassar kicked a rock.

"Come on guys," she said. "Are you telling me you're not up for tackling a new challenge?"

Nassar scowled. "Not at all. I'm up for it, if Tariq goes along." He folded his arms. "But I'm not going alone with you."

"Tariq?" said Zakia.

Tariq ran his fingers through his hair and looked back at the door they had just walked through, "Okay, I'll do it for Elias's sake. He vouched for me when there were rumors swirling around that I was gay. I would have lost my job or worse, if the truth had come out."

"He was a good friend," said Zakia.

"I'm blown away," said Nassar, turning to Tariq. "For that, you may indeed have lost more than just your job."

They walked to the car. "How many people are on duty on a Saturday?" asked Zakia.

"You can't go a whole day without getting into trouble, can you?" Tariq rolled his eyes. "Just one employee today and I know who it is. His name is Leron."

"Good," said Zakia. "Can we get access to the accident report or Elias's personnel file?"

"It's locked up in Rahim, the supervisor's office," said Tariq, crossing his arms. "And we'd be seen."

"Your job will be to distract Leron," Zakia opened the car door and got in. "Are there any security cameras?"

"No. But, what should I say to Leron?" Tariq wiped the sweat off his brow.

"Tell him you've come back from Al Tarife because you are not feeling well and wanted to get out of town. Al Tarife is noisy due to the festival today—it looked festive, anyway—and everyone is out and about. Then you ask him to join you in your trailer to watch a pirated DVD you just acquired."

"That's your plan?" asked Tariq with a snort of dismissive laughter.

"Do you have a better idea?" she asked.

She looked at Nassar. "None here," he said. "Her plan sounds good to me."

150

"Okay, okay," Tariq grumbled, opened the car door and climbed into the back seat. Nassar took the wheel and drove toward the gas well.

Zakia was relieved they saw no cars on the road. She leaned over the front seat and looked at Tariq. He sat there with a grave expression on his face, hands folded in his lap. "We'll text you when we are done," she said. "You'll say it's just your friends in Al Tarife asking if you are feeling better."

Tariq smirked. "How did you know I had pirated DVDs?"

"Lucky guess."

Zakia turned to Nassar. "Do you think you can pick the lock to Rahim's trailer?"

"No need for that," said Tariq. "He has an extra key hidden under the bottom step."

When they got to the gas well, Nassar parked behind the sand dune, with the car turned toward the road in case they needed to leave in a hurry again.

They got out of the car and stood there fidgeting for a moment before Tariq flashed them an uneasy smile and walked off to the office. Zakia and Nassar stayed behind, peeking around the dune, waiting for Tariq and Leron to disappear into Tariq's trailer.

Zakia emptied hot sand out of her shoes. She was beginning to rethink this whole project. It was getting late. By the time she got home it would be past midnight. Even though Dani and Harris were spending the night at a friend's house, she couldn't help worrying. She checked her phone—no reception. Zakia shook her head.

Finally, Tariq and Leron come out of the office and walked to the other trailer.

"Let's move," she told Nassar. The two of them half-crouched while they ran to the office. Scavenging around under the bottom step, Nassar found the key, quickly walked up the steps, and unlocked the door.

"Well done," said Zakia, following him into the office. The place seemed much quieter than on her last visit, except for the constant drone of a large generator.

Nassar locked the door behind them, "Just in case," and looked around nervously. The place was a mess, papers stacked high on a desk and a beat-up filing cabinet. "Where might they have put Elias's file, since he is no longer an employee?" asked Zakia. "And what about an accident report?"

Zakia pulled at the top drawer of the filing cabinet. "It's locked. Darn." She began searching the files on top of the desk.

Nassar pulled out all the desk drawers and rifled through them. "No key here."

Nassar frowned. "What if Rahim figures out we've been here?"

"Hopefully he won't notice; the office is in such a mess," she said.

Just then her cell buzzed with a text. "He's coming." Zakia stiffened, her heart leaping. She looked at Nassar and then nodded toward a small closet behind the desk. "Quick, get in there."

Nassar forced himself into the coat closet and Zakia dove under the desk.

She heard footsteps, coming up the stairs to the office, a voice muttering, and a key in the lock. The door swung open and Leron stepped in. She held her breath as she watched his scrawny legs from under the desk. Had he cared to look, he would have spotted her.

Zakia peeked out, careful not to make a sound and saw him open a first aid box mounted on the wall by the door. He grabbed something and left, locking the door behind him.

Zakia gasped for air, as if she had just done a half mile sprint. "Nassar, are you all right? I thought we were in for big trouble just now."

"It's really stuffy in here," he said, as he squeezed out of the closet.

"Stop taking so many snack breaks," she teased.

As she was about to get up from the floor, she noticed a key taped underneath the desk. She yanked it off and scrambled up. "Look, I think this is the key to the filing cabinet." Zakia straightened up and walked over to the filing cabinet. "Yes!" She unlocked the top drawer and pulled it open. "We're in luck."

Flipping quickly through the files, Zakia found nothing. After a few minutes, she finished rifling through the second set of drawers.

"Nothing in the first two drawers. Let's see the bottom one."

"We're running out of time," said Nassar.

"Okay," said Zakia wiping her brow. She rummaged through the third drawer, while Nassar pulled aside the blinds to see if Leron was coming. She straightened up. "This is curious."

"What is it?" asked Nassar.

Zakia held up a file. "I'm not sure. There's a handwritten note in here, dated April 20 and it's addressed to Rahim."

"Who's it from?"

She frowned. "It isn't signed."

"Keep reading?"

Zakia read it out loud. "This is to confirm that you will eliminate the N.B. problem. You will be well compensated for your loyalty to the company. Instructions attached. Let me know when the problem is resolved. Be sure to burn this note." Her jaw dropped. "N.B. stands for 'nota bene' in Latin, or 'take note' as we would say, but here I suspect it refers to nomadic Berber, implying Elias. What do you think, Nassar?"

"I never had Latin, but that sounds plausible to me."

Zakia added, "I guess someone forgot to burn the note or, perhaps, wanted to keep it for insurance. What kind of instructions could he be talking about?"

Nassar whistled. "I don't know. Is there anything else in the file?"

"Nope, I see staple marks, but the rest is gone."

"That's almost a smoking gun," said Nassar. "It's like the Brits call...cloak and dagger stuff, right?"

"Yes. I kind of like the adrenalin rush of the chase, this is one of the cool parts about journalism." Zakia taped the key back underneath the desk. "I'll take a picture of this and then let's get out of here."

"Sounds good."

When she was done, she replaced the file and shut the drawer, which locked automatically. Nassar hurried out of the office and down the stairs, with Zakia following on his heels. She was so immersed in thought and shocked about what she'd just found that she missed a step and fell.

"Shit," she said loudly, sitting up and rubbing her ankle, which throbbed with pain.

"Shh. Are you all right?" whispered Nassar, hovering over her. "With the noisy generator running,

Leron probably didn't hear anything."

"I hope so," she whispered. "Did you lock the door?"

"No. Damn!" Nassar raced back up the steps, locked the door, and replaced the key.

Zakia got up, dusted herself off, and looked at the trailer where Tariq was still evidently entertaining Leron. "Let's go."

They ran for the car, Zakia wincing with every step. She texted Tariq to return to the car. He joined them shortly thereafter and climbed into the backseat, looking pale and frazzled.

"How did it go?" she asked.

Tariq shook his head. "Leron offered me a soft drink, and I decided to play up my sick act, so I belched after downing it too fast. I made a big deal out of it and pretended to be in horrible pain. Then Leron just tore out of the trailer, yelling that he would get me something for the pain. I almost panicked."

"Maybe you should tone down your act next time," said Zakia, amused.

"I'll say. I was barely able to text you." Tariq continued. "I was afraid I would have to talk Leron out of having you arrested. Leron was back in a flash with some pain medication." He leaned forward in the seat. "Could we get moving? No need to sit around here any longer if you have what you wanted."

"We found one more piece in the puzzle, but not quite hard and fast proof," said Zakia. "But it sounds like Leron likes you."

Tariq groaned. "I have a partner already. Besides he's not my type."

Nassar edged the car around the dune, down the

bumpy road, and back onto the pavement.

"Soon after you sent me the text saying you were done, I told him the pills really helped, that I was feeling much better, and wanted to go back to my friends in Al Tarife. I invited him to join us after his shift."

"Are you really meeting him tonight?"

Tariq frowned. "Not likely. I need to go home now and recover from this stressful experience."

"Sorry," said Zakia. "Will you lose your job if the management finds out what we did?"

"I should be so lucky that I lose only my job," he muttered.

"What do you mean?" asked Zakia.

He gave her a long, steady look. "Remember you thought that Elias's death wasn't just an accident? I was in disbelief at the time. I'm much more convinced now. I'm glad you are relentless in your investigation."

"Me too. Here you can see the picture I just took of the latest piece of evidence." Zakia passed him her cellphone. "I'm pretty sure the N.B. stands for nomadic Berber, in other words Elias."

"That's outrageous," he yelled. "I kept thinking Rahim would never have stooped that low, but I know he is ruthless and crazy ambitious."

"Any idea who might have sent this?" Zakia asked.

"I have my suspicions," he said.

"I think this all points to Sigurd Agnarsson, but we need more evidence," said Zakia.

Tariq nodded.

"It would be helpful if we could find the missing attachment to this note."

Tariq rubbed his temples. "That could be tricky."

Then he leaned back in the seat and closed his eyes until they reached Al Tarife. As they pulled into town, he sat up and leaned over the front seat, beads of sweat on his upper lip. "Keep me posted."

Zakia nodded.

After Tariq got out of the car, Zakia turned to Nassar and said, "Since our paper won't publish my story, we'll keep this last part of our excursion today to ourselves, okay? Jasem will find out eventually anyway. No need to cause turmoil ahead of time."

"Sure, no problem," he said.

After the long drive home, Nassar dropped her off in front of her apartment. All the lights were off in the house. Even the outdoor light, which was always on at night. Then she remembered that her sons were at a sleepover and probably had forgotten to turn on the security light before they left. Zakia let herself into the quiet apartment. The kitchen window was wide open. Maybe it was one of the boys that had burnt his toast and forgotten to close the window. She checked the rooms in rest of the apartment. When she opened the storage closet, she gasped and nearly fell backwards. A hairy, four-inch baboon spider was hanging on a thread right in front of her face. *I have to take it easy*, she mumbled to herself as she slammed the door shut. She tucked a towel tightly underneath the door to the closet. *I'll get the manager to remove it in the morning.*

Chapter Fourteen

In his office on Monday, Jasem looked up from his computer when Zakia knocked. "Come in, Zakia. How was your weekend?"

Zakia felt a pang of guilt and wondered, for a second, if Nassar had told him about their weekend escapade. The thought nearly threw her off. "It was fine. But I have something important to tell you. Is this a good time?"

"Sure. And what might that be?" asked Jasem.

She sat down on the edge of the chair. "I have enjoyed working for this paper, however, due to personal reasons, I need to resign."

Jasem jerked his head back. "Hold on a minute. What do you mean? You're my best reporter."

"I'm sorry. Unfortunately, I have no other choice."

Jasem looked at the ceiling, then back at her. "You can't quit now. I realize you have not had an easy time of it lately, but this is the career you chose. And look at how much good you have done for Morocco, for instance, your story on the economic crisis in the Maghreb area."

"I appreciate the opportunities I've had here," said Zakia wiping her eyes and swallowing hard.

"This isn't because we've decided not to publish the blowout story?" asked Jasem. "I know you would have wanted it published in our paper, but you do understand our dilemma, right?"

Zakia shook her head. "No, it's not that. Benjamin wants us to move to the United States sooner than I had planned, especially after all the trouble in China."

"I can see why he'd want to move. It might also be safer for you to publish the story after you arrive in the United States."

Zakia nodded. "Yes, that makes sense. I will stay on a few days to wrap up the other stories I've been working on. That way I'll also have access to the resources here to continue with the blowout story." She took a deep breath. "Again, I want to thank you so much for everything. It's been a wonderful experience."

"We've worked together for, what…more than fifteen years now. It's not going to be the same without you."

Zakia's eyes met Jasem's. She blinked away a film of tears. Jasem sighed. "Just know that you are welcome back any time."

"Thank you Jasem, I appreciate hearing that." Zakia wiped her eyes.

She went back to her cubicle, walking quickly past her colleagues—who were all either on the phone or typing at their keyboards—sat down at her desk and whimpered. It was silly to cry over her job, but she felt so frustrated at having worked so hard only to have to abandon it all and move to the U.S.

"What's going on?" asked Fatima stepping into the cubicle, her eyebrows drawn together.

"I just told Jasem I'm resigning." Zakia blew her nose.

"What? Why?" Fatima tipped her head to one side.

"Remember I told you Benjamin wished to move

us to the United States? Well, after all that's happened, I finally agreed. It has been too much of a strain on my family and my marriage is barely hanging by a thread."

"I get it. It's not easy. You have put yourself out there, haven't you? I will miss you terribly, but I hope Jasem doesn't want me to take your beat," said Fatima. "Speaking of which, I ran across some information you might find interesting."

"Have a seat," said Zakia.

Fatima squeezed into the seat in the small space across from Zakia's desk. She lowered her voice. "Well, I ran across a compelling source this weekend when I was covering the reception for the opening of an exhibit at the Contemporary Art Museum. I didn't tell Jasem, since he isn't going to print your story anyway."

"What did you find?"

"I found out that Elias turned down a bribe."

"What?" Zakia's voice rose. "Who tried to bribe him? Why?"

"The minister of oil and energy offered him money to keep his mouth shut."

"Well, that fits with my impression of Samara when I met him in China. He's one slippery fellow."

Fatima scribbled something on her reporter's notebook, tore out the page, folded it, and handed it to Zakia. "You need to guard this very carefully, because I don't want her life to be endangered." Zakia unfolded the piece of paper and looked at it. Daliyah was the woman's name. Zakia sucked in her breath. "I'll be careful. I promise."

Fatima went back to her desk. Zakia wrote a piece on the energy conference and the travel piece from China that she'd promised Jasem, skipping, of course, the kidnappings.

Two hours later, she wrote a short e-mail to Fiona telling her that she had the climate data on a zip drive and that she and Benjamin had decided to move to the U.S. They would be leaving in a few days. She skimmed through the climate data on the zip drive and started to mail the first batch of materials to Fiona.

Shortly thereafter, she received a text from Fiona: *Zakia, stop sending the data. I've been hacked.*

A second later, another text came in: *I suspect my phone was being tapped. I'm now using a disposable phone. Call me at 00 718 6488.*

Zakia called her right away and Fiona picked up.

"I think I'm also being watched—this is nuts."

Zakia shivered. "Be careful."

"I will. But, look," said Fiona, "I have to ask you another big favor. In your e-mail you mentioned you are moving to the U.S. Is there any chance you could bring the data in person? It's the safest way for me to get it. And it would give us an opportunity to catch up. You could spend a couple of days here in Iceland with me and do some sightseeing. Can you manage that on such short notice?"

"Well, I'm working on a complicated story and I'm supposed to be packing and organizing things for the move." Zakia's thoughts were racing, all the crazy things happening in her life right now. Was she going to just drop everything and fly to Iceland? She thought about it for a moment, then realized she could do both. "I'll see if I can stop by on my way to Chicago. With your help, I might also be able to visit the Oddleifur headquarters which would be perfect for my story."

"I'll try to help you. But remember, I didn't leave

the project with Oddleifur on a good note."

"Yes, but at least we need to try. I'd like to find out if the order to eliminate Elias came from headquarters. Say, do you think the hackers are related to the assassination attempt on the Pope?"

"It's most likely the same bunch. The fossil fuel industry and associated interests don't like my research on climate change," she said. "It's similar to the tobacco industry; it misled the public for twenty years. In the same way, the fossil fuel industry wishes to carry on with business as usual." Fiona raised her voice. "Can you believe it? They'd rather continue killing the planet's life-sustaining systems than make the transition to renewable energy."

"I think it's all in the money and short term interests," said Zakia, thinking about the land deeds she'd found. "And, of course, power."

Fiona added, "It's not just the money. The oil industry is clearly trying to delay as much regulation on climate change as possible. They equate climate activists and scientists with Communists, because, of course, government involvement will have to be part of the solution to protect our planet."

"The oil industry doesn't seem to get it," said Zakia.

"I think they get it, but prefer to live in denial. You'd be surprised at how connected all this stuff is. We already have the technology for renewables and prices have come down immensely, but oil companies aren't budging. Short term interests, as you said."

"Okay, I'll let you know when I've worked out the details of my trip," said Zakia. "In the meantime, please be careful. We don't know who those people are and what lengths they will go to, in order to silence you."

"Yes, I'm being careful," said Fiona. "But Iceland is not exactly known for having high crime rates."

****

When Zakia Skyped Benjamin that night, he seemed taken aback by her plan. "Why the detour to Iceland?"

"Fiona's computer got hacked and she needs some climate data."

"What does Fiona's climate data have to do with you?"

"Well, I collected the data she needs," said Zakia.

"What do you mean?"

"I took a trip back to the desert near Al Tarife to get her the data." She braced herself for his response.

Benjamin pushed away from his desk. "You did what?" he cried.

"I had to go back to the desert because that's where the weather station is—very high-tech, by the way. Our government has not been cooperating with the climate scientists."

He leaned back in his chair. "How could you go back to the desert, Zakia? Here I have been so worried about you and the boys and you have the gall to take off and do something that stupid. For a second time! How could you?"

Zakia bit her lip and stared down at her hands. She shook her head. "It seemed to be the right thing to do. I owe it to Fiona and our children. Remember climate change." She took a deep breath. "Besides, Dani and Harris had a sleepover that night. They were fine." Zakia was not sharing the fact that she had also returned to the gas well.

163

"I'm running out of patience," Benjamin shouted, throwing his arms up in the air. "What do you owe Fiona? She's not family and you certainly don't work for her."

Zakia fixed him with a cold stare. "Benjamin, some friends are like family. You trust them."

"You are out of your mind," he said. "I've about had it with you."

Her cheeks burned. "I guess you're right. I'm crazy. But now that we're going to start a new life in the U.S., we need to be able to work together better than we are doing now. We have to make some compromises. Remember, I already agreed to the move."

"Yes, you did, thank goodness," he said. "I hope you keep that bargain."

"Benjamin, you know I love you," she said firmly. "It's not my fault Fiona is in trouble. I guess you heard about the assassination attempt on the Pope. Fiona knew that before the news outlets because she is one of the Pope's advisors on climate change."

"I don't know how that makes any difference," said Benjamin, shaking his head. "It's still your safety I'm worried about. If some heinous group can try to knock off the Pope, what makes you think you're not in danger of being eliminated for being such a headache?"

"I'm not the Pope," she said, drily. "I'm just an insignificant journalist."

Neither of them said anything for a few moments. Zakia regarded Benjamin with a steady gaze and he looked at her with narrowed eyes, "I suppose I can't stop you," he said, scowling. "But we are a team here, remember. It would be better if we could talk about your crazy schemes ahead of time before you dive in headfirst."

"I didn't have much time."

"Well, somehow you need to straddle both worlds. We need to pack, remember. I'm sorry I lashed out at you. It's mostly me reacting to my own situation, the fact that I can't be there for you right now."

"I wish you were here already," she said. "But, at least now we will be on the same continent. That's a big improvement. You can come home on weekends from Washington D.C."

"We'll be together soon," said Benjamin with an upturned face.

"I miss you. Okay, I think we have a plan. After you take off with Dani and Harris to Chicago I will fly to Reykjavik and spend two-three days with Fiona before joining you guys. You're okay with that, right?"

"Sounds fine. A mini-vacation to see your girlfriend is not a bad idea," he said, doing his best to sound enthusiastic.

"Thanks for understanding," she said. She wondered just how much vacation time she would have, since she would carry on with her investigation. But she couldn't share that with him either.

****

At work the next day, Jasem called her into his office. When she walked in, he was fuming and pacing behind his desk. "Sit down," he snapped.

"What's wrong?" Her heart sank.

"First of all, why didn't you tell me ahead of time about the second trip to the desert? You seem to be searching for trouble, constantly. What's the matter with you Zakia? What are you trying to prove?"

"Nothing, sir," said Zakia more formally, as if that would help her case. "I just had this sense that I needed to help a friend doing important work. Anyway, who told you?"

"I overheard Nassar talking about having gone to Al Tarife last weekend. When he mentioned your name, I figured it couldn't possibly be anything good. So I pried it out of him."

"Oh, that's too bad."

"He said you drove to a weather station out there."

"Yes, so it wasn't for work, anyway."

"I don't care. You put Nassar in danger and perhaps the Oddleifur Oil employee—what's his name?"

"Tariq."

"Yes. Tariq. He could lose his job as a result, you know."

"I'm not trying to get anyone in trouble. I'm just trying to help my friend prove several aspects of the link between climate change and extreme weather events." Zakia skipped any mention of the visit to the gas well.

"You're really thinking one scientist is going to make a difference?" asked Jasem.

"Step by step, they've been accumulating knowledge on climate change. This is another piece in the puzzle."

Jasem laughed. "I admire your belief that one person can make a difference, in climate change or anything else. But perhaps I have been doing this too long and have grown cynical. There are so many naysayers and skeptics that I wonder if we are going to be heard at all."

"We have to try. I have to, anyway, for the sake of my sons and future generations."

"That's fine. I get it." said Jasem. "Now, getting back to the blowout story, since you only have a short time left before your trip," he added, in a soothing tone, "why don't you just tie up the loose ends on that story, since you can't publish it here anyway and let's move on."

"Sure. But there may be a pattern with what has happened to me in regards to my coverage of the story. I think I might be rattling some powerful people." She wasn't going to telling him about her latest find either, the one implying the elimination of Elias; she would get to it later.

"No, Zakia, Don't even go there." Jasem had an edge in his voice. "You may see it that way, but it could just be coincidences. I think you're going over the top playing with conspiracy theories."

"I don't think it is possible to shut down that part of my brain."

"Well, keep it to yourself. I don't want a word of it breathed here in my newspaper. Do I make myself clear?" Jasem scowled and shook his finger at Zakia.

"Okay, I'll try and wrap up the loose ends." She stood up, sighed and walked out of his office.

Chapter Fifteen

Before leaving work that evening, Zakia got a call. A woman was crying on the other end of the line.

Zakia said, "Hello? Who is this?"

"This is Tariq's mother, Miriam." Her voice quavered. "Tariq passed away."

Zakia gasped in disbelief. "That's not possible I just saw him three days ago." Miriam started sobbing. "He died in a car crash today on his way here to Rabat. He called yesterday and said he was ordered to attend a meeting at his company's headquarters this morning and would visit us tonight."

"I am so sorry. God have mercy on him."

"Thank you. We are still in shock. He had left me your cellphone number. 'Just in case,' he said. I asked him what that meant, but he brushed me off and said you two had become friends."

"I guess we were," Zakia's voice was breaking.

The silence was awkward for a moment, and then Miriam started crying again.

"Is it okay if I come by and visit you?"

Zakia waited in suspense, not expecting Tariq's mother to be welcoming to a stranger, but Miriam's tone shifted and she answered with a warm voice. "Yes, that's fine." She gave Zakia her address.

"Can I come by this evening?"

"That would be kind of you. Our family would be

honored."

Zakia hung up the phone and sat, stunned. Tariq was a young man with a lot of promise and she appreciated how he had gone out of his way to help her.

And now he was dead.

The newsroom was still busy, but Zakia was in her own isolated world. She called home to let Dani and Harris know she would be late. Nura answered the phone and assured her that she would stay as long as she was needed that night. Zakia hurried out of the *Le Journal du Maroc* building and into the street, dodging cars and other commuters on their way home, and hailed a taxi. Tariq's family lived only a few minutes away, in an older part of Rabat. Their house was walled in, old style, as her grandpa's had been.

She paid the taxi and walked to the large wooden door and hesitated. Her desire to know what had happened fought with her reluctance to invade their privacy at such a devastating time. Before she rang the doorbell, she told herself she was simply relaying her personal condolences. The least she could do for Tariq.

The woman who opened the door was short and wearing an elegant long black dress with long sleeves. She had long black hair drawn back in a ponytail. Her eyes were teary and red, but she smiled.

"Hello. You must be Zakia," she said. "I am Miriam. Thank you for coming." She led Zakia through the hallway to a large, beautiful patio with a water fountain in the middle and greenery on one side. She faced Zakia and greeted her in the traditional way, dipping slightly, her hand on her heart. "I am touched that one of Tariq's friends would come so soon."

The woman beckoned Zakia to follow her through

the living room, decorated simply with low-slung sofas lining two of the walls, and a large rich, wine-colored Persian carpet on the tiled floor. Zakia marveled at the octagonal wooden coffee table which stood in front of the sofas. She realized that Tariq came from a traditional family and wondered if his parents thought it odd that Tariq had a female friend who was clearly westernized. It seemed they had no idea he was gay and Zakia was not about to tell them.

Miriam graciously invited her to a small inner courtyard beyond the living room for tea. She beckoned to a young woman, who was also wearing a mourning dress. "This is my daughter, Kamila," said Miriam, drawing the girl toward her and kissing her cheek.

Kamila put her palm on her chest and nodded at Zakia, murmuring a polite greeting when Zakia introduced herself.

They sat down on cushions around a low table that bore dates, almond cookies, fine teacups, and a tall, silver teapot. Zakia told Miriam about her own family, answered questions about her children and husband, and drank some of the sweet mint tea. She was relieved that Miriam did not ask about her friendship with Tariq. Miriam seemed simply glad to meet someone who had a connection with him. Eventually the conversation turned toward Tariq's job at the gas well near Al Tarife and how much his mother had missed him. In a quiet voice, Zakia asked "If you can, please tell me what happened."

Miriam dabbed her eyes with a handkerchief. "The police left just a short time ago. As I mentioned on the phone, Tariq called us last night and said he needed to attend a meeting at his company's headquarters. This has never happened before." She waved her hands, looking bewildered. "My intuition told me something wasn't right."

Zakia leaned forward. "What made you think so?"

"Tariq had told me that the workers never go to headquarters." Pinching the skin on her throat she said, "Do you think my boy was in some sort of trouble?"

Zakia did not want to hurt his mother's feelings. "That's hard to tell." She was tempted to tell her what she and Tariq had been up to, but this was not the time. Besides she had no definite proof.

Miriam stared at her hands. "We were told that just before ten this morning he was in a horrible accident on the highway. It seems Tariq's car swerved off the highway where the guard railing is missing and rolled down the side of the mountain." She gave Zakia another bewildered look. "But Tariq never took risks while driving."

Kamila leaned over and patted her mother on the arm and whispered in her ear.

"Thank you, dear," Miriam said, wiping her eyes.

"I am so sorry," said Zakia, searching for something to say and feeling more and more like she shouldn't have come. "There have been many accidents on that highway. You would think they could put up some more guard railings."

"Yes, but it's too late for my son." Miriam's voice was choked with tears.

Finishing her tea, Zakia realizing that she had probably overstayed her welcome and that it was nearly time for evening prayers, excused herself and stood up. "It's time for me to go home," she said. "I am so sorry about Tariq."

Miriam got up, too, and gave her a surprising hug. Zakia put her arms around her. "Thank you for your hospitality."

Walking towards the entrance they met a tall, heavy man, wearing the traditional long robe, as he let himself in the front door. He looked surprised to see Zakia.

"This is my husband, Sahib," said Miriam and then gestured to Zakia. "This is a friend of Tariq's. Zakia's a journalist, but came from her busy job to express her condolences. We've had some tea. I'll call for a taxi." She picked up the phone on the console table.

"Thank you," said Zakia. She half expected Tariq's father to be upset that a reporter was in their house— under the circumstances—but he smiled at her. "I am glad to meet you," he said. "In fact, I have some information that might interest you, since you were a friend of my son, and a journalist."

Zakia's eyes widened. "What information would that be?"

He pulled out a sheaf of papers from his jacket. "I decided to get the police report. As you probably know, it can take days before the final report is made public, but the secretary at the police station needed money to pay for her summer vacation, so I made a donation. She made me some copies of Tariq's file."

Zakia looked at him, shrugged and said, "I see, and did you find anything, this early in the investigation?"

Sahib nodded. "We were right, I think, in suspecting that there's something odd about this accident."

Zakia wouldn't have expected a conservative family to question the authorities. "How so?"

He looked through the papers and gave her one of the pages with a photo attached. He pointed at it. "Look. There's a second set of tire marks on the ground near where Tariq's car went off the edge. They're fresh, obviously made at the same time. After the most recent rains, the soil still looks moist."

"Are they looking into it?" asked Zakia.

Sahib met Zakia's gaze. "The police said it looked suspicious."

"I'm sure the police will get to the bottom of it." Zakia tried to convince herself more than anyone.

Miriam blew her nose. "We need to wash and shroud Tariq's body as soon as it arrives; the police said it would be soon. It's so awful—mothers are not supposed to bury their children. My poor wonderful Tariq." She began sobbing and her husband drew her near, putting his arm around her.

"I'm so sorry," Zakia said. "I should go. The taxi will be arriving."

"I would like you to take this information and look into it for us," said Sahib. "If you can." He handed her the papers.

"I can do that, but I can't guarantee anything," Zakia hesitated. "Please don't tell anyone that I have this information."

Miriam looked at Zakia, throwing her hands up. "I just want someone to find out what really happened."

"I'll see what I can do. I promise."

The taxi pulled up to the house and Zakia hurried out, clutching the report. The father ran out to her and said. "I hope you will come to the funeral tomorrow morning."

She said she would try and he went back into the

house.

The sadness in the house followed her. She sat in the taxi, trying not to imagine, but picturing the funeral. Tariq's body would soon be at a mosque, and his family would pray over him. He would be buried within twenty-four hours of his passing, as was Muslim tradition.

She wished she had not said she'd go to the funeral. She didn't mean to be disrespectful, but the most religious encounter she had experienced was her parents' Anglican Church funeral many years ago. She sighed.

She thought that Tariq's mother and father were grasping at straws, trying to find out why their son had died. She bit her lip. Had she not asked for his help searching Rahim's office, Tariq would probably still be alive. *This can't be a coincidence.*

****

The next day, Zakia arrived at the office early, before her colleagues, when it was still quiet. She found a new computer on her desk. *Thank you Jasem!* She put the computer she'd borrowed aside. It didn't take long to download her files from the cloud.

She started to outline all the information she had regarding Tariq and the suspicious accident—that was most likely murder. There were few other explanations for his death. She sat back in her chair. Either way, she'd really messed up by involving him so deeply. She thought how nervous Tariq had been the whole time they'd been working together. He had even had a premonition that something bad could happen. *But murder?* If she wasn't careful, she could be next. Zakia shuddered.

She phoned the source Fatima had given her. When a woman calling herself Daliyah picked up, Zakia introduced herself, mentioning where she worked and asked if she had a moment to talk.

"Yes, I have a moment. My boss is out so I have the office to myself."

"And who is your boss?" Zakia asked. "Fatima just gave me your name and said you had some important information to share. But she didn't tell me much else."

Daliyah did not answer right away. "I just want to make sure that you don't publish the information until I'm safely abroad."

"I won't."

"It's a complicated story. I can't talk here. It's too dangerous. Let's meet someplace."

Zakia thought for a moment. There were few places where women could meet in public in Morocco, without eliciting cat calls and other harassment from men. The most convenient was the public baths, the *hammam*. She suggested one located in the neighborhood not far from her office. "Can we meet there tomorrow afternoon?"

"I can't make it until Friday," said Daliyah.

"Okay, Friday. How about 4 p.m.?"

"That will be fine." "How will I know you?"

"I will ask for you by name. And you can see my photo on the paper's website, so you'll know it's me. Thank you for helping."

"It's well worth it."

As Zakia hung up the phone, Jasem strolled up to her cubicle and leaned over the partition. "Can I see you in my office please?" he said, his brow wrinkling.

"Let me finish my notes and I'll be right there."

"Thanks," he said, and walked back to his office.

How unusual, thought Zakia, Jasem rarely left his office to summon anyone. He ordered others to fetch the person.

She grabbed her new computer and walked into his office. "Jasem, it's wonderful, I really appreciate the new computer. That was most kind of you."

"You're welcome. Have a seat."

"What's up?" Zakia settled into his uncomfortable visitor's chair.

"I just heard that Tariq died in a car accident. What's going on?"

"I visited his parents yesterday—very sad. His mother said he had been called in to his company's headquarters and that Tariq told her that's unusual. And his father thinks the car crash was no accident. He obtained a copy of the preliminary report from the police station. It appears there were two sets of tire marks."

"It looks like you might have something there," said Jasem. "If there were two sets of tire tracks, most of the time it's one of two options: either he was run off the road or he was stopped, killed, and then the car was pushed off the road."

Zakia nodded. She had come to the same conclusion, but having Jasem put it out there in the open made it more real.

"When we put all the prior incidents together, I think it points to a cover-up by Oddleifur Oil," said Zakia "Perhaps in cahoots with our own oil and energy minister."

"I think you are right about that." Jasem stared at her.

176

Zakia averted her eyes. "It's my fault he is dead. He would still be alive today if it weren't for me asking for his help."

"You can't blame yourself. He was an adult and made his own choices."

"But..." she started.

Jasem held up a finger. "I wouldn't go there, if I were you."

"That's two people dead—that we actually knew, in addition to the three other victims in the blowout incident. I should think this makes it even more urgent to run the story," she said.

"Nice try, but you know we can't do that. The higher ups have said no. They are not going to change their minds. The issue is too sensitive."

Zakia sat there, gripping her own wrist. *Here we go again.*

"We can't run the story here, but it's clear you have enough to publish the story somewhere else, once you are out of the country."

"I'm willing to stick my neck out. Why aren't you?"

"Zakia, I am planning to retire with a pension and without having made a bunch of enemies," said Jasem. "I still live in this town, remember. Furthermore, I am glad you're leaving now. It's not safe for you to stay."

"I realize that," she said, staring down at her feet. She was eager to meet with Daliyah and then let Jasem know that she had a source that might provide proof of her suspicions.

"You can work from home to finish up your stories, but be careful," he begged her.

"Thank you Jasem for believing in me," said Zakia.

"I will always remember you for having brought me on board as a novice, when most women journalists at the time were hired as glorified secretaries or assigned to report on fluff. You got me started in this business and I really appreciate it, thank you."

"I can't say it has been uneventful having you as an employee." Jasem grinned.

"I will keep a low profile, but I'm actually going to see if I can scrounge up some more information on Oddleifur Oil and Gas. And yes, I will be discreet."

Jasem raised his eyebrows, but Zakia plunged ahead, explaining that she needed to land an interview with Sigurd Agnarsson, the CEO of Oddleifur Oil Morocco. "I can even say that I'm pitching the story to a business magazine, if you like."

"That's not going to work. They'll eventually link you to this paper and we'll be in trouble."

"Remember I have resigned. You cannot be blamed for what I do on my own."

"Yes, but then again, you are putting yourself in danger. They will recognize you."

"I've thought of that," said Zakia. "I'll go incognito. Sigurd Agnarsson has never met me. I'll wear my stunning glasses, which I never use, and my makeshift hijab. I'll tell him I am doing a series on business leaders in Morocco. You know, boost his ego."

Jasem fixed her with a stare and his mouth twitched. "Stunning sunglasses and a hijab." Jasem threw his arms up in despair. "You think that will be enough? You're on your own on this one."

"He won't kill me in his office in broad daylight."

"No, you're right about that. He'll have it done in a

dark alley at night."

Zakia gave him a wry smile, then told him she was attending Tariq's funeral and hurried off to snag a taxi. Jasem's words bounced around in her head. Her guilt regarding Tariq came back full force.

****

Friday afternoon, Zakia walked through a lime-green alley to reach the unassuming, women-only *hammam* where she had arranged to meet Daliyah. At the front desk, she paid the clerk and was greeted by a petite woman who showed her to a large changing room, where she sat on a wooden bench against the wall near the entrance and waited for Daliyah.

Ten minutes later, an attractive young woman wearing a smart business outfit appeared and looked around nervously. It had to be her.

Zakia approached her and introduced herself.

After shaking hands, Daliyah sighed. "I'm looking forward to passing along this information. It's been a burden."

"I understand, but I won't be able to take notes here," said Zakia.

"It's okay; I have photocopies in my bag," she said. "But let me give you the rundown in the steam room where we can probably find a corner that's more private."

The two women undressed, hung their clothes on hooks on the wall above the bench and proceeded to the steam room. It consisted of two huge tiled rooms with domed ceilings filled with steam. There were naked women reclining all over the floor. On the far side of the adjoining room they found a quiet corner and placed their rented plastic mats on the tiles.

Two women were filling buckets from a gushing tap on the wall. Zakia and Daliyah soaped and washed, then rinsed themselves, and settled on their mats on the floor. Then two scantily-clad attendants or *tabayas* arrived and after applying black soap all over them, scrubbed them, giving them a complete skin cleansing. Zakia relaxed in the steam, the first time in a long time that she'd indulged in such luxury. There were many things about Morocco she would miss.

After a final gush of hot water, the *tabayas* moved on and Daliyah launched into her story.

"One of my responsibilities is to open the minister's mail every morning. The past few months I've opened several envelopes with checks to the minister. They were company checks, addressed to him personally, and were for large sums of money."

"Who are the checks from and what do you think they were for?"

"They were from Oddleifur Oil, and they were sent from Iceland," she said. "Since the company has its headquarters there, I guess that makes sense, but I'm not sure what they were for. There have been several permits made out to Oddleifur Oil that went through the normal channels, but this money didn't fit the system. These checks were out of the ordinary; they seem to refer to transfers of state land, which aren't dealt with by our ministry. That's not how it works."

Zakia was ecstatic. "Why are you coming forward now?"

Daliyah looked satisfied. "I've wanted to tell someone about this for a long time, but because of my situation, I couldn't. Now the time is right. I am moving to France in a few days. I want something better in life than to live as a second-class citizen, given the limitations on women, in this country. I have my parents' support which makes it easier."

"Why are you sharing this information about the Minister?" asked Zakia, impressed.

"Samara has made aggressive sexual advances toward me," she said. "I'm fed up with him, and he's obviously involved in illegal dealings, so this is it."

"Fatima mentioned Samara tried to bribe someone at Oddleifur Oil," said Zakia.

"Yes, I put a phone call from Elias Mansur through to the minister, and I overheard part of the conversation. Elias turned down the bribe. Samara was so upset he slammed down the phone."

"Can we get in touch if I need you to corroborate that story in future?"

"Yes, just ask Fatima. She'll know where to reach me." Daliyah told her about some of the documents that she had managed to photocopy. Then she said that she had to go.

"I can't thank you enough. This is incredible."

They walked back to the changing room and got dressed. Before they left the *hammam*, Daliyah took a hefty envelope out of her bag and pressed it into Zakia's hands. "Be careful," she said. "And don't do anything with this until next week when I've left the country."

Chapter Sixteen

Zakia waited twenty minutes in the grand waiting room of Sigurd Agnarsson's office with its marble foyer and lavish water fountain, before the stunning secretary approached her. "Mr. Agnarsson will see you now."

Sigurd strode out from the executive suite and greeted her, his blond hair glistening in the sunbeam from the window. Zakia got up from the sofa where she'd been waiting. "I'm Calandra Sabri."

"I am so glad we can finally meet," he said. He held the door and gently ushered her forward into his office with his hand on her back."

Zakia stiffened. Moroccan men never touched women unless they were somehow related.

"Thank you for taking the time." She felt more on guard. *This could be the man who ordered Elias's murder.* Zakia shuddered, but then reminded herself that she needn't worry—this was not a dark alley.

His office had wood-paneled walls, a massive desk and a separate seating area with a sofa and two lounge chairs. There were poster-sized pictures of Iceland showing hot springs and snow-covered volcanoes.

"So you're interested in writing about how I founded Oddleifur Oil & Gas. Let's sit over here on the sofa." He gestured toward the plush sofa.

"I prefer the chair; my back tends to give me a hard

time after sitting too long on soft cushions." Zakia rubbed the back of her neck.

He sat on the sofa next to her chair and looked at her. "I'm an open book. Ask me anything."

She gestured at the posters hanging on his walls. "What do you think of the weather in Morocco, compared to Iceland?"

"Oh, it's much better here. It's too cold in Iceland for my liking."

"So, do you have family in Iceland?"

"Yes, a daughter, Runa, and my cute grandchild. Runa's mom, my wife, died of ovarian cancer, so it's only the three of us. We spend a lot of time together."

"I'm sorry to hear about your wife." An awkward silence ensued. Zakia looked at her notes, wondering if he was going to tell her anything worthwhile. "So, tell me a little bit about your background."

"I grew up in Iceland, went to a small elementary school and high school in Akureyri up north, then I went to the University of Iceland in Reykjavik where I got my MBA. My dad was a fisherman, like most of my family, but I was not meant to join that tradition. I got seasick even coming close to a boat."

He laughed at his own joke and Zakia forced a chuckle.

"Then what?" Zakia hoped that if he kept talking, something useful might slip out.

"I finished my studies, worked a few years in a local bank, until the economy tanked and the country went bankrupt." For a moment, he appeared lost in thought and looked genuinely distressed.

"That must have been devastating."

"Yes, but I was fortunate. Since my family has

cousins in Norway, I decided to move there. I was lucky enough to get hired by Baldvin Oil Company."

Zakia had been reading a lot about the fossil fuels industry and knew that Norway was a big player, although it wasn't a member of OPEC. "I heard Norway is sort of the Saudi Arabia of the North."

"I guess you could say that. However, Norway scores 'very clean' on Transparency International's rankings for corruption, though recently I noticed they have had a few high-profile corruption cases."

"Do you find corruption is a problem in Morocco as many analysts claim?"

"It depends on how you define it. In many societies, as you well know, certain showing of appreciation is part of the culture. Were you thinking of anything in particular?"

"No, nothing in particular," said Zakia. *I better hold back.*

"When did you establish the Oddleifur Oil & Gas Morocco?"

"Four years ago, I became aware of the enormous progress made on hydraulic fracturing while working in the U.S. for a subsidiary of Baldvin Oil and decided that was the wave of the future. I incorporated my company, Oddleifur Oil & Gas Co. in Iceland, but most of my activities are outside of Iceland. I run the subsidiary here. I like to get projects off the ground, and then move on. But my subsidiary is tightly connected with the head office, which is run by my good friend Halgrim Thorsson in Reykjavik. I pretty much tell him what to do."

"Where did your funding come from to start the company?"

"I gathered some investors together who believed in my project. They are all investors who have placed their bets on fossil fuels and done very well for themselves."

Zakia took notes and nodded. "I'm curious just how you found these investors? You can't just show up at their offices and ask for money."

"Oh no, you're right about that. You need to get plugged into the right trade associations. I've recently become a member of an exclusive inner circle of such an association in the United States. A powerful group of people indeed. They get things done. But I can't say any more on that topic. It's all confidential, I'm afraid."

"I see. Are you positioning Oddleifur Oil and Gas to become a big player?"

"Well sure. Last year, you could say was a breakthrough year. The Chinese bought seventy percent of my shares in the parent company, but decided to keep me on as the CEO here. It was mostly due to the Chinese-Icelandic Free Trade Agreement. It has given Icelandic companies a lot more leeway to expand into new markets."

"Will there come a point when Oddleifur Oil is big enough?" she asked.

Sigurd wrinkled his brow. "No, you have to keep growing or lose market share. Unfortunately, you can never have enough money."

It was such an odd statement that Zakia wondered if he was referring to money for the company or for himself.

She looked at her computer and noticed that they'd already been talking for twenty minutes.

"Do you think you'll continue expanding even if it

hurts the environment and harms indigenous peoples?"

"What do you mean?" His voice had an exasperated tone. "There is always a balance. Here we follow all the laws to the letter."

"I mean the nomadic Berbers. It has come to my attention that you've bought up state lands traditionally used by the nomads and received permits for oil and gas exploration, focusing on fracking, which has affected their water sources. The nomads will not be able to continue their traditional ways in those areas anymore."

Sigurd fixed her with a stern look. "You have no proof of that."

Zakia shrugged. "I don't know about that, except I've spoken to some of the nomads."

His posture stiffened and he waved his hand dismissively. "They will be well compensated."

"Did you know that one of the employees who died recently in your gas well blowout was a nomadic Berber?"

Sigurd raised his eyebrows. "Is that so? Which worker was that? As you know, we lost a few good men in that unfortunate accident."

"His name was Elias Mansur. Is it possible that he uncovered a few discrepancies in your operation near Al Tarife?"

He shifted in his seat and, when he spoke, his voice was ice cold. "This is an unacceptable line of questioning. What kind of stories are you writing, anyway?"

As Zakia faced him, she felt sweat running down her armpits. "Just one more question. What is your relationship with Samara? He seems to be very supportive of your company, at the expense of the nomadic Berber's water rights and detrimental to climate change."

She saw his jaw working, "I have no comment. I'm out of time and this interview is over."

"Is that how you wish to be quoted?"

"I'll be most displeased if you print any part of this conversation." He reached under the end table and pressed a quiet buzzer. "I'll have my secretary walk you out."

"Don't bother. I will show myself out," she said, although she hoped he couldn't hear the loud pumping of her heart. "Thank you for the interview; it has been most interesting."

Zakia almost bumped into the secretary as she headed out the door.

Outside on the sidewalk, she blinked in the bright, hot sun and considered how silence speaks volumes. Sigurd certainly wasn't going to implicate himself in Elias' death, but his whole demeanor suggested guilt. She glanced behind her as she walked, afraid that he might have assigned someone to follow her. She had rattled him—yes, but merely asking tough questions was part and parcel of a journalist's job.

Rather than going back to the paper, Zakia called Fatima and asked to meet her at the café across from their office. She went in and found a seat in a cool, dark corner and took off the sunglasses and the hijab. When her colleague hurried in and sat down across the little table from her, Zakia, in a soft voice, told Fatima all about the interview.

Fatima turned pale. "I think you pushed things too far. What a crazy thing to do. If you thought you weren't in danger before, you've practically sealed your fate now. So what are you going to do?"

Fatima's comments emphasized that she had, indeed, stuck her neck out. *Good thing I used a fake name and a disguise.* "I guess I'll just carry on. I will write up my notes to file for future use—perhaps an American newspaper will publish the story. Anyway, I'll be leaving Morocco in a few days. Besides, I'm not such an important player in the scheme of things. They don't know I have proof of the transactions between Sigurd and Samara."

Then she received a text. She looked at her phone and saw that Benjamin had arrived at the apartment. "Oh, good," she said. "Could you please tell Jasem I had to go home."

Fatima nodded. "Will do."

"Thank you." Zakia hugged Fatima and then hurried out of the café.

****

When Zakia arrived at home, the living room was in an uproar, with boxes stacked everywhere and mounds of kitchenware, piles of clothing, stacks of books, and toys strewn all over the floor. A Beatles tune, *It Won't Be Long*, played loudly in the background. Benjamin shouted at Harris to stop playing with his old action figures and get on with the packing. The moving company had delivered the boxes and since Benjamin and the boys were leaving in three days, he had begun packing in a serious way.

Zakia put her purse and computer bag down and hugged Benjamin. "Hi guys," she said to the boys.

"Hi Maman," said Harris, as he crossed his arms over his chest. "Why do we have to move, anyway?" he whined. "It's not fair. If it weren't for your job, we'd be safe here in Rabat. Why don't you just look for another job?"

"Harris, it's not that simple. There are some really bad people out there and you don't mess with them." *I just finished dealing with one of them. Maybe Fatima was right; I'm crazy.*

Benjamin raised his voice. "Now calm down all of you. We were planning on moving anyway, we are just doing it sooner than planned."

"But what about my friends?" asked Harris.

Dani laughed. "You don't have any friends."

"Yes, I do. And just because they aren't part of the 'trendy' crowd like yours, doesn't mean they don't exist."

Zakia turned to Dani and Harris. "Okay, guys, let's drop it, shall we? It's been a long day and I need some peace and quiet."

Benjamin laughed. "Then you've come to the wrong address. We need to finish packing now. The movers are picking up the boxes tomorrow."

"Already? I completely lost track of the days," said Zakia. "Okay, but please, let's stop the quibbling."

Dani chucked a pillow at Harris. Benjamin gave them a stern look. "All right," said the boys in unison.

Zakia told Benjamin she had to deal with a couple of e-mails and went into their bedroom. A few minutes later, Dani was at her bedroom door. He held a photo in his hand and had a curious look on his face. "Maman, who's this in the picture?"

Zakia swiveled her chair away from the desk. "Here, let me see it."

He walked over, gave it to her, and sat down on the edge of her bed.

Zakia took the photo and had to muffle a gasp. She coughed instead. It was a studio photo of Elias taken right before he went to graduate school. He was wearing a suit and tie and looked dashing.

"You okay?" asked Dani, patting her on the back.

"Oh my, I got something in my throat." Zakia rolled her chair closer toward Dani and eyed the door, hoping Benjamin wouldn't happen to come in.

"Who is this? He looks just like me." Dani sounded excited and gave her an intent look.

Zakia hesitated, wondering how to answer. She had forgotten she had that photo. She looked at the photo more closely and then said. "Oh, yes. He's a third cousin from my side of the family."

"How come I haven't heard about him before?" Dani gave her a skeptical look.

Zakia stroked Dani's hair. "It never came up. We're not close with that branch of the family. It's a long story and a complicated one, so it's better if we have more time to discuss it."

Dani wrinkled his nose. "When? You're always working."

"You leave in a couple of days, but I will join you guys soon after that."

"Okay, but I'm keeping the picture."

"Sure, that's fine." Zakia handed it back to him, like it was no big deal.

"Thanks." Dani gave her a curious look and walked out of the room.

Zakia sat at her desk and sighed. *Close call.* She thought it must have fallen out of the book she'd tucked it into years ago at the bottom row of the bookshelf.

That night they ate couscous, chicken tangine and

melon, spiced with paprika and turmeric, which Nura had prepared earlier in the day. They talked about their sons' final day at school.

After dinner and some TV, Dani and Harris said goodnight and went to their room, Zakia and Benjamin stayed in the living room talking. Benjamin finished his coffee and leaned back on the sofa. He gave Zakia an intent look. "Didn't you have an interview today? Wasn't it with the head of Oddleifur Oil?"

Zakia, surprised that he even remembered, since she'd barely mentioned that she'd been trying to get a hold of him, murmured an affirmative.

"Well, what happened?" asked Benjamin.

"Do you really want to know?" Zakia stood with one arm holding the other at the elbow.

"Yes, I do. I happen to care a great deal about your work, even though you don't think so."

"I didn't get much information out of him. But he had a very fancy office."

"I smell evasion here. What actually happened?"

"Well, I asked him about the blowout, land transfers and his relationship with the oil and gas minister."

"How could you ask him such direct questions? I thought by now you'd know better than to endanger yourself and your family, yet again," The smile had gone from his face.

"And now you're a journalist, are you?" she asked, her tone rising. "Besides, I was disguised and used a fake name."

"That doesn't matter. They can still figure it out. You know better than to mess around with those bigwigs." He rubbed his chin. "Are you out of you mind, Zakia?"

Benjamin looked at her and, behind his anger, she sensed real fear. She might have been reckless in going to Sigurd and exposing her agenda, but she was confident her disguise would work. "I'm trying to investigate an important story. But you have a point. In fact, Fatima said the same thing. I just want to get the necessary information for my story. That is my primary focus."

With a stern tone in his voice, Benjamin said, "If you carry on like this Zakia, I think it will seriously affect our relationship."

Zakia sat in disbelief at his words, but she understood where he was coming from. It had been crazy dangerous, the things she had gotten up to lately. Throw in the fact that she had omitted telling him that Elias was Dani's biological father and there were grounds for a divorce.

"We will have to see what happens when we get to Chicago, but it looks pretty bleak to me," he added. "I strongly suggest you stop getting mixed up in these things. For crying out loud, the next thing you know, these guys will be ready to get you out of the way permanently."

Zakia's stomach hurt as though she'd been punched. "You know I don't mean to endanger our family. But I've never had to deal with such threats before. It's as if I'm becoming part of the story."

Benjamin sighed. "I'll say it again, be more careful. Think before you dive into more trouble."

****

Just before daybreak on Thursday, Zakia drove with her family to the airport to see them off. She walked them to the security line. Standing there while she watched them pull out their passports and tickets, a sudden sense of emptiness struck her and she wanted to go with them. It wasn't possible. She had promised to help Fiona and she wanted to meet with Halgrim in Iceland.

"I'll see you in a few days," she said, her throat closing as she tried to force back the urge to cry. She hugged and kissed them all. Dani and Harris hugged her back but were quick about it; they seemed so grown up now.

Benjamin rubbed her shoulder and muttered about the long security lines. "Be sure to call your sister; if this line doesn't move faster, we might miss our flight."

"Will do," said Zakia. "Give Tahra and her boys my love."

Zakia watched them wind their way through security and then waved at them before turning and walking quickly back to the curb to catch a taxi. To make the day seem less empty, she decided to go straight to work.

She arrived early at the newspaper, but Jasem was already there. When he saw her walk into the newsroom, he stuck his head out the door and called her in to his office.

"Zakia, what have you done now?" he asked before she even had a chance to sit down. "I got a call from the owner of the newspaper. He got a call directly from the CEO of Oddleifur Oil. He was not pleased with your interview."

Zakia's heart sank. She plunked down onto Jasem's sofa. "I can explain…"

Jasem held up his hand, interrupting her. "Didn't

we agree that you were going to be careful and didn't I strongly suggest you *not* interview Sigurd? It isn't as if you haven't had a second chance. Anyway, the publisher has instructed me to fire you."

Zakia shook her head. "But I've already resigned."

"I know. I told him that, but Sigurd had to be satisfied that we were really taking action so that you wouldn't be out there again," said Jasem. "Sigurd was threatening to pull advertising and, even worse, report us for ethics violations to the government."

"That's insane, Jasem."

He shook his head. "It's a moot point, since you're already out of here, but I wanted to let you know that you are in deep muck now. You must be close to uncovering something major."

"Well, that's good to know," she sniffed.

"You know how it works, Zakia," he said. "We can go so far and then we can't go any further."

"But that's not reporting. That's a joke."

His face reddened. "I'm sorry you feel that way. I've had it with you constantly disobeying orders. Don't call me for a recommendation."

Zakia took a deep breath. She had things to do and it wasn't worth it to fight this one out. "Okay, I understand, Jasem." She straightened up on the sofa and blew her nose.

"I'm surprised Sigurd figured out who I was so quickly."

Jasem rolled his eyes. "How many nosy women journalists do you think we have in Morocco?"

"There must be more than ten female investigative journalists by now."

He said sternly, "You, however, are a unique

specimen. Anyway, you're leaving the country shortly. Please, stay out of trouble."

"I am sorry, Jasem. Of course, I'll stay out of trouble."

She excused herself and went straight to her cubicle.

She called Tariq's mom to see if she had any news. When Miriam answered, Zakia said, "Salam Miriam, it's Zakia. How are you? It's been a week now, hasn't it?"

"Salam Zakia. Actually we've passed the eighth-day mark. I've been meaning to call you, but I've been exhausted. Just yesterday, I found something you might be interested in."

"What did you find?"

"I was finally able to clean up Tariq's room. He stayed here a lot. He was a good boy, you know."

"Yes, he was," said Zakia.

"When I changed his bed sheets, I found a file under the mattress with some technical instructions and drawings that looked like they might be from the fracking operation where he worked, but I have no idea."

"What kind of instructions?"

"I don't know. And the first page is missing because it starts on page two. But it must be important for Tariq to have hidden it. As I mentioned, he came by for a visit the Sunday before he died."

Zakia took a deep breath. "Can I pick up the file and make copies of the instructions?" she asked.

"You can keep the papers. I have no use for them."

Zakia asked if she could pick them up right away, but Miriam said it would be better if she could come the next day.

****

Zakia arrived home late that evening. After supper, she heard someone at the front door.

She peered out the peephole into the street, but no one was there.

Zakia made tea and paced in the living room. She fell asleep on the sofa, only to be awakened in the middle of the night by the piercing sound of shattering glass.

She found a brick on the kitchen floor, surrounded by shards of broken glass. "*Merde!*," she swore. A note was attached, "We are tracking you. Iceland will not be safe for you either." Zakia removed the note with trembling hands, put it in her purse, and called the police.

Two policemen arrived twenty minutes later. They examined the trajectory of the brick and bagged it as evidence. Then one of the officers said he would search the apartment and the garden. The other officer took her statement about the incident.

"Do you know who could have done this?" asked the police officer.

"No. I've never had something like this happen before." She refrained from giving them the note. Getting the cops mixed up in her investigation of Elias's and Tariq's murders would not be helpful.

"We'll put an extra patrol car in the neighborhood tonight," he said. "You'd better have someone come and replace the glass first thing in the morning. And keep the door locked at all times."

Zakia went to bed shivering that night, even though a warm wind blew softly through the iron grille of her bedroom window. *What am I going to do?* The smart thing would be to abandon her story, but as a journalist she just couldn't.

Chapter Seventeen

The next day, Zakia, exhausted, arrived at work late and in a foul mood. Though she had been fired, she preferred to go to the office to keep her mind off the incident at the apartment. She started looking for a layover in Iceland on her trip to Chicago. Fatima came to Zakia's cubicle and saw the airline's homepage on her screen. "Shouldn't you have done that a little earlier? Now it will be terribly expensive."

"I already have my ticket to Chicago. I'm just adding a stopover in Iceland. Fiona wants me to visit on the way to Chicago. Anyway, Jasem has paid for the flight. I think he's dying to get me out of here."

"Lucky you," said Fatima. "You look tired. Not sleeping well? You've been through a lot."

Zakia told her about her eventful night. Fatima's eyes widened. "Weren't you scared?"

"Yes, but it's almost commonplace for me now. Anyway, I've taken care of it with the police and since I'm out of there shortly, I'm not too worried."

"Things have not exactly been peaceful these past few weeks," said Fatima.

"I couldn't agree more.

"I will miss you terribly," said Fatima.

"And who am I supposed to divulge my secrets to and vent all my problems? "I'll tell you what; we will get really good at using Skype."

"We'll keep in touch," said Fatima. They hugged each other for a long time.

What will life be like in Chicago without Fatima? Or Jasem?

****

After lunch, she told Fatima she had an errand to run, and left the building. She hailed a taxi and hurried to Tariq's parents' house to pick up the mysterious file that Miriam had found. She hoped its contents would qualify as evidence for her story. As the taxi approached the neighborhood, Zakia heard sirens and saw an ambulance heading towards them. It came at them so fast it nearly hit the taxi and Zakia had a premonition that all was not well. "Could you hurry it up a little?" she asked the driver.

"Yes, Madame."

When they pulled up to the curb by the house, Zakia saw that the door was slightly ajar. She bit her lip and wondered if the ambulance had been at the house.

"Could you please wait while I go in?" she asked the driver.

"No problem," he nodded at the house. "Do you need any help?"

"I'll be fine," she said, even though her muscles were tense.

She rang the bell by the front door, but nobody answered. She hesitated for a moment before pushing the door wide open and walking inside. "Hello?" she called out. "Miriam? It's Zakia."

No one answered, but she saw signs of turmoil when she walked in. In the living room, the cabinet doors and drawers were ajar and broken glassware and fine china were strewn on the floor. Zakia hesitated and then moved through the house making as little noise as possible.

It was clear no one was there, but in every room, personal effects and books were pouring out of drawers and off the bookshelves.

In the inner courtyard, she saw a slick of blood on the floor.

She froze, her heart pounding. She called Miriam's cellphone number. After a few rings, Miriam picked up.

"Miriam, I'm at your house to pick up the file. The door was open so I walked in. It looks like a war zone. What happened?"

"Oh, it was terrible. My daughter and I came home from shopping and found Sahib unconscious on the floor. He's been severely beaten."

"Is he going to be okay?"

"They think so. We just arrived at the hospital." Miriam suppressed a sob.

"I hope he recovers quickly. Did you call the police?" Zakia was breathing in gulps.

"Yes, they said they were on their way to our house. Are you all right?"

"Yes, I was shocked by the mess and I saw blood on the floor."

"I don't care about the state of the house. My focus in on my poor husband now."

"Of course, I understand." Zakia was nearly whispering. "Do you remember where you left the file?"

"On top of the dresser in Tariq's bedroom. It's the second door on the right in the hallway, next to the bathroom."

"Thank you, I'll check and then I'll leave." Her

heartbeat was racing now.

Zakia hurried to Tariq's room. She had a sinking suspicion that what looked like a break-in could be related to Tariq's folder, and she didn't want to be detained by the police.

The file folder was not in his room.

She ran through the house and outside to the taxi.

"What's the matter?" asked the driver as Zakia slipped into the car. "You look like you've seen a ghost."

"I spoke to the woman of the house. Someone assaulted her husband. They're in the hospital. The police are on their way and I think it's best if we get out of here, now."

The driver started the car and pulled away from the curb. "Good idea."

She heard police sirens in the distance. Zakia let out her breath as they reached the main street. She had the taxi driver take her back to the office.

****

Zakia was surprised to see her colleagues had arranged a goodbye party for her. The whole staff had pitched in to buy her a cake, honey and almond cookies, sweets, and plenty of sodas. Someone, probably Fatima, had even strung a banner across the wall that read: *Good Luck, Zakia!*

Zakia thought, *I sure could use some luck.*

After cake and cookies, she said farewell to Fatima, Jasem, Nassar, and the rest of her colleagues. Jasem said he would miss her. She did not tell him about what had transpired that afternoon in Tariq's family home. Zakia was sure Jasem would find out soon enough and would contact her, *never fear.*

Before packing up the rest of her desk, she scanned all the papers she had received from Daliyah and saved them onto a flash drive. By the time she was done, it was almost dark and she could hear the call to evening prayers. When she let herself into her apartment, she saw that the kitchen window had been replaced, and the janitor had swept up the broken glass. But as she walked through the apartment, it felt like something was amiss.

Sure enough, the drawers of the built-in dresser in their bedroom had been yanked out and her clothes scattered on the floor. Zakia searched the apartment, making sure no one was there. Then she noticed the lock on the balcony door had been forced. She stood with her arms crossed while blowing out a series of short breaths. She wasted no time calling Fatima, asking if she could spend the night at her place. Then she called her landlord. She gathered her things and hurried away from the home she had lived in for nearly twenty years. She had no time for tears.

Chapter Eighteen

The next day, on board Flight 311 to Paris via Tunisia, Zakia began to think about her recent experiences. She had put the flash drive from Daliyah and the one from Maati, the scientist at the weather station, together with her passport, in a thin travel pouch under her shirt before she left Fatima's apartment.

When the passengers were cleared to move about the cabin, she got up to use the restroom. On her way down the aisle, she did a double-take when she saw a familiar face a few rows behind her seat. It was the scar-faced man who had trailed her and her sons when they took the taxi to the airport, and again in the terminal before they headed for China.

It wasn't as though she could tell the flight attendant that a lot of bad things had been happening to her lately and that this man might want to harm her.

Why hadn't they just taken her out already? They'd had no qualms about killing Elias or Tariq.

Both Benjamin and her boss had said that she was putting herself in danger—that she could be next—and yet, nothing fatal had happened to her. *Why not?*

Had her position at the paper given her extra protection? Not likely; journalists were being killed all over the map these days. Then it hit her and she felt foolish. Samara had mentioned her father when they'd met on the cruise ship. Maybe her dad's connections and prominence afforded her some protection. She had met many of the VIPs at social gatherings in her parents' home in Rabat when she was a teenager. Her dad used to joke that she was set for life, but she hadn't understood him at the time. She racked her brain. Would any of his friends still have her on their radar? Did any of them still watch out for her?

When she returned from the restroom, she checked that the file with the papers from Daliyah was tucked in the bottom of her bag. It was, but she suspected it wouldn't be for long. She was also interested in seeing if this man was really tailing her or if it was just another coincidence and, if it was the former, how far would he go?

Zakia settled in to wait. As she expected, the scar-faced man got on the flight for the next leg of her trip to Paris. An hour into the flight, without warning, the plane was hit by violent turbulence, which shook the aircraft so fiercely Zakia was sure they wouldn't make it. The oxygen masks dropped, some women started crying, others screamed. Then the captain asked everyone to brace themselves. Zakia said a short prayer. Some fifty minutes later, by some miracle the turbulence was gone. Once it was over, the captain came on the intercom and announced drinks would be served at no charge. Everyone started clapping.

When they were close to landing, but before the fasten seatbelts sign went on, Zakia saw an opportune moment. She got up and went to the restroom, walking slowly past the man so that he would notice that she'd gotten up. She took her time in the bathroom until someone started pounding on the door.

Once she got back to her seat, the woman next to her said, giggling, "Your husband is really charming."

"My husband was here?"

"Yes, he came while you were in the restroom and said you were unable to get seats next to each other, and that he needed a file." The woman looked at her, doubt appearing on her face. "Was that all right?"

"Oh yes, of course," Zakia forced a smile.

Zakia sniffed and, pretending to need a tissue, went digging through her bag. The file was gone. It had worked. Maybe she could take the driver's seat on this one. She resisted the urge to turn around and have another look at the scar-faced man.

****

By the time the plane landed safely at Charles de Gaulle, it was too late to make the connecting flight to Iceland. Zakia was stuck in Paris for the night. She found a quiet corner in the airport and called her cousin, Yvette Laurent, right away. On her way to China with her sons, Zakia had a stopover at Charles de Galle and had briefly connected with Yvette on the phone. Now Yvette said she would gladly meet her at the Gare du Nord train station. They hadn't seen each other for more than five years and Zakia was looking forward to their reunion.

Zakia got on the train and watched to see if the scar-faced man was following her. When the train pulled away without him making an appearance, it looked as if she was safe for now. He must have been satisfied with the papers in the file.

At Gare du Nord, her cousin was waiting for her. She was just a little older than Zakia, but they'd met at family reunions and gotten along well. Seeing Yvette, she immediately missed her parents, but she tried to shove that ache to the back of her mind.

"Bonsoir," said Zakia as they kissed each other on one cheek, then the other, back and forth three times. Zakia felt like an old boot next to her chic cousin, with her long silky black hair and matching skirt and top, with a pearl necklace.

"*Ça va?*" asked Yvette.

"*Bien, merci,*" said Zakia. "Well, after getting over the rather uncomfortable plane ride, I'm not bad—not bad at all. Getting stuck in Paris never seemed problematic to me."

"I'm glad you called," said Yvette. "Your timing was perfect; my husband and our daughters went ahead to spend the long weekend at our summer home close to Nice. I'll join them tomorrow." Yvette led the way out of the train station; the Paris evening was unusually warm and the sidewalk cafes were packed. Yvette touched her on the shoulder. "Maman has been asking about you. She still misses your mother, her favorite sister."

"I miss her too, immensely. I'm so happy I am able to visit you today," said Zakia, looping her arm through her cousin's as they walked toward her apartment. "It has been pretty hectic lately."

They entered an old building and took the rickety, tiny elevator to the third floor. The hallway in her cousin's apartment was covered with family photos. Zakia paused for a moment in front of a photo of her mother and Yvette's mother in their early teens, dressed as flower girls for a wedding. Then she saw one of her father and mother when they were just dating, posing with her grandmother.

"Your dad was so dapper," said Yvette. "We always thought he had to be more than just a businessman."

Zakia looked surprised. "And what would that be?"

Yvette laughed. "Grandma always said he could have played the most convincing James Bond."

"I hardly think so," laughed Zakia, though the idea intrigued her. "Yet, now that you mention it, he did travel in interesting circles. Selling engines for Rolls Royce would have been a perfect cover."

Yvette raised her eyebrows. "The question is—who was he spying for?"

"The Brits, of course," said Zakia.

Being around her cousin almost made her parents come alive again. After Zakia settled into the guest room, Yvette suggested they go out for dinner.

****

Seated at Brasserie Jacqueline, Zakia remarked, "This Boeuf Bourguignon is exquisite."

"Yes, there's an extraordinary chef working here."

Zakia enjoyed her cousin's company over dinner, although, her thoughts wandered to the thief on the plane. Her plan had worked. No one had followed her out of the terminal or onto the train. She needed to plan her next move on the chessboard.

To distract herself, Zakia decided to focus on her cousin. "How is your work going?" Yvette was a neurosurgeon at the university hospital at the Sorbonne.

"With operating in the morning and seeing patients in the afternoon, plus teaching two days a week, you could say I am also quite busy," she said, taking a sip of her wine. "Thank goodness, my husband and the children support me in my work or else I couldn't have managed."

Zakia found it interesting that she mentioned support from the family. That had also been her situation, at least until recently. "I'm afraid that Benjamin and I are struggling right now," she said with her head down. "We're moving to Chicago. Benjamin and the boys have already left and I'm going to join them after my layover in Iceland. I'm not sure how things will sort themselves out when I get there."

"You're moving to Chicago?' Yvette gasped.

"Yes, Benjamin has wanted to do that for a while."

"I'm sure it will work out," said Yvette. "Benjamin is a reasonable person. They sat in silence for a moment, each sipping their wine, and then Yvette brightened up. "So, why are you headed to Iceland?"

"I'm visiting the headquarters of an oil company there which has a subsidiary in Morocco, Oddleifur Oil & Gas. I'm writing a story on a friend of mine who was killed in a fracking accident which seems not to have been an accident after all.

"That sounds like a movie script."

"Yes, it's scary." Zakia filled Yvette in on her arrest and the kidnapping of her boys.

"That's downright dangerous. Don't you worry about your family?"

"Yes, that's why we are moving. We're no longer safe in Morocco."

"Indeed."

"I've made some progress with the investigation of my story," continued Zakia, "but I'm not quite there yet. I'm also bringing some climate data to a friend of mine who is currently doing research in Iceland," she said.

"You're hand-delivering data, in this day and age?" said Yvette. "Why not just e-mail it?"

"Her computer was hacked," admitted Zakia. "And time is of the essence."

Yvette leaned forward. "Unless we speed up our action on climate change, I think it will be too late for our children."

"So, you've been following the climate change discussions. What is the perception among you and your colleagues?"

Yvette shook her head and poured herself another glass of wine. "We are quite perplexed. The politicians have all the information they need to act, yet they seem to be waiting for the next guy to take action first, all in the name of having to protect their country's competitive edge when it comes to trade," she said. "Some of them seem downright corrupt."

If you only knew.

"Anyway, I find it fascinating in one way, it's the biggest scientific experiment ever, but it is also terrifying in another way." Yvette continued, "The impacts of climate change are already visible."

"Yes. It's strange how people listen to their doctors, but they won't listen to the majority of the climate scientists," said Zakia.

"No one questions whether a cancer diagnosis is good science, even though you could be misdiagnosed," said Yvette. "With climate change, it seems that some people prefer to carry on with business as usual—denial is their best bet. If a cancer patient ignored their diagnosis, they would be dead. A strange inertia is going on with the politicians. It's quite unacceptable in my mind. If you do accept the facts, then you need to act on them."

"Suddenly, when it comes to climate change, we all think we are scientists and can have an opinion on the scientific facts," said Zakia.

Yvette nodded solemnly. "*Mon Dieu*, it's a mess."

They lingered in the restaurant longer than they should have, but Zakia appreciated spending time with someone who understood her passion for climate change which seemed to be intertwined with Elias's murder.

Yvette encouraged her to publish her story and not worry so much about whether or not she would get a job in the U.S., or even whether or not Benjamin was going to leave her. "He's a big bear," she said. "He's just afraid for your safety. You're covering controversial issues and you insisted on working in Morocco instead of moving to France after your parents died. You could have, you know. Maman would have taken you in. Why did you take off to get a master's instead and then return to Morocco?"

"France seemed so different," said Zakia. "Morocco is what I've always known, even if it is harder for a career woman there. Tahra didn't like me moving back either. However, with my work, I knew I could make a difference."

"You were always the risk taker. Remember when we used to climb trees together? You climbed higher than anyone. Even if you fell, you weren't afraid to climb again."

Chapter Nineteen

Her flight reached Iceland just after lunch and Zakia was totally taken by the landscape. In contrast to Morocco, they had plenty of rain in Iceland, but the landscape, consisting of lava rock covered in moss and lichen, was barren nonetheless.

Fiona met her at the terminal. Zakia had no trouble spotting her petite, strawberry blond friend. She was wearing an 'I love Scotland' t-shirt.

"Good to see you," said Zakia as she hugged Fiona. "Has it been three years since we last met?"

"Yes, I think so," said Fiona. "You came to visit me in New York on your way to meeting Benjamin in Washington D.C. Here, let me roll your suitcase."

"Thank you," said Zakia, laying a hand on Fiona's back.

They exited the terminal and walked toward the parking lot, while Fiona surveyed her and smiled. "I'm delighted you're here."

"Me too. As I recall, you were doing another teaching marathon at Columbia when we last met," said Zakia. "It must be nice to have a routine like that, traveling to New York from Boulder twice a semester. Does Jack go along sometimes?"

"Yes, he treats me to a show sometimes, when he can get away from meetings at the United Nations. We timed this visit well because I'm finishing my research here, with the help of the data you brought me. I plan to leave just a couple of days after you."

"Iceland definitely is cooler than Paris," said Zakia. She wondered if she'd brought enough warm clothes for the next couple of days.

"This is actually quite warm for Iceland, today at least. The weather can change quickly though."

At the parking lot, Zakia saw Fiona's tiny red electric rental car parked perpendicular to the sidewalk. It had just enough room for two people.

As Fiona wedged the suitcase awkwardly in the boot, Zakia grinned. "Your car reminds me of an oversized toy car."

"Yes, it's kind of cute, isn't it? But it definitely does the job and can go over a hundred and eighty miles without needing to be plugged in."

"I love electric cars. We should all have them, don't you think?" said Zakia.

"Well, maybe you can get one in the U.S. Benjamin's making the big bucks, right?"

"Oh sure," answered Zakia. "He'll happily do that for his unemployed, trouble-making spouse."

Fiona laughed. They drove off toward Reykjavik.

Zakia relayed the spat she'd had with Benjamin, which seemed less of a crisis now that she had left Morocco. She told Fiona a little bit about the latest incidents that she'd endured in covering the story. "I hope I can get some more proof and get this story published soon," she confided.

"Oh," said Zakia. "Before I forget, here's the flash drive with the information from Maati Tawfeek at the climate station. He said he had read some of your articles."

"Thank you so much. I'm glad people are reading my research. Just slip it in my purse there by your feet, please."

The two had been talking so intensely, that Zakia was surprised they'd arrived at the outskirts of Reykjavik already, a sprawling modern city. And in no time, they arrived at Hotel Esjafjøll.

"We're home," said Fiona, getting out of the car. "I got you a nice room with a view of the ocean."

"Thank you. That's wonderful." Zakia followed Fiona into the lobby. She checked in and they went up to put her suitcase in her room. "It's perfect."

"I'm across the hall," said Fiona. "I have a suite with a kitchenette. It's very comfortable. The University of Reykjavik is paying, thank goodness." She unlocked her door and showed Zakia her suite, which had a living room with peach-colored walls and a large framed poster of Monet's *Water Lilies.*

Zakia went back to her room, closed the door and unpacked her suitcase. As she emptied her big purse on her bed to switch to a smaller purse for the evening, she found a small piece of yellow paper that she'd never seen before. Zakia gasped when she read, "Don't think we can't find you in Iceland." Zakia shivered. It must have been placed in her bag by the scar-faced man who had stolen Daliyah's file on the flight to Paris.

I can't win.

****

That night, Fiona suggested they dine at a restaurant right downtown Reykjavik, called Hovedrettabarinn, which was within walking distance from their hotel on the ocean side. On the way there, Zakia was startled to see what looked like a Viking ship in the bay.

"That looks pretty darn close to the images I've seen of the original ones," she said.

"It's an excellent reconstruction," said Fiona with a smile. "In 2000, the Icelanders used it to sail to America as part of the millennium celebrations of Leif Erikson's discovery of America—you know, at L'Anse aux Meadows in Newfoundland. Now it's become a tourist thing, so they make a crossing every three years or so."

They enjoyed their locally sourced grilled salmon and plump pink shrimp with creamed parsnips.

Zakia picked up her wine glass and smiled. "I'm so glad we could meet again. It's been way too long. Cheers."

"*Skál,*" Fiona as she raised her glass and grinned.

They talked about the data Zakia had brought and the latest on Fiona's work. Zakia asked if there had been any more news about the assassination attempt on the Pope. Had they found any suspects?

Fiona shook her head. "No. It's going to take time to figure out who was behind the incident, but I've got some crazy guy following me around here. I have no clue who he is or what he wants."

"The one you mentioned earlier?"

Fiona nodded.

"Have you reported him to the police?"

"I have talked to the police, but they can't do anything," said Fiona. "As long as he is not threatening me and keeping his distance, everybody is allowed to walk the streets, they tell me."

Zakia frowned. "I think it could all be related to my search into what happened to Elias."

"Perhaps. With the latest incident; the guy stealing the file from your purse and leaving you a note, you're definitely moving into unchartered territory," said Fiona. "I think *you* should consider going to the police."

"What good would that do, if they won't even look into your stalker? The note mentioned Iceland, but nothing has happened…not yet, anyway."

"At least they would be put on notice."

"Maybe you're right. But bureaucracy usually kicks in only after the fact." said Zakia.

"Perhaps a body guard like you had in China would be in order," suggested Fiona.

"Right, that would be handy," said Zakia. "On another note, any luck with setting up a meeting for me with Halgrim at Oddleifur Oil?"

"I left him a message, but haven't heard back. Remember, they may not have taken kindly to my approaching them again, since our project didn't exactly work out."

"I'll give them a call then. An interview with him could be very helpful."

After dinner, they walked through the quiet streets back to the hotel. Zakia's thoughts drifted back to her recent incident. *What if the scar-faced man shows up here in Iceland?* It was past ten p.m., but still daylight, so she told herself to take a deep breath and relax. She wasn't in Morocco, but on an isolated, distant island with a low crime rate.

Chapter Twenty

The next morning, Fiona invited Zakia to her office. "I want to download the data from the flash drive you brought me onto my newly secured computer, and then we'll go on a mini sightseeing tour. You need to rest a little after your stressful incidents—I insist. It will do you good."

"I have so much work to do, but I guess it makes sense," said Zakia.

Fiona's guest office at the University of Reykjavik was far better than Zakia's tiny cubicle had been. Fiona sat down and plugged in the flash drive. After a few minutes, her face lit up. "This data is really good, Zakia," she said.

Zakia thought about Tariq. She sighed loudly and frowned.

Fiona paused and looked up. "What's wrong?"

"Well, this gets complicated." Zakia took a deep breath. "I told you about Elias?"

"Yes, dreadful," said Fiona.

"What I didn't tell you earlier was that I got in touch with Elias's roommate, Tariq, at Oddleifur Oil's operation outside Al Tarife." Zakia sighed and rubbed the back of her arms. "Tariq arranged for me to get that data. In fact, Maati was his friend. With Tariq's help, I was also able to get into Oddleifur Oil's office at the gas well that same day. Not a week later, he died in a car crash. Also a suspicious death."

"Oh, that's appalling," Fiona listened with grave interest. "You have gotten yourself in deep, haven't you?"

"I'm trying to find the link between the two incidents."

"It's obvious that you need to push forward with this, even though it sounds dangerous."

"Thanks," said Zakia. "I appreciate being able to talk with you about all of this. Benjamin is getting more and more worried about our safety, so I can't share it all with him anymore."

"That's why we're friends," said Fiona. "Now let's get this done so we can do some sightseeing."

Thirty minutes later, Fiona clapped her hands together and stood up. "All done. Now, let's have our little outing. You can tell me more while I'm driving. First, we'll head to the renowned waterfall, *Gullfoss*."

"Sounds like a plan," said Zakia in a light voice.

****

Fiona drove out of the faculty parking lot and onto the main road heading toward the mountains.

"This landscape is amazing," said Zakia.

"Yes, it's the arctic desert."

"It's so different from our desert in Morocco."

Fiona nudged her. "You ready to talk about your real problem now?"

Zakia shrugged. "Sure. I thought it would be helpful to meet Sigurd Agnarsson for my story. He's the CEO of Oddleifur Oil in Morocco. I pretended to be writing a story on leadership for a business magazine, so I went incognito. After talking about his background, I questioned him about the incident, and he clammed up. Later he had me fired from my job; I'd already resigned, so no problem. I guess my disguise was not convincing.

"You're lucky he didn't put out a contract on you," said Fiona.

"So far, so good." Zakia went on to explain that there had to be connections between Sigurd and the oil and energy minister and that she'd gotten some proof. "And then you have to add in Tariq's car crash. The entities I'm investigating are getting closer and closer to me, trying to intimidate me and eliminating people I've been in touch with. And my family has been put in danger."

"I don't know what to say, except now we are practically in the same boat when it comes to levels of danger," said Fiona.

"Our two situations may well be connected, since we were both contacted by Elias."

"I don't like that possibility at all," said Fiona. "Plus, remember, I was supposed to work with Halgrim, but I pulled out of the project."

"And you are also being stalked," said Zakia.

"Speaking of stalkers, it appears that my stalker has upped his game." Fiona looked in the rearview mirror.

"You mean the guy you mentioned earlier?"

"The very same. Check out your mirror in the sun visor. Do you see the white car back there in the distance?"

"Oh, yes, way back there. So, what does he want?"

"I don't know. I'm alarmed that he's not letting up. I haven't been tailed by car before.

"What should we do?" Zakia's heart was beating faster now.

"Stay the course," said Fiona, though her eyebrows were drawn together.

"Okay." Zakia settled back in her seat, trying not to be obvious as she turned around to see if the car was still following them.

"After lunch you can call Oddleifur and try and set up a meeting. Then we can head for the Blue Lagoon, the renowned hot springs pool. That will be great, since it isn't raining or snowing today. We've had a bit of both lately."

After a short drive, Fiona pointed to a river that broke the landscape in the distance. "Look we are getting close to Gullfoss. It's my favorite waterfall, the largest in Europe. And one of the most mysterious."

"What's so mysterious?"

"The water drops into the unknown in the gorge below, which you can barely see from the edge at the top."

After Fiona pulled into a small rest area, where other cars were parked, she went around to the front of the car and peered behind them down the road. "No sign of the stalker. I think we lost him," she said.

They walked across an open field, and stopped a good distance away from the drop-off in front of the waterfall. A few other tourists were admiring the falls and snapping photos. Zakia leaned over a low railing to get a better view.

"Don't go any closer. It can be slippery. You wouldn't want to fall in," shouted Fiona above the thundering noise.

"No, I wouldn't. My, it's beautiful," said Zakia. When she looked to her left, she saw a man standing there behind the other tourists. He seemed to admire the falls, until he stared at her. He was a tall, handsome man in a thick sweater and an anorak. He nodded, and then returned his gaze to the falls.

Fiona grabbed Zakia's arm. "That's him," she shouted in Zakia's ear.

"What? You mean the man who has been stalking you?"

"Yes."

"But he looks like a regular tourist," yelled Zakia.

"Okay, this is too close for comfort, but at least you've seen him too." Fiona pulled Zakia away from the falls, toward the car.

"That looks obvious," said Zakia as she drew her arm away.

"Well, let's get a move on. The guy hasn't tried anything, but the way he keeps showing up everywhere I go is terrifying."

Zakia wanted to say that "terrifying" is when your sons get kidnapped, but she didn't say that to Fiona, who was already rattled.

They got into the car and Fiona pushed the big button to start the electric engine, which hardly made a sound. "At least you got to see the waterfall, even if it was just a moment," she said.

****

On the way to the Blue Lagoon hot springs, using the car's Bluetooth phone, Zakia called Oddleifur headquarters to set up an appointment with Halgrim for the afternoon the next day. She had considered using a fake name, then decided against it. She figured no one here would be expecting someone to be visiting from Morocco. Hopefully Sigurd hadn't told Halgrim about her interview with him.

Zakia and Fiona arrived at the Blue Lagoon just before closing. Zakia was surprised to see that it looked even better than the images she'd briefly seen on the tiny screen on the flight over. Steam rose against the hills of volcanic rock that surrounded what seemed like acres of mineral rich, light blue water. A few people bobbed like seals in the water. Once she got into the hot water, Zakia felt warm for the first time all day. The fleece she had borrowed from Fiona wasn't quite thick enough.

Fiona swam close to Zakia, "Before your meeting with Halgrim tomorrow, let's go to my friend's cabin on the other side of the island. We can grill a couple of lamb chops for lunch, and then return to the city."

"That sounds like a lovely idea. But is there enough time?" Zakia pinched the skin on her throat.

"As long as we don't bump into stalkers." Fiona had a wry smile on her face.

****

The next day, they got up early to drive to the cabin. Fiona insisted on packing four gallons of water, in addition to the groceries "You can never have enough water. It's an old-fashioned cabin with an outhouse and no running water. And there are no stores nearby," she said.

"That makes sense then," said Zakia. "What a beautiful day with all this sunshine."

"Yes, we lucked out."

They passed the volcanic mountains to their left, as they drove east, circling part of the island in a large loop. The further they drove from the city, the more desert-like the view became. Zakia remembered Sigurd's posters on his office walls, the same barren landscape, yet covered in snow. Must be freezing cold in winter, she thought.

Fiona had just said that they were near the cabin when their car stopped. "Oh no," moaned Fiona, coasting to the side of the road.

"What happened?" asked Zakia.

"I don't know," said Fiona. "I think the motor died. I've had a few issues with the car lately, but this wasn't supposed to happen. And, of course, we have no gas or plug-in stations for miles."

"Why don't we call for help?" Zakia pulled out her cellphone.

"Don't bother. There's no reception out here. It does work at the cabin though," said Fiona, rubbing her arms.

They got out of the car and opened the hood. Fiona looked glumly at the engine. "I used to know how to fix cars, but now it's all electric and computerized and I have no clue."

Zakia groaned. She'd been through enough lately and just wanted to enjoy herself. "We'll have to flag down a car. It can't be that isolated out here?" She pulled out a bag of chips Fiona had stashed in the back seat. "Let's have a snack and relax for a moment," she said. "Somebody is bound to come by soon. Besides, the scenery is superb. Look at those majestic mountains."

Fiona sat down on a rock and took the bag of chips from Zakia. "The scenery is breathtaking," she said. "But the volcanoes can be unpredictable."

"What do you mean?" asked Zakia.

"I heard on the news this morning that Katla—that mountain we passed at a distance after we left town—

has had an increase in seismic activity. It happens all the time with volcanoes. But this is more than the usual amount. It sounds like it might erupt at some point in the near future."

"That's not good news, but I guess people here are used to it, so they know what to do," said Zakia, cautiously eyeing the mountain range.

"Yes, the Meteorological Institute is good at monitoring the situation, enabling the Civil Protection Authority to alert the public. With the *Eyafjallajökull* in 2010 there were no fatalities, only minor injuries. We'll see what happens with Katla."

"Aren't you worried?" asked Zakia.

Fiona was about to answer, when a white car cruised towards them.

"Oh look," said Fiona. "Thank goodness."

"Let's hope he's a Good Samaritan and can give us a hand," said Zakia.

Fiona stood up and Zakia reached into the car, fished around in the back seat for some water. She heard the car slowing down and pulling up on the shoulder behind them. Then she heard Fiona swear.

"What?" asked Zakia.

"It's my stalker," hissed Fiona. "Just act normal. Okay?"

The man got out of his car and walked toward them. He grinned. "So, what's going on ladies? Are you in need of help?"

"We're fine," said Fiona avoiding eye contact. "My car just stopped all of a sudden, but I've got it."

"Fiona," said Zakia, glaring at her. The stalker didn't look dangerous to her and she didn't want to be sitting here much longer, especially with Fiona's talk about an erupting volcano.

His eyebrows went up. "I take it you checked the motor?" he asked.

"Really, we don't need your help," said Fiona.

Zakia stepped around her friend. "Hi, we're just renting this car and have no clue what to do. It just died. It would be great if you could help us." She folded her arms in front of her and tried to act tough.

"Okay, let's check it out," he said.

Zakia stood and watched him while he examined the engine. Fiona stood on the other side of the car, frowning. Zakia gave her a "thumbs up" and Fiona shook her head.

The man wiggled some wires, unplugged them, and then hooked them up again. "Try the engine again."

Fiona just stood there.

"Well," he said. "I haven't got all day. I'm on the clock."

She grumbled, but got in the car and, on the second try, it started.

The man straightened up, slammed the hood, and wiped his palms together, looking satisfied. "Voila! Anything else I can do for you ladies?"

Zakia thanked him, but Fiona stepped out of the car with a doubtful look on her face. "As a matter of fact, it would be nice if you stopped following me."

He gave her a cheeky grin. "That's not possible. I was assigned by MI5 to keep an eye on you. With so many climate scientists threatened recently and the assassination attempt on the Pope, we're not taking any chances. I do have to catch a plane this afternoon, but not to worry; we'll still keep an eye on you."

"I see." Fiona breathed a big sigh of relief.

"Glad to be of service," he said "Unfortunately, we don't announce what we're doing. My name is Ian Blackstone, by the way. Just don't let on that you know who I am."

Fiona and Zakia introduced themselves.

Ian tipped his head at them, walked to his car, got in, and made a U-turn, back toward Reykjavik, while Zakia and Fiona stood there, their mouths open.

"Phew!" said Zakia and blew out air.

"We got lucky," Now, let's get going. We'll be arriving at the cabin shortly."

****

Soon Zakia saw a chestnut-colored cottage jutting out of the flat, wild landscape, heather and low-lying shrubs growing all around. It looked homey.

"Here we are." Fiona pulled up the lane and came to a stop in front of the door. "How do you like this place?"

"I thought you said it was rustic. It's beautiful, and it's no small cabin either."

"Well, 'rustic cabin' is a relative term. We have electricity, but no running water as I mentioned. However, the cabin has plenty of space; in fact it has three bedrooms."

"That's nice."

After they lugged the water bottles inside, Fiona looked happy at last. The fear of her stalker seemed gone. "Okay, let's start the grill, shall we?"

"Good idea." Zakia followed Fiona out to the deck. "Wow, what's that rumbling? And look at that dark cloud to the south."

"I see it. It's coming from the Katla Volcano and the rumblings are small earthquakes—the seismic

225

activity I mentioned. We have them all the time. But the major volcanoes are constantly tracked." Fiona eyed Katla while she started the grill and placed a couple of lamb chops on it. "According to Norse mythology, it's Loki, a Norse god, tied up underneath the earth, that causes the earthquakes. But this sky does look quite different from the norm. Let's keep an eye on it. And we should call the CPA to get the latest updates on evacuations, since I didn't think to register my mobile for automatic updates. At least I have their number."

"Thank goodness for that." Zakia sighed.

They began their lunch on the deck. Every so often, a cloud of smoke spewed from the volcano and there were more rumblings. Fiona kept a partial eye on it. "Okay, the rumblings are more pronounced now. We'd better check with the CPA. I'll put the phone on speaker so you can hear the latest status report. They also speak fluent English or we'd be in trouble. My Icelandic vocabulary consists of just a handful of words."

After Fiona entered a number and pressed "9" for English, they could hear a tape running: "This is an update: The status of Katla Volcano is 'red' for 'high alert'. Katla is projected to erupt in about an hour. If you are in the vicinity, you need to evacuate now, for your own safety," said the female voice on the tape. Fiona clicked off the phone and stared at it.

"Yikes, that's doesn't sound good. Which direction?" said Zakia.

"Southwest. The lava is predicted to flow just short of Reykjavik,"

"Are we in danger?"

"It will be a close call. We have to leave

immediately and see if we can make it past the potential path of the lava flow before the volcano erupts."

"Why can't we just stay here until it's over?"

"Because the lava may well come all the way here, not to mention the ash cloud and we don't want to chance it. We have enough time if we go now."

"We can't just take off? Don't we need to close down the cabin first?"

"Yes, we need to leave everything locked up and safe." Fiona grabbed the plates and rushed to the kitchen. "I'll take care of the dishes. You make sure the gas on the grill is turned off. We have ten minutes and we should be out of here."

With a pounding heart, Zakia checked the grill, then ran to the front entryway, grabbed a gallon of water which hadn't been put away and hustled it out to the car. She then returned to find Fiona in the kitchen, frantically washing the dishes. "Do we really need to do the dishes?" called Zakia in a shrill voice.

"You're right, I'm not thinking." Fiona set down the plate in her hand. "If lava flows in this direction, there's no point in worrying about dirty dishes. It will all be incinerated. Let's get out of here."

Fiona drove as fast as she could. Thirty minutes later, Zakia watched, awestruck, behind them as the Katla volcano erupted with a huge bang and colored the sky with its pyroclastic fireworks in bright red and orange. Then an ash cloud began to overtake the blue sky, creating an eerie darkness. Fiona drove like a madwoman and Zakia worried they might veer off the road before being overtaken by any lava flow.

****

After a harrowing drive, Zakia and Fiona arrived in

227

one piece, but exhausted at the outskirt of Reykjavik where their car died—again.

"We did it!" cried Fiona breathing heavily. "We beat the lava flow. Look how it's going straight down to the ocean over there beyond the ridge, burning everything in its path."

"Fantastic!" Zakia hugged her friend, laughing and crying at the same time. "That was so close. I can't believe it. What if the car had broken down earlier? I was so scared."

Returning the hug, Fiona said, "You and me both. I'm not very religious, call it Catholic lite, but I want to thank God on this one."

"I second that motion."

They got out of the car. "Now we just have an easy walk to the hotel. Let's go!"

Zakia hesitated. "What about our bags?"

"We can get those later. We'll have the car towed in the morning."

As they started walking into the city center, the ash was falling all around them like snow. "Where are all the people?" asked Zakia. "This looks like a ghost town."

"I'm sure the authorities told everyone to stay indoors because of the ash and the sulfur in the air."

"I'm glad I had my scarf." Zakia had wrapped it as a makeshift mask across her face. "The ash is irritating, but the rotten egg smell is awful."

"Yes, pungent." Fiona held a tissue up to her nose and mouth. "Oh my, I guess you missed your meeting with Halgrim this afternoon."

"Darn, you're right. I'll try to reschedule it for tomorrow morning before my flight out."

After a twenty minute walk through the ghostly silent streets, they caught sight of their hotel, its lights gleaming in the strange darkness. When they arrived at the entrance, they brushed off their ash-covered clothes. Zakia noticed a flash of light coming from the corner of the building. She saw a face in the light. It was someone lighting a cigarette. Then it was gone. She could have sworn it was the scar-faced man.

"Did you see that, the scar-faced man just looked at us from the corner of the building? That's the man who stole my file on my flight to Paris. He's here in Iceland," said Zakia in a hushed, trembling voice. She shuddered.

"Oh, dear," said Fiona as she put her arm around her and they hurried into the hotel.

Chapter Twenty-One

Zakia was surprised to see so many guests huddled in the lobby. They were talking amongst themselves and looking out the window at the huge cloud of ash.

Walking toward the counter, Fiona turned to Zakia. "We'll need new keycards now, unless you grabbed them when we left the car."

"No, I just snatched my passport, pocketbook, and phone."

The desk clerk looked at them curiously as they told her that they'd left their belongings in the car when it broke down, after narrowly having missed the lava flow. "Are you all right? You look a little frazzled."

"It was more adventurous than we expected," said Fiona. "But we need new keycards, please."

"No problem. I remember you two, room 306 and 311." She handed them new keycards. "Oh, I received a phone call for Zakia Karim. Someone from Oddleifur Oil called and said your meeting was canceled."

Zakia swore under her breath. "I'll phone them back, thank you." She turned to Fiona. "I'm still going to meet with Halgrim—somehow."

"Good luck with that."

Zakia and Fiona trudged to the elevator.

The elevator opened on their floor and they agreed to meet later to have some dinner. "I need a shower to get rid of this ash," said Fiona.

"I'll call Oddleifur. I'm sure they'll understand that I need to meet with Halgrim tomorrow morning before my flight."

Zakia entered her room, closed the door, and suddenly was hit by the whole incident. The great escape from the lava flow, hadn't felt real. Then Scarface showed up. *Was it really just my imagination?*

She sat on the bed, checked her phone and saw that the Wi-Fi was working. She messaged Benjamin and signed on to Skype, her hands shaking. He responded immediately. When he appeared on her tiny phone screen, looking worried sick, Zakia could barely keep her composure.

"Zakia, thank goodness, I've been worried. I heard about the volcano erupting on the radio this morning. Are you okay?"

"It was awful," she said. "However, I'm fine now. I want to hug you, but seeing you on the screen is better than nothing."

"Are you close to the affected areas?"

"Not anymore. We're back at the hotel, but barely an hour ago, it was dicey," she said. She told Benjamin everything that had happened—the trip to the cabin, the volcano erupting, and the terrifying drive back to town.

"Jeez, that's incredible," said Benjamin, his eyebrows rising.

"We were very near the lava flow's course, but somehow we were able dodge its path."

Benjamin thought about that for a moment. "I'm glad you are all right." The disagreements they'd had seemed unimportant compared to surviving a volcanic eruption.

Zakia sniffed and nodded. They talked a bit more

and then signed off. "Give my love to Dani and Harris. I'll see you soon."

Zakia was happy that things seemed better between her and Benjamin. Perhaps the fact that she was headed to the U.S. soon made for new dynamics between them.

Then she called Oddleifur Oil. They had shut down the office due to the ash cloud, but a few employees were still there, including Halgrim's secretary. Zakia used flattery to persuade the woman that she needed to reschedule their meeting. Somehow it worked; Halgrim could see her for half an hour in the morning.

She took a shower, and then put on her pajamas and a terrycloth bathrobe from the closet. She crossed the hallway and knocked on Fiona's door. Fiona too, was in her PJs. As Zakia entered the suite, Fiona laughed and said: "Great minds think alike. Shall we order room service?"

Zakia strode over and sat down on the sofa. "How about pizza?"

"Sure."

Fiona ordered the pizza, and then sat down next to Zakia. "I gather you talked to Benjamin. Was he mad?"

"Not this time," Zakia said. "He could hardly blame me for the volcano erupting."

"Don't worry. You'll be in the U.S. with him soon enough and everything will be boring as usual. Just the way he likes it."

Zakia laughed. "Let's watch TV for a bit. I hope the pizza gets here soon. I'm famished. It's a shame we barely got to taste your delicious lamb chops."

"Yes, too bad," said Fiona as she turned on the TV and flipped through the channels, all of which showed coverage of the volcano.

"My goodness, they don't know the half of it. We should have filmed our close call," said Zakia.

Twenty minutes later, their pizza arrived. As Zakia watched the BBC anchor summarize the damage, she felt a chill when she saw the impact the volcano had had in the small town closest to the volcano, the place was knee deep in ash and one person had nearly died of asphyxiation from the gases.

"Let's see if there's a movie. I need a distraction from today's events," said Fiona, handing Zakia a slice of pizza.

"Good idea."

They watched an Alfred Hitchcock movie late into the night. Fiona fell asleep and Zakia went to her room. She didn't know what time it was when she finally fell asleep. It seemed she was always on high alert these days. She missed Benjamin's snoring.

****

Zakia slept fitfully. She had nightmares about explosions, only the volcano turned out to be the gas well and then she saw Elias there and tried to warn him, but couldn't get to him in time. And then it blew and she woke up.

While she lay there, groggy and disoriented, she heard a knock on the door. It was Fiona—she practically bounced into the room. "I feel so grateful I'm alive today," she said. "Come on Zakia, let's go see what's for breakfast, maybe there are crepes today. They're delicious. Oh, by the way, I also got a hold of the car rental place. I told them about our crazy drive. They will pick up the car and deliver our things to the hotel by noon."

"Wonderful, thanks."

Zakia got dressed, feeling out of sorts, while Fiona sat on the bed, waiting for her. Zakia thought Fiona had way too much energy. "I had a terrible nightmare last night and now I'm exhausted."

"You'll be fine after breakfast," said Fiona. "But what was the nightmare about?"

Zakia was reluctant to admit she was dreaming about Elias. But she told Fiona anyway, describing as briefly as she could the explosion and the feeling that she had been responsible for his death.

"I took nearly two weeks to read his e-mail," said Fiona.

"I guess we both let him down by not responding to his e-mails. But had I done things differently, maybe Elias would still be with us," said Zakia.

"You couldn't have saved him." Fiona folded her arms. "You've just had a nightmare," she said. "You can't make that into something else. You're supposed to combine work with a break on this trip. Benjamin thinks you're on vacation, remember. So try to enjoy yourself at least a little bit."

"That's easy for you to say," Zakia bit her lip, because the nightmare had brought something else to mind too, and she was bursting to tell somebody. She was sure Fiona would understand. She sighed and sat on the desk chair.

"I need to tell you something terribly important. It will come as a bit of a shock, so I'm glad you're sitting down."

Fiona looked alarmed. "What is it?"

"This could ruin my life." She paused, thinking. *Maybe I shouldn't tell her.* Then she continued, "You see, Dani is Elias's son, not Benjamin's. There! I've said it." She looked at Fiona expectantly.

Fiona flopped backwards on the bed, her mouth falling open. "What? Why didn't you tell me earlier?"

"I've never told a soul, except my sister. Surviving the volcano together, I feel our friendship has become very special. You're the only friend who could understand. I hadn't had the heart to tell Benjamin or Dani, let alone Elias and now he's dead. What a fool I've been."

Fiona got up and put her arm around her friend. "No, it's a very delicate matter. Don't blame yourself."

Zakia shook her head, but said nothing.

Fiona said, "Look, I barely knew him, but Elias seemed like a nice man. Why didn't you tell him, poor soul?"

Zakia sighed, "I'll tell you the story from the beginning. When I was dating him and he talked about marriage, I was very torn and my sister said it would be a bad idea. You even said he seemed too conservative."

"Oh, I guess I did say that."

"Anyway," continued Zakia, I thought about it, and since he clearly wasn't interested in my pursuing a journalism career, I made my decision. I broke up with him and shortly thereafter I met and fell in love with Benjamin."

"How did you know that Dani was Elias's and not Benjamin's boy? Did you take the test?"

Zakia sighed. "No. So I wasn't sure at first, but he's the spitting image of Elias. Thank goodness Benjamin didn't meet Elias or he'd have figured it out."

"I'm sorry Zakia. What a tough spot you're in."

"I argued with myself for days on end—before and right after Dani was born, but came to the conclusion that telling the people involved would ruin my life and Dani's."

"Why?" asked Fiona, looking surprised.

Zakia shook her head sadly. "Oh, think about it. Dani would be considered a bastard in Morocco, since I married Benjamin and not Elias, his biological father. By not telling the world, Dani appears to be Benjamin's boy, part of a respectable family."

Fiona was quiet for a moment, studying the Picasso poster over the bed. Then she looked at Zakia steadily. "I am sorry you didn't confide in me. I know we weren't that close at the time. I'm sorry you had to experience this alone."

"We're talking now," said Zakia.

Fiona nodded. "Does Benjamin suspect anything? And are you ever going to tell Dani?"

"Benjamin did become a little suspicious about my relationship with Elias, especially after I started investigating his death. But I have managed to downplay it for now."

"And Dani?"

"He could have suspicions," said Zakia. "As the boys were packing for the move, Dani found a photo of Elias. He asked who it was and I lied and said it was my third cousin and that I would tell him more when I got to Chicago."

Fiona looked at her intently. "And? That seemed to satisfy him?"

"Yes. Thank goodness. But now I will have to clear things up when I get to Chicago." In a sarcastic tone she added, "I can't wait for that to happen."

"Oh, my," said Fiona. "Will you tell Benjamin?"

"Yes. I had decided, originally, to let Dani know

when he turned eighteen, but now that Elias is dead, it doesn't make any sense to wait five more years. Of course, it could cost me my marriage. But I can't keep it from them anymore." She knew she sounded too confident about revealing this secret, but she hoped Benjamin would not leave her as a result, though he would have good grounds to do so.

Looking flustered, Fiona stood up and walked to the window. "My goodness, that's a heavy burden you bear. All I can say is that I'm glad I didn't have children. Jack and I have had a happy marriage without them."

Zakia shrugged. "Well, I wouldn't want a life without my sons, they're terrific. Anyway, I'm glad I finally told you. It's a relief to talk about it. Now my focus is on finding out what happened to Dani's father."

"That is understandable," said Fiona. "Well, we'd better get going or we'll miss breakfast. I don't think the ash cloud is too bad today. I heard the hotel has face masks at the front desk for the guests who want to venture outside. I can walk you to your meeting at Oddleifur this morning, if you like. It's just a few blocks away. Then I'll drive you to the airport this afternoon."

The breakfast room was all abuzz. They saw a long line for the crepes. Checking the rest of the buffet table, Zakia felt ravenous. "You get the crepes; I'll find a table."

"Good idea," said Fiona.

As Zakia turned to find a table, a fragment of conversation caught her attention. An elegant lady with blonde hair, wearing slacks and a thick wool, Icelandic sweater, was headed back to her table from the buffet and was talking to some other tourists while waving her arm. "I just heard on the news that all of Europe is paralyzed. Again," she said with a heavy sigh. "No planes going in or out of any airports in Europe. Just like what happened with the other volcano in 2010…what was it called? Eyafalla…or whatever."

"Eyjafjallajøkull," said one of the locals standing nearby.

"Thank you," said the woman in the Icelandic sweater.

"Really?" said Zakia, addressing the woman. "That can't be. My flight to Chicago is this afternoon."

"Not likely," said the woman, fixing her with her intense, grey-blue eyes. "All flights have been grounded due to the volcanic ash cloud." She held out her hand to greet Zakia, expertly balancing a big plate brimming with crepes and sausages in the other. "I'm Ellen Larsen."

"I'm Zakia Karim," said Zakia. "We were on the other side of the island and barely made it back yesterday. We experienced the ash cloud firsthand out there—a frightful experience."

"I can imagine," said Ellen. "Do tell me more."

Fiona arrived, holding two plates loaded with crepes. "What's all the excitement about?"

"Ellen, this is Fiona McPherson. Fiona, meet Ellen Larsen," said Zakia. "Ellen says all flights in and out of European airports are grounded. Do you want to join us at our table, Ellen?"

"Actually, my husband is just coming, but thank you."

Fiona nodded knowingly. "If the wind is blowing into the jet stream, then closing the airports makes sense. Volcanic ash contains glass crystals, not just ashes. If a plane flies through the ash it can destroy its engines," she said. "I think that is a sound decision. Did you tell Ellen about our little outing yesterday?"

"I only just got started," said Zakia.

Ellen sighed. "I told my husband we should have vacationed on Oahu. Rarely does anything inconvenient happen there, even if it's a volcanic island."

Zakia hid a smile. It appeared from the way that Ellen dressed that she didn't lack any funds. She was probably in her late fifties. "Please excuse us, then. I guess we'll see you around if we are going to be stuck here," said Zakia.

She followed Fiona to the table and they began eating their crepes. They talked about Zakia's interview at Oddleifur Oil headquarters. Zakia asked Fiona on a whim if she would join her for the interview with Halgrim.

"I don't think that's a good idea."

"If you come, you could get him out of the office while I pretend to be writing notes or something, giving me a chance to look through his files."

"Wait a minute. How do I get him out of the office?"

"I found out that the famous chess board from the 1972 World Chess Championship between the American Bobby Fischer and the Russian Boris Spassky, played here in Iceland, is housed at Oddleifur Oil's headquarters. Halgrim considers it a unique souvenir from the Cold War days and has to show it to all his visitors."

"How come I wasn't shown it the last time I was there?"

"That's the difference between a journalist and a climatologist. We do different kinds of research. Maybe he ran out of time when you were there."

"Okay, since it's for a good cause, I'll go along with your little scheme. But I don't like it."

"Thanks Fiona, I owe you big time."

Soon the breakfast room was empty. They were the last ones there.

Zakia got more hot tea and cupped her hands around the mug. "Ah, nice and warm," she said. "You forget how warm Morocco is until you leave."

"It's colder than usual for this time of year. But we should get going. We need ten-fifteen minutes to walk to Oddleifur's offices.

Zakia and Fiona helped themselves to masks at the concierge's desk before leaving the hotel. Two blocks later, Zakia stiffened. Across the street, rifling through the books displayed on stands on the sidewalk, stood the scar-faced man. She nudged Fiona and, when he wasn't looking, discreetly nodded toward him.

"What is it?" asked Fiona.

"That's Scar-face."

"Are you sure?"

"Yes, definitely not a mirage," said Zakia.

"So, now what do we do?"

"Just act naturally," said Zakia.

Chapter Twenty-Two

When they arrived at the appointed hour at Oddleifur Oil's headquarters, Fiona remarked it was one of the newest buildings in Reykjavik. They were welcomed by a young secretary with long blonde hair. She asked them to have a seat in the large foyer. Five minutes later, a tall, muscular man came into the lobby, looking much friendlier than Zakia expected. He definitely had Viking genes, she thought. She stood to greet him.

"Zakia Karim, I'm with *Le Journal du Maroc*. Thanks for taking the time to meet with me. Volcanoes are so inconvenient, aren't they?"

"Yes, nice to meet you. I'm Halgrim Thorsson, they call me 'Grim' for short," he said with a laugh. Then he noticed Fiona and said sternly, "Fiona, what are you doing here?"

"I asked her to come with me. She's a friend of mine. I told her of the famous chessboard that's housed here that she missed when she was here the last time. Fiona is an avid chess player," lied Zakia. "I figured after my meeting with you, it would not be an imposition to show us the chess board."

"Uh, I guess that should be all right," said Halgrim in an uncertain tone. He turned to Fiona, "Would you like some coffee while you wait?"

"Yes, please. That would be nice."

Halgrim nodded at the secretary seated behind the desk.

"That was quite a scare with the volcano erupting," said Fiona.

"Yes," said Halgrim. "But at least no one was killed. Come this way." He waved Zakia into his office. "What can I do for you?"

Might as well get straight to the point, thought Zakia. "I'm doing research for an article on hydraulic fracturing, and since you have a company in Morocco, I wanted to see how it all works from here."

Halgrim's grin faded, for just a moment, but he quickly recovered. "It would be my pleasure. Have a seat."

"Thank you." Zakia sat in an armchair across the large desk from him. Halgrim offered her coffee or tea. Zakia declined.

"What do you want to know?" he asked. Halgrim steepled his fingers, oozing confidence. For ten minutes Zakia asked him about the technicalities involved in fracking. Then she zeroed in on the blowout.

"I'm sure you know about the accident outside Al Tarife in Morocco," said Zakia.

"Yes," said Halgrim, "A tragic accident."

"I have heard such accidents are pretty rare. What happened? Was it human error?" asked Zakia.

Halgrim leaned forward and cleared his throat. "I can't comment on that. We're still investigating. We follow all the local laws to the letter."

"I see," said Zakia. "And you don't think there might have been foul play involved?"

"What are you talking about? Where did you get that idea?" He frowned.

Zakia gave him a noncommittal look. "Just wondering."

"Our fracking operations are starting to take off in a big way in Morocco. This is our first gas well using predominantly local labor, offering employment to people who otherwise wouldn't have a chance."

"That's good," said Zakia.

"No other subsidiary company in Morocco employs such a large percentage of locals as we do, including in management positions," continued Halgrim. "We are quite proud of our approach."

"Perhaps this time it didn't work out so well," said Zakia, knowing full well he was evading her questions.

"As I said, we are still investigating."

"Could there have been issues between the workers and the supervisor?"

"That would be highly unlikely."

"I heard that another employee died a few days after the accident—in a car crash."

"That has nothing to do with us. It happened outside of the company property."

"I see." Zakia nodded and took more notes. She realized she wasn't going to get any more information out of Halgrim and wanted to stay on relative good terms to take the next step. "Might Fiona and I see the chessboard now?"

"Yes, I'll take you to the room we made specifically for it. We call it the 'erudite study.'" Halgrim grinned.

"Oh, wait a minute. I should probably clean up my notes for a minute while they're still fresh. Why don't you and Fiona go ahead? I'll wrap up here at your elegant desk, and then have the secretary show me the way."

Without a word, he headed out the door, but left it ajar. She could hear him speaking to Fiona as they walked down the hall.

Zakia moved to Halgrim's chair. She opened the desk drawer on the right and found several files. She rifled quickly through them. In one file called *Pending Issues* she found an e-mail from Sigurd Agnarsson that said, "Relating to the expansion plans, the major N.B. problem has been eliminated." Zakia gasped and replaced the file in the drawer. Next, she opened a file named Trade Association. She saw Sigurd's name typed at the top of a long list of names. It was the minutes from a meeting entitled "The Dirty Network." What an odd name, thought Zakia. Sigurd's name was followed by a George Stevens. She made a mental note.

Before she could read on down the list, she heard footsteps in the hallway. She quickly pushed the file back in its slot. No sooner had she closed the drawer and started scribbling in her notebook, than the secretary stood at the door with a harsh squint on her face. "Can I help you Madame?"

"Oh, hi there, Mr. Thorsson said it was all right to clean up my notes. I'm so bad at balancing my notebook on my knee. I always prefer a desk. I'm done now. Would you kindly show me to the room with the famous chessboard?" Zakia was dripping with sweat.

"My pleasure," said the secretary.

"Wonderful. Thank you," said Zakia, taking a deep breath.

She joined Halgrim and Fiona admiring the chess pieces in the study.

"You got your notes all sorted out?" asked

Halgrim.

"Yes, thank you. I was just thinking what an amazing game Fischer played. My, look at those chess pieces. They're very plain," said Zakia. "You'd think the famous players would have demanded some elaborately carved versions."

"Usually the players' hands are so clammy from nerves, they would tarnish the finish on fancy pieces," laughed Halgrim.

"I'm more inclined to think someone would have walked out with a chess piece as a souvenir," said Zakia. "There are a lot of pieces to keep track of."

"The players can easily tell," said Fiona.

"Yes, indeed. There's no chance of that happening" said Halgrim.

"Anyway," said Zakia eager to leave. "Thank you for taking the time to meet with me and for letting us view this historic chessboard up close."

"What a treat it's been," said Fiona.

Halgrim ushered them through the hallway and to the lobby where they made their way out of the building.

"How did it go?" asked Fiona, turning to Zakia. "Any luck?"

"Perhaps," said Zakia. "Let's not talk about it here."

Chapter Twenty-Three

At breakfast the next morning, Fiona raced through the buffet before Zakia had even picked out what she wanted to eat. While she was standing by the food, contemplating her choices, Ellen showed up. She told her that the flights were still grounded. "Now they've said five days."

That didn't fit in with Zakia's plans at all. She loved Fiona, but Zakia was ready to leave Iceland and get away from Scar-face.

Zakia helped herself to piping hot oatmeal and then joined Fiona at their table. She appeared to have loaded up on every last crepe—Zakia wondered how she stayed so thin.

"I can't believe it," said Zakia as she tasted the oatmeal. "Now Ellen says the airport is closed for another five days."

Fiona seemed unperturbed. "It's a precautionary measure."

Zakia had another spoonful of oatmeal. "The thought of five more days is getting me claustrophobic," she said. "It's one thing planning a mini vacation, but this is a forced stay and I don't like it. And what about Scarface?"

"Call the police, why don't you?" said Fiona.

"I did, this morning," said Zakia. "I got the same answer you did. But I skipped mentioning the Morocco incident. It would get too complicated." said Zakia.

"You're probably right about that," said Fiona.

Fiona went to work and Zakia focused on her story in her room, wondering about the connection between Scarface and Oddleifur.

****

As she congregated that evening with Fiona and the other tourists in the hotel dining room, Zakia's head was filled with possibilities of conspiracy. Fiona tugged Zakia toward the buffet to admire the assortment of hot dishes, each with a label identifying the dish; there were fish species Zakia had not seen in Morocco.

"They serve a tasty supper here," said Fiona, looping her arm through Zakia's. "I hadn't really noticed it earlier. I always ended up eating somewhere closer to my office. But since it's included in the price, it makes sense to take advantage now, since the air is unpleasant outside."

"Yes, and look at the mussels; that's a real treat, my favorite, but I'll pass on the whale meat." said Zakia.

"Me too," said Fiona.

They had a long discussion on the pros and cons of whale hunting.

Twenty minutes into their dinner, Ellen and a tall, stylish man showed up at their table. "This place is full. May we join you?" said Ellen.

"Yes, by all means," said Zakia.

"This is my husband, David Larsen. David, this is Zakia Karim and Fiona McPherson. We met yesterday at breakfast."

"Nice to meet you," said David, as he sat down next to Fiona, Ellen settled in beside Zakia.

"We just got back from the Icelandic History Museum," said Ellen. "It's interesting the way Iceland got its independence from Denmark—in a peaceful manner, before the end of World War II."

"I had no clue." said Zakia.

"A proud country," said Ellen, and then turned to David. "Honey, let's check out the buffet table."

Ellen got up and David smiled at them. "Excuse us," he said. "We'll go help ourselves."

Fiona watched the Larsens make their way through the buffet line with an amused look on her face. "They seem like an interesting couple," she said.

"Perhaps," said Zakia. "We've only just met, really." Fiona and Zakia were deciding whether or not they had room for dessert when Ellen and David returned, their plates loaded with mussels in one hand, desert in the other.

"What brought you to Iceland?" asked Zakia, pushing the idea of dessert out of her mind.

"We flew in from Minnesota and we were going to spend two days here on our way to Norway, where we both have cousins," said Ellen. "We had reserved a cabin on the Ekspressruten, the cruise ship sailing along the Norwegian coast. We were supposed to leave from Bergen and sail all the way up to Kirkenes, north of the Arctic Circle. Then, of course with this volcano erupting, we had to cancel. It was a nice idea. Maybe next time."

David ate one of the mussels on his plate. "Delicious. Oh, I also had a meeting scheduled with the CEO of a subsidiary of an up-and-coming oil company that has its headquarters here in Iceland, but unfortunately he got stuck in Paris on the way here due to the ash cloud."

Zakia took a sip of her wine. "I'm guessing it must be Oddleifur Oil, the only large oil company in Iceland."

He gave her a curious look. "It is. Do you have some interest in oil companies?"

Zakia hesitated. She did not know who she could trust these days. "Could be."

Ellen looked at her husband with a frown and then smiled and turned to them. "What about the two of you?"

Zakia answered first. "I'm a journalist from Morocco on my way to Chicago."

"And I'm a climatologist doing research here," said Fiona.

Ellen laughed and waved her hand dismissively. "Climate change research. Well, it does provide employment for you scientists, doesn't it? I heard a scientist on Wolf News explaining how global warming is actually caused by sunspots or solar variability, not human activity. I mean, really now, the ice age, then the warming period—it's all cyclical isn't it? There is nothing we can do about it, right?"

"I wouldn't say that," said Fiona, her cheeks flushing."

"And where does your funding coming from?" asked David, concentrating on another mussel on his plate.

"I work for the National Center for Atmospheric Research in Boulder, Colorado."

"Really?" asked David.

"Yes," quipped Fiona, "And where do you work David?"

"I'm an investor at T.P. Moyers. We invest money on behalf of the large pension funds."

Fiona looked at Zakia with a satisfied smile. "Ah, important players in the war against climate change."

"What do you mean?" asked David, giving her a questioning look.

"It's like this," said Fiona, leaning back in her chair. "The sooner we take serious action to address climate change the less it will cost us. Investments must be shifted from the fossil fuel industry to the renewable energy companies."

"The market indicates that investing in oil and gas is still where you would get the most return," David countered. "Right now with the abundance of supply, the price of oil has dropped, but that is bound to change soon. As an investor, I have to focus on profits. Renewables are only now becoming competitive. All the talk of regulations to address climate change is just a way for the governments to gain more control of our society."

"I disagree." Zakia shook her head. "You have to look at the big picture. When the impacts of climate change result in hurricanes, droughts, and sea level rise, the government agencies will need to step in. There will be an awful lot more of that."

"I guess you have a point there." David's shrugged.

"On another note, are you by any chance familiar with an inner circle of any international oil and gas trade association?" asked Zakia.

"I've heard of a few trade associations, but I'm not familiar with an exclusive circle. But, I've been in touch with several high ups in the industry.

"Any chance you might have heard of George

Stevens?"

"No, the name is not ringing a bell. But I can make a few inquiries. Where did you come across his name?"

"Oh, I just saw it on a list I think might be important in the research for an article I'm writing.

"Speaking of research," Fiona looked at David and sighed. "Sadly, the oil industry has focused on doubts in the climate science and has published misinformation to delay action on climate change."

At that, David's face turned slightly red. "I think one has to keep in mind that science has uncertainties. In the meantime, the world still runs on fossil fuels. What do you say to the millions of people in China, just coming out of poverty—that they should go back to their farms and starve?"

His voice was loud and Zakia noticed that people in the room were turning to look at them. Ellen was visibly annoyed.

Fiona grinned. "Ninety-seven percent of climate scientists agree that climate change is happening and that human activity is the main cause. But the oil industry has suppressed that information. And while we continue to debate the *facts*, the Chinese people are choking on their own pollution. We have already lost precious time with these fictitious debates on climate change.

"Really?" said David.

"Yes. It's the same misinformation approach that was used when the tobacco companies duped the public on the dangers of smoking so they could continue to make large profits," said Fiona.

"That was outrageous!" said Ellen. "I did pick up the news about the Paris Agreement on climate change and two degrees, but I really don't get it," said Ellen.

"By setting a target, the idea is that everyone can focus on reducing carbon dioxide emissions which function as a warming blanket, heating the earth," said Fiona. "This way, we will avoid the most devastating consequences. We need to keep the *average* global temperature increase below two degrees Celsius compared to pre-industrial times."

"Who cares about two degrees anyway, ten degrees would sound ominous," said Ellen.

"For the last ten thousand years the temperature range has fluctuated by only about one degree Celsius. Now with our carbon dioxide emissions we are pushing two degrees." said Fiona.

"As regards warming, the last few winters in Minnesota have been colder and we've had more snow than we've had for many years," said David, taking a bite of his chocolate cake.

"As it happens, I'm focusing on extreme weather events in my research," Fiona said. The cold winters are following the pattern of climate change. It induces a weakening of the normally straight jet stream in the northern hemisphere, creating waves which allow polar blasts to penetrate far south in the United States."

"That makes no sense whatsoever," said Ellen.

"Remember, climate change refers to changes in long-term *averages* of daily weather," sighed Fiona. "There can be many variations in the weather, such as a heat wave or snow storm, but the temperature on average is still increasing."

Ellen rolled her eyes.

Zakia elbowed Fiona and got up from her chair. Fiona looked at her, startled, but took the hint, turned to the couple and smiled. "It was nice to meet you. We'll be off then, going to take a stroll if the air has improved. Maybe we will meet again tomorrow."

"I'm sorry I got everybody riled up, but for my job I need to be on top of this stuff," said David. These are important issues and I'm an open-minded human being. Oh, and I'll check into this George Stevens fellow you were asking about."

"Thank you," said Zakia.

"Have a good night," said Fiona.

The Larsens wished them goodnight and Fiona followed Zakia through the lobby and outside.

****

"You handled David's questions very well. I was getting all worked up. How dare he ask where your funding is coming from."

Fiona shrugged. "That doesn't bother me. If everyone was transparent about their funding, we would have fewer problems, I'm sure. It's the hidden funding used by these fossil fuel companies and others denying climate change that will definitely lead us on the path to disaster."

"Good point," said Zakia.

Fiona's jaw clenched. "David's obviously investing in the very same companies that are spewing out disinformation about climate change, hoping that the confusion will block or at least stall regulations to cut carbon emissions. Only, he wasn't aware of the misinformation."

"That's unfortunate."

They had just reached the shopping district when Fiona grabbed her by the arm and started pulling her across the street.

"What was that for?" cried Zakia.

"Act normal," whispered Fiona. "There's that guy again, Scarface, from yesterday."

Zakia sneaked a look and felt a jolt of adrenalin. He looked even more menacing in the semi-darkness. She took a deep breath, but started coughing. "Where is your MI5 body guard when we need him?"

"That's a good question," said Fiona, glancing behind them nervously.

"I don't like this," said Zakia. "I wish the ash cloud would blow away, so we could get off this island."

Zakia thought about her sons kidnapping, but she didn't want to frighten Fiona. They walked past the storefronts. Zakia kept glancing at the man, who would stop and look at his phone every once in a while, as though he didn't notice them. She and Fiona ducked inside Café Roasti, ordered a latte and a hot tea, and sat down on a comfy-looking red sofa. Zakia waited, expecting to see their stalker, but he didn't follow them into the café. "Shouldn't we go to the police?" asked Zakia. "He's clearly following us."

"I'm not sure. We still don't have proof of any wrongdoing."

"Too bad," said Zakia, glumly.

"Well, let's not have it ruin your stay here. We still have some time together. I'm almost done with my project, but I do need to work all day tomorrow. If you like, we can meet at the café where I take my usual afternoon tea on the way back to the hotel," said Fiona. "It's cozy and they have delicious macaroons."

"That's nice, but I can't focus on my writing all day again. I guess I'm getting 'island fever.'"

"Why don't you work in the morning and visit the

national museum in the afternoon? That might distract you. Besides, it would make a great destination piece."

"I couldn't go anywhere alone with this crazy stalker on the loose."

Fiona sipped her latte. "Wait a minute, I thought you were Zakia the Fearless who returned to the desert after being arrested the first time."

"That's different, that's on my turf. Here, I don't have my bearings and don't even speak the language."

"Then why don't you see if Ellen and David are available to join you?"

"Now, why would I want to hang out with climate change deniers?"

Fiona laughed. "It's good practice. You can try in a civilized manner to tell them what is really going on."

"Okay, I'll visit the museum with the Larsens, and then I'll question David on his investments if I get the chance," said Zakia, warming to the idea. "He said he was going to talk to Oddleifur Oil. Maybe he has information I can use for my article."

****

Fiona was gone by the time Zakia woke up on Friday morning. Now she just had to convince the American couple to go with her to the museum. She'd have to pretend she enjoyed their company. It was a good thing that Fiona had done most of the arguing the evening before.

She found the Larsens sitting at breakfast and walked over to them. They both looked up and David seemed happy to see her, his wife, less so.

Zakia smiled pleasantly. "Good morning Did you sleep well?"

"Yes, wonderfully," said Ellen, looking at her

suspiciously.

"And you?" asked David.

"Very well, thank you. It's nice to see that the ash cloud is diminishing, don't you think?"

"Finally. We've barely seen the sun for a week now," said Ellen. "It's about time."

"Yes, indeed," said Zakia. "I'm glad I caught you this morning because I was wondering if you would like to join me to visit the National Museum this afternoon. Fiona has to work and I'd love your company."

"What a splendid idea," said David. "We would like that very much."

"No, you see," said Ellen. "We were thinking of going to the Blue Lagoon again."

David looked at her. "You're forgetting the ash cloud. It's probably closed."

"Oh, that's right," said Ellen.

"Besides you don't want to miss the National Museum," said David. "There's that exhibit on polar expeditions that you wanted to see. It's on our list."

"Okay," she said, sounding perturbed. "I guess that would be a good distraction from all the talk of volcanoes these days."

"We're all stuck here," said David. "We might as well make the best of it. Besides, it's not often you meet people who aren't afraid to mix casual conversation with a little political and scientific debate."

Zakia frowned and Ellen leaned over to her and said softly, "We don't talk about money, religion, or politics in our circles in Minnesota. David's always getting himself in trouble by not following that rule."

"I say it's always good to get things out on the table," he responded. "I'm from New York, originally. We're usually direct, some would say brash."

"That's settled then," said Zakia. "I need to work this morning, but I can meet you in the lobby when I'm done. Shall we rendezvous at about one this afternoon?"

"Sounds like a plan," said David.

****

Working in her hotel room, Zakia searched some more to find out who might be behind the threats to climatologists—were they related to the oil and gas industry? She ate the bland soup of the day from room service and missed her Moroccan spices.

At one p.m., when Zakia got off the elevator to meet Ellen and David, she saw them at the far end of the lobby, talking with Scarface. She stood there, frozen, then turned on her heel and pressed the elevator button again. They were so busy laughing, she hoped they didn't notice her. She almost canceled her plans to go with the Larsens, but decided she might find out more about Scarface by going.

When Zakia returned five minutes later, Scarface was nowhere to be seen. She chatted with the Larsens for a moment, and then they began walking to the National Museum. David had already mapped their route and Zakia followed him with Ellen. They strolled down Skothusvegur road and made a right to Sudurgata. The air pollution was much less than the previous days.

In the corner of her eye, Zakia saw Scarface again, far behind them. The Larsens seemed oblivious to his presence, engaged as they were in an energetic discussion about renowned explorers of the world's last frontiers.

Soon they arrived at the National Museum and entered the modern, well-lit lobby to purchase their tickets.

David insisted on paying for all three tickets.

"No, you needn't," said Zakia.

"No problem. I got this one," he said.

"Thank you very much," said Zakia graciously.

They spent over an hour touring the polar exhibit, which showed an overview of the polar expeditions and the debate over who had reached the North Pole first, Robert Peary, Frederick Cook, Roald Amundsen, or Admiral Richard Byrd. The Larsens kept up their lighthearted banter over their favorite in the race. Amundsen's story seemed to be the most convincing in the end.

Over coffee in the museum's café, Zakia said, "David, I was thinking about our conversation last night and I wanted to ask if you'd heard that the Rockefeller Brothers Fund and the Norwegian Sovereign Wealth Fund, among others, have divested in whole or in part from fossil fuels."

David took the bait, "Yes, only that was a dumb move, I think," he said. "When it comes to influencing companies, my theory is that it is better to be on the inside to move the company in the right direction. Once you divest you no longer have any influence over the company."

"Dr. McPherson attempted to do something similar," said Zakia. "Oddleifur invited her to explain the science of climate change. By the third meeting, she realized they were only interested in using her for their green-washing PR campaign. Without any regulations on climate change, they'll just carry on with business as usual. They blame it on competitiveness concerns, which could be tackled, in part, if we put a price on carbon or implement a cap and trade program."

"Well, honestly in a capitalist system, competition is very important," offered Ellen. "A price on carbon is really just a tax. That's not going to fly. And the cap and trade system in Europe was pretty much a flop."

"If we move into dangerous climate change, there won't be much to compete over," said Zakia. "The focus will be on dealing with one climate crisis after the other, or trying to address conflicts due to climate change impacts—like water and food shortages due to drought."

David looked perplexed. "Yes, but I can't be ahead of the game and make risky investments, since I invest on behalf of the large pension funds."

"Fossil fuel investments will become stranded assets. If you're still invested in oil and gas when the ship goes down, you'll clients will lose everything. Not a wise investment strategy, I should think."

"I know about stranded assets. Yet, the oil companies will try to hold on as long as possible," said David. "That's why they are fighting regulations."

"Exactly," said Zakia. "We have all been counting on the market to value the natural resources correctly, but the impacts of climate change caused by burning fossil fuels are not taken into account," said Zakia. "Have you looked at Oddleifur Oil in this context?"

"Is this on the record?" asked David.

"No," she said.

"I don't think they are strategically well positioned

for long-term returns in a low-carbon society. But the jury is still out," he said.

"I wonder how far they will go to protect their interests," she said.

"By the way, I was able to find out about George Stevens. I heard he was an oil executive, heavily involved in an oil and gas trade association. Here's his email." He handed Zakia his card where he'd scribbled George's email on the back. "I'm sure he's heard of my employer, as his company has used us on several occasions.

"Thank you. I appreciate that,"

"Do mention my name. Then he's more likely to respond to your e-mail." David smiled. "I understand that he's retired to DeKalb, outside Chicago, to be closer to his granddaughter."

"That is good news," said Zakia. "I'm headed for Chicago."

"Look, Zakia, I know you and Fiona are passionate about renewable energy, and it's not like I have my head in the sand and am not aware that we have to transition to renewables. But it's not going to happen overnight," said David.

"In the meantime, Oddleifur has started fracking in Morocco and plans on expanding," said Zakia.

"Well, for now fracking is worth it," said David. "And it's better than coal in regards to climate change. That's why they say natural gas is a bridge to renewables."

"Unfortunate the scientists say that if you take into account the methane leaks, fracking is the same or worse than coal with regard to climate change. There are also local environmental problems which are not taken into account. And, an increase in earthquakes."

"I guess fracking will still be debated in the U.S for a while at least," said David. "I did notice New York State adopted a moratorium. And fracking has also been banned in Bulgaria, France, Germany, Ireland, and the Netherlands."

"I hope other states in the U.S. come to their senses soon, because even if the methane leaks are addressed, burning fossil fuels, in whatever form still emits carbon dioxide," said Zakia. "By the way, have you had access to Oddleifur Oil's accounts?" Being blunt was a gamble, but David didn't flinch. Bribes to Samara might show up in one form or another.

"Yes, they look straightforward, as far as I can tell," he said. He finished his latte and then leaned in to her. "You know something that you're not telling me, don't you?"

Zakia's shoulders stiffened as she all of a sudden noticed Scarface casually leaning against a nearby pillar. Zakia stifled a gasp. He wore a button-down shirt, a dark blue sweater, and khaki pants. He looked as if he were waiting for a tour group, he must have been eavesdropping.

Ellen seemed to notice her discomfort. "What's the matter, Zakia?"

Zakia tore her gaze away from Scarface and forced a smile. "Nothing. I just had a sharp cramp in my foot. I have them on occasion. It just lasts a moment or two, and then it's gone."

"I'm sorry to hear that," said David.

"Anyway, as I was about to say," continued Zakia. "I'm not sure that Oddleifur Oil is completely above board in its operations."

Just then, Scarface walked right up to their table. Zakia froze, and then got angry. She convinced herself he wouldn't do anything to her here.

David saw him and stood up to shake his hand. "Hello Rostek. Fancy meeting you here. Did you take the afternoon off?"

Rostek nodded and gave Zakia a sly grin. "I heard this exhibit was very good, so I thought I'd catch it before it ends."

David turned to Zakia. "Let me introduce you. "This is Rostek Bukowski. He works for Oddleifur Oil and they arranged for him to give us a tour of a couple of the historic sites here in Iceland. He's an analyst there. Rostek, this is Zakia Karim, a journalist from Morocco."

"Nice to meet you," said Zakia, as she clenched her fist under the table. By staying angry, she was able to subdue her fear.

Ellen nodded.

"May I join you?" asked Rostek.

"Certainly," said David. Rostek sat down on the extra chair and David continued, "Zakia here was trying to convince me to invest in renewable energy. She thinks your company is going to become a hydrocarbon dinosaur, with stranded assets."

"Those aren't my words," said Zakia.

"David, quit trying to stir up a fight," said Ellen.

"That's okay," said Rostek. "Zakia, I heard you mentioned fracking. I think you should stop talking about things you know nothing about."

Zakia took a deep breath. "Excuse me! As it turns out, I know quite a bit," she said.

David looked puzzled as he picked up the

animosity between them. "Well, Zakia doesn't know what you do. Why don't you tell her about your job at Oddleifur Oil, Rostek?"

"I'm involved in lots of different projects," answered Rostek, his eyes flicking over Zakia. "For the most part forecasting threats to the company to make sure they are dealt with quickly and preventing any damage."

David shook his head. "You do whatever you can to protect the company—loss prevention. That sounds like risk management to me."

"Yes, that's right, an expanded version of it," said Rostek, directing his gaze at Zakia.

Zakia shivered, wanting to tell David and Ellen not to trust this man. That his real job was to threaten her and frighten her off the story.

Rostek smiled at Zakia. "Nice to meet you all, but I have a meeting," he said, standing up. He shook everyone's hands and when he took Zakia's, he held it a little too long before he narrowed his eyes and released her. Then he walked away.

Zakia's heart was hammering like she'd had a gun held to her head. She made a mental note to ask Fiona about going to the police. No doubt he was threatening her.

Ellen, checking her watch said, "Oh, it's five o'clock; the museum is closing. We better head out. Zakia, would you like to join us tomorrow for an outing to the contemporary art museum?"

"Yes, I'd love to. I have some work to do in the morning, but we could leave at noon perhaps."

"Good, then we have a plan," said David.

On the walk back to the hotel, Zakia kept thinking

about Rostek. She realized she had provoked him by talking to the Larsens about fracking. His goal must be to keep her from scaring off one of Oddleifur Oil's potential investors. A chill ran down her spine.

Chapter Twenty-Four

Zakia got back to her room and e-mailed George Stevens right away, remembering to mention David. The tension of meeting Rostek had worn her out. She decided to take a nap before dinner.

She had just closed her eyes when she heard a knock at the door.

Zakia went to answer it and opened it a crack, expecting to see Fiona. Instead two menacing-looking men forced themselves into the room and closed the door. Right away she recognized one of them; it was Rostek. The other was tall and looked like he might be from the Middle East.

"What are you doing?" she shrieked.

The tall man clapped his hand over her mouth. "Be quiet," he said. "Or we will hurt you. Understand?"

Zakia nodded and stared at Rostek her eyes narrowing.

The tall man removed his hand and took a roll of duct tape out of his bag. "We are taking you with us, and if you make a fuss we will kill you." He shoved her hard onto the bed. "Do you understand? Don't mind Rostek, I'm in charge. The name is Ahmed."

Rostek stood next to him, watching her closely.

She trembled. "Who do you think you are?"

"You'll find out soon enough," said Ahmed. He pulled a large, dark trench coat out of his bag and threw it onto the bed, "Put this on. Now!"

Zakia did as she was told. Once she had the coat on, Rostek grabbed her wrists, held them tight in front of her, and fastened a long plastic zip tie around them.

"What's going on, Rostek? Please don't do that," she begged him. "That hurts."

"You'll be fine if you cooperate. Just shut up," said Rostek. Then he measured some duct tape and as Zakia watched, wide-eyed, he tore off a strip and then taped it over her mouth.

"Now just come with us. Don't try to call attention to yourself. Or else…"

Zakia starting to panic, tried to calm herself. *I can't fight these guys. I might as well cooperate and see what happens.*

They put a hijab with a niqab on Zakia's head that covered all but her eyes, then rolled a scarf over her wrists and hustled her out of the room and into the hallway. Zakia looked longingly at Fiona's door, wishing she would magically appear.

As they pushed Zakia down the hallway, she tried to make eye contact with a housekeeper as the woman stepped into the corridor to take some towels off her cart, but she took one look at the men and turned away.

They walked past the elevator, to the back stairs, one man in front and one behind Zakia, pushing her the whole time. She tripped on the stairs and was dragged back on her feet. They were moving so fast that she didn't see any opportunity to run. Less than ten minutes after they'd barged into her room, they reached the parking lot at the back of the hotel.

There were a few cars, but nobody else in sight. They shoved her into the backseat of an old Volvo and sped off.

Zakia's mind was racing. How long would it take Fiona to realize she was missing? Zakia's phone and purse were still in her room; if Fiona called her cellphone and didn't get an answer, would she investigate any further before dinner?

After driving for ten minutes, Rostek stopped the car abruptly at a red light. Zakia lunged for the door. She managed to open it and was about to throw herself out, when Rostek gunned the Volvo and Ahmed grabbed the back of the trench coat and pulled her back in.

"Don't do that again," said Ahmed. "Your children may be in America but that doesn't make them safe."

Zakia slumped in the back seat.

Rostek drove out of town and soon the road looked familiar. The ash cloud was letting up, but she had no idea where they were headed.

"If you keep your mouth shut, I'll take the tape off your mouth now," said Ahmed.

Zakia nodded and leaned forward. Ahmed lifted the niqab and then ripped off the tape. She blinked away tears at the pain.

After a few miles, they pulled up at a small hotel that she recognized. It was the one next to the Blue Lagoon.

"Ah, are we going for a swim?" she asked, trying to curtail her fear with some humor.

Rostek turned around and grinned at her, but Ahmed smacked him on the head with his hand. "Stay focused," he said. "If you had done your job, we wouldn't have to do this."

They parked at the back of the old hotel. The two

men got out of the car and started arguing, but Zakia couldn't make out what they were saying.

She scooted closer to the car door. The entrance to the hotel was but a few feet away, up a small, steep hill.

Rostek and Ahmed continued arguing. She thought they spoke Icelandic, but, by the way they were gesturing toward the car, it clearly involved her. Zakia watched them, biting her lip. Ahmed poked Rostek hard in the chest. Rostek turned red and took a swing at him.

Zakia leaped out of the car and made a run for it.

With her hands bound and breathing heavily in the polluted air, she did not make much progress. The grass on the hill was wet. She slipped as she climbed.

Then she fell.

She struggled to get up, straining to see with the niqab obstructing her vision and tripping on the trench coat. Ahmed pounced on top of her. He got up and jerked her back on her feet. "Stop trying to run away," he said frowning. "It will just make things worse for you. Rostek has suggested we kill you right now and get it over with."

Rostek rolled his eyes. "You're so sentimental, Ahmed," he said.

"Shut up, Rostek. I'm not a killer," muttered Ahmed.

Zakia went cold.

They hustled her to the back entrance of the hotel, which seemed deserted.

"Closed for renovations," said Ahmed as if he had read her mind. He leaned forward and tore the hajib and niqab off her head. "The workers have gone for the day. There's nobody here but us."

They walked her up two flights of stairs and into a

suite. There they shoved her into a chair and cut the zip tie around her wrists.

"Okay," said Zakia, rubbing her wrists. "What do you want from me?"

"You've brought this on yourself by causing so much trouble," Rostek said as he pulled a gun from under his coat.

Zakia drew in a shaky breath.

"We have our instructions," said Ahmed. "Now listen very carefully. We work for some people who are not happy about your work. You are to stop all your prying into the fracking accident or any related activities. Is that clear?"

Zakia rolled her eyes. It wouldn't do to let on how scared she was. "You have been watching too many movies. You could have just e-mailed me and spared yourself the trouble."

This time, Ahmed laughed and Rostek told him to shut up. Then Rostek leaned into her, his face so close she could feel his warm, garlicky breath. "You are quite powerless now. Why don't you give it up? There are interests involved that are much bigger than you can imagine."

"Isn't this Iceland, where freedom of the press is respected? If I do get my piece published, what will you do to me?"

"Then we will call in some guys from Bulgaria to help us out," said Ahmed, giving Rostek a pointed look. "They kill people without leaving a trace. They are very good at what they do. You should understand your predicament now. When you were arrested in Al Tarife, and when your children were kidnapped in China, some would get the message, but you just carried on. You must have a guardian angel to have lived this long, but now your luck has run out. I don't know why my boss didn't instruct us to kill you right away. Let this be a final warning. Don't write about the blowout or talk to anyone about Oddleifur Oil. Is that clear?"

"I'll think about that," said Zakia, her mouth dry. "Rostek, you know that my friend and I saw you following us earlier. I'm sure she's notified the police by now."

"Not to worry; you won't be seeing Rostek anymore," said Ahmed.

Rostek scowled at his partner.

Ahmed smiled at her in a way that made Zakia's lips tremble. Then he turned to Rostek. "Go ahead, do the honors. Since you've been itching to do something violent for a long time."

Rostek looked at Zakia with an arched eyebrow, then aimed the gun at her. "This might hurt," he said.

Zakia looked him straight in the eye, blinking back tears, willing her voice to stay steady, "Go ahead—make me a martyr."

In an instant he flipped the gun, landing the barrel in his hand, raised his arm and in a flash brought the handle down hard on her head.

Everything went black.

Chapter Twenty-Five

When Zakia came to, her head throbbed and her right arm was numb. She felt wet, though she wasn't cold. She realized she had been stripped down to her underwear. As her eyes adjusted to the dim light, she saw that she was lying in the lagoon with water up to her chest. Her right hand was tied to the railing connected to the ramp at the water's edge. She tried to wriggle out of the zip tie, but it was impossible. She started shaking, aware that she was lucky to be alive.

Why had they bothered to leave her in the lagoon? Were they coming back for her?

She didn't know how late it was.

Should she cry out for help? She was afraid they might come back. Her head hurt and she wondered how long the lagoon would be closed for renovations and what time the workers would come in the morning. Then she remembered it was Friday. She could be stuck here until Monday morning.

She lay there, feeling woozy. Then she thought she saw movement along the far edge of the lagoon.

Was she imaging things?

She heard voices. One of them was female.

Zakia turned her head and tried to pull herself as much as possible out of the water. "Help!" she cried as loud as she could.

Two people came running. A blonde-haired woman

knelt beside her. "Oh my god, you've got a lump on your head the size of a golf ball." She touched Zakia softly on the shoulder.

Zakia reached up gingerly with her free hand to feel the bump, and almost passed out.

The man, nearly bald, started fiddling with the zip tie on the railing. "Don't worry. We'll get you out of here. Are you hurt anyplace else?"

Zakia shook her head. She felt like she was going to throw up.

"You need to call the police," the woman said to the man.

He frowned. "We'll get to that, but first I need something to cut this plastic zip tie with. I think there's a penknife in our car. Pia, run and get it please, while I help this poor woman."

She nodded, looking pale, and ran off.

"Who did this to you?" he asked, helping her sit up.

"I'm not quite sure," said Zakia, trying not to vomit. "Someone doesn't like my asking questions."

He frowned. "What do you mean?"

"I'm a journalist. My name is Zakia."

"I'm Thor and my friend's name is Pia," said the young man.

The woman returned with the penknife and cut her free. Thor and Pia dragged her slowly out of the pool. Zakia was shivering in the cool night air, Thor gave her his coat.

"Thanks," she said.

"We'll drive you to the hospital," said Thor.

"I'll be fine, just drop me off at my hotel. I'm very tired," said Zakia.

They drove her to the hospital anyway, where a nurse called the police and Fiona.

Zakia was examined and diagnosed with a nasty concussion. Thor said he and Pia needed to leave and Zakia thanked them profusely. While she was waiting in the examination room to see if she would have to be kept overnight, the nurse brought her some hot tea and it wasn't long before a police officer arrived. He introduced himself as Captain Gunnarsson and asked if she was able to make a statement.

At that point, Fiona—biting her lip—walked into the room with the Larsens in tow. Fiona elbowed her way past the captain and hugged Zakia. "You stood me up for dinner."

Zakia started sobbing. "I was so scared," she said.

The Larsens said they would wait in the hallway and left the room.

"You gave me such a fright," said Fiona. She pulled the hair back from Zakia's forehead, wincing at the sight of the bump. "I was worried when we couldn't find you, and you didn't answer your phone. Who did this to you? Was it the stalker?"

"Yes. His name is Rostek." she said pulling herself together. "I don't think certain parties want me to publish my article."

Captain Gunnarsson cleared his throat. "I hate to interrupt, but I need to file a report."

"I understand," said Fiona. "I'll join the Larsens and we'll go and look for the cafeteria. I'll check back in a little while to see if we can take her home tonight."

The captain arched his eyebrow when Zakia explained that the attack was most likely in retaliation for her investigation into Oddleifur Oil. She wasn't sure that the captain could help her. She figured Rostek and Ahmed wouldn't be showing their face in Reykjavik for a while. She informed him how two employees of Oddleifur that she knew, had died in Morocco—one was incinerated, the other had died in a car crash.

Rubbing his chin, he said, "Is that so? This sounds like an international issue. I'll get in touch with Interpol." But, judging from his glum expression, Zakia thought this could be a dead end.

She asked him if the grounded flights would be allowed to take off anytime soon. "Not just yet," he said.

This made her stomach clench, but she was hopeful. At least if she couldn't get off the island, maybe Rostek and Ahmed would be caught in Iceland after all.

The officer said he would meet her again at the hotel with his assistants to investigate the initial scene of the kidnapping. They were already checking the Blue Lagoon. As he was gathering his things to leave, Fiona showed up. She had been informed that Zakia should spend the night in the hospital, but Zakia waved her off. "I just want to go back to the hotel and sleep," she said.

"But you've had a serious concussion," said Fiona.

"Well, what are they going to do about it? They'll just keep waking me up all night to check on me," she said.

After a few moments, the nurse walked into the room, smiling. "I just spoke with the doctor and he said you're free to go. We'd like you to check in with your primary doctor when you get back home." Zakia thought, where is my home now?

****

Back at the hotel, Zakia's bravado evaporated. David parked the car right by the entrance where Fiona and Ellen walked Zakia into the lobby. Captain Gunnarsson and two police officers were waiting for her. "We need to examine your room now and prefer that you wait here until we're done."

Zakia felt dizzy. The thought of returning to her own room, in which she had been so recently violated, gave her the creeps. "I think I've had enough excitement for the evening. I'll wait here, if Nurse Fiona will allow me to have a drink."

Fiona told her no, no drink, but that she could arrange for some tea at the bar next to the lobby.

The captain and his officers left to investigate her room. As Fiona stood by, the Larsens said goodnight, each giving Zakia a hug and promised to help however they could.

Facing the Larsens, Zakia said, "Would you mind staying here a few more minutes? I need to talk to you." They looked at her curiously, but followed her into the bar. They all took a seat around a small cocktail table and ordered drinks, tea for Zakia.

"What's so important that it can't wait until tomorrow?" asked Ellen.

Zakia took a deep breath. The headache had receded somewhat, but this was going to be a difficult conversation. "I need you to know that one of the kidnappers was Rostek from Oddleifur Oil."

David looked shocked. "That's not possible. Oddleifur is not a criminal entity," said David, looking pale. "They're not the mafia."

She pointed to her forehead. "This says otherwise. At least there are criminal elements safeguarding their interests. I think certain parties don't want me to publish my article."

"What are you working on?" asked David. "Surely, this doesn't have anything to do with the investments we were talking about earlier."

Zakia closed her eyes against the headache that was again engulfing her. "It has to do with fracking, climate change *and* investments in oil companies," she said. "The kidnappers warned me not to write about Oddleifur Oil and fracking," she hesitated, "or to talk to you about Oddleifur Oil. I assume that's because you are considering investing in the company."

Ellen's face had turned ashen. David shook his head. "This is hard to take in. Did you tell the cops everything?"

"Not everything, not yet," she said. "But they're connecting with Interpol."

Silence ensued while the waiter brought them their drinks.

Zakia took her tea.

"Look, I'm telling you that there's more going on with Oddleifur Oil than meets the eye. I urge you to tread with care or withdraw from any involvement with them."

David rubbed his eyes. "I just can't believe it. Rostek seemed like an amicable guy."

"My goodness, we spent a whole afternoon with him," said Ellen, hugging herself. "Do you think we are in danger too?"

Fiona crossed her arms. "Rostek has been trailing us for a couple of days."

"Oh no!" said Ellen. "Why didn't you tell us he was stalking you after he showed up at the museum?"

"I was afraid of him, and I didn't want to appear paranoid. There's an awful lot that's been going on in the last few weeks. You can't imagine. And it's hard to prove." Zakia took a deep breath and continued. "The police will probably be asking you questions, too, because I mentioned that you knew Rostek professionally." David and Ellen listened intently.

Ellen patted her husband on the knee. "Well, David, I guess you're going to have to find another investment opportunity. I, for one, don't think you should pursue this one any further." She gave Zakia and Fiona a half-hearted smile. "I am really looking forward to leaving this island."

"Well, it hasn't been boring," said David.

"I wonder if Rostek was acting on behalf of the company, or if he is working for someone else," said Zakia.

David rubbed his cheek. "That's a good question, Zakia. This whole operation doesn't seem right. Either way, I am going to call Oddleifur Oil in the morning and cancel our meeting."

"I'd wait until we are on board the plane, hopefully soon," said Ellen, drily. "How about you call in sick?"

"Whichever approach you use, please be careful." Zakia told them about the kidnappers threatening her family. Eventually, the Larsens excused themselves and went up to their room, wishing Zakia a speedy recovery.

Zakia said she wasn't ready to sleep just yet and stepped over to the bar counter where she ordered more tea and Fiona joined her and asked for a glass of water.

"I'm freaked out with the thought of sleeping in my room tonight, do you mind if I stay in your suite for a couple of days? I can sleep on the sofa."

"Of course I don't mind. But we can share my king-sized bed, no problem."

Zakia grinned at her friend. "How did you manage to bring the Larsens along on your rescue mission to the hospital?"

"They were asking to see us for dinner, and, when you were nowhere to be found, they also got worried and wanted to help in the search. Then we got a call from the nurse, and shortly thereafter, the police showed up. We all took off to the hospital."

"That's interesting. I thought we wouldn't get along with the Larsens after your discussion at dinner the other night, but then again, we were very civilized with each other at the museum."

"I hope your experience today has started to make them think a little differently," said Fiona.

"It's hard to ignore kidnapping and assault," Zakia blurted out. "But we have to figure out a way to make climate change that vivid for everybody. The way extreme weather events are becoming the new normal—that's what should frighten people. It's not that fun to have your house flooded out, time and time again, as we've seen happen in England, the Philippines, the Caribbean and so many other places."

"It's sad, isn't it," said Fiona. Abruptly she straightened up. "Oh, no," she said.

"What?" asked Zakia.

"What are you going to tell Benjamin?"

Zakia waved her arm, pretending to blow her problems away. "You know, I'm so exhausted right now that I don't care what Benjamin thinks. Besides, if he gets mad and can figure out a way to get us out of this godforsaken place with criminals roaming the streets, more power to him."

Fiona laughed and shook her head. The two talked until Captain Gunnarsson came down. "I've left your personal effects in the room. And the door is locked," he said.

"I'm not sleeping there again," said Zakia. "I'll get my things shortly. Thanks, and please keep me posted."

"I don't think we'll see your kidnappers anywhere nearby," he said. "But I'm posting an officer outside the hotel tonight, just in case."

Zakia and Fiona went back to Zakia's room, gathered her things and took them to Fiona's suite. She took a shower and got into her pajamas. When she was settled in bed, Fiona said, "I hope you're able to sleep tonight. If you like, we can watch a movie again."

"That sounds great," said Zakia. "It will distract me from my throbbing headache."

"Let's hope that doesn't last long. Soon you'll be due for more pain killers. In the meantime, I'll look for a can of chicken soup I bought as backup." She rummaged in the cabinet.

"Found it," she said.

Zakia watched as Fiona bustled around in the kitchenette. Then Fiona walked over to her and showed her the flash drive with the climate data and asked, "Where should we keep this? I added my own research to the flash drive as well, just as a precaution. I thought somewhere in the kitchen might be good."

"What if we put it in a zip locked bag in the electric kettle?"

"So you can boil it every time you're making tea?"

"No silly, then you take it out. The point is to hide

it in plain view. No one would guess to look there.

"As long as we don't boil it accidentally." Fiona found a zip lock bag in a drawer and put the flash drive in it.

"Right," said Zakia. "As it turns out, I have my own crucial flash drive. See." She pulled it out of her bag and showed it to Fiona. "It has information I haven't shared with you. It's really hot, but it can't be boiled either. Let's put them together, join forces so to speak."

Fiona opened the zip locked bag and Zakia popped her flash drive into it.

"There, all set," said Fiona. So what is on yours? Something juicy, I presume. Let me get the soup and you can tell me all about it."

Fiona joined Zakia on the bed. Zakia told her about the meeting with the oil and energy minister's secretary and the bribes the minister had received from Oddleifur Oil.

"You should give that information to the police," said Fiona.

"I'm still trying to figure it out." Zakia took a spoonful of soup. "But they'll get it eventually."

Fiona looked dubious, but held her tongue.

"Good soup. Thank you." Zakia stretched. "I have to Skype Benjamin now and get some sleep. I feel as if I've been run through a washing machine."

The bump on her head was still painful and, when she went into the bathroom to brush her teeth, she saw it didn't look great, either. She certainly couldn't Skype with Benjamin looking like that. She hadn't decided what she would tell him, but if she texted or phoned him for a few days, she wouldn't have to deal with it.

So she texted him that she was too tired to Skype and that she just wanted to get some sleep.

He texted her back: *I miss you.*

****

Zakia woke up on Saturday, with Fiona gently shaking her. "Just checking that you are all right," said Fiona.

"I'm okay," said Zakia. "Thanks."

A bit woozy, she stood up and wandered to the bathroom, her forehead still throbbing where the gun handle had struck her. The swelling was a little less than the night before. With a hat she would look almost presentable.

"The visibility is pretty good now," called Fiona as she looked out the window. "The ash cloud has dissipated considerably."

"That's great," mumbled Zakia as she brushed her teeth.

"Okay, I'm heading for breakfast," said Fiona. "Take your time; I'll see you down there."

Zakia heard the door shut behind her. She was relieved that Fiona wasn't hanging over her. When she walked toward the closet, the floor creaked, and her heart missed a beat. *Now, take it easy.*

Zakia got dressed and brushed her hair. The dizziness was going away, but once she was out in the hallway her shoulders tightened. She was relieved to see a cleaning woman smiling at her as she passed by on her way to the elevators. She got to the dining room just as Fiona and the Larsens were sitting down from a trip to the breakfast buffet.

"Wonderful! You're just in time Zakia. We are not quite done," said Fiona.

Zakia moved to the buffet, filled her plate with eggs, whole wheat toast, and herring, and then joined them.

David and Ellen smiled at her. "Good to see you looking almost chipper this morning," said Ellen.

"You gave us quite a scare," added David.

"I'm fine," she told them. She then cut off any more inquiries about her wellbeing by digging into the eggs and herring.

"Did you hear the news?" Ellen asked. "I seem to have become the newscaster on volcanoes and ash clouds. Anyway, I've heard from the desk clerk that flights are definitely resuming tomorrow."

"Finally. That's wonderful," said Zakia, feeling a little dizzy. "I never thought I'd be so eager to get to the end of a vacation. This one has been overwhelming, to say the least."

"Yes," said Fiona. "Zakia is starting to get a serious case of cabin fever."

Everyone laughed. "So tell me," said Ellen. "What exactly happened at the Blue Lagoon?"

Zakia gave them the tamer version. She didn't want to scare them too badly.

Ellen laid her hand on Zakia's shoulder: "Oh my goodness, how awful."

Zakia added, "They said there are much bigger forces at play here; that I didn't have a clue."

"What exactly are you investigating in terms of fracking?" asked David, frowning.

She wasn't sure if David and Ellen were ready to hear the whole truth, but decided to tell them all about the fracking blowout, anyway.

"I can't believe it," said Ellen.

"Yes," said Zakia, starting to sniffle. "I knew the man who went up in flames. His name was Elias. We both studied at Columbia University where I got my master's in journalism, he became an engineer." She gave Fiona a knowing look.

"The accident sounds horrific," said David. "But I understand such blowouts seldom happen."

"Yes," said Zakia. "It turns out such events are indeed rare. But I've evidence that it was arranged to look like an accident."

"So you are saying it was sabotage," said David.

"It looks like it."

"Wow, this sounds way over the top. Have you talked to the police?" asked Ellen.

"No. It seems the police in that area may be in cahoots with Oddleifur Oil."

"And how do you know that?" asked David.

Zakia filled them in.

"My goodness. That's intense." said Ellen.

"In the Arab world, when events like this happen, as a journalist, you get the message and you lay low with the story. But when my sons were kidnapped, I knew it was more serious."

"I should say so," said David. "It's outrageous."

"And now you've had your second warning. Or is it the third?" asked Fiona.

"I guess it's the third." said Zakia as she took a sip of her tea. "I know they must have some illegal dealings going on in order to expand the fracking operations, but I'm still piecing together the clues and haven't got all the evidence I need yet."

Ellen and David looked at her in disbelief.

"I don't get it," said David. "There are a lot of

people fighting fracking in the U.S., the protesters are arrested if they fail to get the required permit. And, of course, you have the usual anarchists who take advantage to create chaos in the peaceful protests. But no one is kidnapped or killed."

David frowned. Ellen put down her fork and shook her head. No one at the table was eating anymore.

Zakia had wanted to educate them, but hadn't wanted to end the conversation on such a dire note. She had an idea. "Why don't you two come to our suite for dinner tonight and I will make my famous Moroccan dish? Fiona loves it. It will be our last supper together since the flights resume again tomorrow. Shall we say seven p.m.?"

"Thank you," said Ellen after getting a nod from David. "That would be a wonderful send off on our last night."

"Good. See you then," said Zakia. "I hate to leave this food uneaten, but I am exhausted. If you will please excuse me, I am going back to bed."

"Yes, of course," said Ellen. "Get some good rest now."

"I think I'll head to our suite, too. I have some e-mails to answer," said Fiona.

"We're heading out, more museums..." said David.

When they got up from the table, Fiona and Ellen walked on ahead, but David pulled Zakia aside. "Look," he said, in a low voice. "I know that you are good-hearted about helping save the world and all of that, but it seems to me that you and Fiona are getting in too deep."

"What do you mean?" asked Zakia

"I'm worried about you. I don't deal with these sorts of things, but I've heard nasty stories." He rubbed the back of his neck. "I always dismissed them as tall tales, but it seems like things can get pretty ugly when investments are threatened and people feel their fortunes slipping out from under them."

Zakia swallowed hard and nodded. "You mean I was right in what I said yesterday, there can be criminal elements involved."

"I didn't want to say it in public or in front of my wife, but yes, I guess the tall tales have some truth to them."

"Thanks for the confirmation," said Zakia. "I'll keep that in mind."

She caught up with Fiona in the lobby and they took the elevator together. When they were back in Fiona's suite and had closed the door, Fiona sighed. "Are you calling Benjamin?"

Zakia's headache throbbed. "Oh, yes," she said. "But I think I'll skip mentioning the warning David just gave me."

"What warning?"

Zakia explained what David had said. "That's not exactly reassuring." She shivered.

"So it's all cloak and dagger operations from here on out." Fiona chuckled, "If he could, I'm sure Benjamin would reach through the computer and haul you off to Chicago."

"At least I can tell him we are finally getting out of here," said Zakia.

"Yes," said Fiona. "There's that."

Chapter Twenty-Six

When Zakia woke from her nap, she found a note from Fiona. She had gone to her office. Zakia decided it would be good to get some work done, rather than dwell on yesterday's incident, so she sat down at the desk and opened her laptop.

She outlined her story and it started coming together. She called the police to see if they had made any progress on the kidnapping. She managed to reach the desk of Captain Gunnarsson. He informed her that the kidnappers had not been found. "We're following up on all the leads," he said. "We are patrolling your neighborhood. Are you feeling better today?"

"Much better, thank you."

"You'll let me know if you remember any additional facts regarding the incident."

She clenched her jaw. *And I thought Iceland was supposed to be a peaceful place.*

Zakia decided to surprise Fiona for lunch. They had agreed that it was okay for Zakia to walk around town alone as long as she stayed on crowded streets.

She showed up at Fiona's office. The door was open and Fiona, intent on her computer, didn't hear her coming. "Hello," said Zakia.

Fiona turned around and smiled. "You look like you've regained your strength," she said.

Zakia nodded. "The headache is nearly gone and

I'm hungry. Where shall we go for lunch? This time it's my treat."

"Oh, I don't know," said Fiona. "Let's make it a quick one. I would like to wrap up a few things before we leave. The extra days here have really made a difference. I'll be able to present my results in London early next week."

Zakia frowned. "I'm sorry I've taken so much of your time."

"It wasn't your fault," said Fiona.

"Okay, let's go to that café that you said serves delicious quiche."

"Fine with me," said Fiona.

At Fenagurs Café, they both ordered the quiche with ham and cheese. Fiona took a bite of hers and gave Zakia an amused look. "Do you think the Larsens have become more enlightened than the first time we met them?"

"I hope so," said Zakia. "Maybe they'll think about their grandchildren's future a little differently now."

"It's sad that we have lost so much time due to the deniers." Fiona dabbed her mouth with her napkin. "On another note, any news from the cops yet?"

"No, I called this morning and they've still had no luck finding the kidnappers."

"Well, with flights about to start up again, those thugs are probably sitting at the gate as we speak," said Fiona. "But I should think the police have that avenue covered."

"Yes, but they could have left on a ship, obviously an option, not just airplanes," said Zakia, playing fitfully with her hair.

"You're going to be fine. Relax."

Zakia needed to throw herself into her work; that was her standard approach to these recurring jitters. Having a lot of free time did not help her. She finished the last bite of her quiche, drank her iced tea and got up from their table, "Right then, I will go by the grocery store to buy the ingredients for our dinner. And then I'll head to the hotel to start cooking."

"Wonderful," said Fiona. "I'll probably stop by my usual café to work a little and enjoy my last teatime in these parts. Then I'll be back at our suite directly."

"I wish I could join you, but I need to get on with the cooking," said Zakia.

"Okay, see you later," said Fiona.

They hugged each other and Zakia hurried out the door.

****

Precisely at seven p.m., the Larsens knocked on the door. Fiona welcomed them in.

"Here we are," said Ellen. "At least we didn't have to worry about traffic, no congestion on the elevators. How are you two doing?"

"Fine," said Fiona. "Zakia is much better today. Would you like some dry sherry to start with?"

"That would be nice," said Ellen.

"Wonderful, thank you," said David.

They sat down in the living room area where Zakia joined them. Fiona handed out glasses of sherry. "Sorry I didn't find any sherry glasses, just these water glasses," she said. "But at least we don't have to use the plastic cups from the bathroom."

David took his glass and offered a toast. "To Zakia," he said. "For fighting climate change and criminal elements, surviving a kidnapping, and making

288

dinner."

"Skál," they all said, clinking their glasses.

David sipped his sherry. "I'm glad we got together for a last time. After you left yesterday, Ellen and I have been talking some more about climate change and I did a bit of research too," he said. "We now realize that I have an obligation to the pension fund investors not to have them end up with stranded assets. Renewables are a viable alternative. It turns out electric car companies and renewable energy producers are turning a sizeable profit these days."

Zakia grinned. "Glad to hear it. I'd like to interview you sometime to see what you come up with." She walked over to the kitchenette to check on the food. The couscous and vegetables were tender and the lamb roast was medium rare.

"On that hopeful note, let's eat, shall we," she called.

"What a good idea," said David.

They settled around the table while Zakia brought in the dishes. She set the regular couscous between David and Ellen.

"Oh, what's this?" asked Ellen.

"It's couscous with lamb," said Zakia. "Fiona gets the gluten free couscous." With much fanfare, she set the gluten-free dish next to Fiona.

"Oh, that's wonderful," said Fiona. "I thought I'd be relegated to eating just meat and vegetables."

"I bought some gluten-free couscous in Rabat before I left," said Zakia. "Bon Appetite!"

Everyone dug into their food, complimenting Zakia on her cooking.

"This has been the strangest trip I have ever taken,"

said Ellen. "We were just stopping here on the way to Norway. I've done it several times earlier, visiting my cousins in Stavanger. Our daughter went over last year with her husband and their two young children. To get stuck here for several days as we have been, and then meeting you two, has been an amazing experience."

Fiona put down her fork and knife and took a sip of water. She was very quiet and looked pale.

"What's wrong?" asked Zakia "Are you not feeling well?"

"I don't know what's going on," admitted Fiona. "But now I have the worst headache and nausea."

"It's not the couscous, is it?" asked Zakia. "I hope I haven't gotten them mixed up."

"I don't think so. My allergies usually don't affect my digestive system until a couple of hours after the meal."

"Well, what's bothering you?" Zakia wrinkled her brow.

"I don't know. I think I need to lie down." She stood up and gripped the edge of the table. "I'm aching all over and I think I'm going to throw up."

She doubled over and started crying. "My head hurts," she wailed.

David and Zakia helped Fiona to the sofa. Ellen reached for Fiona's half-empty glass of water, offering it to her.

"No, thank you," whispered Fiona.

Zakia bent over Fiona and patted her on the arm, as she squirmed in pain on the sofa. Zakia looked at the Larsens mumbling, "I've never seen Fiona like this before."

"We better call a doctor," said David. He walked

over to the desk, found the hotel info booklet, and flipped through it, looking for the front desk number. "Anyone remember the number for the front desk or the emergency number?"

Ellen, set the glass of water down on the end table. "The emergency number is 1-1-2."

Fiona began shaking. Then she groaned in pain. "Something is very wrong," she said, a tremor in her voice, holding her hand to her forehead. Then her eyelids fluttered and closed. She stopped moving.

"She's passed out," sobbed Zakia, shaking Fiona. "Fiona, stay with us. Wake up."

David looked up from the phone. "It's ringing. Yes, hello we have a woman who is very sick at Hotel Esjafjøll, room 306. Please hurry." He paced a short circle with the phone to his ear. "She just ate some meat, vegetables, and couscous, and is getting sicker by the minute. No, she hasn't vomited. Yes, she's unresponsive." He looked at his watch. "Ten minutes, you say? Make it five!"

Fiona, huddled on the sofa, pale and breathing rapidly. Zakia shook her head repeatedly. "Oh, my God, this is awful!"

It seemed like the longest time before the paramedics came. One of them, an energetic woman, turned to Zakia and asked her if Fiona had a history of seizures, heart disease, or stroke? They started an IV and whisked Fiona onto a stretcher, barely squeezing it into the elevator. The Larsens ran down the stairs, with Zakia, her head throbbing again, following at a slower pace. All three of them stood outside as Fiona was loaded into the ambulance. "I'm riding with her," said Zakia, looking sharply at one of the paramedics, who shrugged.

The ambulance took off into the night, its sirens blaring. Zakia took Fiona's hand and squeezed it. Her hand was limp.

****

At the hospital, Fiona was lowered from the ambulance and Zakia was told to go sit in the waiting room. It was the same room she'd been in just a day earlier. She touched her forehead; it felt like the bump was almost gone. After a few moments, the Larsens showed up, looking worried. "How is she?" asked Ellen.

"Still not responsive," said Zakia.

They sat in the waiting room, each in their own thoughts. After a few minutes, Zakia said, "This place smells so sterile. It's so unpleasant."

"I agree," said Ellen. "I'll see if I can find some coffee," she added, and left.

Zakia paced up and down the room, trying to collect her thoughts. Fiona had been so violently ill that Zakia's own stomach convulsed. She and Fiona had been through so much together. She couldn't even think of what might happen next.

Two hours later a doctor walked into the waiting room, looking very serious. "Are you Fiona McPherson's family?"

"We are her friends," said Zakia as she stood up.

"Well, we need to contact her family," said the doctor. "Do you have that information?"

"Her spouse, Jack Thompson, works in Colorado and she has a brother in Edinburgh," said Zakia, embarrassed that she hadn't thought to call Jack earlier. She rummaged through her purse. "I have Jack's mobile number." Zakia pulled out a planner from her purse and dictated the number as the doctor wrote it down on his clipboard file.

"How is she?" asked Zakia.

"We are doing all we can, but she is deteriorating fast." He hesitated and gave Zakia a curious look. "The symptoms don't add up. They are consistent with poisoning, but she's also losing some hair. It's very peculiar, but we need to run more tests. Did she say anything to you about having cancer or any other illness?"

"What do you mean?" cried Zakia. "She's always been in good health. And how could she be poisoned?"

The doctor looked baffled. "Well, we need to think of all the possibilities."

"Can we see her?" asked Zakia. "Is she awake?"

"No, I'm afraid she's in no condition to receive visitors."

"Well, can I just peek in on her at least?" Her voice was shrill.

Ellen stepped between Zakia and the doctor. "It's okay, Zakia. Let's sit down for a minute. Let the doctors do their job."

Zakia mechanically sat down on the sofa.

David came over and put an arm around Zakia, "I think we need to go back to the hotel and get some rest."

Zakia shook her head. "I'm staying right here, thank you."

Ellen sat beside her while David had a hushed conversation with the doctor. Then he came over and stood before Zakia and Ellen. "Ellen and I can go get something to eat. Do you want us to get you some dinner?"

Zakia sniffed. For a fleeting moment, she thought about the lovely dinner she had worked hard to prepare. She shook her head. "I'm not hungry, but thank you."

Ellen got up from the sofa and whispered to David. Then she turned to Zakia. "We have decided to stay on in Iceland for a few more days, until we know more about Fiona."

Tears welled up in her eyes as Zakia said, "Thank you very much. I'm calling Jack right now and I'm sure he'll be here soon. But I appreciate the company," said Zakia. "I'm so glad we met."

"Then we'll head back to the hotel for the night," said David. "Get some sleep. We'll be back tomorrow." They both gave her a hug and left.

Zakia tapped in Jack's number on her cell. He answered right away.

"Zakia, the hospital just called me," he said. "What's going on?"

"Fiona is very sick. I cooked dinner in Fiona's suite for an American couple we befriended at our hotel. I made a separate couscous dish for Fiona. Just minutes into the dinner, she got very ill; said she felt nauseated, had a splitting headache, and ached all over. Now she has deteriorated to the point where the doctors are worried and they think she might have been poisoned. They're running tests. "I'm so sorry," she said. "I hope it wasn't my cooking. I bought the gluten free couscous in Morocco, but the box hadn't been tampered with."

"Now calm down," he said. "I'll take the first flight out of Denver tomorrow. I'll be there early Monday morning."

"I wish you were here already. I'm still in a daze. I hope the tests will tell us something."

After they hung up, she called Benjamin. It was early evening in Chicago and she'd caught him making dinner with the boys. She told him what had happened to Fiona. "I'm so sorry, Zakia," he said. "I hope she recovers real soon."

Listening to Dani and Harris talking in the background, she said, "I can't wait to join you guys."

"Well, it sounds like you'll be in Reykjavik a little longer," said Benjamin, "But I understand you have to be there with your friend. And, we're fine here."

She talked with Dani and Harris for a few minutes about their summer activities. They had already made friends in the neighborhood and seemed to be adjusting. They had even found a Jiu Jitsu school.

"But I miss you, Maman," said Harris. "When will you be here?"

"It will just be a few more days, I miss you too."

After she hung up, Zakia thumbed through some old magazines that she couldn't read—Icelandic was not something she'd learned at school. She tried to make herself comfortable on the sofa, but she dozed fitfully all night, waiting for the nurses to give her an update on Fiona's condition. They had placed her friend in isolation, as a precaution, until the tests came back. The nurses indicated that she could have a long wait.

****

The next day stretched forever. The doctors told her the lab reports came back negative for any viruses, or rat poison, or any of the other poison that could have been used. But Fiona was still unconscious. They questioned Zakia about what Fiona had been doing and eating, and her health in general. They could not explain what was wrong with her. Her hair had started to fall out in large clumps. She was having problems breathing. They sent blood and urine samples to London to a forensic lab they used for the difficult cases.

The Larsens showed up in the evening with Chinese food. They tried to coax Zakia back to the hotel to sleep, but she refused again. She wanted to be there for Fiona.

She made herself as comfortable as she could for a second night in the waiting room and drifted off.

****

The next morning, Zakia was awakened by a touch on her arm. It was Jack.

"Jack?" she said in a sleepy voice. "You got here early. What time is it?"

She sat up, disoriented. She had dreamed that she was running in Central Park in New York City, looking for Fiona, and all the women had no hair. Now, here was Jack, looking at her with a sad face. Then she remembered that she was camped out in the waiting room at the hospital in Reykjavik.

"It's not so early. Here drink this," he said, handing her a cup of coffee. "It's nearly eight o'clock."

"Thank you." Zakia took a sip of the coffee.

Jack was red-eyed, as though he'd been crying, and was hung over with jet lag.

"I'm so sorry, Jack."

Zakia put the cup down and they hugged for a long while.

"Did they let you see her?" she asked.

Jack ran his hand through his hair. "For a little bit,"

he said. "She looks terrible. She's lost a lot of hair and looks so frail, hooked up to all those machines. I had to wear a gown, mask and gloves, since she's in an isolation ward."

"Did the doctors give you an update?"

"Yes, they still haven't figured it out," he said, biting his lip. "They said her kidneys, spleen, and liver are damaged and she can barely breathe on her own."

Zakia sighed and took his hand. "This is surreal."

Jack, sniffled. "I can't believe it. I just talked to her three days ago. She said she was unusually tired, but looking forward to coming home after a quick stopover in London."

Zakia didn't say anything.

He shook his head. "Can you tell me what happened right before she got ill? I'm confused by all of that."

Zakia related the events of the day leading up to the dinner. Jack listened with a fixed gaze, and then rubbed his eyes. "Look, I'm not taking this in yet. I think I'll just find something to eat. I'll be right back."

After he left, Zakia wandered to the hallway outside the isolation unit. The nurse at the desk gave her a stern look, but told her she could go in for a few minutes. Then she helped Zakia put on the gown.

Zakia sat by the bed and took Fiona's hand, which felt cold even through the gloves. Fiona drifted in and out of consciousness, muttering to herself. She did not look like the vivacious woman who had picked Zakia up at the airport barely a week ago. *How could this be happening?*

At one point, Fiona woke up and looked at her. "Oh, there you are, Zakia. I'm sorry, but I don't feel well."

Then she started to vomit and a nurse came running and shooed Zakia out of the room. By the time she returned, Fiona was already asleep again. Then the doctor came in and said he wanted to speak with Jack. Zakia asked him what was going on, but he said he needed to talk to her next of kin. Then he left.

Jack returned to the isolation ward fifteen minutes later. His face looked even more haggard with the mask on. "How is she doing?" he asked Zakia.

"The doctor said he wanted to speak to you." Zakia looked at the wall clock. "I'm sure he'll be back shortly."

"Good," said Jack. He gestured to the chair. "Do you mind? I'd like to sit with her now. "

"No, not at all. I'll be in the waiting room if you need me."

Jack settled into the chair and held Fiona's hand. Zakia paused in the doorway, watching long enough to see Fiona wake up and cry, "Jack!" Then Fiona started weeping, "What's happening to me?"

Jack leaned over her on the bed, holding her hand. "Shh, I'm here," he said. "It's going to be all right."

Zakia hoped he was right.

Zakia and Jack took turns sitting at Fiona's bedside. Between bouts of vomiting, Fiona slept most of the time. She wasn't able to eat. She barely tolerated the IVs and painkillers. A slew of doctors rotated in and out of her room, concerned about the test results that were expected back from London.

The evening passed in slow motion. Zakia barely touched the food Jack had brought her from the cafeteria and spent only a few moments on Skype updating Benjamin. The Larsens came by and met Jack. Ellen brought Zakia a change of clothes. Everyone was somber and distracted. They rolled a cot into Fiona's room for Jack, and Zakia slept in the waiting room for a third night. The nurses by this point had brought her blankets and a pillow.

The next morning the hospital was already quite busy when she woke up. She folded her blanket, put her pillow on top of it and walked to Fiona's room just as the doctor walked out.

"Any news, doctor?"

He nodded to the room. "You'll need to talk to Jack," he said. "We've still to receive the results from London. Due to budget cuts, there seems to be a bottleneck. But we should hear back very soon."

"Thank you," said Zakia. Gowning up, she walked into the room and saw Jack, hunched over in the chair, sobbing. Fiona lay in bed, asleep, breathing in ragged, erratic bursts now.

She put her arm on his shoulder. "Jack, what happened?"

He sat up. "Can we go out in the hallway?" he said. They both removed their protective gear.

They walked down the hallway together. Zakia asked, "Has she been awake this morning?"

"No," said Jack. "Not at all."

In the waiting room, Jack stood by the window.

"You know, Fiona's been my life." He looked at Zakia with an unfocused daze. "The doctor just confirmed that she's dying. Her organs are shutting down."

"Dying? That's not possible. She's going to get better," said Zakia. "Do they know which poison it is?"

Jack shook his head. "I heard mention of radiation poisoning because of the hair loss, but I don't think they are certain."

Zakia felt dizzy and sat down.

Jack turned away. "I want to get back to Fiona," he said and walked back to her room.

Zakia stayed in the waiting room, blinking back tears. Fiona had been given a death sentence and it seemed that the doctors were still not sure of the cause. The next few hours, Zakia took turns with Jack at Fiona's bedside, but he refused food or water.

All that day, Zakia hoped Fiona would wake up by some miracle. Jack asked her to call the one Catholic priest in town to come in and administer the last rites, even though Fiona was a lapsed Catholic. He also asked her to call Fiona's brother in Edinburg. Zakia's call was greeted by an answering machine. She left a brief message.

The priest came and went and the hospital buzzed all around her, but she didn't notice. That night, she settled again into her less than luxurious accommodations in the waiting room, though, to be truthful, she no longer saw it as a hardship. The Larsens were kind enough to bring her computer, so she researched poisons, keeping in mind Fiona's symptoms. There had to be something, but the only symptoms that matched were the result of such farfetched poisons, they'd be out of the question.

****

The next morning, a nurse woke her, with a soft touch on the arm. "Fiona died in her sleep during the night." Zakia shook her head and started weeping.

"It was a merciful death," said the nurse. "She

could have been in agony for weeks."

The nurse looked at Zakia with compassion. "Do you need anything?

Zakia, sniffling, look up at the nurse. "No, thank you."

The nurse left and Zakia sat on the sofa, blew her nose and stared at the ceiling. This wasn't right; Fiona was young and perfectly healthy. She wiped her eyes and tried to compose herself. As she walked to Fiona's room, she could hear Jack crying.

Chapter Twenty-Seven

Zakia felt numb. Fiona looked so peaceful—no more suffering. Zakia offered her condolences and left Jack to sit with Fiona's body. She would call Fiona's family to give them the news. Fiona's brother was already en route.

She went back to the hotel for a shower, and then went to the lobby and found they were still serving breakfast in the dining area. She wasn't hungry, but knew she needed to eat. There was no line at the buffet. Most of the tourists had left once the airport had re-opened.

The Larsens found her crying over her crepes.

Zakia looked up from her plate. "She passed away in her sleep last night," said Zakia, blowing her nose. "I can't believe she's gone."

"Oh, no," said Ellen, "I am so sorry," she said, giving Zakia a hug.

"We were going to the hospital this morning. No point now. How terribly sad," said David.

"The doctor said she was lucky the illness didn't drag on for many weeks with excruciating pain as it could have done."

"Is there anything we can do?" asked Ellen.

Zakia shook her head. "I don't think so," she said. "Jack is still there and I hope to connect with his family. Will you join me for breakfast?"

Ellen and David helped themselves at the buffet and returned to Zakia's table. All three ate in silence. Zakia had just given up on her crepes when she saw two police officers walk into the dining room. They made their way straight to her table, frowning.

"What's going on now?" muttered Ellen.

Zakia hoped that the police had news about Fiona's death. But she didn't recognize these two police officers.

"Are you Zakia Karim?" asked the female officer.

"I am," she said.

"We understand that you were Fiona's McPherson's friend," she said. "I'm Detective Boghildur."

"I'm glad you're here," said Zakia. "Fiona was healthy three-four days ago and then all of a sudden..." She couldn't speak for a moment.

The police officers looked at each other. "That's what we want to talk to you about. We'd like you to come with us to the police station and answer a few questions."

"I am happy to help," said Zakia.

Zakia stood up and so did David. "I'm David Larsen, this is my wife, Ellen," he said. "We knew Fiona, too, and we were there the night she got sick."

"Yes, we'd also like a word with you two," said Boghildur. She turned to Zakia and said, "Why don't you ride with us?"

****

At the police station, Zakia followed Boghildur to a room down a hall, where they took their seats across a wooden table.

"Zakia, I know you are rattled and confused, but

we need to know what happened. Given the symptoms described by the doctor, we are considering food poisoning as a cause of death," said Boghildur.

She could barely focus on the officer's words. "The doctor mentioned poison, but they weren't sure what was wrong with Fiona," said Zakia.

"Yes, but her illness may have been induced by food poisoning," said Boghildur.

"Food poisoning? Like Salmonella? I cooked the lamb thoroughly."

Boghildur raised her eyebrows. "I'm sorry, I misspoke. My English isn't so good. I meant that her food was poisoned."

"You mean murder?" asked Zakia, her heart sinking. She had thought so, but hearing the officer voice it out loud made the possibility even more real.

"Yes, that's right. We checked with the hotel, they threw out the food that was left on the dinner table, so that evidence is gone."

The officer stared at her, as if waiting for Zakia to volunteer some vital information. Zakia said nothing, and Boghildur said, "Do you know what might have poisoned your friend?"

"I have been wondering about that, but no, I have no idea," said Zakia with a sigh.

"How was your relationship with her," said the officer. "Were you fighting? Were you jealous of her— a famous climatologist?"

Zakia drew a quick breath, "Are you implying that I had something to do with her death?"

The officer looked at her unperturbed. "We have to check out all the possibilities. You flew to Iceland, after not having seen Dr. McPherson in three years. You've been talking and texting on the phone with her. What can you tell us about this?"

"You took Fiona's phone and you've been investigating me?" asked Zakia, feeling nauseated. "Wait a minute, am I under arrest?"

"At this point we are only asking you for a statement. You are considered a person of interest, that's all. You have a right to a lawyer, but most people don't ask for a lawyer unless they are charged with something."

Zakia sat for a moment, her bottom lip trembling.

Boghildur toyed with her pen, "Let's run through the whole incident from top to bottom the night Fiona got sick, shall we."

"Okay," said Zakia and took a deep breath, "Fiona and I invited the Larsens to join us for dinner at our suite. I made couscous and lamb for everyone, but a separate portion of gluten free couscous for my friend, Fiona, because she is, I mean, *was* gluten intolerant. I had brought it from Morocco. I have an extra box of couscous in my suitcase I can give you, if it can be of any help."

After sending a text, the detective said, "That is useful. My officers are going through your room right now."

"Was the dish in the suite the whole time?" asked Boghildur as she took notes.

"Where else would it be if I cooked it and we had dinner in the suite?" said Zakia.

Boghildur gave her a sharp look. "Was Fiona sick before dinner?"

"No, she was in excellent health. She never gets sick and exercises three-four times a week, at least. I mean exercis*ed*. Oh I can't believe it," said Zakia, choking up. "Excuse me," she said and drew a tissue from her bag to wipe her tears.

"Well, you must try to think if you can recall any additional information that might shed some more light on this case. All we have so far is that you gave Fiona a separate dish of couscous which no one else ate and, within four days of your meal, Fiona McPherson is dead."

Zakia stared at the officer. Her head started buzzing. Her eyes wandered to the window. The seaside looked inviting, in contrast to the tension-filled room.

"The tests sent to London are expected in very soon. Hopefully, that will shed some more light on the case," said the detective.

Zakia brought her hand to her chin. "Why haven't you found the men who kidnapped me nearly a week ago? Might they have something to do with this?"

Boghildur looked up from her computer. "We are still working on that case, but I don't see a connection at this time." Boghildur closed her computer. "Okay, we are done for now. You may go, but we will need your passport and want you to stay in Iceland for the next few days."

Zakia felt uneasy about handing over her passport. "My passport? Is that necessary?"

"It's just a formality."

Zakia pulled her Moroccan passport out of her purse, hesitated, and handed it to the policewoman.

Boghildur looked at it and stuck it in her folder. "We'll be in touch," she said, getting up from her chair.

"Am I free to go now?"

"Anywhere in Iceland," said Boghildur.

****

Zakia met the Larsens outside the police station. "Thanks for waiting. Let's talk when we get back to the hotel." She blinked in the bright sunlight. Fiona would have been glad to see that the ash cloud was gone. Once in the lobby, Zakia invited the Larsens to her suite. Zakia couldn't face going alone to the room she'd been sharing with Fiona.

When they got to the suite, Zakia was going to offer them a glass of sherry, but found that the cops had removed the bottle.

Ellen settled down on the sofa. "It seems the police think you're a suspect," she said with a curt tone. "How could they?"

"It's probably routine procedure. To be more accurate, they used the words 'person of interest.'" With little sleep the last few days, Zakia was ready to drop. She went into the kitchenette and poured three glasses of water. "What did they ask you about Fiona and me?"

"They asked us all about you. Whether you and Fiona had been fighting. How long you had known each other and so forth." Ellen paused. "And whether you were a couple."

"What?" asked Zakia. "I'm married. So was she."

Ellen shook her head. "That's no problem in this day and age."

"It is, where I come from," said Zakia, shaking her head.

David chuckled, "Enough of that. We told them in all honesty that we had only just met. We said our conversations had focused a lot on climate change, investments, and the oil and gas industry. We said we did not see you and Fiona arguing."

"I appreciate that."

"And we told them your dinner was delicious," added David, smiling.

"Thank you," said Zakia with a slight grin. She remembered she hadn't told Boghildur about the assassination attempt on the Pope and that Fiona had worried she might be a target, as one of his advisors. When she was feeling less rattled, she'd ring the station and inform the detective.

"We do believe you're innocent," said Ellen.

"I appreciate that," said Zakia. She wished she could take a nap, but she wasn't sure she could sleep.

"However, we did mention that you had run into problems investigating the death of a nomadic Berber in a fracking blowout in Morocco." said David. "The Icelandic police seem kind of naïve, if you ask me."

"Yes, well, I'm beginning to understand that this is much bigger than I thought. There are huge sums of money at stake," said Zakia. "I seem to have stuck my hand in a beehive. Or maybe my head, more like it."

"In certain countries, I guess that can lead to people being eliminated," said David.

"You've been watching too many movies," said Ellen.

"It's hard to tell," said Zakia. "I'd be devastated if Fiona was killed to warn me off. But she was also an advisor for the Pope's encyclical, so she may have been a target because of that."

"I didn't know she had connections to the Pope," said David. "Oh, I remember now; I read about an assassination attempt a few days ago. Could this be related?"

"Might well have been," said Zakia. "She was deeply involved as one of his main advisors."

"This all sounds terrifying," said Ellen.

"I am going to see if I can get some leads on what might have happened," said Zakia. "I'm sure the police are just doing their job, but I hope they will fill us in."

The three of them sat there in silence for a moment before Ellen slapped her knee and stood up. "Who's hungry?" she said. "It's almost dinnertime."

"I'm not hungry, but I guess I should eat something," said Zakia.

They were about to leave when someone knocked on the door.

Chapter Twenty-Eight

Jack stood at the door with a pained stare.

Zakia invited him in and David and Ellen offered him their condolences. They talked about Fiona for a few minutes, and then Ellen said, "Let us know how we can help. We're just going for an early dinner, if you'd like to join us."

Jack shook his head. "I'm going to try and get some sleep." Turning to Zakia he said, "Do you have a moment?"

"I'll pass on dinner," Zakia to the Larsens. "I'll just order room service."

"Oh, that's too bad. We have already booked our flight back to Minneapolis for tomorrow," said Ellen. "We both have to get back to work. So this is goodbye then, I guess."

"I understand," said Zakia. "I'll miss you two. Thanks for all your help. I'll keep you posted."

"Thank you." Ellen gave her a tight hug.

"I also have to thank you," said David. "For everything." He gave Zakia a hug and a kiss on the cheek and he and Ellen left.

Jack settled down on the sofa. Zakia took the dirty glasses to the sink.

"Thank you so much, Zakia, for staying on," said Jack. "Oh, I meant to tell you earlier, you can just stay here in the suite. I've already arranged for another

310

room." He asked Zakia if she'd had a chance to contact any of Fiona's relatives.

"No, I've been at the police station."

"The police station?" He grimaced.

"We were all three at the police station, being questioned."

"What on earth for?"

"The police think Fiona was murdered."

"My Fiona, murdered?" Jack jerked back on the sofa.

Zakia walked over to him and touched him on the shoulder. "I'm so sorry," she said softly. "And you should know that I'm considered a person of interest."

Jack rubbed his neck. "That's outrageous. That's the most ridiculous thing I've ever heard."

"I'm glad you see it that way."

He took Zakia's hand and looked up at her. "I think you should get a lawyer—the sooner, the better."

"Why do I need a lawyer? Wouldn't that make me look more suspicious?

"It just makes sense. I can talk to somebody at the American Embassy to get a recommendation."

They spoke a while longer and then made plans to connect with a lawyer the next day, as Zakia became more and more afraid of her own situation as a person of interest. Finally, Jack excused himself to get some sleep.

****

After Jack left, Zakia realized that she was tired and hungry. She ordered the shellfish soup from the room service menu. She missed Benjamin and their boys now, more than ever. She hadn't spoken to Benjamin since Fiona had died. She tried to straighten up the suite a little bit, but the sight of Fiona's personal belongings brought tears to her eyes. No wonder Jack had gotten another room. She would help him pack Fiona's things in the morning.

Her soup arrived, and she sat at the dining table with her computer and got on Skype. Benjamin answered right away. It was early afternoon in Chicago.

"Zakia, I've been thinking about you. How is Fiona?"

Zakia started sobbing. "Benjamin, I have terrible news. Fiona died in her sleep last night."

"Oh no."

"The police suspect she was murdered."

"Murdered?"

"Yes, they think she was poisoned, though they haven't any proof yet."

Benjamin sucked in his breath. "There's been so much commotion lately. Are you in danger? I think you should come home now."

"I can't." She cried harder. "They took my passport."

"What! Why?"

"Because I'm a person of interest. I cooked the meal the night Fiona became ill, including gluten free couscous for her that no one else ate. They think I had something to do with it."

"So you are a suspect in a murder case," Benjamin's voice was shaky.

"Not quite. A person of interest is not a suspect— yet." Zakia wiped her eyes.

"Now what happens?"

"I'm sure that once they get done with their investigation, they will give me my passport back."

"Okay, let's look at the bright side; you haven't been arrested, so that's good, I guess. Had you been arrested for murder in Morocco, you'd be in real trouble. As far as I know, Iceland has a legal system that actually works."

"Jack said I should get a lawyer. He'll check into it tomorrow."

"He's right. How's he holding up?"

"Pretty distraught."

They fell silent for a while. Zakia wished he was with her.

"Remember you are strong, Zakia, and you will get through this!" Benjamin held his eyes fixed on hers.

"I hope so, Benjamin, I really hope so. Kiss the boys for me. Love you!"

After they hung up, Zakia sat for a moment, fatigue washing over her. If the police thought Fiona was murdered, she needed to find the killer. Especially, since she was—as Benjamin pointed out—almost a suspect.

"Okay, let's think straight now," she said out loud. Zakia spent the next hour going through her list of contacts, e-mailing colleagues and sources all over the world for help. "What do you know about a poison that causes symptoms of radiation poisoning? What kind of poison can go undetected?"

She took a long shot and Tweeted out her questions and posted them on Facebook. People would wonder what she was investigating now, but she didn't care. She wanted results. Two hours later, Zakia heard a knock on the door. She opened it. It was Jack again. He was wearing pajamas and a robe, and looked pale and drawn.

"I'm sorry to bother you. I can't sleep. I thought I'd get some company because I'm going nuts."

She invited him in. "I was just about to make tea. Would you like some?" Zakia's voice was monotone.

"Yes, please. That would be nice."

Zakia busied herself boiling the water, being careful to remove the zip lock bag with the flash drives, and then she set out the cups. At the same time, she kept checking on Jack, who was sitting slumped on the sofa, staring at the ceiling.

"I was trying to think who would want to kill Fiona," said Zakia.

"She was a climatologist, after all, and they've been harassed and threatened in the last few years, but murder—that's never happened before, to my knowledge."

"So, you really think it was related to climate change? I mean related to the assassination attempt on the Pope?"

"We may have gotten to that point, sadly. Fiona ruffled a lot of feathers and she was moving in powerful circles. I worried about her a lot."

"But murdering a climatologist? What would that achieve?"

"Those with interests in not addressing climate change are trying to get them so frightened that they'll stop their research on climate science and focus on other areas of science."

"I guess I have read something about the threats." Zakia brought the tea to the coffee table and started pouring. "Sugar?"

"Just plain." He took his cup. "There's this climate change professor I met once who experienced the whole gambit, from Climategate to attempts at muzzling his academic freedom. He has also had death threats."

"Do you think the same people could have killed Fiona?" Zakia sat down next to him on the sofa.

Jack looked tired. "I could contact him. We haven't been in touch lately, but I know he received white powder in the mail. It wasn't anthrax, thank heavens. He's a decent fellow, just doing his job. It's outrageous."

"Would you share this with the police?"

"Of course. Now that you mention it, when I got to my room after my previous visit, I had a phone call from the detective in charge, asking to meet with me tomorrow. She didn't go into any details though. After our conversation earlier, I thought it was just routine procedure."

"I wonder what that's about." asked Zakia. "You weren't even here when she got ill, so what can you add to the story?"

"It's probably just background information they want. I was just thinking back to when Fiona and I first met. It was on Pearl Street in Boulder. You remember—the charming pedestrian street?"

"Yes, I remember. It's pretty small, but a delightful place for a stroll."

"I just can't believe that Fiona is gone, forever," Jack was not able to stop the tears rolling down his cheeks. Zakia placed her hand on his. He cried, but this time, he tried to muffle it.

"Can I help you with the funeral arrangements?" asked Zakia.

"Yes, please." Jack sat there for a moment, with a slack expression. "I wouldn't mind if you accompany me to the funeral home. Fiona and I agreed we would both be buried in her family plot in Scotland, so there'll just be a memorial here."

"Of course."

Jack got up to leave.

See you tomorrow, then," said Zakia.

"Hopefully, I will fall asleep this time. Thank you for the tea."

"You're welcome."

She walked him to the door, opened it, and there stood Detective Boghildur, with another police officer.

Jack looked at them. "It's almost midnight. What's going on?" he asked in a loud voice.

"This doesn't concern you," Boghildur answered. She looked at Zakia and said, "Zakia Karim, you are under arrest."

"What?" cried Jack.

Zakia gasped for breath. She was so stunned she could hardly speak. "I was just at your office earlier today and answered all your questions." Her throat tightened.

"You are charged with the murder of Fiona McPherson. You have the right to remain silent, anything you say, can and will be used against you. Furthermore, you have the right to a lawyer. We will also contact the consulate for you."

Jack put his arm around Zakia. "I'm Fiona's husband and I demand an explanation. Zakia is like family to me."

Boghildur looked at Jack with interest. "We are so sorry for the loss of your wife and we appreciate your cooperation in our investigation. But, we have grounds to arrest Zakia."

Jack looked red in the face. "Now just a second, what are you saying?"

"The tests results finally came back. Your wife was indeed murdered. We will go into the details at the station."

Other hotel guests, in their pajamas, had come out into the hallway to see what all the commotion was about. Jack folded his arms and Zakia said softly, "I'll cooperate with the police, Jack. I'm innocent and I'm confident they will get to the bottom of this."

Boghildur nodded in approval. "Please follow me. We won't cuff you if you cooperate."

"Can I get my purse?"

"Yes," said Boghildur. "But make it quick."

Zakia hurried into her bedroom, found her purse and stuffed her phone and laptop in it. Then she gave Jack a hug, and followed Boghildur down the hall. The other police officer walked behind her.

"I'll be in touch real soon," called Jack after her.

Chapter Twenty-Nine

On the drive to the police station, Zakia's mind raced. How could they think she would have murdered her friend and mentor? And who had actually killed her. Zakia still hadn't told the Icelandic police about Fiona's involvement with the Pope.

As they entered the police station, she bumped into a man walking out. He mumbled something she thought sounded Icelandic, turning to give her an apologetic look. He recognized her. And smirked.

Zakia suppressed a gasp. It was Halgrim from Oddleifur Oil.

Before she could collect her wits to say anything, he'd walked off.

"Come on," said Boghildur. "We've got a meeting to attend."

Zakia, shaken by the sight of Halgrim, was led into an interrogation room and asked to sit across the table from Boghildur. "Your lawyer will be here soon," she said as she flipped through the files stacked up on the table.

"You're making a big mistake. I did not kill Fiona," said Zakia.

"We're just following procedure."

An officer came in, carrying a slim file and handed it to Boghildur. She opened it and started reading. The officer turned to Zakia and asked if she wanted a glass of water.

"Yes, please," said Zakia with a quaking voice.

Zakia slumped in her chair. The officer brought her a glass of water and she took a sip.

"Thank you."

Twenty minutes later, a woman wearing a dark suit walked in and shook Zakia's hand. "My name is Ida Oskarsdottir and I will be your lawyer. I was sent by the American Embassy, courtesy of Jack Thompson. He gave me a quick rundown on what happened."

Even though it was after midnight, the woman looked sharp and focused.

"Please thank Jack for me. I can't believe this."

"Will do," said Ida, pulling documents out of her briefcase. "Let's see what we can do."

Boghildur looked up from her files. "Thanks for joining us at such a late hour, Ida."

"No problem." Ida settled into the chair next to Zakia's. "What do we have here?"

"Your client is charged in the murder of Fiona McPherson, a Scottish climatologist who was doing research at Reykjavík University."

"On what grounds?"

"The poison that killed Fiona was sent to a lab in London. The forensic experts there determined the poison to be polonium-210, a rare poison. It's almost impossible to detect in humans. Ingesting it has only one outcome—death. There are no antidotes. It is only available on the black market in certain Eastern European countries and Russia."

Zakia was speechless. She had read about the polonium poisoning of a Russian spy that had defected to the UK, but had dismissed that poison in Fiona's case because it was, indeed, too hard to obtain.

"What does that have to do with my client?"

"She prepared the dish which only Fiona ate the night she became ill and died four days later."

"Have you any proof of that?" asked Ida.

"Not exactly, the food was disposed of before it could be tested. However, we have just been informed that Zakia has a criminal record for terrorist activities in Morocco."

Ida looked at Boghildur with surprise, and then turned to Zakia. "Well now, that paints a different picture. Could I have a few moments alone with my client?"

"Certainly," said Boghildur. She left the room.

Zakia explained, "I was arrested in Morocco, but it's not what you think." Zakia flushed, "I was never convicted of having ties to terrorists. That was misinformation because I was investigating a story and may have trespassed on private property."

Ida sighed. "Yes, I've heard of people being framed in those parts of the world. It's unfortunate. I think we can address that issue. However, I think there may be some loose ends here in Iceland. The question is where did the police get that information?"

"Oh, jeez," said Zakia. "I saw Halgrim Thorsson, leaving this place as I was brought in."

"What does he have to do with Morocco?" asked Ida, frowning.

"Oddleifur has a subsidiary in Morocco and I have been investigating a story about corruption and murder carried out by that company."

"It sounds like you have made some enemies along the way."

"It seems that way." Zakia laid out all she had experienced since the blowout, while Ida took notes.

After she finished, Zakia threw her hands in the air. "What evidence do they have against me in Fiona's murder case?"

"No one knows much except that you are a suspect in a murder case because you cooked the food that may have contained the poison that killed Fiona. Coupled with terrorist activities, it doesn't look good, but I'm still optimistic," said Ida, fixing Zakia with a reassuring smile that looked practiced.

"Tomorrow, I mean, this morning," said Ida, "we will go to the lower court, which is right next door, for the arraignment, where you will be formally advised of the charges, and you'll be asked to enter a plea to the charges. The court will then decide whether you will be released pending the trial," she said.

Zakia made a noise of protest and Ida held up her hand. "You will be questioned by the judge. Just stick to the facts. Don't volunteer anything. The judge will then ask what you plead—'guilty' or 'not guilty' and you'll say 'not guilty'. Is that understood?"

"Yes," said Zakia, her chin fell to her chest.

"They will book you now."

"Wait a minute. What about bail?"

"Not if the case involves terrorism."

"That stinks."

"In the meantime, your things will be registered and put in storage," said Ida.

"Can you do me a favor?" asked Zakia.

"That depends," said Ida.

"Please contact my spouse, Benjamin Atkins, let him know that I'm okay. Here's his cellphone number."

Zakia showed Ida her phone. She swallowed a lump in her throat.

"No problem." Ida wrote off the number.

"Thank you. One more thing."

"What's that?"

"Can you bring me my computer, please?"

"As far as I know, you can't have anything in the holding cell, but I'll check and get back to you."

"Thank you."

"You and I will talk more tomorrow," said Ida. "Try to get some sleep."

"I doubt I'll be able to sleep."

An officer led Zakia off. They took her fingerprints and snapped a photo of her. Then she was led to a holding cell with just a bed, a plastic mattress and a toilet.

Zakia was living a nightmare. She curled up on the bare mattress, turned toward the wall, and let the tears flow.

****

The courtroom was modern, yet spartan. The only people there were Zakia, her lawyer, the prosecutor, the bailiff, and the judge. After setting out the case and asking Zakia some questions, the judge looked down at them from her raised bench.

"You have been charged with murder. How do you wish to plead?" asked the judge, looking at Zakia over her glasses.

Zakia turned toward her lawyer and Ida nodded. "Not guilty." Zakia made sure her tone was matter-of-fact.

After taking notes, the judge looked up. "I have decided that because of the issue of terrorist activities and, since you are not a resident in this country, you're a flight risk. Therefore, you will remain in custody until the trial. The court date is set for June 23."

Zakia couldn't believe what she'd just heard. This was Iceland, not Morocco, and she was going to jail for a crime she had not committed. She put her head in her hands and sobbed. The bailiff led her out of the courtroom and Ida followed them.

****

She felt as if she was watching someone else's experience. She squinted her eyes and twisted her neck as if it was sore, wondering about the possibility of not seeing her children again for a long time.

After they left the courtroom, Ida excused herself to make a phone call. Two guards walked Zakia back to the police station and into the interrogation room. Shortly thereafter, Ida joined her.

As Ida took a seat opposite Zakia, she looked at her with a sympathetic smile. "You're holding up pretty well!"

"How can they just put me in jail like this?" Zakia slammed her hand on the table.

"I understand you're upset, but it's a temporary measure, since you've been denied bail; called 'detention on remand.' The police are still investigating the case."

"I hope they figure it out soon because I did not kill my friend."

"I'm sure you didn't." Ida's voice sounded hollow.

"Too bad the judge didn't think so."

Ida stretched and stood up. "Yes, that was unfortunate. I'm sorry we weren't able to get you out of here. Now you will have to be held in custody until the court case comes up. It's in less than two weeks. But at least you will move into nicer quarters at the women's prison.

"Were you able to contact Benjamin?"

"I didn't talk to him, but I left a message. Look, be patient. I'll meet you at the penitentiary in a couple of hours to see that you're settled in. The prison is at Kopavogur, just south of here."

Ida left and an officer walked in. "Come with me, please," he said, nodding to Zakia.

He led her down the hallway to the back entrance, where a van was waiting. "Wait a minute," said Zakia. "Can I have my computer now?"

The police officer shook his head, "No."

"What do you mean—no? It's my livelihood. That's the only tool I have to stay sane under the circumstances."

"The rules are the same for everyone, a mechanic, a banker, or a journalist. However, I will ask at the prison. Perhaps they will allow it since you are in a foreign country and don't speak the language."

"I appreciate that." Zakia clutched at her chest.

****

At the prison, Zakia thought she'd landed on another planet. Moroccan prisons looked nothing like this. In fact, the prison wasn't very different from the hotel she just had been staying at, minus pictures on the walls and no curtains.

After her intake, she was shown around by a tall, thin inmate with blonde hair. She introduced herself as Helga. Zakia's cell had a window with discreet bars, a desk and chair, a bed with sheets and a blanket, plus a sink and toilet. And even a flat screen TV. The door to her room, however, could only be locked from the outside.

Down the hall from her room were the shower facilities and a common room with a kitchenette she would share with eleven other inmates.

"It's amazing," said Zakia.

Helga grinned. "I heard a prison warden visiting from the U.S. say to our prison director that he might as well give the keys to the inmates, since we have so many freedoms and amenities."

Helga started laughing and Zakia was so exhausted that she felt lightheaded, even giddy. She laughed too.

Zakia and Helga sat down on the sofa. Helga turned to her and smiled. "I was convicted for several robberies I committed to support my heroin addiction. Finally, I got caught, but here I'm getting treatment."

Zakia nodded, unsure of what to say.

"Enough talking about me. Zakia, what's your story?"

Too tired to go into details, she gave Helga a shortened version.

"That sounds like a nightmare from the third level of hell," said Helga.

"That's one way of putting it. I've seen a lot of nasty things as a journalist, but nothing compared to this."

Helga nodded.

"So what's the routine here?" asked Zakia.

"We get up, get dressed, and eat breakfast in the cafeteria," said Helga. "The food is, in fact, quite edible. Then we do either kitchen duty or laundry. After that there are courses, such as needlepoint or knitting, computer classes, or you can do your own courses online. Some have studied law here. We have a computer room with limited access to the internet."

"That's good," said Zakia, yearning for her own computer. She wondered what Dani and Harris were doing at that very moment. It had to be early morning in Chicago. Then she realized she'd lost track of what day it was. She needed to keep sharp. Forgetfulness would not help her case.

"Oh, I almost missed the most important part. Visiting hours are from five to seven p.m., starting tomorrow for you."

"That's good news," said Zakia, though she didn't mean it. The only good news would be finding Fiona's killer and getting the hell out of here. "Not likely that I'll get any visitors. My husband is in the United States with our two sons."

Helga looked at her with empathy and then walked her back to her cell. Zakia spent part of the day doing laundry and the rest staring at the ceiling in her cell and wondering who might have killed Fiona. If she'd had her computer, she was sure she could break the case.

Chapter Thirty

The next day, Zakia had just returned to her room from kitchen duty when a guard arrived with her computer. Zakia was so thrilled she hugged the guard. Then she gasped and pulled away. Moroccan women do not hug strange men, or men they know, for that matter, unless they were family. *What's gotten into me?*

The guard was a big fellow and he just smiled.

"I understand that the computer means a lot to you," he said, in a kind voice. "However, this is quite unusual, a big exception to the standard procedure."

"Thank you," said Zakia, "with all my heart. Now I can help find out who really killed my friend."

The guard nodded. "I hope you do. Here's the official spiel. You have been authorized to use your computer with full access to the internet. Here is the username and password." He handed her a strip of paper. "But be discreet. This is a special privilege."

"I will. What a relief. Thank you very much."

Zakia knew that the first thing she needed to do was to contact Benjamin. But what could she tell him? That she was in prison? She dreaded hearing his response.

She paced her room, going over what she would tell him. *Hi Benjamin, they think I murdered Fiona, but don't worry; jail here is pretty nice.*

With a long, low sigh she forced herself to sit down

and sign onto Skype.

When he signed on, Benjamin looked perturbed. "What's going on Zakia? Where are you? I got this strange voicemail from somebody claiming to be your lawyer that said you've been arrested. Is this going to be the new standard? Because..."

Zakia interrupted him. "Absolutely not. Hear me out. I've been formally accused of murdering Fiona. The court date is June 23. That's in ten days."

For once, Benjamin had nothing to say. He just stared at her.

She told him that Fiona had been poisoned with polonium-210 and that the police assumed Zakia was responsible, since she had made Fiona's last meal.

"That doesn't make sense," said Benjamin. "There's no way that making a meal could make you a murderer. There has to be intent."

"That's my point! However, because someone tipped them off about my arrest in Al Tarife, they think I could be a terrorist." she said. "I bumped into Halgrim on the way into the police station. He was heading out. He might have shared that information."

"But you weren't even indicted in that case."

"I know. But I have to stay in detention until the court date. They're worried about the flight risk, since I don't live here and could be a terrorist."

"I'm sorry about that. It's outrageous!"

"I agree. Thank goodness Jack arranged for me to have a lawyer. She left you the voicemail. Her name is Ida Oskarsdottir. She's sharp and very helpful. That's how I got my computer into the prison."

"She sure has her work cut out for her."

"You could say that," said Zakia. "Here at the

prison, in the meantime, they keep us busy with chores and I'm using all my free time chasing leads to figure out how I ended up here in the first place."

"Good, then you have your hands full, too. I thought the legal system in Iceland was better than Morocco's. Now, I'm not so sure, I'm furious—the incompetence!" said Benjamin. "I see no point in my scrambling to get over there right away. Someone has to focus on Dani and Harris. Tahra's out of town for a couple of days."

Zakia wiped her eyes. "I understand. I'm so run down I've hardly had any energy to get angry. But with my computer, finally, I can do what I do best, search for answers, find out what really happened. I'm so sorry about all of this. "

"Me, too." Benjamin stared down at his hands. "But remember, this will be sorted out soon enough. Keep me posted. And remember, as your dad used to say, *chin up*—you'll get through this!"

"Thanks."

They talked for a few more minutes about how Dani and Harris were doing and then signed off.

Zakia sat for a moment with a heavy heart. She was in a mega mess this time. She wasn't sure if Fiona's murder was tied in with Elias's and Tariq's, but she was determined to find out. Three murders in a row could not be coincidental.

She called Jasem on Skype. She told him about Fiona's death and that she herself had been accused of murdering her.

"That's the wildest story I've heard in a long time," said Jasem.

"Yes, well, I'm living the nightmare. But look, this

is my cell," said Zakia. She turned her computer around so he could see her surroundings.

Jasem squinted into the screen. "It doesn't look like jail. It looks more like a cheap hotel room. Does it have room service too?"

"No," Zakia chuckled. "It's a standard jail cell in Iceland."

Looking somber, she said, "On another note, I think the three deaths, Fiona, Elias and Tariq—are related."

He gave her an incredulous stare and then asked, "What's the status of *your* case?"

"Well, we need to find the killer," she said. "Otherwise, I'm going to be in jail for a long time."

"At least, there's no death penalty in Europe," said Jasem.

"Thanks," said Zakia. "That's a comfort."

Zakia asked him if he had any ideas about who might be able to purchase polonium-210 in Eastern Europe or Russia. And was there any connection to Oddleifur Oil?

"That's going to be tricky to establish," he said. "But I'll do some poking around."

After they hung up, she went straight to the Interpol site and spent as much time as she could, skimming over the wanted posters of international criminals, looking for Rostek and Ahmed. She had no luck. She wondered if the Icelandic police had engaged with Interpol in her case. They seemed to have given up on tracking her kidnappers. The police seemed to have all their focus on her now. She could probably thank Halgrim for that.

Frustrated, she took a break to do her chores in the

laundry room. There she found Helga folding towels.

"How's it going Zakia?" asked Helga.

"All right, I'm still trying to get used to the routine here." said Zakia as she moved a load of sheets from the washing machine to the dryer.

"I've been thinking about your story," said Helga. "You mentioned an oil company in Morocco that had ties to Iceland. You were so upset and tired, I hesitated to ask at the time, but was it Oddleifur Oil you were referring to?"

"Yes, that's right. Why do you ask?"

"I met the daughter of an executive at Oddleifur Oil right here in prison last year. She was released six months ago. Her name is Runa Agnarsson."

"Wow!" said Zakia. "That is interesting."

Helga nodded. "She defrauded her family and friends for millions of Icelandic Krona, that's like tens of thousands of dollars.

"How did she do that?" asked Zakia

"She lied to them for years. She claimed that she had cancer and was being treated by a specialist at a clinic in Switzerland."

"How tragic," exclaimed Zakia

"Yes, it was all over the papers here at the time. One of her friends, who happened to be vacationing in Switzerland, wanted to look her up while she was undergoing treatment there. He discovered no such clinic in the town Runa had mentioned. She was actually lapping up the sun on the Riviera," said Helga, moving a stack of towels to a shelf.

"How extraordinary! How long was she in for?" asked Zakia.

"She spent two years in here. Her father visited her

regularly with her little girl, his granddaughter. He forgave her for stealing the money and he's even helping her pay back the debt to the family members and friends."

"Amazing," said Zakia, trying to reconcile the Sigurd she knew with this family figure that Helga was talking about. "It gives a whole other picture of her father, Sigurd Agnarsson. I actually met him in Morocco."

Helga snorted, "Parents! What suckers they are. They are so easily manipulated by their children. I'm glad I don't have any children."

"Poor man," said Zakia, surprised. "I almost feel sorry for him. Yet, it's conceivable that he's involved in my arrest and the killing of six people that I know of, three of them friends of mine. And who knows how many more?"

"That's terrible," said Helga. "I wouldn't have guessed."

Zakia began folding sheets with extra vigor. "He really is an evil man. I guess it's a bit like the Mafia; you love your family members, yet you have no problem burying an enemy alive in a concrete grave."

Helga shook her head, looking thoughtful. "Not the kind of man you want to have as an enemy."

Zakia shivered, even though the laundry room was hot as an oven.

****

That night, Benjamin didn't Skype as he said he would. Zakia sat waiting by the computer, but his icon showed that he was not available. She started worrying that he was upset with her and giving her a message with the silent treatment, but it didn't make sense. He'd sounded more concerned than mad and he'd never gone silent before.

She thought about Skyping with one of her sons, but her stomach was so tied up in knots, she decided not to. *What good would it do to talk to my sons from jail? That would just freak them out.* First, she needed to find out what Benjamin was up to and what he had told them. Then she would decide what to do next.

She forced herself to eat the white bouncy fish balls at dinner and was surprised to find them quite tasty. She went to sleep, worrying about her marriage, her family, and work—everything. She wondered who would kill such a wonderful person like Fiona. Then she pondered whether she was going to spend a number of years in jail.

****

The next day began early with the usual chores and work on her own case. Zakia kept signing on to Skype, wondering if Benjamin was going to call her. She hadn't received so much as an e-mail from him. Maybe he'd tried to call or text her, but her cellphone had been taken away. She rested her head in her hands. At ten that morning, a voice came over the speaker instructing her to report to the visitors' room. She was done with her chores and was in her room reading e-mails from some of her colleagues. She wondered why she was being asked to go to the visitor's room. Visiting hours were in the afternoon, Helga had said.

The visitors' room was an ordinary room, with no glass panel dividing the visitor from the prisoner. Zakia sat down at a table and waited.

She was trying to figure out who it might be, when a familiar figure walked into the room.

"Benjamin! I can't believe it!" Zakia jumped up from her chair and threw herself into his arms. They hugged like they had rarely done before. Zakia started to cry and even the otherwise staunch Benjamin sniffed, holding back tears. He looked exhausted from his trans-Atlantic flight, and perhaps even older.

She pulled away to look at him. "Oh, I've missed you so much. You can't believe it. I'm so sorry all of this has happened."

"I missed you, too."

"I've been so worried about you, Dani, and Harris after Fiona was killed." She felt stricken at having to admit this, but she continued. "I think her death is related to the work I've been doing, but I can't be sure. Are our boys *safe*?"

He took her face gently in his hands and looked at her with a solemn expression. "Wait, Zakia, now it's my turn to talk. Everyone is fine at our end. Dani and Harris are safe with your sister. She is taking extra precautions. We were all just worried sick about you. I had to see you. Something is always awry with you ever since the blowout, and now this."

"I still can't believe it." Zakia sniffed. Now that he was here, she didn't have to be strong all by herself.

"I am staying in your suite, by the way. I guess there aren't that many people staying at the hotel since the airport opened again, so they seem to have been waiting for you to come back."

"Well, that's nice." Zakia smiled.

Benjamin rubbed his eyes. "I must say I was surprised when I entered the prison. Not much deprivation going on around here."

"I'm told it's all part of the rehabilitation process.

The recidivism rate is about twenty percent instead of over fifty percent as in most prisons around the world."

He looked at her with concern. "Take a deep breath. You're all right—no need to give me a speech."

Zakia inhaled. She was more comfortable reporting than she was being mired in this mess. "I'm trying to figure out who else Fiona interacted with before she died," said Zakia. "With all the focus on me, the real killer is going to get away. We've got to move quickly."

"Give the authorities a little bit more credit," said Benjamin. "And from what Jack tells me, you have the best lawyer in Iceland."

"I hadn't heard that, but I'm grateful," said Zakia. "Jasem and I talked on Skype about where one could find polonium-210. He's digging into who would have access to it. I also found out more about Sigurd from an inmate here." She filled him in on Helga's story.

"I wouldn't expect anything less of you. You'll keep searching for answers. But you must stay hopeful in your own case too. We all know they have arrested the wrong person."

Zakia leaned into Benjamin, relieved that he was not angry. Yet, she wondered about her fate, bogged down as she was in a case that seemed to grow tentacles in all directions.

Chapter Thirty-One

She'd only been there a few days, but Zakia fell into the routines of jail. Her body was there, but her mind was always elsewhere, trying to solve her own case. She made a list of people who would have had contact with Fiona and places she would have gone. With the trial looming, she had no time to waste. She wanted to have new information by the time she met with Ida again. By tracing Fiona's steps, she hoped she could track down the killer. On that terrible day that set everything into motion, Fiona had gone to work, they had had lunch together, Fiona had returned to work and then Zakia had gone to the grocery store.

Something was missing, hovering at the back of her memory, nagging her.

She went to lunch late, to a near empty cafeteria and tried to remember elements that were eluding her. She was eating a sandwich when Helga came and sat down beside her. "Any progress on your case?"

"No luck yet," said Zakia.

"So sorry." Helga looked downcast. Then her expression brightened into a smile. "I'm getting a cup of coffee; can I get you one?"

"Actually, I prefer tea, thank you," said Zakia. "I have looked, but we seem to have run out of teabags."

"Oh, I'll check in the kitchen. There's an extra box in the back somewhere, I'm sure."

Helga left and Zakia sat there, thinking.

Then it hit her.

Hadn't Fiona mentioned that she was going to the café for tea before dinner on the day she got so sick? How could Zakia not have remembered that detail until just now?

Helga came back carrying a steaming cup of tea and another of coffee. Zakia smiled, took the tea, and thanked her. "You just helped solve my case." She stood up. "I have to call my lawyer. Thank you."

"Well, you're welcome." Helga rubbed her chin. "I'd hoped we could sit and chat."

"Another time." Zakia hurried toward the door while balancing her cup.

In her room, Zakia researched how the Russian ex-spy had been poisoned. Sure enough the poison was in his tea.

She Skyped with Jasem right away.

"I have a theory," she said.

"Wait a minute, I have news," he said, cutting her off. "I've talked to some of my friends working in the shadows and I'm thinking the closest person to have the right connections would be Sigurd himself. Four years ago, Sigurd tried to bring fracking to Bulgaria. My source says he was involved in some shady deals with some government officials and the Bulgarian organized crime syndicate, which often work together."

"That's the Sigurd I know," said Zakia.

Jasem nodded. "And to think you went to his office. Anyway, he hit a wall when the government adopted a ban on fracking, but it appears he still has some dealings over there. He could easily have gotten in touch with the 'right' person in Bulgaria or Russia and agreed to pay him to procure polonium-210."

"It's not likely he poisoned Fiona himself." Zakia felt sick to her stomach.

"That's right. He probably assigned one of his henchmen to perpetrate the crime in Iceland."

"Of course, that makes sense. Sigurd is resourceful."

"You're lucky they didn't kill you too," Jasem said. "It has occurred to me that prison is probably the best place for you right now."

Zakia nodded, staring down at her hands. She had to concentrate on getting out of there and she had to put Sigurd behind bars.

"But we need proof," she said.

"Yes. However, technically, that's difficult," said Jasem. "You see, polonium-210 is hard to trace because we already have a tiny bit of the substance in our bodies. The question is how did they get it into Fiona? You have to actually ingest it for it to kill you. That explains why they accused you because you'd made her last meal."

"I think I have the evidence that will show that it wasn't me." Zakia had a gleam in her eye.

"And what might that be?"

"Fiona stopped at a café for a cup of tea on the way to our suite the day she got sick. It must have been in her tea."

"That's it! You must get that information to your lawyer and the police as soon as possible," He grinned.

"I'm about to do that," said Zakia. "I wanted to touch base with you to see if you had any more information. Do you have a paper trail for Sigurd's activities in Bulgaria?"

"I'll see what I can find."

"Thanks! On another note, I have some other news regarding the case," said Zakia.

"Good, let's hear it."

"Helga, an inmate, told me a couple of days ago that she'd met Sigurd's daughter, Runa, right here in jail."

"What a strange coincidence. Is she still there?"

"No she was released six months ago." Zakia told Jasem what she'd learned about Runa.

"It's so sad when offspring do such things to their parents," said Jasem. "Well, that could explain his determination to scale up the fracking venture."

"Killing for money seems rather extreme for someone like Sigurd, don't you think?" asked Zakia.

"Happens everywhere, even with people from law-abiding Iceland," said Jasem.

She signed off, took a deep breath and walked to the control room.

The prison guard in charge asked, "Can I help you?"

"I'd like to make a call to my lawyer," she said. "I think I have had a breakthrough in my case."

"That's good news," he said and smiled. "The phone is right over there."

Zakia pulled Ida's business card out of her pocket and entered the number. Her hands were shaking. When Ida heard the news, she was very pleased. "This might be the break we've been hoping for," she said. "I'll get in touch with the police right away. Can this Jasem send me whatever information he has on Sigurd?"

"He's still working on it, but I will ask him," said Zakia.

The rest of the day went by in a blur. Benjamin came back during the normal visiting hours. He too thought her lead was promising. Then he asked her if she was ready to talk to their sons yet. "They miss you."

Zakia sighed. "I'll admit I've avoided talking to them. How do you explain to your sons that you're in jail?" She wiped her eyes.

"I haven't told them anything, said Benjamin, gently. "I just said you were very busy and didn't have time to talk, but this isn't going to last. I think you should tell them now. Let's talk to them together."

Zakia sat for a moment, working up her courage, and then went to fetch her computer. When she returned to the visitors' room, Benjamin smiled at her. "Just be honest. They understand much more than you give them credit for."

"Okay," said Zakia.

The boys connected on Skype right away. "Maman," said Dani. "We haven't heard from you for days. What's going on?"

Harris elbowed him. "Hi Maman, where have you been? I miss you so much. Dad said you were busy, but he wouldn't say with what."

"Hi boys," she said. "I've missed you too. It's a complicated story. Listen carefully."

Zakia told them that her friend Fiona had died of radiation poisoning and that their Maman had been arrested for murder, since she had prepared Fiona's last meal. Dani looked shocked and Harris rubbed his eyes. "Wait, are you in jail now?"

"I'm afraid so," said Zakia. "But it's not like you think. Jails here are more like a youth hostel. Only you're locked in at night. The most important thing to know is that we have made great progress on the case to prove my innocence."

Harris nodded in disbelief, his chin trembling, and Dani scowled. "Why didn't Dad tell us?"

"He thought it would be best if you heard it from me," she said.

They were silent for a moment. "Are you going to be there forever?" wailed Harris.

"No, the trial is in a few days, then we'll know more." she said. "I'm sure they'll find the real killer before long."

Harris was crying and Dani looked at her, dumbfounded.

"Listen," said Zakia. "We don't know how this is going to play out so I need you to be strong."

"We'll do that," said Dani.

Harris sniffled. "I miss you. Please come home soon."

"Here's what I need you to do," she said. "I want you to carry on with your activities, but be extra careful and don't go out without your aunt until we get back. That will be best." *I just said 'until we get back'. At least my subconscious is hopeful.*

"So, somebody killed Fiona," said Dani. "Are they coming after us next?"

They both looked at her with wide eyes. Zakia didn't know what to say. She didn't want to make them any more worried than they were already.

Benjamin cleared his throat. "No, that's highly unlikely. But please do as your mother says and mind your aunt."

"Dad, when are you coming home?" asked Dani.

"I'll stay with your mother a few more days," he said.

They talked with Dani and Harris for a little longer. Then she asked to talk with Tahra, and explained what was going on in more detail.

Her sister looked very concerned, but hopeful. "I'm sure we'll see you back here before you know it," she said. "You know how Papa, bless his soul, would have been all over this. It's clear you inherited his courage."

"I wish," said Zakia before signing off.

When she went to bed that night, she hoped with all her soul that Tahra was right—that she would be home soon.

****

On Monday, Zakia was working in the prison kitchen when she was called to meet someone in the visitors' room. She washed her hands and hung up her apron. She hoped it was Benjamin stopping by for a visit again. She felt stronger now that he was in town.

The guard who met her at the visitors' room wasn't saying much. He asked her to take a seat as her visitor was being authorized and would be there soon. That piqued her interest. Benjamin was already in the system.

She recognized the tall, good-looking man who walked into the room. It was Ian, the stalker, who had turned out to be MI5.

"Hello," he said, extending his hand. "Not where I expected to see you."

"Yes. Hello. This was not according to my plan either." Zakia shook his hand.

Ian sat down at the table opposite to Zakia. "We followed Fiona for six months before she was killed.

There have been several threats on the lives of climate scientists in recent months. Delaying action on climate change is clearly a threat to the UK, so our mandate at MI5 was expanded to include the protection of our scientists, wherever they might be."

"If you were supposed to protect Fiona, then why was she killed?"

"I had an emergency in the UK and my replacement got grounded at Heathrow when the volcano erupted. I got here as soon as the air cleared for flying. I have no doubt we failed in our mission," he admitted in a flat voice.

"Yes, I'd say you did," she retorted.

"This was a peculiar case," he said. "But, it looks like we might be near the end of it."

"How so?"

"With your lead on Fiona's teatime habits, I was able to work with the Icelandic police to piece together how she was poisoned."

"Did you find polonium-210 at the café she used to stop by?" asked Zakia, her hopes rising.

"Yes, the teapot was still there."

"That's good news," she said. "But wait, weren't other people poisoned?"

Ian shook his head. "Thankfully, not. It seems Fiona had her own special teapot at the café, and she insisted it not be washed, just rinsed, as is the tradition in many Scottish homes."

Zakia nodded. "Oh that's right."

"Plenty of polonium-210 residue was found in the teapot. Hence, the prosecutor has dismissed the case."

"Thank heavens." Zakia took a deep breath, holding back tears.

Ian sat silently, watching her.

Finally, she collected herself. She still didn't understand how everything was pieced together. "I've read about the Russian spy poisoned with polonium-210. It took him three weeks to die. How come Fiona died so quickly?"

Ian shook his head. "For a small woman like Fiona, it took only a tiny increase in the amount of poison, and that, added to her condition, made her death much quicker than that of Alexander Litvinenko."

"What do you mean by 'her condition?'"

"Fiona was a smoker, right?"

"Yes, she used to smoke, but she quit eight years ago. What are you saying?"

"Tobacco leaves contain radioactive material, particularly polonium-210. Polonium-210 is present in tobacco smoke as it passes into the lungs," he said. "Even if the concentration of polonium-210 in the tobacco is relatively low, this concentration accumulates in the lungs of smokers. This is what happened to Fiona. Intense localized radiation doses occur at the bronchioles, which happened in her case."

"I never knew that could happen."

"Yes, her smoking, together with the higher dose of polonium-210 in the tea, was enough to bring her to a quick death."

Zakia could hardly breathe. It was difficult to think of the pain Fiona had endured.

"In a way it's a blessing she didn't linger. Litvinenko died a horrible death."

They were both silent for a moment, Zakia absorbing the information and Ian watching her with much sympathy.

"So it wasn't in the couscous I cooked for her," said Zakia, taking a deep breath and releasing a sigh. It was bittersweet news. She was relieved to be exonerated, but felt again the loss of Fiona.

"That's right," said Ian. "It may take a few hours, but you'll soon be released."

"But wait, what about the actual murderer?"

"It's possible that the men who kidnapped you might be the culprits. What do you remember about the kidnappers?"

Zakia told Ian how Rostek had stalked her in Morocco. She explained the awkward introduction to him through the Larsens. "He said he was working for Oddleifur Oil," she said. "I'm sure David Larsen could verify that information." Her head was spinning.

Ian nodded and wrote notes in a small, leather notebook.

"If it was him, would he have killed Fiona on orders from Halgrim Thorsson," Zakia wondered. "Or do you think he was working directly for Sigurd?"

"We don't know at this point, but we're bringing Halgrim in for questioning. We haven't been able to track down Rostek or Ahmed yet. It turns out that Rostek was a recent Polish immigrant to Iceland and was already wanted by Interpol before he even arrived here. I don't know how he managed to get his work papers."

"I do have another question," said Zakia. "How did Fiona's killer get the polonium-210? My understanding is that it is extremely difficult to acquire."

"We think the polonium-210 was transported by ship, as the planes were grounded. We traced it to Bulgaria, where it had been bought from a Russian, formerly employed by a nuclear facility. We'll continue to assist the Icelandic authorities on this one."

Zakia told him about Sigurd's ties to Bulgaria. "You've done some good work," he said, looking impressed.

"I've been investigating Oddleifur Oil, but I wonder if there are some bigger entities behind this. I feel like we're just scratching the surface."

Ian nodded. "If you have any more information about Oddleifur Oil, we'd love to have it."

"I have something on Sigurd that might help," she said. "But I need your assurance that I can use it in a story."

Ian hesitated. "I don't see why not. Why don't you contact me as soon as possible after you get out of here?"

Zakia nodded. "Now what?"

"As soon as your paperwork is done, you'll get your passport back and you'll be free to travel," he said, his tone gentle.

Zakia choked back a sob, relieved that her nightmare was over. Ian pulled out a handkerchief and handed it to her and she blew her nose. "Thank you," she said.

Just then, Benjamin entered the room. "I came as soon as Ida gave me the news. What a relief."

"Oh, thank God," said Zakia. She stood up and hugged him.

"This is almost unbelievable. I'm so glad you'll be out of here very shortly," said Benjamin. I'm going to order tickets so we can leave right after Fiona's memorial service the day after tomorrow."

Ian cleared his throat and Zakia turned to Ian.

"Sorry, I almost forgot. Ian this is Benjamin Atkins, my husband." She looked at Benjamin, "Ian Blackstone is from MI5."

"Nice to meet you," said Ian.

"Likewise," said Benjamin. "What's your role in all of this?"

They all sat down around the table and Ian explained how, thanks to Zakia's brainpower, they had figured out the means used to poison Fiona.

"There's just a slight problem. I'm off the hook, but they still haven't found out who poisoned her."

"So the killer is still at large?" Benjamin said, clearly concerned.

"Yes," said Ian. "Hence, we need to have extra security in place for the two of you."

"Fine," said Benjamin. "But it won't be for long. We're flying out right after Fiona's service."

"Good," said Ian. "I'll get right on it."

A prison guard stepped into the doorway, with a smile on his face. "Zakia Karim, we have a release order for you. Please follow me. We'll get your things, then you'll sign the paperwork, and I'll walk you to the exit."

Zakia and Benjamin hugged again and she shook hands with Ian, who was grinning. "I'll get you that information we talked about," she said.

She walked out with the guard and met Ida in the hallway. "Well, this was a much faster release than expected. I'm glad it's over."

"Me too," said Zakia. "But they still have to catch the murderer."

"Yes, but I'm sure the police will catch him, especially with MI5's help."

Ida walked her through the paperwork and in less than an hour, Zakia met Benjamin at the exit. He had a cab waiting for them.

As the cab wound through the busy streets of downtown Reykjavik, Zakia reflected on all the time she'd spent in Iceland with Fiona. She still couldn't believe her friend was dead. As if he could sense her thoughts, Benjamin took her hand and squeezed it.

When she walked in to the hotel, it felt like she'd been gone for years, rather than a few days. The hotel clerks greeted her enthusiastically. Back at her suite, she connected with her boys over Skype and gave them the good news. They whooped with joy and she could see Tahra crying in the background. Knowing her family was in good shape, Zakia thought, now all I need to do is get to Chicago and finish my article. Except there's one problem—the killers are still out there.

Chapter Thirty-Two

When she woke up the next morning, Zakia nearly fell out of bed, expecting the prison wall on her left side. She felt her heart thumping before she remembered that she was safe. She wasn't kidnapped. She wasn't in jail. She was at the hotel in Reykjavik, curled up in bed next to Benjamin for the first time in what seemed like years.

Benjamin got up and showered while Zakia turned on her computer. When he stepped out from the bathroom he shot her a worried look. "Are you going to be able to fly home with me?" he asked. "Or are you going to stay and continue to probe Fiona's death?"

His statement saddened her. Benjamin had been through trying times and had supported her in her career, even though he didn't always like it. "Of course, I'm going home with you," she said with a cheery voice.

Benjamin smiled, leaned over and kissed her. "I've missed you," he said, sliding his hand down her back.

Zakia batted him away. "Why don't you take a walk," she said. "I have some work to do."

Benjamin laughed, got dressed, and announced he was going out. "The latte is better down the street than here at the hotel," he said. "Do you want me to bring you one, too?"

"No thanks, I'll pass," she said. "I prefer to make

tea."

Almost as soon as he left, the phone rang. It was Ian. "I'm following up on our last meeting. I wanted to give you an update before you leave and ask you a few more questions while the details are still fresh on your mind." he said. "I'm in your lobby. Can you come down?"

"Sure. I'll be there shortly."

Zakia dressed quickly and hurried to the elevators. She thought about taking the stairs, but she had too much history with those stairs.

When the elevator doors opened in the lobby, Ian was waiting for her.

"What's up?" asked Zakia.

"Let's find a quiet corner, shall we?"

Zakia led him to the back of the bar, where she settled into a sofa and Ian sat down in an armchair across the table from her. She sat with her arms by her side, still in a daze from all that had happened. *At least I'm free.* She wondered if anything would ever be the same.

"I just wanted to catch up with you before you leave because you mentioned you had more information about Sigurd."

"I have information not only about Sigurd, but I can tie him to a prominent member of the Moroccan government."

Ian's eyebrows shot up. "Go on."

She told him about the copies of the money transfers she'd received from Samara's secretary, as well as the land transfers she'd found.

"Do you have those copies?" he said with a sparkle in his eyes.

350

"No, I'm afraid not," she said.

After Ian sighed, she was quick to explain, "But I scanned them onto a zip drive the day before my hard copies were stolen on my flight to Paris."

"Good thinking," he said. "You'd make a great agent. You see, when Fiona's office was searched a few days ago, they realized that her computer had been stolen and, if she had any other storage devices, they were gone, too. And the cloud back-ups were canceled. So I reached a dead end on that front."

"Well, I've got the solution to that problem. Fiona knew her work was vital and had been hacked recently so she saved it onto a flash drive. She didn't trust the systems enough to put it on a cloud."

"Where is it now?" asked Ian.

"With all the unfortunate incidents taking place these past few days, I flat out forgot that it's hidden in Fiona's suite. Let's see if it's still there."

"But the police searched the room. "

"We stored both flash drives in a zip lock bag in the electric kettle in our suite."

"What do you mean?" asked Ian.

"I figured that flash drives you hide it in plain view, as for instance, a kettle, would not be found.

"That's impressive."

We put both our flash drives in a zip lock bag."

Ian stood up. "Let's hope they're still there."

Zakia laughed. "Lucky for us, Benjamin moved into my suite, and since he only drinks coffee, he will not have boiled the flash drives."

"That's a relief."

The two of them walked to the elevator. She noticed that despite his easygoing demeanor, Ian seemed keenly aware of his surroundings.

On the way to the suite, he asked her about Fiona's research.

"She'd done a number of studies on the link between climate change and extreme weather events and was wrapping up an article on that very topic the day she was poisoned."

Zakia could see Ian's mind making rapid connections. "I see," he said.

"I think this information needs to get to the climate scientists at Reykjavik University," she said.

Ian nodded. "Since you and Benjamin are leaving shortly, if you entrust me with the flash drive, I will deliver it to the university."

The elevator opened on their floor and there stood Benjamin. Turning to Zakia he said, "You weren't in our room and I was getting worried."

"You were quick," she said. "Did you get a latte?"

"I didn't want to be gone too long," he said, in a sheepish voice. "But I got my latte, thanks." He turned to Ian. "How's the case coming along?"

Ian swept his hand through his hair. He looked tired, Zakia thought. They all did. "I think we might have another lead," said Ian. "Again, with your wife's help."

Benjamin turned to her with a smirk. "Can't leave it alone, can you?"

Zakia laughed. "You should know me by now. Don't worry; I'm still going home with you. But right now, we need to retrieve some flash drives."

"I haven't seen any flash drives," he said. "Jack already took all of Fiona's things."

"Probably not the flash drives," she said.

Ian and Benjamin followed Zakia into the suite. They watched as Zakia walked over to the kitchenette, opened the electric water kettle, and pulled out a zip locked bag with two flash drives in it.

"*Voilà!*" she said.

"One more mystery solved," said Ian.

****

Early Wednesday morning, Zakia woke with a fright. She had dreamt that Rostek was pushing Fiona's head under water in the Blue Lagoon and Zakia was tied up and couldn't stop him. She tried to sleep some more, but gave up and was about to get out of bed when she noticed Benjamin was sitting on the sofa with a book on his lap, watching her.

"Good morning. You're up early."

"Yes, I've been ready for a while now, just waiting for you to wake up so we can have breakfast together."

Benjamin wasn't talkative in the morning and Zakia was grateful for the silence. It was the day of Fiona's memorial. Zakia was enveloped in her own grief. Benjamin ordered a taxi to take them to the memorial service, and then on to the airport. The church was within walking distance, but he didn't think it was a good idea to walk. "We should probably take some precautions," he said, "even if we have a security detail."

"You're being paranoid," she said, but she didn't protest after he shot her a look of concern.

"I'm playing it safe. Too many things have gone wrong already."

"Poor Fiona," said Zakia.

They checked out, rolled their bags out of the hotel and got into the taxi.

Zakia was surprised by the large turnout from the university and the local community, in addition to family members from Scotland. Fiona's body was already en route to Scotland. The memorial service was dignified, with a bagpiper skirling sad tunes that pulled at Zakia's heartstrings. She started to weep, thinking about what a wonderful friend and mentor Fiona had been. Benjamin put a firm arm around her shoulders.

After the service, she met Jack and gave him a tight hug. "I'm so sorry Jack. And thank you for arranging for Ida to take my case."

"I'm glad you could make it. I was worried about you languishing in jail."

"At least now moving to Chicago, we can easily visit you in Boulder."

"Benjamin told me your flight is early so you won't make the gathering this afternoon."

"Yes, I'm sorry, but I must get back to my boys."

"God speed."

"Thank you. Take care of yourself," said Zakia.

"I will. See you soon."

The congregation moved to the church stairs to greet the priest and other parishioners, but Zakia didn't feel up to it. She was relieved they needed to get to the airport and could make a quick exit.

Just as she and Benjamin were turning to go, she glanced down the street and saw a man who looked like Ahmed, but he was so far away she couldn't be sure. The man gave her a little nod and her stomach turned.

She put her hand on Benjamin's arm. "We need to go," she said.

He gave her a sharp look. "What's wrong?"

She forced a smile. "I'm just exhausted and want to

354

get to the airport so we can get under way to see our boys. The sooner, the better."

Benjamin let out a breath. "There's my wife back."

Zakia pulled him along to the taxi that was waiting up the street from the church. They got in and he instructed the driver to get them to the airport. *"Tout suite."* He gave Zakia's arm a squeeze. "We'll be home before you know it."

Zakia nodded, resisting the urge to turn around to see if they were being followed.

At the airport, they rolled their bags into the terminal, checked in, and were lined up at the security screening. Benjamin stepped through without a problem. When Zakia started to step through, one of the guards stopped her. "Miss, is this your case?" he asked.

"Yes," she said. "Is something wrong?"

"We need to search it. Please step over here."

"Yes sir," said Zakia, starting to sweat. *Now what?*

He started digging around in her case, "I'm afraid you can't take this on board," he said, holding up a half-empty water bottle.

"Sorry," she said. "I forgot I had left it in there." *I'm getting paranoid.*

He tossed the bottle, repacked the items and Zakia was on her way. She sighed as her eyes went up, looking heavenward.

****

The sight of Dani and Harris waiting for her at the O'Hare airport made her eyes shine. She pulled them to her and kissed and hugged them until they pulled away.

"Maman," Dani said. "Everyone is watching us. We need to go." Benjamin stood by, smiling.

Tahra was the last to hug Zakia. "Hello, stranger. I

missed you."

"I missed you too," said Zakia, wiping away a tear.

Walking to Tahra's car, Zakia gave her phone a brief glance. She had an e-mail from George Stevens. It would have to wait until the morning.

Harris said, "Why are you grinning Maman?"

"Oh, it's just another piece of the puzzle of the never-ending story I'm working on that may be falling into place. Let's not think about that now." They had Chinese takeout for dinner, which Zakia found odd. Tahra did not like Chinese food. Right after dinner, Zakia collapsed in bed with her story swirling around in her head.

Chapter Thirty-Three

Early next morning, Zakia woke up in a cold sweat. This time she'd dreamt that she'd drowned in the Blue Lagoon. It was still dark, but she heard Benjamin snoring next to her and remembered she was safe in her sister's condo in Chicago.

She slipped out of bed and turned on her computer. She read the e-mail from George. He had received her e-mail, had connected with David and was willing to meet her when she got to Chicago. George asked that she call to set up a time to meet. It was too early to call, so she moved to the next e-mail. It was from Ian. He wanted her to call him on Skype as soon as possible.

She snuck out to the living room, carrying her laptop.

When he answered, Ian looked pleased to see her.

"I didn't expect to hear from you so soon," he said. "Isn't it the middle of the night where are you are?"

"Almost," said Zakia. "I'm jetlagged and can't sleep. Must still be on Icelandic time."

"Good," he nodded. "Zakia, are you still available to help us? We know you have done research on Oddleifur Oil, and you were closest to Fiona. Your journalistic skills will also come in handy."

"Sure. How can I *not* help?" said Zakia. "Fiona was one of my dearest friends."

"Thanks. The last two days have been productive,"

he said. "Halgrim's in custody and claims, of course, he had nothing to do with the poisoning. Rostek was finally found, in a most improbable place, the reconstructed Viking ship in the harbor." The police had received a tip from someone on a boat in the harbor that had seen light coming from the Viking ship late at night. It was Rostek using his cellphone trying to signal a ship outside the territorial waters.

"I'm relieved you have Rostek in custody. At Fiona's memorial service, I thought I saw Ahmed not far from the church when we were leaving," said Zakia.

"Why didn't you contact us?" asked Ian. "That was foolish. We had our security detail close by."

"I guess I was so grief-stricken I wasn't thinking straight," she said.

"I'll say. Well, for heaven's sake, please call me next time." Ian rubbed the back of his neck.

"There won't be a next time."

"I hope you and your family are okay."

"Yes, we're fine. I'll stay out of trouble."

Ian chuckled. "Knowing you, I doubt that. Anyway, it turns out Rostek was hired by Sigurd. Sigurd was in fact in Iceland a few weeks ago to set it all up, according to Rostek."

"Really?"

"Yes, according to him, Sigurd had planned the poisoning of Fiona in great detail. He hired Rostek to carry it out. The fact that you came along and looked guilty by circumstantial evidence just made it easier. They were also trying to get you out of the way. A long prison sentence for you would have just about covered it."

"That's horrible." Zakia, once again, was flooded

with pain over her friend's demise. "What was his motive?"

"We suspect it might be related to Fiona's status as an advisor to the Pope and as part of an international expert group of climatologists calling out fracking as a contributor to climate change. This publicity was upsetting the Moroccan oil minster's plans to mislead the public in order to facilitate fracking rather than transitioning to renewables."

Zakia was silent.

"The Icelandic authorities have put out an arrest warrant for Sigurd on Interpol," added Ian. "Unfortunately, there is no extradition treaty between Iceland and Morocco, even if they were to arrest him at his Rabat office."

Zakia wanted to make sure Sigurd didn't get away. She said calmly, "If my sources are correct, Sigurd was bribing the oil and energy minister of Morocco to expand his fracking operations."

"Yes, it appears your source is reliable," said Ian. "The repercussions are going to be immense."

"Now that the regulations aimed at reducing carbon emissions seem to be picking up speed after the Paris Agreement, the fossil fuel industry must be worried that their shareholders will indeed get stuck with stranded assets, as they had refused to believe it was possible. I imagine there's a lot of money at stake." Zakia frowned.

Ian's shook his head. "What do you know about Sigurd's personal situation? Was it the usual greed or were there other motives?"

"Well he was paying back money to the victims of his daughter's crimes." Zakia gave Ian the information she had received from Helga.

"Yes, we found something to that effect too."

"Furthermore," said Zakia, leaning back on the sofa, "when I interviewed Sigurd he said he had become a member of an exclusive inner circle of a large oil and gas trade association, headquartered in the U.S. I think he had aspirations that he and his company would someday hit the big leagues. Crazy ambition can motivate people. Perhaps all of these things have turned him into a criminal, though you couldn't tell by looking at him."

"That's an interesting point," said Ian. "Call me if you remember or come across anything else about Sigurd."

"I'll be in touch." Zakia signed off Skype.

At this point, her sons and their cousins were up and about. Dani and Harris hugged Zakia good morning and were thrilled she was home. They asked if she could do something fun with them and their cousins in the afternoon. She said they could go to the Art Institute of Chicago in the afternoon and then get ice cream. The four boys jumped around, yelling: "Yes, we get ice cream!"

Benjamin got up and made himself a cup of coffee and sat on the sofa with the morning paper, smiling at Zakia. Tahra soon joined them, gave her sister a big hug, and made breakfast for everyone. The condo was abuzz with activity, but Zakia couldn't let herself get carried away by all this togetherness; she still had several murders to solve. At about ten a.m., Zakia announced she needed to make a phone call and disappeared into the bedroom.

Zakia reread George's e-mail. She had no

information on him, except that he had been an oil company executive. Zakia called the local number.

A pleasant-sounding voice answered the phone. "George here."

She introduced herself and he sounded pleased that she'd called.

"I understand you want to talk to me as soon as possible. Could we meet for lunch today? I'm in town on business, but I leave tomorrow for a long weekend with Amy, my granddaughter." said George.

"Yes, I would appreciate that. You name the place and the time and I'll be there," said Zakia. "I have plans this afternoon at about two, but I'm free until then."

"How about meeting at Lou's Steak House at noon?"

"See you there." Zakia knew she had to do some more research on George before lunch.

She got back to her e-mails and found one from Gail, one of her classmates from Columbia. Gail specialized in health reporting, so when Fiona got sick, Zakia reached out to her. Now her friend had written Zakia about the possibility of a job at *The Chicago Post*, where she had worked some years ago. "I know you will be in Chicago soon, if not already," said Gail. "Do get in touch with Roberta Windward and say hello from me. I will write her too."

Zakia wrote Gail back, thanking her, and then e-mailed Roberta asking if she could visit the paper. She thought about attaching her resume but decided against it; she didn't want to seem too forward.

****

It was two minutes after noon when Zakia arrived at the posh restaurant in downtown Chicago. It was well-lit and smelled scrumptious. Most of the diners were dressed for business. She hoped lunch wouldn't break her bank now that she was out of work.

A host took her name and ushered her to George's table in the back of the room. He was a grey-haired, pleasant-looking man who stood up slowly when she arrived at his table. He wore a blue blazer, grey slacks, and an ascot tie. He had a cane hanging on the chair next to him.

"Are you Mr. Stevens?" asked Zakia

"Yes. And you must be Zakia Karim. Nice to meet you. Do call me George," he said as they shook hands.

"It's a pleasure to meet you. Thank you for taking the time to meet me on such short notice."

"Please, have a seat," he said, gesturing to a chair.

Zakia settled herself in. "Thank you."

He took a sip of water. "David mentioned you'd get in touch. He said that you are a journalist working on a story about a blowout accident in Morocco and tying it in to climate change somehow."

"That's right," said Zakia.

"David may have mentioned I've retired from an oil and gas company."

"Yes, he did."

"David also told me about how you'd met in Reykjavik and how you and the climate scientist…Fiona, was it?"

Zakia swallowed hard. "Yes, Fiona McPherson."

"Seems that you and this Fiona played a big part in convincing him that climate change is much more serious than he thought. David has begun advising his pension fund clients and others like me to move away from fossil fuel stocks and put our money in renewable energy instead."

"That's wonderful news." She smiled.

George glanced at the menu, and then turned to Zakia. "So what did you want to speak with me about?"

"Mainly, what you know about Sigurd Agnarsson."

"Perhaps we should order first." Abruptly, George returned his attention to the menu. "I suggest the small portion of their renowned steak. That's plenty for one person. It's really good."

I guess I mentioned a touchy subject. She opened the menu and scanned it. "Sounds like a fine idea."

The waiter came over and they each ordered a small steak. After the waiter left, George wiped his forehead and said. "Where were we?"

"You were about to tell me about Sigurd."

"Well, there's not much to say. I've met him briefly at a meeting."

"That's all you have to say?"

"Yes," said George. "I think you misunderstood what information I could help you with today."

"Is that so?" Zakia caught herself getting angry.

"I'm just doing David a favor."

"Well, I've done my homework, George. I've been in touch with your granddaughter. I tracked Amy down online."

George stood up from his seat and started to reach for his cane.

Zakia put up her hand. "Please wait. Amy's going to call you in a moment. She said she'll make sure that you'll be quite frank with me." George sat down again with a pained look on his face.

"You know you are using my most precious possession against me."

"In this game, I've learned to use whatever is available. Your granddaughter, as you well know, is a climate activist. She's eager that I talk with you. It's her future we're dealing with."

Just then, George's cellphone rang.

He answered it. "Yes. George here. Oh, hi Amy." He just listened. Then he spoke into his phone again, "You really didn't give me a chance, did you?" George slumped in his chair. "Yes, all right. We'll talk more later. I love you too. Bye now."

George looked up at Zakia. "You win," he said as he clicked off the phone. "Amy sends you regards. She drives a hard bargain."

"So, you were saying," said Zakia.

"I'll start at the beginning. And yes, I was a member of the Dirty Network."

"The Dirty Network?" asked Zakia, leaning forward.

"The Dirty Network, of course, is just a nickname. But it's the inner circle of the international oil and gas industries' largest trade association. Until recently, I was a member of the network and we met periodically at a country club outside Houston. The mission was to protect our interests. We were all successful executives and wanted to make sure it stayed that way."

Zakia's mouth fell open. She pulled out a pad from her purse and began scribbling notes.

"You have to understand that in the oil industry we have scientists examining factors that can impact our industry in the long term, say thirty to fifty years into the future. Already in the 1980s, our own scientists told us that climate change was increasing as a result of burning fossil fuels. We soon realized even then that policies to address it would affect our profitability. We decided that it was in our best interest to make sure that this news didn't reach the public."

"That's unbelievable." Zakia's eyes widened.

"It gets worse. The Dirty Network members agreed that they would start a number of campaigns to cast doubt on the climate change science and discredit what their own scientists had confirmed in order to deceive the American public. We started all sorts of think tanks and other front groups designed to discredit climate scientists, focusing on the doubt that still existed in the science to distract the public from what was really going on."

"Exactly what the tobacco industry did," said Zakia. "And they were sued, weren't they?"

George frowned. "The oil and gas industry used the exact same playbook and some of the same actors too. And yes, tobacco companies were sued and now one of the oil companies has been sued for securities fraud as we speak."

"What does that mean?"

"It means a company is lying to its investors. In this case, the stockholders were lied to regarding the risks climate change and its regulation can have on the company's bottom line, thus affecting the value of their shares."

They were silent for a moment. Zakia noticed that George was looking off into the distance.

"Back then, I was focused only on my job, making money for my company. I've since retired as the CFO, but I'm still on the board. I'm ashamed to say that I went right along with the whole campaign to feed disinformation to the public so that we could continue business as usual, making huge profits while delaying any regulations that would mandate cuts in carbon emissions."

"But you have since had a change of heart?" asked Zakia.

George smiled. "Let's say things have changed in my personal life. For years Amy has been on my case about climate change. I love her to bits, but I thought I knew better, so I would just change the subject."

"How old is your granddaughter?" asked Zakia.

"Amy's twenty-three now," said George. "Wait a minute...I have a photo of her." He pulled out his phone. "Let's see if I can get this thing to work."

Zakia sat silently, watching him.

"Here we are, Amy and me," he said, handing her his phone.

She saw a photo of a smiling young woman, sitting beside him on a park bench. Each had an arm on the other's shoulder.

"Ah, yes. Much better than the one I saw of her on the internet. You look like you have a loving relationship," she said.

He beamed. "We do. She's sharp, a real go-getter. She organized sit-ins to force her college to divest from fossil fuels. She barely got to her classes, so she only just graduated last year. I was upset with her, but I still wasn't getting the message."

"What made you change your mind?" asked Zakia, handing him back the phone.

He took the phone and pocketed it. "I am eighty years old. A month ago I found out I have galloping colon cancer."

"I'm sorry to hear that," said Zakia.

"Having just a few months left has put things into perspective in a whole new way. I spoke to my pastor who's a member of an interfaith group focused on caring for God's creation, including the climate system. Then I had a serious talk with Amy and started reading up on the Intergovernmental Panel on Climate Change—the IPCC reports," he said, giving her a pointed look. "I assume you are familiar with them?"

Zakia nodded. "Yes, I am."

"Well, the consequence of all of this is that I now deeply regret my earlier actions and feel a need to make some drastic changes. Your determination is the push I needed to get my story out there, make it public before it's too late."

"I'm glad to hear that."

"Wait up, I'm not done yet."

"Right."

Their steaks arrived. Zakia cut a piece of meat, but George left his plate untouched.

He looked at her with a pained expression. "The next part is hard for me to tell you."

"Please go on."

"A few weeks ago, The Dirty Network had another meeting. Sometimes we had speakers show up, but this time I heard talk of a new member joining us. An Icelander, introduced as Sigurd Agnarsson, visited the meeting."

Zakia's jaw dropped.

"Sigurd went on a tirade, talking about all the challenges his Oddleifur Oil Company was up against. I'm sorry to say that your name came up, as well as that of Fiona. Sigurd explained how you and Fiona were in cahoots and were a threat to the industry's interests. He mentioned Halgrim's failed project with Fiona and that you were investigating a blowout at his fracking operation. In addition, he brought up Fiona's work with the Pope and her presenting new data confirming important aspects of the climate science. The network was in an uproar." He smiled and sat back. "You caused quite a stir."

"Oh my goodness! That's scary." Zakia's stomach was churning. She wasn't sure if she would be able to eat the rest of her meal.

"A couple of the members said the best thing would be if we took Fiona out of the equation."

"They said what?"

"I know. I could hardly believe it myself. In all my years in the network, I've never heard anything like it."

"This is unbelievable," she said. "It sounds like a Mafia meeting."

George sighed. "I was dumbfounded. Different ideas raced through my head. If I were to speak out against them, I figured, I would be next on the hit list. I convinced myself it wasn't possible that they, being serious businessmen, would take part in a conspiracy to commit murder, so I kept silent throughout the rest of the meeting. I was praying no one would notice how sick I felt. I left the meeting and flew home. Ever since then I've been struggling with my conscience."

Zakia was silent.

"Then four days ago, David contacted me about you wanting to meet with me. He mentioned a climatologist had been murdered in Iceland, and my suspicions were confirmed. I didn't tell David." He rubbed his eyes with his handkerchief. "I regret that I didn't speak up at the meeting. I was in disbelief. Now I feel guiltier than ever."

The waiter came by to check on them and George waved him away. "We're fine, thank you."

The horror of Fiona's death washed over Zakia once again. She knew that Fiona was murdered, but to think that a whole group of men had wanted her dead really disturbed her. And she wondered if she was meant to be eliminated too. She didn't dare ask, but stayed focused on Fiona. "You have to go straight to the police, the FBI, or both," she said.

"In due time. I'm not in a rush to go to jail. They will know where to find me."

Zakia needed to concentrate and not be swept away by emotion. "I don't know what to say. This is a real scoop for a journalist, but I'm thinking of Fiona." She realized it was more important than ever to get this information out to save herself from the same fate Elias, Tariq and Fiona had met.

George looked down at his plate and wiped his eyes again. "I didn't tell Amy about the Dirty Network, only that I was meeting with you to talk about climate change. I figured she would walk away from me. I risk losing her, but I hope she understands that I'm making amends."

"I'm sure she will."

They were silent for a while. Zakia pushed the steak around on her plate and George seemed to lack any appetite.

"In searching for Fiona's killer, I have been working with MI5," said Zakia. "Fiona was Scottish, you see. But we couldn't quite figure out Sigurd's involvement. We have circumstantial evidence, but this definitely fits the puzzle pieces together. So, I take it

Sigurd was paid to arrange the murder?"

George nodded. "Yes, that was discussed later in the meeting, almost as a joke, allowing me to believe they would never follow through with it. In addition, Sigurd was invited into the Dirty Network as a special member."

Zakia forced herself to keep from grinning, wanting to contact Ian right away with this explosive information. Then she straightened up all of a sudden. "Wait a minute, there's a slight problem with all of this."

"What would that be? I've told you everything."

"Where's the proof?"

"Oh, yes," said George. He dug into his pocket and brought out his phone. "When my old cellphone died a month ago, Amy insisted she accompany me to buy a smart phone. 'Join the rest of the world,' she said. I asked her how to use it. After a short introductory course, she said I should just play with it and I would figure it out."

"At the Dirty Network meeting, I quickly got bored when they were going through the minutes from the last meeting."

"They wrote minutes?" asked Zakia.

"Yes, we were that arrogant, I'm afraid," he said. "So I pulled out my phone to play with it, as per Amy's instructions. I pushed some buttons or icons or whatever you call them, and a red light started blinking." He smiled at her. "Thinking it would make a noise, I stuffed it quickly back into my pocket. When I got home, I realized I had inadvertently taped the meeting."

"Amazing!" said Zakia.

"Dumb luck," he said. "Of course, I don't know what to do with the recording."

"No problem. Let's have a look." Zakia took his phone and hit the play button and heard men speaking.

"It's about an hour-long meeting."

"Would you mind e-mailing me the file?" Zakia handed him the phone.

George laughed. "I have no idea how to do that either. Here, you do it."

Zakia brought up his e-mail and sent the audio file to herself. She gave him his phone. "I'm going to pass this along to my MI5 contact," she said. "When you go to the FBI, just give them the phone. They will know what to do with it."

"Well, it's a relief to get all this off my chest. We'll see what kills me first, the cancer, sitting in jail, or losing my granddaughter's affection."

"Hopefully, Amy will realize that you have done the right thing. Thanks for having the courage to come forward with all of this," she said. "I'll send you a copy of my article. I hope it will be published in one of the big newspapers."

"I'm counting on you now."

"Indeed."

"Then that's settled. You could say grandpa got a conscience in the end." George smiled.

"And you can't imagine what this will mean for your granddaughter and future generations."

George smiled at her, though he looked downcast and Zakia could see that he was worn out from the conversation. "I'm going to pay for this lunch. You can get going, if you like. You said you had plans this afternoon."

Zakia thanked him again and stood up to leave. He pulled himself up from the chair and slowly walked around the table. She reached out to shake his hand and he responded by giving her a hug. "I'm so sorry about Fiona," he said.

****

Zakia hailed a taxi and returned to Tahra's condo. She poked her head into Harris and Dani's room, where they were playing video games with their cousins. She found Benjamin in the kitchen, loading the dishwasher after lunch with Tahra and the boys.

"Hi," he said. "I'm glad you are home. Tahra took off to run errands."

She put her bag on a kitchen chair and kissed him. "Me, too, though this probably feels more like home to you than it does for me at this point."

He dried off his hands. "You'll soon settle in and we'll find a place of our own. How was your lunch? What was the important news that this man had to tell you about?"

"*Mon Dieu*, it blows my mind, this is so big," said Zakia. "We should sit and have cup of tea."

He filled the electric kettle and set it to boil. Zakia sat down and pulled out her notes from her bag. While Benjamin prepared the tea, Zakia told him all about her meeting.

Benjamin didn't say much until he brought the two cups to the table and sat down. He looked Zakia in the eyes and said, "Do you know what this means?"

"Yes, I'm afraid so," she said. "I'm part of the story now, big-time, but it seems like my lucky break, in terms of being published. And, I hope as a consequence, all the guilty parties will be brought to justice. It will also contribute to saving future generations from worse climate disasters."

Zakia sipped her tea, but Benjamin just pushed his cup away. "Can't you see how dangerous this information is? Isn't there a way you could publish under a pseudonym or give the story to an established reporter in Chicago? I don't like the sound of this Dirty Network. It's way too risky for us. We'll be getting death threats next."

Zakia couldn't believe what she was hearing. Benjamin didn't know about the threats she'd received in China and Iceland. She pressed her lips tightly together and shook her head. "You're not serious? Publish under a pseudonym?"

"Oh, yes, I am." Benjamin rubbed his chin. "I'm thinking about your safety and the safety of our family."

"No way, that's going to happen. I won't publish under a pseudonym or hand it off to another reporter." Zakia narrowed her eyes.

Benjamin knuckles tightened. "I think you should at least consider it."

"You mean whether I should consider giving up my career?"

"Perhaps."

"I don't think I'm ready for that."

They stared at each other for a moment, before Benjamin said: "That's it. I can't live like this anymore. I've said it earlier, but now I have to draw the line. This is our family's safety we're talking about."

"I care about that, but what safety will our family have when climate change really takes its toll? Here I have evidence of a whole industry working against addressing climate change, which will affect the safety of everyone on the planet. They have delayed action by twenty years or more, funding politicians *not* to address the problem. Besides, we're talking about the murder of at least three people here. How can I not publish?"

"You should turn it over to the police," he said in a low stern voice.

"Yes, I could do that, but they're already investigating the murders. By publishing, the whole world will know about the disinformation that's been spread. Furthermore, I will get my scoop article out there. I'm bound to get a job then." Benjamin didn't answer, but looked down at his teacup. Zakia got up, stormed into their bedroom, and stopped short of slamming the door.

Clenching her jaw, she zipped through her e-mails on her computer and saw that her contact at *The Chicago Post* had asked to meet her tomorrow. She Skyped with Ian and gave him the mind-boggling news from George. He was thrilled. She did not, however, share with Ian that her marriage had now reached a new low point, perhaps rock bottom.

"This information from George is a huge break in the investigation," he said. "If what he told you is true, the case can be wrapped up in short order. Not only to arrest Sigurd, but also to bring down anyone else involved in this. I'll get in touch with the FBI."

"I'll send you a copy of the recording. George said he was going to see the FBI himself."

"Good, maybe they'll take him into protective custody."

"That may not be necessary. With his cancer, he hasn't got long to live. I hope he can get a lesser sentence, since he's turning over information. And he's agreed to go on the record with me for my story."

Ian smiled. "Good work!"

"Thanks," she said. "But, one thing doesn't compute, why wasn't I mentioned as a person to be eliminated? Why only Fiona?"

"That's a mystery to me too. But you could be next on their list."

"Thanks. That's not very reassuring." Zakia stayed focused on the story to avoid letting fear get the better of her.

"Not much I can tell you. Just be extra careful," said Ian.

"Right, I'll be in touch soon."

Zakia thought about Benjamin's fear of death threats. *He's right.* She shivered. *But at least this information about the Dirty Network isn't out there yet, so I have a little time to wrap up the story.*

Chapter Thirty-Four

The next morning, the feeling of uneasiness still lingered in the condo.

After breakfast, Dani and Harris left for the swimming pool with their cousins. Tahra sighed and said it was good to have Zakia home, but that she was late for a dental appointment. With that, she too was gone.

That left Zakia and Benjamin sitting at the table, giving each other awkward looks. Zakia wondered if their lives would ever be the same.

Benjamin cleared his throat. "I know that you've had a lot on your mind, but I hope you remember the lecture series I was able to arrange at the Business School at the University of Chicago. I start teaching on Monday, so I have to go in today to get organized."

"Of course, that's great. What are you teaching?"

"It's a joint program with the World Bank on economic development and poverty reduction."

"I guess that covers the recently agreed-upon Sustainable Development Goals you mentioned earlier."

"You got that right," said Benjamin. "We'll see if the students pick up on the importance of the goals in an economic perspective."

"Good luck with that."

"Thanks. At least it will allow me to stay in

Chicago for a few weeks."

"Wonderful," said Zakia.

She was glad he wasn't heading straight back to Washington D.C., as he'd have done otherwise, now that she was in a precarious situation. "Then we'll have a chance to do some catching up."

"Yes, I hope so," he said. His posture was stooped. He reached for Zakia's hand. She took a deep breath and put her hand in his. She ran her other hand through her hair.

"I love you," she said. "And I appreciate your shouldering so much of the work with Dani and Harris while I've been gone. I couldn't have done it without you." She leaned over and kissed him.

"You must believe what I said. We'll have to put some work into this."

Zakia felt torn. Must she weigh their marriage against the future of the planet? She had expected there would be a lot of sacrifices to combat global warming, but she was not sure she was willing to sacrifice her relationship with Benjamin.

"Well?" he asked.

Zakia looked at him, biting her lip, "I think you should consider taking the children with you to Washington D.C.," she paused. "That way they will be safer."

Benjamin's mouth fell open, "What do you mean? We're splitting up?" His brow wrinkled.

"No, silly, it would just be until this all blows over in a few weeks. At the end of the summer, you'd bring them back."

Benjamin took a deep breath, "Say, that's a great idea. As soon I'm done with this lecture series or if need be, I'll just cancel it." He kissed her hand.

"Good, then that's settled," said Zakia as she withdrew her hand. "You better go organize your lecture series," she said. "I'm going job hunting. I have an interview with the *Chicago Post* today."

"Okay," he said. "Please stay out of trouble. Maybe the newspaper could hire you to do stories about the arts."

"Not likely," she said. *He doesn't get it.*

Benjamin left the room to get ready for work and Zakia cleared away the breakfast plates. After he left and the door shut with a resounding thud, Zakia took a deep breath.

She had to get her piece published so she and Benjamin could put all this trouble behind them.

****

That afternoon, Zakia got another e-mail from Ian. Her heart began pumping faster. Maybe he had another lead on Sigurd. The four boys were back and after lunch had settled in to watch a movie in the living room. Zakia was concerned that her sons were not getting outside enough, but dismissed the thought. She would deal with that after the article was published. She told Tahra she was going to get some work done, locked herself in the bedroom, and Skyped with Ian.

Ian appeared to be in high spirits. "Thanks to your latest lead, Sigurd was arrested in Paris last night. He claimed he was attending an annual meeting arranged by one of the oil industry's trade associations, though we're not sure if anyone else from The Dirty Network was present. We're still investigating."

"That *is* good news." Zakia let out a huge breath.

With Sigurd, Halgrim, and Rostek in custody, at

least three bad actors were locked up. She thought about Ahmed still at large and a chill ran down her back.

"Yes, we are pleased. On another note, we checked with the scientific community; it turns out Fiona's work confirms that climate change is indeed causing more and more extreme weather events, surpassing any natural climate variability. In addition, she has been able to prove some correlation between specific extreme weather events and climate change."

"That's wonderful."

"Sigurd isn't saying much, but we've confirmed that the fossil fuel industry got word of Fiona's research and were attempting to stop the information from coming out. Fiona had e-mailed a friend at the University of Pennsylvania. Someone must have hacked her e-mails."

"Yes, she told me." said Zakia.

"Not to worry; her findings are being corroborated as we speak. It's all in the timing now. However, the fossil fuel industry might still want to throw a wrench into the latest round of negotiations on the implementation of the Paris Agreement." said Ian.

"How come you know all of this?"

Ian grinned. "I've been boning up on climate change, since I was assigned to protect Fiona."

Zakia said, "To tell you the truth, I'm not surprised the industry is trying to delay action. They're probably more desperate than ever now."

"Should be interesting," said Ian. "Anyway, we are interrogating Sigurd and pressuring him to give us the names of the other members attending the meeting of the Dirty Network besides George Stevens. We want

Sigurd to confirm who gave him his marching orders to arrange the killing of Fiona. That will corroborate George's list."

Zakia was happy that the case was moving along. "Has Sigurd confessed arranging for Elias's murder? And Tariq's?"

"Not yet, but the investigations of the so-called accidental deaths of Elias and Tariq are being reopened and his shady deals with the oil and energy minister are being looked into. No doubt, Samara's in big trouble in Morocco."

"Is Samara going to be arrested, too?"

"We're working on it with our Moroccan counterpart, but it's going to take a while," said Ian. "And who knows if he'll actually be given any prison time."

Zakia wondered what her situation would be in the future. Could she ever return to Morocco?

She made Ian promise to keep her updated.

****

After signing off with Ian, Zakia showered and dressed quickly.

"Good luck with your interview," said Tahra who was back from the dentist.

"Thanks, gotta run!" she said, and zipped out the door. As a safety precaution, she had called a taxi to pick her up at the condo, rather than walking to the bus stop a few blocks away.

From the lobby of the paper she was directed to the newsroom, where she stood awkwardly until one of the reporters looked up and pointed her in the direction of the editor's office.

An assistant smiled at her. "You must be Zakia

Karim. You're early."

She showed her to a beat-up sofa in the corner of the small room, piles of newspapers occupying one end of the sofa. "Please wait here. Would you like some tea or coffee?"

"I'd like some tea, please."

Thirty minutes later, the managing editor arrived. She was smartly dressed, in slacks and a bright red blazer. Her smile was warm and genuine. "Hello. I'm Roberta Windward. And you are Zakia Karim, I gather."

"Yes. Glad to meet you." Zakia shook her hand.

"Let's go into my office."

The office was bigger than Jasem's, with a big desk and a plump sofa.

They both sat down on the couch. "So you're a friend of Gail's?" she said. "And you've been working in Rabat, Morocco, for *Le Journal de Maroc*. That's exciting."

"Yes. I was given a lot of leeway in reporting on some engaging and complex stories. But I covered a lot of beats, too."

"Had you worked there a long time?"

"Over fifteen years. It's a small, independent paper, so normally we cover more controversial topics than most of the other papers in that part of the world."

Roberta nodded, but she looked serious. "It's a luxury to have that freedom."

"How so? You must have a large news budget here." Right away, Zakia regretted having said so. "That's part of the reason I was so grateful to get an interview. I'm eager to prove myself in a larger setting."

Roberta shifted in her seat and said, "You're looking for a position?"

"Yes, that's why I'm here," Zakia said in an uncertain tone.

"You are aware that the newspaper industry has taken a huge downturn because of digital media."

"Yessss," Zakia clasped her knees tightly together.

"I'm so sorry. I misunderstood why Gail had sent you here. I'm afraid we can't offer you a position."

"I am so sorry for the confusion," Zakia felt herself flush.

"I wish we could offer you something. The truth is, we are on our third round of layoffs and it's been an excruciating process. We've had to let a lot of wonderful people go."

"I'm sorry to hear that." If the *Post* was laying off reporters, then what were her chances of getting any journalism job in the Chicago area? The market would be flooded with people like her looking for work. Only they'd be locals.

Roberta touched her shoulder, looking sympathetic. "I realize this is not easy for you. I would be very pleased to offer you a position here if only I had one available."

Zakia nodded and took a deep breath. *Time to move to plan B.* "I have an article I would like to see published. Would you be willing to read it and perhaps publish it as a freelance piece? I can give you a draft of it, if you like." She took a deep breath. "It's about nomadic Berbers, climate change, oil and gas, and murder."

"That sounds intriguing. We can take a look at it, no problem. How soon can you have it ready?"

"Three days?"

"All right, that works. If it's a good article we will print it and perhaps you can become a regular contributor." she added, with a slow smile.

"I'd like that."

Zakia left Roberta's office feeling a bit more uplifted than she expected, having been turned down for a position. Now all her energy was redirected to her story. She knew there would be repercussions when it was finally out, but despite Benjamin's dire predictions, she believed that she and her family were safe in the United States. Besides, she wanted to make a difference, especially in light of what had happened to three of her friends at the hands of Sigurd. She didn't want their deaths to be in vain.

Chapter Thirty-Five

At dinner that night, Zakia focused on the family. She helped Tahra cook a great Moroccan meal of chicken, green olives, onions, and lemon, spiced with ginger and cumin. Everybody devoured it as if they hadn't seen food for days. Tahra's dining room was rather small, but they all crammed together, creating a cozy atmosphere.

"Tahra I've been meaning to tell you how much I appreciate all your help with Dani and Harris while I was away. I am so grateful," said Zakia.

"Oh, that's what families are for, isn't it?"

"I guess, but not all have such a wonderful sister, mother, and aunt."

"Okay, don't go overboard. You can invite me out to a fancy dinner one day." Tahra grinned.

"Sounds like a plan. After my article is published, you name the time and place."

"I'll hold you to that."

During dinner, Benjamin didn't seem as apprehensive as usual. He laughed and joked with their boys and Tahra's. It started to feel like home.

Benjamin had come home late and they had not had time to talk, but after the plates were cleared, Tahra went to her room and the boys disappeared into the living room, he took Zakia's hands in his.

Zakia smiled, "How did your work go today?"

"Oh, I'm still preparing. The first lecture isn't until Monday," he said. "What about your interview? Did it go well?"

Her shoulders slumped and the smile was gone, "It didn't, I'm afraid. It was the usual answer. They don't have any positions. In fact, they are laying off journalists everywhere."

Benjamin looked startled. "Then what are your options?"

Zakia's mouth twitched a little bit. They'd been married long enough for him to know that she would not accept that answer and walk away.

"I pulled out Plan B—I offered them my article."

"I figured," said Benjamin. "How did that go?"

"Well, right now, I'm just happy that she's willing to look at it. The *Post* is a top-notch paper and if my article is published there, it may give me some good job leads. But I have to have it ready in three days."

"That's a tight schedule, isn't it?" asked Benjamin.

"I have to hunker down and get it done or it will never get published."

Benjamin kissed her. "You have to promise me that this isn't going to cause us any more trouble."

"I can't anticipate every crazy person out there," she said. "But I seriously think there are fewer chances of danger finding us here."

"I keep thinking about Fiona's death. It really shook me up," he said.

"It's not like I'm going to forget what happened. I was the one in jail, remember? But we'll put it all behind us, as soon as possible." said Zakia. "I just want you to understand why this is so important. I'm doing it for our sons and their children." And especially Dani, thought Zakia.

Benjamin looked at her, his expression full of hope, worry, and love. "I do understand," he said. "I'm not trying to be unreasonable."

"I know, and I'm very grateful," said Zakia with a loving smile.

Zakia and Benjamin cleaned up the kitchen and she announced she was confining herself to their bedroom to organize her notes and write a first draft.

Before she knew it, it was midnight. Dani and Harris were fast asleep, her sister was in her room reading, and Benjamin was watching the late news on the TV.

She printed out what she had so far. She still needed to work in the information about the whistle-blowing secretary. It looked like the start of a big shakeup in the oil industry and any other parties interested in doing their bidding. Alongside the Paris Agreement, which called for a shift to low-carbon energy, she hoped her story would be a wake-up call about what was going on behind the scenes.

****

Zakia got up Saturday morning before anyone else did and continued working on the draft. Benjamin got out of bed, left the bedroom, and returned with a cup of tea for her.

"Hard at it, I see," he said, standing beside her. "You know, I'm against what you're doing, publishing under your own name. We'll have to think about safety at every step of the way. And I'll consider whether or not I should take off with the boys. Right now, I'll make breakfast for the whole gang."

"Thank you." Zakia went back to work.

Over the next two days, she tapped away on the keyboard, double-checking facts and adding background information. Benjamin and Tahra took turns coaxing her to eat and supervising the four boys.

The night before her story was due, Benjamin looked in on her. "Are you almost done Zakia? Or will this be one of those all-nighters again?"

"I'm almost done. I just need to check something from one of my sources," she said.

"I do love you so," said Benjamin. "Even if I worry about you and get frustrated."

"Yes, I know. I love you too," said Zakia.

Her shoulders were tense and hurting. By 2 a.m. she was finally done. She read it one more time and wrote a quick e-mail to the editor at the *Post,* attaching the article and her list of sources for fact checking. Then she clicked the send button.

She walked into the living room and looked out the window. Tahra's neighborhood was quiet and peaceful. Nevertheless, now that the article was out of her hands, she felt uneasy. Ahmed and the members of The Dirty Network were still at large. *And they probably have other henchmen.* She needed to get in touch with George and find out what, if anything, he had heard about his former associates.

****

With her story filed, Zakia couldn't sit still, wondering what the editor at *The Post* would think. It was long for a newspaper article and would run better as a series. She knew that Jasem, for example, would have cut it down. She debated whether or not to call the editor to see if she had any questions, but decided that it would be better to turn her mind to some other task.

She took her sons and her nephews to the crowded beach at Lake Michigan, but the water was too cold, even in June, to do anything more than dip their toes in, so they sat on a blanket by the shore, had a picnic, and soaked in the sun.

She started house hunting, keenly aware that she needed to secure a job in Chicago first; otherwise it made more sense to move closer to Benjamin's job in Washington, D.C. She perused the ads in *Editor and Publisher* and *MediaBistro* and sent out resumes.

****

It wasn't until Wednesday that she got an e-mail from the editor. "Due to the sensitivity of your article, we must refrain from publishing it. We thank you for your understanding."

Her stomach hurt, her hands went limp.

"What's up, Zakia?" Gail was in the middle of taking a coffee break when Zakia called. "Are you still job hunting? I might have another lead."

"No, that's not what I'm calling about." Zakia explained what the editor had told her, read the e-mail she'd received, and then gave Gail a quick summary of her article. "It's a hugely important story, and I've backed it up with hard evidence. I don't understand." She sighed.

"It sounds like a real scoop to me and it will probably shake up a lot of people," Gail's voice had risen a notch. "If what you are saying is true, a lot of folks are likely going to prison."

"Yes, there are no guarantees, but I hope this story will get the ball rolling."

"Well, give me a little time and I'll talk to another friend at *The Post* to find out what happened."

"Thanks, Gail. I really appreciate it."

"Hey, you were always there for me when I needed support, especially, when I was struggling with my business reporting class."

"Let me know what you find out, and thanks." Zakia hung up the phone and went to the kitchen to make some tea. Thirty minutes later, Gail called back. "Here's the deal," she said. "Clearly, there are strings being pulled by the paper's ownership. I heard through the grapevine that the owners have a lot of investments in oil and gas."

Zakia's heart sank. "That explains it."

"I'm afraid so," said Gail. "Look, I think you should keep trying. Send it out to a few more papers and see if anybody bites. It might take a while to land, because you are making waves and newspapers aren't exactly doing investigative reporting these days. Sensational stories about celebrities have pretty much taken over."

Zakia hung up. She was so frustrated she wanted to scream.

She decided to go for a walk through the neighborhood. She forced herself to focus on her surroundings. The flowers were in full bloom. But she couldn't help feeling as though she was letting everybody down by not getting published.

Out of nowhere a car with tinted windows swerved right in front of her. Zakia froze, and then stumbled into a small park next to the sidewalk. The car took off and Zakia ran home as fast as she could. She called Ian and told him about this latest incident. He said she mustn't leave the house under any circumstances.

When Benjamin got home from the university, he

called the police. They thought it might have been Zakia who was mistaken, that the car may have been kids on a joy ride.

"Okay," said Benjamin. "That's it. You can't publish the article, Zakia."

"You don't really mean that."

"Oh, yes I do. You could have been killed today. It won't be enough for me to take off with the boys. You are in danger. Whistleblowers rarely win."

"I heard back from *the Chicago Post*. They're not publishing the article and probably none of the other big papers will either, so this could all die down shortly."

****

After dinner she decided to give George a call. She went into their bedroom and closed the door.

"Zakia, it's good to hear from you. I've been meaning to call you, but I've been busy wrapping up my will and talking with the FBI."

Zakia didn't know what to say. "How's that going?"

"Well, they haven't arrested me yet," he said with a laugh, and then he sounded more serious. "A few of my former associates are in custody, but it's all been hush-hush. I have been watching the papers, but so far, no one has broken this story. How's your article going?"

Zakia sat down on her bed. "That's part of the reason why I am calling," she said. "My article is finished, but *The Chicago Post* turned it down, even though they originally indicated it looked interesting. They said it was due to its sensitivity. One of my friends tipped me off that the ownership has connections to the oil and gas industry."

"That's not surprising. Many of the media outlets are being bought up by industry moguls."

"I know, and the chances that any of the other big papers will publish it, are miniscule. But I'm not giving up," said Zakia. "You don't happen to own a newspaper, do you?"

George laughed. "No, but I have a good friend who owns an independent newspaper. He and I go way back."

"Which paper?" she asked.

"It's a small one, but with lots of integrity," he said. "It's *The Hudson Tribune*."

Zakia frowned. She wanted so badly to get her article published in a major newspaper, but she would be lucky to get it published anywhere, at this rate.

"I'd be happy to introduce you to him," said George.

"That would be wonderful," said Zakia. "Thanks."

****

The Hudson Tribune was a small newspaper, as George had indicated, but when she spoke to the owner, Raymond Butterfield, he sounded enthusiastic about her story and about publishing it. As soon as it went to press, he would let her know. Then he would overnight a few copies to her and post it online the next day. Zakia was thrilled but still a little sad that only the readers in the Hudson Valley would have access to it.

Early Friday morning, after receiving a text from Raymond, Zakia got up, pulled on her robe, and rushed to the front door. As she picked up the package on the front stoop, she looked up and stiffened when she saw a towering, muscular man on the sidewalk. He began walking toward her. She noticed he was armed.

391

Zakia was about to run back into the house when he yelled, "Hello, I'm here for your protection, courtesy of Ian Blackstone. The name is Charles Hayden."

Zakia let out a burst of air, "What a relief. Thank you. I'm Zakia. Give Ian my regards." Zakia brought the package inside. Raymond had made good on his word.

She found four copies of the *Tribune* in the package, her story prominently featured above the front-page fold with the headline: *The Dirty Network behind murder of Climate Scientist—How the Oil Industry Has Forced Delayed Action on Climate Change*. The subheading noted that several oil company executives had been accused of securities fraud. The editor had managed to acquire some photos of some members of the Dirty Network being arrested.

"Yes!" shouted Zakia. She sat down at the breakfast table and read the article. She was ecstatic. The editor had made few changes. She had placed the blowout incident and murder of Elias and Tariq at the front end of the article.

Tahra walked into the kitchen, yawning. "What's all the ruckus?"

"My article got published. Look at these headlines." Zakia grinned.

"That's wonderful news. Congratulations!" Tahra gave her a big hug.

Benjamin had already left for work, so Zakia sent him a quick text and gave him the site for the online version of the paper. He called her back.

"Zakia, I take it you met our security guard," said Benjamin.

"You might have mentioned it earlier. I was

freaked out."

"I was late and totally forgot. Sorry. But even with him out there, I think we are in more danger than ever now that your story is out. It's no longer just Oddleifur Oil, but all the oil companies that will be after you—and us."

"You may be right about that."

"However," said Benjamin. "Congratulations are due. It's a fabulous piece. Fancy an accident, which was not an accident, could lead to the shakeup of a whole industry. But now you have to be even more careful with *everything* you do."

"Yes," she said with a smile in her voice.

Zakia walked on air that whole day. She and Tahra cooked a meal of couscous and Moroccan lamb tangine with honey and apricots for dinner that night. She and the family toasted her success with champagne that Benjamin had brought home.

"I'm not happy that we need a body guard," said Benjamin. "But I'm proud of your article. It's excellent," said Benjamin. "For all the danger you've put us in, you have done an immense service to the public. I hope we stay safe and that all this tension blows over soon. I hope you have a less risky career from here on out."

"I'm sure we'll be safe here after all this has blown over," said Zakia, looking at the boys. "Of course, it's hard to predict the future." She knew she wouldn't forgo an assignment she was passionate about.

****

Over the next couple of days, Zakia started getting phone calls and e-mails from all over, some praising her, some contained threats—which she ignored. Her story had been picked up by the wires services and on social media it had gone viral.

Jasem had read her story as it was reprinted in a liberal newspaper out of the U.K., *The Sentinel*, and he was thrilled for her. "You managed to bring the oil and energy minister under fire. Rumor has it he'll spend time in prison," he said. "I only wish we could have published your story ourselves."

"Me, too. Next time, perhaps." Zakia knew full well that would never happen and that she was not likely to find employment in Morocco in the future, but she was happy that Jasem was still talking to her. She missed him, Fatima, and Nassar.

On Monday, in the midst of the flurry over her article and her newfound celebrity, George called. "Have you seen the TV news?" His voice sounded weak.

"No, why?" asked Zakia.

She waited while he had a horrible coughing fit. Then he came back on the phone. "Sorry about that. I think you ought to tune in to the news. All the members of The Dirty Network have now been arrested, except me."

"Well, I'm glad they're in jail, and you're not," said Zakia, her heart sinking. "How did you get off?"

"I'm now in hospice care, so my lawyer was able to have the court grant me an exception on humanitarian grounds," he said. "If I recover, I'll go to jail. But I don't have much time left."

"I'm sorry to hear that, George. I appreciate your help. You made it possible."

"Oh, no. Your article got the ball rolling and allowed me to redeem myself. You must be getting a lot of publicity and several job offers, I should think." George started coughing again and Zakia heard a female voice in the background talking to him. She heard him say "yes, dear" before he came back on the phone. "Sorry about that."

"That's okay," she said. "Is that Amy I hear in the background?"

"Yes. We patched up things and are now spending every moment together."

Even though she couldn't see him, she could hear from the tone in his voice that he was happy. "Thanks again for all your help," said Zakia. "I'm glad this story is out there so the world can understand what's been going on and take more serious action on climate change."

Zakia hung up the phone with a mix of emotions. That was probably the last conversation she'd have with him. Even if he had been part of The Dirty Network, he'd come around. If he weren't in such poor health, he could have helped the cause, now that he understood how it was all tied together.

Zakia had already received job offers in New York and San Francisco, but that afternoon, she received an offer from a small, progressive paper in the heart of the city, *The Chicago Press*. She accepted right away and was told she could start immediately.

****

George's funeral was held on a beautiful day, the third of July. Amy had called Zakia to tell her he'd passed and to insist that she come to the funeral. "Grandpa would have wanted you there," she said. Zakia took the afternoon off and, accompanied by Benjamin, attended the service at the New Episcopal

Church, north of the city. The eulogy given by the pastor was very touching and made her think about so many deaths of good people she'd known—Fiona, Elias, Tariq, and now George. She was glad it was over. She and Benjamin walked out of the church and decided to loop through the cemetery adjacent to the sanctuary before going to the parking lot.

They strolled among the trees, pointing out tombstones from the Civil War period. Zakia stopped in front of a small structure that looked like a mausoleum, with delicately carved angels at the entrance.

"It must be a rich and large family buried here," she said to Benjamin.

"I think so," said somebody behind them.

Zakia stiffened. They turned around to see Ian standing behind them, with a big grin on his face.

"Ian! You startled me," said Zakia. "What are you doing here?"

"I thought I'd see how you were doing on this side of the pond," he said.

"I don't believe that for a moment," said Zakia.

Ian's smile faded. "Actually, I have something to talk with you about." He looked at Benjamin. "Do you mind if I have a word with Zakia alone?"

Benjamin looked at him, astonished, but walked away.

Zakia folded her arms. "This isn't a social call, then?"

Ian shook his head. "First, I wanted to let you know that Ahmed was arrested in Iceland, finally. Now for the real reason why I popped by. My boss sent me. I am to offer you a job working for MI5."

"A job?" Zakia tipped her head to one side. "But I

just got hired by a local newspaper. Why would I want to give that up?"

Ian looked amused. "You wouldn't need to give it up. This would be more of a, shall we say, 'moonlighting' job. In fact, your job as a reporter would be a perfect cover."

Zakia looked at him while thumbing her earing. "Just what kind of a job do you have in mind?"

"An analyst." He shrugged slightly, as if it were no big deal.

Zakia rubbed her chin. "Oh, I see. And by 'analyst' you mean 'spy.'"

"You might say that, but I can't give you all the details at this point."

"Well, I'll have to think about that," said Zakia. "I wrote my first paper on spies in high school, on women spies. I discovered espionage was the second oldest profession in the world."

"Fancy that," said Ian.

"I guess it's the chase and the adrenalin rush that always attracts me when I read spy novels or see the movies. It's not that different from chasing a story as a journalist, I guess."

"Of course, we do have some of that in the real world too. You'd be perfect for the job. You are smart and good at investigating issues. There are a lot of people out there like the members of the Dirty Network and Sigurd. We need more people like you, with ideals and integrity. Anyway, you think about it," he said with a smile.

"You flatter me," said Zakia. "Thanks for the offer." But she worried about Benjamin's reaction.

"So you'll contact me when you've decided?"

asked Ian, shoving his hands in his pockets.

"Of course," said Zakia, her voice noncommittal. It was too big a decision to make right now. At least she'd have to sleep on it.

Ian wished her well and said he hoped he would be getting a positive response from her soon.

Zakia watched him walk across the cemetery, picking his way around the gravestones until he reached the street, got in his car and drove off. Benjamin walked over to her and took her hand and said in a calm voice, "What was that all about?"

Zakia gave him a hug, her brain racing. Her heart was pumping at the offer Ian had just made, but now wasn't the right time to talk to Benjamin about it. Perhaps he need never know. "Ian was giving me an update, they arrested Ahmed."

He looked at her with raised eye brows. "So, why couldn't I hear that?"

"Oh, you know these spy characters," said Zakia while she picked lint off her dress. "They make even simple things into cloak and dagger business. They need to feel important."

Benjamin shook his head. "I'm glad all that's behind you. We need to start a new chapter in our lives here in Chicago. With your new job, we have so many more opportunities. We might even be able to afford a comfortable house."

Zakia nodded. In order to really begin their new chapter, she needed to tie up one important loose end. She had promised Dani that she would talk with him about the picture of Elias he had found that she had portrayed as a distant cousin. Now it was time and she hoped Benjamin would understand. "Speaking of new chapters, I need to talk to you and the boys about a serious family matter," said Zakia.

Benjamin looked surprised. "What can that possibly be about? Should I be worried?"

"I can't tell you right now. It has nothing to do with my work and no, it does not affect our safety. We'll find a convenient time for everyone soon, I'm sure."

Zakia smiled at Benjamin and held his hand, as they walked out of the cemetery. She heard the breeze blowing in the trees and the sound of the church bells. It had been a crazy two and a half months and she wondered what the next few months would bring, starting with the day of the family meeting. On the way out, she turned to close the small, wrought-iron gate and saw a large statue of an angel with her hands out, as though ready to embrace her. She smiled. The sight of the angel gave her goosebumps. She thought about Elias, Tariq, and Fiona all meeting untimely deaths. By all rights, she should be dead, too. She wondered, not for the first time, who her guardian angel was.

"Thank you," she said quietly and turned to join Benjamin on the sidewalk.

A word about the author…

Originally from Norway, living in Colorado, Halvorssen has focused on teaching law and writing on environmental issues, especially climate change. Her first law degree is from the University of Oslo, Norway. She has a masters of law and a doctorate in law from Columbia Law School, New York.

Before pursuing an academic career, she was an Executive Officer at the Norwegian Ministry of Environment. She is a member of the International Law and Sea Level Rise Committee of the International Law Association. Halvorssen is Director of Global Legal Solutions, LLC, an international think tank and consultancy.

She is also a member of the Rocky Mountain Fiction Writers, the Lighthouse Writers Workshop, the Colorado Writing School, and the International Thriller Writers.

Thank you for purchasing
this publication of The Wild Rose Press, Inc.

If you enjoyed the story, we would appreciate your
letting others know by leaving a review.

For other wonderful stories,
please visit our on-line bookstore at
www.thewildrosepress.com.

For questions or more information
contact us at
info@thewildrosepress.com.

The Wild Rose Press, Inc.
www.thewildrosepress.com

Stay current with The Wild Rose Press, Inc.

Like us on Facebook

https://www.facebook.com/TheWildRosePress

And Follow us on Twitter
https://twitter.com/WildRosePress

CPSIA information can be obtained
at www.ICGtesting.com
Printed in the USA
FSHW020651121218
54421FS

9 781509 223855